"THE PERSON WHO COMMUNICATED WITH THE GUARDIAN WAS MY SON . . ."

Admiral Morrow looked at Spock incredulously.

"Your—" Kirk doubted that Morrow could have looked more thunderstruck if the conference table had come to life and danced a hornpipe. It was a full thirty seconds before the admiral could speak. "I apologize, Mr. Spock . . . but your personnel records never . . . "

He cleared his throat. "At any rate," Morrow continued, "the important thing is that contact was established. What your son did once, he may be able to do again. Where is he?"

"I am afraid that will be impossible, Admiral," Spock said levelly, but something shadowed the dark eyes for a moment. "My son has been dead for five thousand years."

"This book brought back all the excitement and wonder of the very first STAR TREK episodes . . . Not only does credit to the skill of the author, but to the entire genre of STAR TREK writing."
—Andre Norton,
Nebula Grand Master

STAR TREK®
TIME FOR YESTERDAY
A. C. CRISPIN

POCKET BOOKS

New York   London   Toronto   Sydney   Tokyo   Singapore

POCKET BOOKS, a division of Simon & Schuster Inc.
1230 Avenue of the Americas, New York, NY 10020

STAR TREK is a Registered Trademark of
Paramount Pictures.

A VIACOM COMPANY

This book is published by Pocket Books, a division of Simon & Schuster Inc., under exclusive license from Paramount Pictures.

ISBN: 0-671-03857-5

First Pocket Books paperback printing April 1988

10 9 8 7 6 5 4 3 2 1

Printed in the U.S.A.

Excerpt from "The Love Song of J. Alfred Prufrock" from *Collected Poems 1909–1962* by T. S. Eliot, copyright 1936 by Harcourt Brace Jovanovich, Inc.; copyright 1963, 1964 by T. S. Eliot. Reprinted by permission of the publisher.

Excerpt from "Being to Timelessness As It's to Time" copyright 1950 by E. E. Cummings. Reprinted from *Complete Poems 1913–1962* by E. E. Cummings by permission of Harcourt Brace Jovanovich, Inc.

This book is dedicated to my friend Deb Marshall, who patiently listened, enthused (as only she can) and encouraged me from the moment of Zar's conception, through the long years of gestation, and proudly midwifed the printed birth with champagne, flowers and hugs. Thanks, Deb.

Acknowledgments

For editorial criticism, advice, hand-holding and an occasional (well-deserved) kick in the pants:

The Whileaway Writers Co-op: Teresa Bigbee, Deborah Marshall, Anne Moroz and, of course, Kathleen O'Malley (who is truly a rare bird, genus *rubricatrix splendiferous*)

Special thanks also to Jannean Elliott for patient, long-distance listening

My friends Howard Weinstein, Bob Greenberger and Dave McDonnell

Rusty Wornam, who discovered D'berahan's secret identity

Also:

Merrilee Heifetz, my agent—who sold it

Karen Haas—who bought it

David Stern—who edited it

For scientific information pertaining to black holes and other astronomical phenomena (any errors are exclusively my own):

Dr. Robert Harrington of the U.S. Naval Observatory, the man who saved Centaurus from a horrible fate, for information on Alpha Centauri and its three stars

ACKNOWLEDGMENTS

Dr. Harry L. Shipman of the University of Delaware, author of *Black Holes, Quasars, and the Universe,* for patiently explaining event horizons and Schwarzchild radii to a liberal-arts major with screaming math anxiety

Vonda N. McIntyre, for suggesting the EMP effect

Thia Rose, for information on the side-effects and treatment of head injuries

For information on ancient weaponry, swords and armor:

Robert Adams, author of the *Horseclans* books

In addition, I'd like to acknowledge the *Star Trek* authors whose creations and/or characters I've referred to herein:

Diane Duane, Brad Ferguson, John M. Ford, Jean Lorrah, Vonda N. McIntyre and Howard Weinstein

To every thing there is a season, and a time to every
   purpose under heaven:
A time to be born, and a time to die; a time to plant,
   and a time to pluck up that which is planted;
A time to kill, and a time to heal; a time to break
   down, and a time to build up;
A time to weep, and a time to laugh; a time to mourn,
   and a time to dance;
A time to cast away stones, and a time to gather stones
   together; a time to embrace, and a time to refrain
   from embracing;
A time to get, and a time to lose; a time to keep, and a
   time to cast away;
A time to rend, and a time to sew; a time to keep
   silence, and a time to speak;
A time to love, and a time to hate; a time of war, and a
   time of peace.

                                          —*Ecclesiastes*

There will be time, there will be time
To prepare a face to meet the faces that you meet;
There will be time to murder and create,
And time for all the works and days of hands
That lift and drop a question on your plate;
Time for you and time for me,
And time yet for a hundred indecisions,
And for a hundred visions and revisions . . .
            —T. S. Eliot
               "The Love Song of J. Alfred Prufrock"

being to timelessness as it's to time,
love did no more begin than love will end;
where nothing is to breathe to stroll to swim
love is the air the ocean and the land

.   .   .   .

love is the voice under all silences,
the hope which has no opposite in fear;
the strength so strong mere force seems feebleness:
the truth more first than sun more last than star
               —e. e. cummings
                  "Being to Timelessness As It's to Time"

Introduction

Way back in high school, when my guidance counselor asked me what I intended to do with my life, I told her that I wanted to be a writer.

I was lying.

I didn't have the faintest idea what I wanted to do with my life. I just knew that I had to tell her *something* to get her off my back and, since I liked to read books, writing them seemed like something I might want to do . . . someday. As I recall, she gazed at me sadly, then said, gently, "But what do you want to do to earn your living?"

Wise lady, Mrs. Duckett. Writing is *not* an easy way to earn a living (most people who do it full-time make less than $8,000 annually—many *much* less) and, as James Gunn sagely says, "Anyone who can be discouraged from pursuing a career in writing, should be."

So I went to college, then I got a job, as any sane person who enjoys eating regularly should do. My few writing attempts during a creative writing course in college were quickly forgotten. I had absolutely no urge to write anything.

Until one November day in 1976 when I found myself staying overtime at my job at the U.S. Census Bureau, saying, "What if?" And then typing: "Doctor McCoy picked up his rook and plunked it down again, taking one of his opponent's pawns." Line followed line, and a *Star*

Trek story began emerging from the typewriter—*Yesterday's Son*. To be honest, I didn't really write that book . . . *it* wrote *me*.

I was obsessed. I bought a used IBM typewriter for $400 (a fortune to me, then . . . I had to borrow the money from my credit union and pay it back at the rate of $18 a month, and there were times I scraped to make that payment), but by that time, I'd have mortgaged my soul to keep going. Writing fever is worse than gold fever, and I had it bad. Every night I'd call my long-suffering best buddy and read her whatever I'd produced that day. It's a wonder Deb didn't move to Outer Patagonia to escape.

By the time I was three chapters into the story, it had become more than a lark, more than "just fooling around" —I wanted to *sell* that book. And there was a little voice inside me that kept whispering I would sell it. Even when I snarled at it to shut up, that the entire notion was nuts, the little voice in the back of my head kept insisting that the book would be published—somehow, someday. It whispered at me the entire year it took to write the five drafts of the novel. It continued to whisper when the manuscript was submitted. It whispered for the next three *years,* while the fate of the book hung in limbo.

But you know the rest, if you read Howard Weinstein's introduction to *Yesterday's Son.*

What you may not know is that the story not only got published, it surprised everyone by becoming the first *Star Trek* book (excluding the movie novelizations) to make it onto the *New York Times* bestseller list. Since then, that occurrence has become fairly commonplace, but at the time, it was a minor phenomenon.

(And you, the readers, were responsible for putting it there, so I'd like to thank each and every one of you who plunked down your hard-earned cash and bought the novel. While I'm on the subject, thanks for buying this one, too. Maybe you should pick up a second copy for a deserving friend, as long as you're in the bookstore. I wouldn't object . . .)

All kidding aside, the success of *Yesterday's Son* gave me

the opportunity to become a full-time writer, and I now realize that, all those years ago, I was telling Mrs. Duckett the truth—I just didn't know it then. I never wanted to be anything else than a writer.

But when *Yesterday's Son* was released in 1983, I thought I was finished being a *Star Trek* writer. Zar's story was over, as far as I was concerned.

Hah!

Then in 1985, I was sitting at my word processor, and my treacherous mind suddenly said, "What if?" again. And, so fast I could scarcely believe it (about a month, as I recall), I had a contract to write a sequel . . . the book you're holding in your hands.

Oddly enough, a couple of months after I contracted to write *Time for Yesterday,* many of the fan letters I received began asking if I'd ever considered doing a sequel to *Yesterday's Son.* Telepathy? Empathy? A *Star Trek* group consciousness? Your guess is as good as mine . . .

Speaking of fan letters brings me to my real reason for writing this. Since the advent of my first *Star Trek* book, I've gotten literally *hundreds* of letters. (Most with an SASE, bless you, Howie!) The overwhelming majority have been the kind that gladden a writer's heart. So far I've answered over five hundred, and am currently about fifty to sixty behind. (I'm always behind, so if you write me c/o Pocket Books, please be patient. If you just want a quick response to a specific question, or an autograph, try enclosing a stamped, self-addressed *postcard.*)

I love hearing from fans, please believe me. I really enjoy knowing what you think about what I've written. However, *answering* dozens of letters does take time away from my writing schedule. Especially since fully three-quarters of the folks who write ask me the *same* question. So I'm taking this opportunity to respond en masse to that most-often-asked question, which is:

"I want to write/am writing/have written a Star Trek *book of my own. How do I get it read and published?"*

I'm truly sorry to say this, but you probably *don't.*

Pocket Books no longer reads unsolicited *Star Trek* manuscripts, as they did back in 1979 when *Yesterday's Son* was submitted. Due to the overwhelming number of submissions they have received, they now only read and purchase manuscripts submitted by professional literary agents. My editor tells me that they currently have books scheduled for *years* from now.

So what is my best advice for people who want to sell a *Star Trek* book? It's to write an original book or two set in your own universe. Rewrite until your book is good enough to publish (aye, there's the rub!) and then keep submitting it to publishers until it's sold.* When that happens, you'll be able to get an agent without much difficulty. Your agent will submit your *Star Trek* novel, it will be read, then *maybe* Pocket Books will want to buy it. (And, yes, they're the only company with the legal right to publish *Star Trek* novels.)

Unless you're dead-set on becoming a professional *writer*, that's a lot of trouble to put yourself through just to get a *Star Trek* book submitted. And nobody makes a decent living off simply writing *Trek* novels. You can't sell enough of them.

If you're dead-set on becoming a professional writer, my advice is about the same: Write in your own universe, sell your books, get a reputation in the field, then Pocket Books will be pleased to read your *Star Trek* manuscript when your agent submits it.

Believe me, I understand the attraction writing *Star Trek* stories has for *Star Trek* fans. It's a siren lure . . . wanting to put words in the mouths of characters we know and love so well. And for me (and for other writers I know), part of the enticement is that it's much *easier* to write *Star Trek* stories than to write original stories.

To me, writing a *Star Trek* novel is like swimming in a

---

*For proper submission format and procedures, go to your local library and consult books such as *Writer's Market* and *Fiction Writer's Market*. (They also contain lists of literary agents and their addresses.) You can also learn a lot about markets, submission procedures and the like from taking courses given at local colleges, attending writers' seminars and workshops, etc.

nice heated pool. You grow tired, you get exercise, but it's comparatively effortless. But, as I discovered when I began working on other original stories, plotting one of my own novels, or the first book in my upcoming *Star Bridge* series, writing in my own universe was like trying to swim in the cold ocean surf. You have to work harder just to stay afloat; making headway is slow, difficult going. (For example, I've been working on one book of mine, *Suncastle*, for five years.)

But writing stories set in your own universe is infinitely worthwhile . . . though there are times when you have to keep reminding yourself of that. There are days when you feel as though you can't write another page, another paragraph . . . sometimes even another word.

But you do. If you're a writer, you can't stop.

Best of luck to all of you out there. Here's hoping you enjoy reading *Time for Yesterday* half as much as I enjoyed writing it.

Ann Crispin
August 1987

Historian's Note: *Time for Yesterday* takes place after the events chronicled in *Star Trek: The Motion Picture* and Howard Weinstein's novel *Deep Domain*.

Prologue

SECOND-IN-WAR CLETAS PACED nervously before the guarded door to his Sovren's office, toes squishing inside his boots with every stride. Even through the thick stone walls of the fortress, he could still hear the dull booms of thunder, the furious hissing of the rain. His dark gray cloak was black with water; it dripped soggily, but Cletas barely noticed the discomfort—he was too tired, too worried, too miserable.

The torches in their wall sconces flickered in the draft as the door opened and Voba, the Sovren's aide, peered out. "You can come in now," he whispered, stepping into the hall. "Ingev and Reydel are just finishing up their report on the range we can expect from the new—what do they call them?—catapults."

Cletas beckoned to the aide-de-camp, a short, slight man with reddish hair and a comical blob of a nose. "How *is* he tonight?" he asked, pitching his voice for Voba's ears alone.

The wiry little man shrugged. "The damp is playing rough with his leg," he said, *sotto voce*. "But is it true what I heard? That today the High Priestess of the Danreg foretold—"

Cletas silenced the aide-de-camp with a glare, knowing that his refusal to speak would be taken as assent, even so. Voba flushed angrily as he signaled the guards to open the door.

Cletas stepped into the study, a small, almost cozy

1

chamber in comparison to the rest of the fortress. His empty stomach lurched, then knotted with anxiety. As the three figures seated at the massive inlaid table turned toward them, Voba announced formally, "Second-in-War Cletas requests audience, sire."

"It looks more like Second Cletas should be requesting a hot meal and bath," the Sovren said, his mouth quirking in what Cletas, from long association, recognized as a smile. "Come in and shed that waterlogged cloak! You're dripping on my rug."

Cletas swung the steaming folds off his shoulders, nodding to Ingev and Reydel, First and Second Heavy Weapons Commanders, as he crossed the planked floor (avoiding the brightly woven blue rug with his wet footgear), then saluted and dropped to one knee, head bowed. "My liege."

"Tonight is hardly the night for formality, Cletas," his Sovren said mildly, one slanting eyebrow rising with amusement. "Sit down and ask Voba to help you off with those boots. I could hear you squishing from out in the hall."

As Voba wrestled with the Second's feet, the Sovren turned back to his other two officers. "So we can expect nearly twice the range of the experimental model?" he asked. "What about the size of the stones?"

"We can adjust the size of the throwing-cup from that of twice a man's helmet to nearly half a meter in diameter, sire," Ingev reported. "Of course, the heavier the stone, the shorter the range. Perhaps 450 meters at most for the biggest missiles, those weighing more than twenty-five kilograms."

"Good. Shore up the bankings on the paths they must travel and check the drainage."

"Yes, sire," Ingev and Reydel murmured, rolling up their vellum lists and drawings.

"Voba, please bring the Second something to eat," the Sovren said to his aide-de-camp, as Cletas moved his chair to join them at the table. "Will you have sufficient troops and draft vykar to move all six of the machines, Commander Ingev?"

Ingev, a short, squat man with the bowed legs of a

cavalryman, exchanged a sideways look with his tall blond Second-in-Command. "We could use another 120 troops, my liege," he said, after a moment's thought. "Twenty for each machine."

"Very well. Cletas, see to it that Commander Ingev is detailed 120 of your auxiliary infantry. Most of them should have time to rejoin their companies before they engage. The catapults will only be useful while the enemy is crossing the Redbank, *before* we engage."

The Second-in-War caught himself before he could grimace outright, but the keen gray eyes opposite him had picked up his reluctance, he knew . . . they missed very little. "As you order, sire," he said, stiffly.

Ingev and Reydel were already standing. "Have we your leave, sire?"

"Of course," the Sovren nodded, sketching a salute in answer to theirs. "Try to get some sleep."

As their footsteps faded in the hall outside, Cletas turned to his Sovren, his protest no longer hidden. "A hundred and twenty infantry fighters, my liege! That's a whole company and more I may lose if they can't rejoin their ranks. And for what—to nursemaid and push along those—those—" he sputtered to a halt, realizing he was on the verge of insubordination. *"Why,* sire?"

"Because, Cletas my friend, those catapults may spell the difference between outright defeat and stalemate for us. I don't dare even think the word 'victory'—that would be rank folly considering the odds we face." The Sovren's lean face was hard and drawn beneath his clipped black beard and moustache, and his gray eyes held his Second's with a bleak intensity. "But the Asyri, the Kerren, and the Danreg have never seen anything like what we've so painstakingly built, and the terror their hordes will feel when faced by a sky raining boulders will cause them even more harm than the rocks themselves."

"But can you be sure the things will actually *work* in a combat situation? They've never been tried—"

"Oh, yes, they have. Not here, not now. But they'll work. Have I been wrong before?"

3

Cletas ran a hand through his salt-and-pepper hair in tired resignation, thinking of all the changes the Sovren had introduced in the twenty years he'd known him. *New ways of counting, of measuring, even of speaking and reading . . . lamps, drainage systems, schooling the children, riding the vykar in addition to hitching them to wagons, better armor, smelting iron instead of the softer, more malleable bronze . . .*

"No, my liege. You haven't been wrong," he admitted. "Still . . ." He grinned ruefully. "I wish we didn't have to try them for the first time in the last battle we both may see. If you've finally made a mistake, I'd hate to miss the chance to say 'I told you so.'"

His Sovren's mouth softened into a genuine, rare smile. "I'll keep your wish in mind." He rolled up a parchment map, his hard, long-fingered hands moving with his customary quick efficiency. "Did you meet with your spies, or did they all drown on the way?"

"We met, sire," Cletas said. "The situation hasn't changed much. Heldeon of Danreg Ford has set up camp on the northern slope of Big Snowy, and this afternoon the War Queen Laol and Rorgan Death-Hand met with him there. They talked for about two hours, then rejoined their troops.

"My informant said that the meeting was interrupted by the discovery of three spies, which caused some finger pointing, but then they calmed down and shared wine and broke bread like the best of friends. Even the rain couldn't damp the greed in their eyes as they looked down at New Araen."

The Sovren's face retained its usual impassivity, but Cletas was quick to note the sagging of his big shoulders. "So we can't even hope they'll cut a few of each other's throats before they open ours," he said softly, bitterly. "And with this rain still continuing, Moorgate Plain will be so soft the enemy will scarcely need shovels to dig our graves. Presuming they have the decency to bury us, which is doubtful."

Cletas nodded, knowing that, although he could no longer hear the downpour outside, his ruler could. "If this rain keeps up, we might as well forget about fighting. The troops won't be able to march, the catapults won't roll, and the cavalry will look like pottery figures ready for firing."

"We'll need two days of sun in order to have decent footing."

"I know," Cletas agreed, staring gloomily into the savory stew Voba slid in front of him. Absently, he broke off a chunk of hard reddish bread and began chewing on it. "We may be forced to abandon the cavalry flanks if the ground is this bad. After all that drilling . . ." he sighed. "Vykar Troop Commander Yarlev will cry, you know."

The Sovren ignored the levity this time, his eyes intent on his Second's face. "The meeting with your spies and scouts," he said. "How did it go? Something is disturbing you. I could feel it as soon as I saw you."

Cletas shivered a little, thinking of all the times his Sovren had somehow sensed matters that he would have rather kept secret. At times it frightened him to realize that this man, so different physically from his adopted people, was also different *inside*. He *thought* differently, in some manner Cletas couldn't explain. He could sense thoughts and emotions and, sometimes, the coming of death.

"I'm sorry, old friend," the Sovren said gently. "Did I rattle you again? You ought to be used to it by now. But what about the rest of your report? Is the Redbank still flooded? Has the High Priestess of the Danreg pronounced the battle oracle yet? When will they march?"

"No," Cletas said heavily, "she hasn't pronounced it yet. We know that Heldeon's people—and, for the moment at least, we can include Rorgan Death-Hand's Asyri and Laol's Clan Kerren also—won't fight without it. As for the river, my sources estimated that they won't be able to cross the Redbank until day after tomorrow at the earliest. More likely three days."

The Sovren watched him intently as Cletas spooned gravy onto his bread. "Then what *did* happen today? Voba knew something, too . . . I could tell. What is it?"

The Second took a huge bite of the gravy-sopped bread and chewed, while trying desperately to think of a way to phrase his news. Perhaps if he started with the plan he'd developed, it wouldn't seem so . . . final. Cletas swallowed the bread, aided by a swig of rochab wine. "The High Priestess, Wynn," he began, "is Heldeon's daughter, in addition to her service to the Goddess."

"So?"

"She's a widow, who lost husband and child two years ago in an Asyri raid. Not a lass anymore, but still of bearing age, my liege . . . they say her father values her counsel more than any of his clan chiefs. And, it's reported, likely looking . . . tall, with—"

"I repeat, *so?*" The Sovren's voice was as hard and flat as his eyes now, and Cletas felt himself flinching away from the palpable wave of anger emanating from his ruler. "Explain what all this has to do with her battle oracle, damn it!"

"Sire," Cletas met those nearly colorless eyes, then, all his resolutions toward subtlety forgotten, blurted, "it's been nearly a score of years now since the Lady Araen—the Goddess keep her—passed the Final Veil. If you wish, it could be a matter of State, no true union! Consider it, my liege, please!"

"Cletas, if you're implying what I think you're implying, you're out of line." The Sovren's face was drawn, its harsh, angular planes making him appear almost inhuman. "If I've misread your admittedly disjointed statement, then clarify your meaning."

"My meaning, sire, is this: If the High Priestess Wynn could be captured *before* she can pronounce the oracle for the coming battle, then the Danreg will be thrown into confusion. Their troops may even refuse to march."

One slanted brow rose in surprise. "Hmm . . . Cletas, that's a far more logical suggestion than most of the ones the Council voiced today. Do you think a small raiding party could engineer such a capture?"

"I would volunteer to lead it personally, my liege," Cletas said. "Tonight." He braced himself. "However, that only constitutes the first part of my plan, sire. Once the woman is within our walls, it may be possible to . . ." he hesitated, searching for words, "it may be possible to . . . reason . . . with her. Convince her that an alliance by marriage would benefit both our peoples. Bride-raiding is common among the Danreg, something they will excuse if done for the purpose of honorable marriage."

With an abrupt, furious movement, the Sovren stood up and turned his back on his Second-in-War. Cletas went on, stubbornly, "Heldeon's people hold the ties of blood-kin and marriage-kin so sacred that they would never fight against one of their own. If you could convince this woman to ally with you in a State handfasting, Heldeon might even be moved to *join* our cause. At worst, he would withdraw his troops to avoid the sin of raising sword against one who is blood-by-marriage."

As Cletas finished, the Sovren began pacing, and even his limp (caused by a spear he'd taken through his left thigh years ago) could not mask the anger plain to read in every stride. "Did the Council put you up to this?" he asked tightly. His face was still impassive, but his eyes made the Second shudder, knowing he'd reopened an old—but still agonizing—wound.

"No, sire," he said, forcing himself to gaze steadily at his ruler. "It might be a way to save New Araen, and that's all I'm thinking of . . . that, and the fact that you've been alone too long. Nineteen years . . ." He hesitated, thinking of his own Marya and their son and daughter, trying to imagine life without them. "That's too long to be alone."

"I spent seven years in total solitude, once. I'll manage," the Sovren's voice was curt. He stood with his hands clasped behind his back, facing a wall painting he'd done twenty years ago, when his stronghold was first built. The Second had never understood the subject matter—stars, and an outspread hand, beneath an odd, disklike shape. Once he'd asked his ruler what it meant, only to be told, "It's a message for someone who hasn't been born yet."

The Second dragged his thoughts back to the present with an effort—there was something strangely hypnotic about those painted stars. They weren't just white specks of light the way they appeared in the nighttime sky, but tiny spheres

7

of all colors, hanging like scattered jewels against the black background. Cletas had never seen stars like that.

"Sire, won't you even consider my plan? It could mean life instead of death for all the Lakreo Valley. Would it be such a terrible price to pay, to take a consort? Heldeon has nearly eight thousand troops, and if he could be swayed to our side . . ."

The Sovren sighed, turning back to face him, weariness of more than body cloaking him, shadowing his features beneath his thick black hair. "Very well, Cletas. I promise to consider the second part of your plan, assuming you're successful in capturing the woman tonight."

"Thank you, my liege."

"But you're *sure* she hasn't given the battle oracle yet? Third-in-War Trebor Damas mentioned that there was some kind of ceremony going on up on the hillside today, and that the High Priestess was speaking."

Cletas sighed. *Here it is, then. I should have known I couldn't keep it from him.* "I'm positive about the battle oracle, sire. What the High Priestess announced today was that she'd had a Sending concerning *you.*"

One eyebrow went up in wry amusement. "Me? And how stands the Lady Wynn's record in these matters?"

"She . . . has never been wrong, sire. At least, not that my sources could discover," Cletas admitted.

"Cletas, you look as though your favorite hunting cat had died. What is it? What did she say?"

The Second-in-War forced himself to meet those tired gray eyes. "She said: *'Only if he who is halt walks healed, if he who is death-struck in battle rises whole, only then can victory slip from us—then only will the Goddess turn Her face away.'*"

This time the eyebrow nearly vanished beneath the black hair. "Indeed," the Sovren said slowly. "So, today Wynn, High Priestess of the Danreg, who has a perfect record in her prophecies, foretold my death in the coming battle."

"But, sire—" Cletas made a helpless gesture. "Maybe this time, she's wrong."

"As my own estimable sire would remark," the Sovren paused, clearly remembering, "'fascinating.'"

"Is that *all* you can say?" Cletas snorted indignantly. "A few moments ago you looked ready to break me in two for suggesting you take another consort, and now, when I tell you it's been prophesied that you won't survive this battle, you just look mildly interested"—he thumped his fist on the table with exasperation—"and quote your *father?* Was *he* as coldblooded?"

"Well, actually, no," the Sovren said, amused at his Second's outburst, "both of us are rather warmblooded, by comparison with the rest of you. By about three degrees, or so."

Cletas gave him a measuring glance. "This must be a night for revelations," he said. "I've never heard you mention your father before. Does he still live? Where is he?"

The gray eyes softened suddenly, wistfully, in the stern face. "My father . . ." he mused. "Someone I haven't seen in more than twenty years, now." He twisted a heavy silver wrist-guard absently, not looking up. "I still miss him, you know? Almost as much as I miss Araen. I knew them both such a short time . . ."

"Is he dead?" Something about his Sovren's manner of speaking made Cletas think not.

"Dead?" The ruler made a small sound, almost a chuckle. "No, he's not dead."

"Is he . . ." Cletas hesitated, "like you?"

"You mean physically?" The Sovren ruffled the hair over his ears, hair deliberately left shaggy to disguise his most obvious "difference." He'd learned early that minimizing his differences made his rule easier. "Yes, I definitely take after his side of the family, Cletas."

"Was—is—he a ruler too, my liege?"

"Well . . . no, not really. Actually, the last I knew, he was a Second-in-Command, like you, my friend. He serves his ruler as loyally and well as you do me. Together, the two of them have had at least as many adventures, and their exploits have become legendary."

9

"Great warriors, eh?"

"When necessary, Cletas. But most of the time they tread the paths of peace."

"Would that we could, too, sire," Cletas said, trying to envision such a land. "Is there any chance you could summon them? We could use two such fighters, now."

Slowly the Sovren shook his head, the expression in his eyes faraway, as though he were looking at something wonderful he could never have again. "No, Cletas. They are farther away than mere distance. If you rode hard for all the days and nights left in your life, and your son and then your daughter rode for all the days and nights of theirs, they could never even draw near to them. Finding them would be as impossible as pulling down a handful of stars . . ."

His words trailed off, then, after a moment, he straightened, his voice hardening. "Come on, Cletas. Let's go over those armory requisitions Trebor Damas sent over. We haven't much time left."

Chapter One

THE FOG WAS a tangible thing, muffling the ocean at the foot of the tall, plunging cliff, concealing the jagged rocks awash in surf beneath its woolly blanket. Even the *whoosh-boom* of the mighty Pacific, here at romantically dubbed Lands End, was reduced by the fog to faint slurping noises that echoed and rebounded eerily in the heavy mist. The man standing by the edge of the cliff was at one moment wrapped in almost total silence, then the next, could clearly hear the mournful barks of the sea lions gathered on the protruding rocks and navigational buoys.

A newborn breeze began whipping his dark wavy hair, and he knew from long experience that it spelled death for this particular fog. San Francisco mists were tenacious, but the wind always won in the end, herding them out to sea, breaking them against the hills, smothering them in the valleys.

For a moment the man felt a sudden pity for the fog, helpless before the air currents. *You're getting morbid,* he told himself. *Stop it right here, or you'll spend the rest of the day depressed. Besides,* he checked his wrist chrono, *lunchtime was over ten minutes ago . . . you're late.*

But he made no move to turn and retrace his steps back to the dully gleaming parabolas and towers of Starfleet Command. After all, what good was rank if you couldn't take an extra half hour for lunch once in a while? It wasn't as if his aide, Lieutenant Thasten, would shake an accusing blue finger at him . . . the Andorian would appreciate the chance to catch up on her workload from this morning. He kept her busy . . . *must remember to put her in for a promotion,* he made a mental note. *Anyone who can keep my office as organized as Thasten has for the past few years has earned the equivalent of a battlefield commission* . . .

He began walking through the moving fogbank, immersed in memories, memories that crowded his mind whenever it wasn't fully occupied with work. The echoes in the mist sounded like a voice, and his mind shaped the sounds into the words he'd heard so often those last three months . . .

Jim . . . how soon can I go home, son? Jim, I hate this place . . . Familiar pain stabbed him, dulling now after six months, but still there. For a second he was back in that austere little chapel in Riverside, Iowa, knowing that in a few minutes he would have to carry the little box to the rows of wall crypts and slide it into the newest one . . . the polished bronze plate identifying the niche as the final resting place for the earthly remains of his mother, Winona Kirk . . .

The hiss of a two-seater messenger skimmer jerked him back to San Francisco and the present. It swooped down, hovering a half meter above the clifftop, and the pilot, a young lieutenant, leaned out, her manner at once respectful and urgent. "Admiral Kirk, Admiral Morrow requests your presence, sir."

James T. Kirk hastily swung up into the little snub-nosed vehicle, and the lieutenant lifted them with a rush even before he'd finished activating his safety field. Lands End dwindled away beneath him as he looked down; then, as the craft banked and turned east, Kirk watched the amber-orange towers of the Golden Gate Bridge emerge from the white fogbank like the ethereal spires of some fairyland.

"What's up, Lieutenant? Where are we going?"

"My orders were to take you to central headquarters, sir,"

the lieutenant said, her expression carefully neutral. "Admiral Morrow did not tell me why, though he did say it was urgent."

Minutes later, the skimmer docked in the central shuttle bay at Starfleet Command, and Kirk headed immediately for Morrow's office. He was still wondering why the commander, Starfleet, had summoned him, and spent a few moments mentally reviewing the status of his current assignments. Nothing wrong there—he was ahead of time on most of them, and, barring bureaucratic snafus (a continual menace), all would be completed on schedule.

His boots clicked impatiently up to the lifts in the northern tower and the admiral scowled, seeing that all were in use. He forced himself not to fidget as he waited, his hazel eyes traveling impatiently over the magnificent vista of San Francisco and the Bay visible through the fifty-story sweep of plex filling the tower's lobby with polarized sunshine. The fog was completely gone, now, and Sol turned the pale bronze, gold, and white lobby into a shining marvel, broken only at ground level by splotches of green, vermilion, and cobalt-colored plants.

Come on, come on, he thought, forcing himself not to turn and stab the lift button again. *Morrow said it was urgent . . .*

The lift chimed softly, apologetically, behind him. "Level 43, Section 17," Kirk announced, stepping into the glassy bullet.

The lift deposited him in the corridor before the admiral's office. As the entrance portal hissed out of his way, Kirk was startled to find himself facing Lieutenant Thasten, who was just leaving. "Thasten, what's going on?"

"I brought your things, Admiral," she said, indicating his packed travel bag sitting on the carpet in the reception area. "Do you know when you'll be back, sir?"

Kirk grimaced. "I didn't know I was *going* until this moment. I'll let you know, Thasten. In my absence, please ask Commander Arex to attend the services for Captain Ikeya and the *Constellation*'s crew."

"Yes, sir."

Kirk turned away to find Morrow's aide busy keying his voder. "Admiral Kirk is here, sir."

"Please go right in, Admiral," he said, almost immediately, then ushered Kirk into Morrow's private office, the admiral's travel bag grasped firmly in his topmost talons.

Harry Morrow was waiting for them, his dark, handsome face drawn and sober. "Hold the questions, Jim," he said. "One of our ships is in trouble. We haven't got much time. *Cochise* is standing by. I'll brief you as soon as we're underway."

Kirk nodded, taking his bag from the aide. Morrow pressed a button and a vid-screen wall swung aside, revealing a small transporter unit with two pads. As they stepped up, the aide spoke softly into a communicator, then Kirk felt the familiar sensation of displacement as the walls shimmered, then solidified, revealing a different location.

The first person he saw as he stepped forward into the *Cochise*'s small transporter room was his former First Officer. "Spock!" he exclaimed, striding over to the Vulcan. "What the hell are *you* doing here?"

"Admiral Morrow sent for me," Spock told him. "I just arrived."

"You're looking well," Kirk said. "How long has it been?"

"One month, six days, seventeen hours, nineteen min—"

"The question was rhetorical, Spock—as you very well know," Kirk broke in, grinning. "It's good to see you."

"And you, Jim."

"Gentlemen," came Morrow's voice from behind Kirk, "I hate to break up old home week, but we don't have much time."

Kirk turned to follow the admiral. "All right, Harry, let's hear a few of those answers you promised me. Where are we going? Why all the secrecy?"

Morrow nodded. "The secrecy is because you're still James T. Kirk, media darling, and I didn't want reporters getting wind of this situation. The last thing we want is a panic."

"A *panic?*" Kirk's good-natured smile faded.

Morrow nodded. "The briefing room is this way, gentlemen."

As they left the transporter room, the barely felt vibrations of the ship's engines altered, and Kirk realized they'd already left Earth orbit at full impulse power. *Morrow wasn't kidding about being in a hurry,* he thought, following the admiral. *We must be halfway to Pluto already. Where are we headed? Which ship is in trouble?*

Cochise was one of the Hermes Class I Scouts, with a usual complement of about 200 crew and officers. But as he trailed Morrow's broad back through the nearly empty corridors, Kirk realized that the ship must be running with just a skeleton crew.

The admiral led them to the small briefing room, activated the security screens, then waved them to seats. "We have a big problem, gentlemen. Something is threatening the Federation, something with a potential for destruction that is . . . limitless, I suppose. Worse than Vejur, much worse. The aspect of the problem that is our immediate concern is Alpha Centauri B, and the *Kismet,* a Federation courier ship which is now stranded about 100,000,000 kilometers from the star."

"Stranded?" Kirk leaned forward, frowning.

"Yes. It's been there for nearly sixteen hours now, helpless, its computer system entirely shorted out."

Spock's eyebrow climbed nearly to his hairline. "The entire system? Most . . . unusual. The backups are nonfunctional?"

Morrow nodded brusquely. "It's all part of what's happening to Alpha Centauri B. The star has been enveloped by a wave of time displacement that is speeding up its aging. It's consuming itself at an incredible rate—converting its hydrogen into helium as though millions of years were passing in minutes. We're evacuating the population of Kent to Centaurus, praying that we have enough time to finish before the star swells into a red giant and engulfs its planets. That could happen as early as twenty hours from now, by some estimates."

Kirk stared at the admiral, stunned. Alpha Centauri was a triple star system. Alpha Centauri A was a yellow sun slightly larger and brighter than Sol, orbited by Centaurus and fourteen other, uninhabited planets. Alpha Centauri B was its nearby (thirty to forty A.U. distant) smaller, orange companion. Both were distantly orbited by a small red dwarf, a flare star named Proxima Centauri. Kirk had known that Proxima Centauri was the closest star to Earth's solar system before he could read.

Alpha A had shown signs of instability for hundreds of years, but its slight fluctuations were negligible on a stellar scale. Kirk had never heard of any problems with Alpha B—under normal circumstances, both stars should have remained unchanged for billions of years. Alpha B was orbited by six planets. The most Earth-like one, Kent, had been settled by humans over a hundred years before. Kirk had visited there more times than he could recall.

He also owned property on Centaurus, only one system away . . . a valley he'd bought over the years and named Garrovick Valley, in honor of his first captain. Kirk had a brief, piercing memory of his little cabin there, the hours of peace and quiet—of fishing in the Farragut River.

It took him a moment to find his voice. "And the *Kismet?* It's caught in this . . . wave . . . of accelerated time, too?"

"No," said Spock, positively. "Logic dictates that if it had been, everyone aboard would have been killed instantaneously. Aged and fallen to dust before they could even realize what was happening to them."

Harry Morrow was nodding agreement. "Right. Though they had to explain that to me in words of one syllable too, Jim, so don't look like that."

Kirk *had* been feeling stupid. "You'd think I'd have gotten used to it after all these years of working with Vulcans. So what *is* the problem with the *Kismet's* computers?"

"The EMP effect," the commander of Starfleet told him. "Any massive thermonuclear reaction—whether it's from a bomb or a star—causes an electromagnetic pulse that shorts out computers—and communications. Anyway, the ship is drifting in space, and if it's there much longer . . ." He shrugged, making a curiously final *flick* of his fingers.

"Can we get close enough to the ship to rescue the crew without getting caught by the EMP effect ourselves?" Kirk asked.

"I don't know," Morrow said. "Communication is impossible, of course, since their systems are down. Our deflector shields will protect us—that's how they're managing to evacuate Kent—but as to whether we can get close enough to the ship to attempt a rescue . . ." He frowned, shaking his head. "*Kismet* got caught by the EMP before it had enough warning to activate its shields. All we can do is get there as fast as we can and see what we can do. My science staff is working on the problem of how to stay shielded and still use the transporter . . . though, as you know, we've never figured out a way to do that yet."

"I will offer my assistance to them," Spock said. "What is our ETA?"

Morrow's eyes flicked to the chronometer. "At warp eight, we should be there in about fifteen hours."

"Cutting it pretty close," Kirk muttered.

"We only found out about it an hour ago. *Kismet* was in communication with Kent when it was hit, but it took awhile for the news to reach us. Communications from the evacuation area have been sporadic and confusing, as you might guess."

"What percentage of the population of Kent has currently been evacuated?" Spock asked.

"Our last report said seventy-five percent."

"Hell of a lot of people left, then," Kirk said grimly. And then, because he *had* to know, he said, trying to keep his concern from showing, "I gather this won't affect Centaurus?"

"Alpha B may engulf or sear the outermost gas giants in the Centaurian system," Spock said, his quick glance at his friend acknowledging the reason for Kirk's anxiety, "but Centaurus itself should be far enough away to escape the heat. As to the cosmic rays . . ." He raised an eyebrow at Morrow.

"We've got special planetary shielding rigged," the admiral told them, "to deflect the rays. Don't worry, Jim, your valley will be safe. I still remember the fishing there."

Kirk sighed. "Thanks, Harry."

Spock steepled his fingers, a familiar gesture to Kirk from all the briefings they'd shared over the years. It meant he was thinking hard. "You said this was only one aspect of a larger problem, Admiral Morrow," the Vulcan said. "Is that larger problem, by any chance, connected with the loss of the *Constellation* ten days ago?"

Kirk stiffened, glancing quickly from the Vulcan to the admiral.

Morrow nodded, reluctantly. "Yes, it—"

The admiral was interrupted by the signal above the door flashing. When he keyed it open, a Tellarite ensign hurried in, saluting, her tiny eyes crinkled with anxiety. "This message just came in for you, Admiral. Priority One, sir."

Morrow reached for the cassette the younger officer held out. "Thank you, Ensign."

While he watched the admiral scan the message, Kirk's mind flashed back to Morrow's revelation about the *Constellation* and her fate. He'd known her captain, Carmen Ikeya, for over ten years. She'd been the first woman to command a starship, though now there were several others. He could see her in his mind's eye, almond eyes beneath unruly salt-and-pepper hair, a reckless, "give 'em hell" grin on her lined face. Whatever had happened to Carmen—and it was apparently more than the official Starfleet designation of "missing, presumed destroyed"—Kirk was willing to bet she'd gone down swinging.

His musings were interrupted by Morrow's soft curse. The admiral's broad shoulders sagged suddenly. "What is it, Harry?"

Spock, too, was leaning forward in his seat, though his expression, as usual, remained unreadable.

Morrow shook his head. "I just got confirmation that the *Kismet* carried a passenger. I'd hoped that perhaps he'd been delayed somehow and wasn't aboard . . ." he sighed, "but he is."

"Who is? What passenger?" Kirk was beginning to feel as if he'd fallen down a rabbit hole.

"I wanted to talk to the three of you together," Morrow went on mumbling, half to himself. "You're such a well-known team, so I ordered him to catch the next ship for Earth."

"'The three of us . . .'" Kirk looked over at Spock, who nodded solemnly at him. "You're telling me *Kismet*'s passenger is . . . Dr. Leonard McCoy."

"Yes."

Chapter Two

"OH, SHIT," KIRK SAID. "This is a hell of a mess."

"Indeed," agreed Spock.

Morrow nodded grimly.

Spock finally broke the ensuing dismal silence. "Admiral Morrow, perhaps you might explain the entire problem —and why you felt 'the three of us' were uniquely suited to advise you."

Morrow took a deep breath. "First, remember that this is all Priority One Secret. *I* wasn't given the complete picture until day before yesterday. Only the Secretary General of the Federation Council, and four other people—two of them theoretical physicists—know everything that I'm going to tell you."

Kirk watched the admiral, wondering why the theatric buildup—he'd known Harry Morrow for years, and drama wasn't his style. *It's as though he has to nerve himself up just to put it into words.*

"More stars than Alpha Centauri B are dying prematurely," Morrow began. "I expect Mr. Spock has seen articles in scientific journals speculating on the sudden increase in star deaths." He glanced over at the Vulcan.

Spock nodded. "Yes. Statistically, there have been fully ten times as many star deaths in our galaxy as there should have been during the past two solar months. Astronomical physicists have been unable to account for this increase, but, extrapolating this trend to include stars of ten-plus solar masses, the projected result is indeed disquieting—"

"You mean terrifying," Morrow interrupted. "What you haven't read in those articles is the reason for these star deaths."

He paused, and Kirk guessed, "More of these time waves?"

"Yes. Fortunately, until yesterday, none of the stars that had been affected has had inhabited planets. But now Alpha Centauri B is dying. Picture what one of those waves of accelerated time would do to Sol. Or 40 Eridani. Kent has a population of fifty million. What's the population of Vulcan?"

"Seven billion, seven hundred and fifty-two thousand —as of the most recent full-count census."

"And Earth has nearly twice that many." Morrow rubbed his forehead as though to ease a headache. "I've ordered every freighter, every pleasure yacht, every Starfleet vessel within range to assist in Kent's evacuation. We just *might* make it."

"And the *Constellation?*" Kirk asked. "What happened to it?"

"The ship came out of warp too soon," Morrow said. "It—" He was interrupted by the bosun's whistle. The admiral activated the small vid-screen. "Morrow here."

"Admiral," the communications officer was a middle-aged Native American man, "I've just received a shielded signal from the Secretary General of the Federation Council."

"Decode and patch through to me here."

A moment later, he scanned the translation, his face drawn and gray with shock. "Neutrino detectors have located signs of growing instability in Canopus. The secretary general wants to know how many Federation-registered vessels in that sector could be used for evacuation purposes."

Morrow activated the screen again. "Lieutenant Buck,

respond that I'll have to do some checking," he said, slowly. "I don't know how many private yachts we may be able to commandeer. Inform the secretary that I'll get her an answer as soon as possible."

Morrow switched off the unit, his expression a study in frustration. "Two inhabited planets in the Canopus system," he growled. "Eight billion people. I'm afraid this briefing will have to wait until I get that information through to T'Kyra. Jim, I'll need your help to chase down some commercial shipping figures. Spock, report to the scientific team."

During the next hours, Kirk pushed his worry about McCoy to the back of his mind, forcing himself to concentrate on the difficult task of tracing the routes and schedules of potentially available cargo ships in the Canopus sector. Once he looked up at a diffident, "Sir?" to find the Tellarite ensign waiting with a pot of coffee and a plate of sandwiches. He ate them mechanically, hardly noticing that they were his favorite, chicken salad. It was only when his fingers marched blindly across an empty plate that he realized he'd been ravenous.

The coffee he drank black, grateful for its scalding energy boost. When he got up to find the head, he looked at his chronometer and was startled to realize he'd been sitting there for nearly five hours.

Two pots of coffee, a sonic shower, and a twenty-minute nap (when he inadvertently nodded off over his figures) later, he had finished the analysis Morrow wanted. Kirk keyed the final data into the banks, then transmitted copies of his findings to Morrow. His eyes were gritty and raw as he rubbed them, trying to will away a throbbing headache. *Ought to get my eyes checked,* he thought, standing up and stretching. His back creaked.

I've only been awake for thirty-four hours, he thought, disgustedly. *Must be really getting old. Time was when I could put in thirty-six hours and still be ready for a fight.* For the first time in hours he let himself think of Bones, wondering how his friend was faring. *It's got to be hell, trapped in that little ship with all the systems dead, blind and deaf, waiting for that star to swell up and swallow them* . . .

The portal slid aside and Spock entered. The Vulcan, Kirk noted sourly, appeared far more rested and alert than he had any right to look. He raised an eyebrow at Kirk's expression. "Are you all right, Jim?"

The admiral nodded wearily. "How long till we reach *Kismet?*"

"We are almost within sensor range of her last recorded position now. Admiral Morrow said he could use our help on the bridge, since *Cochise* is carrying a minimal crew."

"Good. Anything is better than sitting around worrying."

The two officers headed for the bridge. Though the scout ship was much smaller than the heavy cruisers such as the *Enterprise,* it was designed along similar lines. Kirk stood for a moment looking at the captain's seat, the viewscreen, each station, and drew a breath of contentment to be back in space, with the feel of a ship beneath his feet. It was impossible to feel happiness, of course—Bones was out there, in danger. But it had been months since he'd even left Earth orbit.

It's only when I'm back out here that I realize how much I miss it, he thought. *I leave something out here when I'm planet-bound . . . a part of my soul.*

"Jim, can you take the helm?" Morrow asked, turning in the captain's seat to regard him. "I just sent my helm officer and navigator down to the shuttle deck, in case we locate them."

"Aye, sir," Kirk said, giving his best "eager ensign" salute and heading for the control and navigation console.

"Mr. Spock, please take the sensors. I want a constant monitor."

"Understood, Admiral," Spock murmured, assuming his station beside the science officer.

"Are we clear, Mr. Spock?"

"Yes, sir. Our best orbit for sensor scanning will be at a distance of 120,000,000 kilometers, Admiral, and we will need to maintain our shields. The EMP emanations are continuous."

"Very well. Ahead one-quarter impulse, helm. Heading three-four-two, mark four."

Kirk found himself scanning the console for the proper controls. *Wish Sulu were here.* He set the course, then eased the switch up in its slot. *Cochise* glided smoothly on her way.

Alpha Centauri B stood out clearly in their forward screens by now, as a small yellowish-orange sphere slightly smaller than the sun as seen from Earth.

"I am detecting considerable neutrino activity, Admiral," Spock said. "Alpha B could begin expanding into an orange giant at any moment."

"Magnification on forward viewscreen. Increase filters."

Alpha B rippled larger, then larger still. Kirk stared at the star. *Look at those sunspots. Never seen so many. And the solar flares!*

"Any sign of *Kismet,* Mr. Spock?"

"Negative, Admiral."

"Increase speed to one-half impulse, Jim. Same heading."

"Aye, sir." Kirk found he was falling back into his days as an ensign helmsman on the *Farragut.* His fingers danced over the controls with fewer and fewer hesitations.

Slowly, *Cochise* settled into orbit around the star. *At this rate, it'll take us days just to circle it,* Kirk thought anxiously. Yet he knew they couldn't afford to miss the tiny *Kismet* on their sensors—they wouldn't get a second chance. If, indeed, they were granted a *first* chance.

The electromagnetic wave disrupted communications, so they could not even check on how the evacuation of Kent was proceeding. Kirk guided *Cochise* in her orbit, keeping a careful watch on their power levels. "Admiral," he said, after nearly an hour had passed, "keeping our screens up at full capacity is draining our power reserves faster than projected."

"How long can we keep searching at this rate?" Morrow asked.

"Not more than another two hours," Kirk told him. "Did

the *Kismet*'s last communication give her location coordinates?"

"Yes," Morrow said. "Her last reported location was where we entered orbit."

"But she's had nearly thirty-two hours to drift away from there," Kirk pointed out.

"Inertia," Spock said, nodding approvingly at his former captain. "Logically, we cannot afford to ignore the fact that a body traveling at any given speed tends to remain at that speed unless acted upon by an outside force."

Morrow rubbed his forehead. "I see what you mean . . . but can we afford to take the chance that we'll miss them by skipping part of our search pattern?"

Kirk took a deep breath. "Can we afford *not* to?"

"How fast was *Kismet* going when she encountered the EMP wave?" Spock asked.

"She was due for a brief message relay at Kent," Morrow told him, "which is why she came out of warp. If Captain Perez was following a textbook approach, he should have been traveling at three-quarter impulse power."

"That gives me something to go on, then." Working with feverish haste, Kirk set up the problem on the navigation computers, double-checking his figures, remembering to allow for the increased buffeting of Alpha B's solar wind on a powerless—but still gliding—vessel. He fed all available data into the computer, then asked it to plot a projected course in three dimensions. Moments later, he had his answer.

"Spock, it's been a long time since I did anything like this. Will you check my figures?"

In his absorption, Kirk had forgotten that he wasn't in command. Spock glanced at Admiral Morrow for permission, who nodded. Kirk transferred his data to the science console, then sat tensely, trying not to think that McCoy's life might depend on what they did in the next few minutes.

The Vulcan straightened after a moment. "Verified," he said, glancing over at Kirk. "Logically, that is where they should be."

"All right, Jim," Morrow said, after looking over the projection, "lay in your course. Warp factor one."

Cochise leaped ahead beneath Kirk's fingers. Twenty minutes later, Kirk announced, "We've reached my projected coordinates, Admiral. Decreasing to sublight."

"Any sign of them, Mr. Spock?"

"Nothing, Admiral."

"Implement standard search grid. Slow to one-half impulse."

Kirk piloted *Cochise* through the maneuvers of the search grid automatically, his mouth dry with anxiety. What if he'd been wrong? *We might have passed them by already. Bones could be ten thousand kilometers behind us, on that ship with no life-support systems . . . he could be dying, right this minute, they could all be dead . . .*

Ten minutes . . . Fifteen . . . Thirty . . . One hour.

One hour and twenty minutes.

"Power status, Jim?"

"We can maintain full shielding only another fifteen minutes," Kirk said quietly, feeling despair settle over him like a shroud. "If we search any longer, we won't be able to keep up our shields long enough to get away ourselves."

Morrow's dark features held nothing but sympathy. "We'll search, then. You did everything you could, Jim. Don't look like that."

Kirk shook his head, numb with the realization that this time, they weren't going to pull a miracle out of thin air. This time, they were—

"I'm picking up something." Spock's flat tone held an undercurrent of excitement.

"Kismet?" Morrow leaned forward.

"Verified, Admiral. The vessel is dead ahead, heading mark three point four-two."

Kirk felt relief wash over him, relief that was almost immediately replaced by increased tension. *Are we too late? Are they still alive?*

Cochise approached the drifting courier ship. Except for her emergency running lights, she was dead in space. "Well, we've found her," Morrow said, to nobody in particular, "now, how do we contact her? All her communication systems are down. She can't see or hear us."

Cochise's science officer, a woman named Lisa Washington, turned to regard the image on the forward viewscreen. "Send someone out to knock on their airlock?" she suggested, deadpan.

Despite his worry, Kirk's mouth twitched at the picture her suggestion conjured up. "Too bad we can't, Lieutenant." Then, abruptly, he straightened in his seat. "Hey, that's *it!* We'll knock on their hull!"

"Huh?" Washington said, frowning.

"Fire our phasers over her bow, just close enough to rattle them a little! Do it in a regular pattern, so they know we're here!"

Spock was already nodding. "It could work, Admiral Morrow."

"Let's try it. Jim, fire when ready."

"Aye, sir. Firing phaser one." Kirk pressed the firing button, and the deadly beam shot out.

By firing in shorter and then longer bursts, he was able to create a pattern. He gave them the old "dot-dot-dot, dash-dash-dash, dot-dot-dot" of the SOS, repeated it, then, on impulse, followed it up with "shave-and-a-haircut."

Then they sat waiting, rigid with hope and fear, praying for some sign of life aboard the crippled vessel. Kirk found himself wishing they could drop their screens, just for a second, so their sensors could lock onto the crew and beam them aboard, but he knew that was impossible. The next move was up to *Kismet*.

Five minutes crept by. Ten.

"Should I signal again, Admiral?" Kirk asked, trying to keep his voice level.

"Yes—no!" Morrow was on his feet, his gaze never leaving the viewscreen. "The airlock's opening!"

Automatically, Kirk increased the magnification, so they could all make out a bulky figure in a thruster suit, hanging against the backdrop of space and the side of *Kismet*'s hull.

As they watched, the figure unclipped a safety line. The lock cycled again, opening to disgorge three more figures in ordinary spacesuits. As each spacesuited figure left the airlock, the occupant of the thruster suit hooked them together with the line. In ten minutes, there were two thruster suits, with ten spacesuited figures linked to each. With their white, slightly reflective suits, they resembled misshapen pearls strung together, suspended against a velvet case of infinite blackness.

They'll have to use the manual overrides when they activate the thruster suits, Kirk thought. *The computers won't work. They'll have to mentally compute their trajectory and how many seconds of thrust to allow.*

"How will we get them aboard?" Lieutenant Buck wondered.

"If they get close enough, that's where we use the shuttlecraft," Morrow said. "If we turn *Cochise* so our hangar deck entrance faces away from the star, the ship's bulk will block the EMP. We can drop our forward shield long enough to let the shuttle leave and return."

"Shuttle deck," Morrow continued, into his intercom. "Ready cargo shuttle *Onizuka* to retrieve *Kismet* crew."

"Aye, Admiral. Standing by."

"They've triggered thruster ignition!" Kirk said.

He watched, mouth dry, as the thrusters cut in, sending the suited figures zipping toward *Cochise*. Each of the linked spacesuits jerked, in turn, as the line tightened, then was towed willy-nilly behind the thruster operator. *Like a giant game of crack the whip,* Kirk thought. *There are going to be some stiff necks and backs tomorrow.*

Finally, just after both pearl strands of spacesuits passed the forward viewscreen at a distance of several kilometers, Kirk saw the braking thrusters fire. *Did they gauge it right? Will they stop where the shuttle can reach them?*

"Shuttle deck here," said the intercom, a minute later. "We have them in range. Navigator Ferguson says we'll be launching in a minute. Stand by to drop number four deflector shield."

An excited *whoop* went up from the bridge crew. Kirk sat poised, waiting to drop, then reactivate, the screen.

Finally, after what seemed an interminable interval—but was actually about fifteen minutes—Ferguson's contralto reported: "We have them, Admiral Morrow. They're A-OK. Shuttle deck doors are closing behind us. You may reactivate number four deflector."

Kirk held himself together long enough to trigger the shield, then leaped up to grip Morrow's hand. The admiral's eyes were shining. "We did it!"

"Thank God," Kirk said softly. Relief washed through him, making him feel light, free. He smiled when Morrow slapped him on the shoulder.

"Put yourself in for a medal, Admiral Kirk," Morrow chortled. "If it hadn't been for you we'd never have figured out where they were."

"Just a little logic at the right time." Kirk's grin grew so broad it felt as if it might split his face. "Guess after all these years some of it finally rubbed off on me, right, Spock?"

The Vulcan stood surveying the celebrants, hands clasped behind his back. "Admiral, with your permission, I would like to join the medical team on the shuttle deck."

Morrow nodded. "You can both go. As soon as McCoy's able, notify me and report to the briefing room. We've got a lot to discuss."

Kirk and Spock reached the shuttle deck just as the last of the spacesuited figures was helped out of the crowded confines of the *Onizuka*'s storage compartment. "Do you see Bones?"

"There." The Vulcan pointed. Both officers hurried over to a spacesuited figure that sat slumped on the shuttle's cargo ramp, obviously having trouble removing its helmet. As they approached from the doctor's blind side, Spock triggered the emergency release mechanism at the rear of the helmet, suddenly freeing the stubborn headgear. McCoy's irascible tones abruptly emerged. "—stupid damn idiotic spacesuit—*ouch!*"

Kirk lifted the helmet out of the doctor's hands, then stepped around to face his former chief surgeon. "Easy, Bones. Spock and I went to too much trouble to rescue you, just to watch you knock yourself out with your own helmet."

Leonard McCoy's jaw dropped with an almost audible *clunk*. "Jim? *Spock?* What the *hell*—?"

Somehow the doctor was on his feet and suddenly, without knowing quite what he intended, Kirk had both arms around his friend and was thumping him on the back—and being thumped in turn. They laughed until they choked, and then, just as their laughter was threatening to turn into something far more embarrassing, Spock ostentatiously cleared his throat. "If you two intend to continue, I shall wait for you in the briefing room."

McCoy mock-glared at the Vulcan. "Why, you coldblooded sonofa—"

"Now, Bones," Kirk interrupted hastily, smothering a grin.

McCoy glanced at him, then a slow, reluctant smile lightened the doctor's haggard features. "Hell, I couldn't be mad at Lucifer himself right now—especially if he just helped save my life. How the hell are you, Spock?"

"I am well, Doctor," the Vulcan replied, only his dark eyes revealing his relieved pleasure at seeing his sparring partner again. "Gratified to find you in such good—if profane—spirits."

"Come on, let's get you out of this suit," Kirk said. "I hate to rush you, after the trip you've had, but we've got an emergency on our hands, and Admiral Morrow—for some reason we don't yet understand—wants our advice in trying to solve it."

"Is that why he ordered me back to Earth?"

"Apparently," Spock said. Together, he and Kirk helped McCoy pull off his spacesuit. Kirk's nose wrinkled.

The doctor bridled at his expression. "I've been living in this double-damned thing for the last fourteen hours, Jim. You were no bed of roses after the Tholian incident,

30

remember?" And I haven't had a bite to eat in more than a day—not that I wanted to eat much after the artificial gravity cut out. Good thing their infirmary had plenty of anti-nausea medicine. I had so many patients I barely had time to worry. What a mess!"

"I imagine we can delay long enough to get you a shower and some food," Kirk said, as they made their way through the crowded shuttlecraft deck.

"I don't know as my stomach's *that* settled, yet. I haven't done a spacesuit drill since basic . . . hanging there, feeling like every part of you is falling forever . . . in different directions." The doctor gulped, shuddering. "Even that damned transporter is better than being towed through space. I hope to hell I *never* have to go through that again."

"Small chance of that," Kirk reassured him. "We're back in warp drive, heading for Kent to pick up as many refugees as *Cochise* will hold before we go back to Earth."

After the doctor had taken his shower and the three officers had shared food and coffee in the small galley, they informed Admiral Morrow that they were assembling in the briefing room.

While they waited for Morrow to arrive, Kirk lounged back in his seat, looking across the table at McCoy and Spock, wondering just how many times he'd sat with these two men trying to solve tough problems before. *It's been a long time since we've worked together . . . hope we haven't lost the old touch.*

Kirk hadn't seen his former medical officer in nearly a year. Until yesterday, McCoy had been teaching a course in Xeno-anatomy at the Starfleet medical school on Prima, parsecs away.

Kirk hadn't seen much of Spock either, though they were at least stationed on the same world. The Vulcan was an instructor at Starfleet Academy and spent much of his time accompanying his students on training details.

"Despite everything, Jim, you look great." McCoy's craggy features were tired, the lines around his eyes and down his cheeks etched so deeply with fatigue that his eyes looked sunken. But their blue was as bright as ever.

"Thanks, Bones. I've been trying to keep up the workouts."

"How is Peter?"

"Fine," Kirk said. "Mom's death hit him hard at first, but the resiliency of youth . . ." He shrugged, turning to look at the Vulcan. "By the way, Spock, how are the cadets? Whipped 'em all into shape yet?"

"It is a never-ending struggle, Admiral," Spock said, straight-faced. "Many of them are human, and they tend to . . . infect . . . the others."

McCoy grimaced. "Vulcans have no honor, Jim. He knows I'm too tired to muster a comeback, so he's taking advantage of me."

"You'll be here awhile, is my guess, so you'll have plenty of time to resharpen the old wit, Bones."

"Yeah," the doctor agreed, pensively. "No telling when I'll get back. My class is probably offering up sacrifices to Hippocrates—I had a test scheduled for today. It's anyone's guess when they'll get it."

The door slid open, and Harry Morrow entered. "Dr. McCoy, I'm glad you're safe." He shook hands gravely. "Have Jim and Spock explained why we're here?"

"No. But I gather that something is happening to Alpha Centauri B—that it's going to blow up, or something."

Spock was already shaking his head. "No, Doctor, it will not explode. But what *is* happening to it is fully as dangerous for Kent. Very soon it is going to swell into an orange giant, then it will cool slightly to become a red giant."

"What *will* happen to Kent?"

"When Alpha B begins to swell, it will engulf all of its planets—not to mention several of Alpha A's gas giants."

"What about Centaurus?" McCoy asked quickly. The doctor had lived on the planet for some years, and it was still his official residence of record.

"Safe," Kirk reassured him. "They're shielding it."

"But if we evacuate all the people on Kent—" McCoy began.

32

Spock shook his head. "The problem does not end with Alpha B, Doctor. Admiral Morrow has explained that several other stars are also aging at a greatly accelerated rate, due to waves of time displacement that are causing them to speed up consumption of their internal hydrogen."

"You want to explain all that in Standard English, Spock?" McCoy glared at the Vulcan. "Preferably words of one syllable? Remember, I'm a doctor, not a—"

"Cosmological physicist," Spock supplied, as the medical officer groped for a term. "Very well." He steepled his lean fingers and thought for a moment. "Perhaps the best way to begin is to remind you that stars, like living beings, possess finite lifespans. When they have converted enough of their internal fuel supply of hydrogen to helium, they die."

"I know that much," the doctor growled.

"Good," said Spock, unruffled. "Small or medium-size stars, like Sol—or Alpha A and B—swell into red giants, then dwindle into white dwarfs. The lifespan of a small-to-medium-size star is approximately ten billion years, plus or minus one or two billion."

"I thought you implied this was an *immediate* problem," McCoy observed sarcastically. "Doesn't sound like anything I should stay awake nights worrying over."

Spock made a small, impatient sound . . . not quite an "ahem." "Dr. McCoy, since there is nothing you or anyone else could do to prevent the natural or unnatural consequences of aging in a star," the Vulcan raised his eyebrow, "staying awake worrying about the eventuality constitutes a completely illogical reaction."

"Don't, Bones," Kirk put in hastily, seeing the light of battle in the doctor's eyes. "We're with you, Spock. Go on."

"Very well. The larger the mass of the star in question, the shorter its lifespan. Massive, heavyweight stars will exhaust their internal supplies of hydrogen in only ten *million* years or so. The star then balloons outward, becoming a red supergiant, and ultimately explodes—a supernova."

"And that's been happening a lot lately?" Kirk remembered Morrow and Spock's previous talk.

"Correct, Admiral. To be more precise, there has been a marked increase in star deaths of *all* types."

"What happens to the supernovas?" McCoy asked, intrigued in spite of himself. "Do they just blow themselves into atoms?"

"The correct plural is supernovae, Doctor. Yes, some stars do just that, becoming clouds of ionized hydrogen we term nebulae. Others, however, collapse back into themselves. Those with lesser mass become neutron stars. The remains of the most massive stars, however, collapse into gravity wells so intense that not even light can escape."

"Black holes," Kirk said.

"That is the popular term for the phenomenon."

"But we've discovered them before," the doctor protested. "They swallow up anything that gets trapped within their gravity pulls, but mostly that's just space gas or dust, and occasionally a stray asteroid or something. They've never posed a threat to a planet!"

"You mean they haven't *yet*, Doctor," Morrow cautioned. "But that's because the explored universe is a big place, and there aren't many of them. But with more developing —possibly many more . . ." he trailed off with a shrug and an expression that spoke more eloquently than words. "I received word only hours ago that Canopus is affected."

"Canopus, too?" McCoy was visibly upset. "I've got an old friend who retired on Serenity."

"Starfleet is currently evacuating the population of the system," Morrow said. "We just hope we can move eight billion people off two worlds before the star goes supernova and its interior collapses. Fortunately, our estimates indicate we'll have several months, so we can probably save those lives. Canopus is a younger star than Alpha B."

The commander, Starfleet, sighed. "But it's too late for Carmen Ikeya and the crew of the *Constellation*."

"What happened, Harry?" Kirk asked. "I knew Carmen, you know."

"So did I." Morrow rubbed his eyes tiredly. "We can only guess at *how* it happened, but we know *what* happened. *Constellation* came out of warp too soon and emerged in real space within the event horizon of a new black hole just discovered in Sector 87. There was a Cepheid-class star there, just like Canopus, named Achernar—*was*. Now there's a black hole, and the *Constellation* is trapped within it."

"Can't it get out?" McCoy demanded.

"No, Doctor." Spock was matter-of-fact. "The nature of a black hole is that it exerts such a pull of gravity that *nothing* can escape—not even light itself. Hence the term 'black' hole."

"And the starship's been swallowed up?"

Spock hesitated. "Time, space, and gravity are intermingled terms when discussing black holes, Doctor. Insofar as the crew of the *Constellation* are concerned, their lives were snuffed out by the enormous gravitational stresses within the hole approximately 6.7 nanoseconds after crossing the event horizon—the point of no return, to express it colloquially."

The Vulcan misinterpreted McCoy's shocked stare for lack of comprehension. "A nanosecond, Doctor, is one-billionth of a second. If their engines were still functioning, they may have experienced perhaps an additional nanosecond or two—"

"Damn it, Spock!" the doctor snarled. "You ought to know by now how sick and tired I am of listening to you rattle off facts and figures cool as a cucumber when you're talking about *people*—sentient beings—*dying!*"

"Doctor, I am as distressed by this development as you are," the Vulcan replied levelly, "but raising my voice or evidencing extreme agitation will hardly help the *Constellation*. Even though their image will remain on our gravitational sensors for all eternity, the ship and its crew are gone."

"You mean the *Constellation* is still *there?*" Kirk was confused. "How can it be on our sensors if it's been destroyed?"

Spock expressed frustration with a small sigh. "It is difficult to explain without recourse to equations, but to the distant observers—us—the *Constellation* will remain trapped within the event horizon forever, like an insect in amber."

"Huh?" McCoy frowned. "Why?"

"Because *observed* elapsed time virtually ceases once the event horizon is crossed. To our sensors, the *Constellation* is there, and will be there, for all time. But from the point of view of anyone aboard the vessel, the starship was destroyed immediately."

McCoy glanced at Kirk incredulously. "Waitaminit, Spock. Are you trying to tell me the *Constellation* is in two places at once? That's crazy—impossible!"

"No, Doctor." The Vulcan permitted himself another sigh. "But to explain more fully would require time we do not have. I am afraid that I must ask you to accept my explanation on faith."

The medical officer snorted, but, after a warning glance from Kirk, subsided. "Okay. I believe you. But why is all this happening? What made the *Constellation* miscalculate coming out of warp?"

"We don't know for sure, it all happened too fast," Morrow said. "Matter of fact, if it hadn't been for the team of scientists monitoring the black hole, she'd have been listed as just another missing vessel."

"'Know for sure,'" Kirk repeated. "You have a theory, then?"

"Not me," Morrow smiled wryly. "You think I understand that kind of math? R't'lk of Hamal is the one who correlated the data. She believes that the *Constellation*'s chronos were running fast, so the ship came out of warp too soon."

Kirk tried unsuccessfuly to fathom that theory. "The *chronos* were wrong—but that's impossible! There are back-up systems, fail-safes, computer tie-ins—!" He shook his head stubbornly. "Starships measure time by stardate. It's the most accurate time constant ever discovered—"

Kirk broke off, hearing his own words. Sudden comprehension began coalescing in his mind.

Spock was already nodding. "I see," the Vulcan said slowly. "The Hamalki physicist was not suggesting that the

Constellation's time-keeping *devices* were at fault. Instead, Professor R't'lk is theorizing that *time itself* was running too fast aboard the vessel."

"What would that do?" McCoy asked.

"For one thing, if that is indeed the case, it would mean that Captain Ikeya and her crew were already dead when her ship crossed the event horizon. Aged and disintegrated into nothingness between one breath and the next."

"Well," Kirk said, feeling a little sick, "at least they didn't suffer."

"They would've never known what hit them," Morrow agreed.

"Admiral Morrow," Spock said, with quiet urgency, "in following this possibility through to its logical conclusion, I conjecture that R't'lk also believes this speed-up in time is responsible for all the premature star deaths?" The Vulcan's eyebrow rose inquiringly.

Morrow nodded. "My compliments, Mr. Spock. It took me nearly ten minutes of explanation to comprehend all the ramifications of what they were trying to tell me—and you figured it out like *that,*" he snapped his fingers.

"Now you've done it," McCoy muttered slowly. "As if his head weren't swelled enough already . . ."

The Vulcan ignored the doctor. The angular planes of his face tightened and even as Kirk watched, the faintly greenish skin paled visibly. "This is . . . most alarming," he said, his voice a near-whisper. "If this phenomenon continues, it will mean the end . . ."

"Of what?" McCoy asked blankly.

"Everything."

"You mean . . ." The doctor's hands closed on the table as though he wanted to reassure himself that it was still solid. "Spock, are you talking about the end of the *universe?* How? They discovered the first black hole over two hundred years ago, and we're still here."

"Indeed we are," the Vulcan agreed, but his calm voice held a hollow ring. "But if time were to be speeded up, or run irregularly, it would create enormous stresses on the space-time fabric, Doctor. We live in an expanding universe, but its motion, for the most part, is only detected by examining the redshifting in the spectra of distant stars and galaxies."

McCoy nodded slowly. "Okay, I remember about that. It's hard to picture, though."

"It may help you to visualize this expansion if you think of the galaxies as individual seeds in a seedcake dough. When the dough begins to rise, the seeds move away from each other. The motion of galaxies in our universe is somewhat analogous."

"So what does this have to do with star deaths and black holes?" Kirk asked.

"We do not really know what the end of the universe will be like, Jim. We can only theorize—and most of the prevailing theories today agree that billions of years from now, the stars will have burned themselves out to ash, or collapsed into black holes—which will then engulf most of any remaining matter before dying themselves. The universe will end, as T. S. Eliot said in 'The Hollow Men,' 'Not with a bang, but a whimper.'"

Kirk tried to imagine an infinite void, bare of matter, even of atoms. Nothing but a few scattered decaying protons or electrons, perhaps. "And you think this decay might be speeded up, so the universe ends much sooner than it otherwise would?"

"It is possible, Admiral. We also do not know what effect many black holes appearing would have on the fabric of space-time. It could be that poking too many holes in an expanding universe would result in massive rips—rather like punching holes in a mesh that is being tugged on from all sides. Eventually, it would unravel completely. Of course, the cosmos has at least four dimensions, not two," the Vulcan added meditatively.

"Who gives a hell how many dimensions there are?" McCoy demanded, throwing his hands up. "Does all this mean we're going to blink out like soap bubbles tomorrow?"

"Hardly, Doctor," Spock said, in a tone of excessive

patience. "The universe is approximately fifteen billion years old. If it ages normally, it will last more than a trillion years. The immediate danger here is presented by the star deaths, and how long it will take before any 'rips' begin to appear."

"R't'lk has already calculated how long we have to stop this," Morrow said, glancing down at a printout. "Since the phenomenon is originating in our own galaxy, we have approximately ninety days before the damage will become irreparable."

"Ninety days!" Kirk felt his heart trying to squeeze itself out of his chest, then begin to slam in hard, fast, waiting beats. Adrenaline rush made him shake. "Harry, if you called us in here just so we could update our wills, I wish you'd let me die in blissful ignorance." He took a deep breath, controlling his wash of fear with an effort, thinking hard. "But there's got to be something we can do about this, or you wouldn't have called us. And why the three of us, as opposed to all the officers in the Fleet?"

Kirk thought he heard Spock murmur, "Logical," even as Morrow gave him an approving glance. "You're right, Jim. I *did* have a special reason for needing you three. We've discovered the source of the time-distortion waves that are causing time to accelerate, and it's located in Sector 90.4."

"You mean Gateway? Are you saying the *Guardian* is causing all this?"

Sector 90.4 was located in one of the older portions of the explored galaxy, a desolate stretch of space containing only a few burned-out black dwarf stars plus a scattering of rocky planetoids. The only marginally habitable world (it possessed an oxygen-nitrogen atmosphere, but no life) was the one the Federation had code-named "Gateway."

Gateway was covered with ruins from a civilization so unthinkably ancient that little was known about it even after years of study by Federation archeologists. The only intact structure (if one could call it that) was the monolithic stone wheel that called itself "The Guardian of Forever."

The Guardian was sentient, self-aware, yet nonliving as

Kirk understood life. It was also a time portal possessed of vast and quixotic powers—able to project the entire history of a world in minutes. Any observer foolhardy enough to jump through its central opening ran the risk of altering history; the time portal instantly transported travelers back to whatever world and time requested.

The *Enterprise* had discovered the Guardian years ago, by tracing the "ripples" of time-displacement the entity gave off. Kirk, Spock, and McCoy had been the first men to use the time portal. Nightmares about that "trip" still occasionally woke Kirk, leaving him lying wakeful in the dark.

The admiral was jerked out of his memories by Morrow's voice: "I'm afraid so, Jim. And, since you three discovered the Guardian, I thought you might have some insights."

"Precisely what is the Guardian doing?" Spock inquired.

"Nobody is sure about anything except that it will no longer respond to questions, and that the nature of those time-displacement waves it gives off has altered. They are now being emitted at widely varying intervals."

"And those waves are speeding up time?" McCoy asked. "Is that why the stars are aging and dying prematurely?"

"We don't know any more about these emissions than we did about the old ones, Doctor," Morrow said. "It's equally possible, I suppose, that all these years the Guardian has been *slowing down* the aging of the stars to lengthen their lifespans. We just don't know."

"It said that it had been there 'since before our sun burned hot in space,'" Kirk mused. "We knew it had many strange powers, but I never dreamed it was capable of anything like this. Have the archeologists on Gateway been able to get any response from it at all?"

"None," Morrow said. "It hasn't responded to any inquiries or attempts at communication for—" he glanced down at the report in front of him, "for 174 Solar days now. We lost contact with the current archeological team and the patrolling ship two months ago. We're presuming the worst."

"Have you tried a telepath?" Spock asked suddenly.

"A *telepath?*" Morrow's eyebrows rose. "No, that is one thing no one has tried. What makes you think a telepath might be able to communicate with the Guardian? As far as I know it's actually some sort of incredibly advanced computer, isn't it? Besides, there aren't that many espers around."

"At the time the Guardian was first discovered, Spock was one of the scientific team chosen to study it. He knows as much about it as anyone living," Kirk told the admiral, with a sharp glance at the Vulcan.

"I know," Morrow said, his eyes never leaving Spock's face. "I read his report several times. It never mentioned that he had attempted a mind-meld with the time portal."

Kirk heard McCoy's soft, indrawn breath, and knew that the doctor was remembering, just as he was, the identity of the person who had successfully contacted the Guardian mentally. Hastily, he began, "Spock's theory that the Guardian can be contacted by a mind-meld is—"

Without looking at him, the Vulcan raised a hand, and Kirk subsided into uneasy silence. "No, Admiral Morrow, I did not attempt telepathic contact with the Guardian. I saw it done, however."

"Since the Guardian is one of the best-kept secrets in the Federation," Morrow said evenly, "I think I am justified in requiring you to identify this individual."

"A young Vulcan relative of Spock's—" Dr. McCoy began, then Spock turned to the medical officer with a spark of amused affection in his eyes. "I appreciate your attempt to protect me, Doctor, but such a grave situation requires nothing less than the truth." He faced Morrow again. "Admiral, the person who communicated mentally with the Guardian was my son, Zar."

"Your—" Kirk doubted that Morrow could have looked more thunderstruck if the conference table had come to life and danced a hornpipe. It was a full thirty seconds before the admiral could speak. "I apologize, Mr. Spock, for intruding on your privacy, but your personnel records never . . ." He cleared his throat. "However, as you said,

41

the situation is extremely threatening. But I had no idea . . ." Morrow cleared his throat again. "At any rate, the important thing is that contact *was* established. What your son did once, he may be able to do again. Where is he?"

"I am afraid that will be impossible, Admiral," Spock said levelly, but something shadowed the dark eyes for a moment. "My son has been dead for five thousand years."

Chapter Three

Spock watched Morrow trying to recover from this second, greater shock. The Vulcan kept his features from betraying his amusement. *That is the second time he has opened his mouth, then closed it without emitting any sound . . .*

"Perhaps I should explain," Spock gently offered.

The admiral nodded wordlessly.

"Approximately 14.5 years ago, now, the *Enterprise* was assigned to observe the imminent nova of the star Beta Niobe, as well as warn the inhabitants of the planet Sarpeidon of their star's fate. But we discovered when we beamed down that all the inhabitants had taken refuge in their planet's past. Through a mischance, Dr. McCoy and I were also thrust through their time portal into the planet's last ice age . . . some 5,000 years ago."

Spock glanced over at McCoy. *He is surprised that I can speak about what happened with such equanimity. Before Kolinahr, I could not have done so . . .*

The Vulcan turned his gaze back to Morrow. "In Sarpeidon's past, we discovered Zarabeth, a woman who had been wrongly exiled to that harsh time period alone. It would have been fatal for McCoy and me to remain in the ice age, and equally deadly for her to go back through the portal. We had to leave her there."

"And she was . . ." Morrow trailed off delicately.

43

"Zar's mother." Spock nodded. "I had no idea, of course, that he had been born until we analyzed prehistoric records the *Enterprise's* computers had copied from Sarpeidon's main library. Zar had painted his own likeness on the walls of Zarabeth's cave. There was," he steepled his fingers before him, "a pronounced resemblance."

"I see," the admiral said. "But how did you get back there to meet him, if that world no longer existed?"

"T'Pau secured permission from the Federation Council for me to employ the Guardian to visit Sarpeidon's past," Spock replied. "Zar then returned to the present of 14.5 years ago with me."

"And Starfleet Command never knew?"

"Admiral Komack did," Kirk spoke up. "We told him the whole story, after the Romulan mess was over and Zar had gone."

"Romulans?" Morrow was looking increasingly dazed.

"They tried to take over Gateway. Spock and Zar were most of the reason they failed."

"Was that when the archeological expedition was massacred?"

"Yes," Spock said. "I believe the details were mostly supressed under the heightened security prevailing after the incident."

"And Zar? Where did he go? I gather he was an adult?"

"Zar was about twenty-eight," Spock said, the memories racing through his mind in a series of flashing mental pictures. "After the battle for Gateway, he elected to return to Sarpeidon's past. The planet's history showed that he had, in fact, returned—and he did not want to chance creating a paradox, after all we had gone through to safeguard the integrity of the time-stream."

"I see," Morrow said, after a long moment's pause. "And I appreciate your honesty, Mr. Spock. Be assured that I'll respect your confidence. Back to the problem at hand, you say your son contacted the Guardian telepathically? How many times?"

"Once," Spock said.

"Twice," Kirk corrected. The Vulcan turned to him, his

eyebrow rising in surprise. "I saw him do it right after he first came through," Kirk explained. "He . . . told me that the Guardian was alive, but not in any way that he understood life. He said that it communicated with him."

"Fascinating," the Vulcan commented. "You never told me."

"Frankly, I completely forgot about it until this moment."

"And you also saw him in contact with it?" Morrow asked, turning to Spock.

The Vulcan hesitated, searching his memory so deeply for the precise sequence of events that for a second he was back there, feeling the chill slash of the wind, hearing its everpresent moan, and seeing Zar, his fur cloak whipping about him, hand touching the unthinkably ancient stone of the Guardian. Seeing him—and knowing, again, the pain of his leaving. *I did not want you to go,* he silently told that vivid memory-image. *I almost went after you . . . scarcely a day has gone by since, that I have not thought of you and wished you well, across the years . . .*

Spock came back into the present with a rush, realizing Morrow was waiting. "The second time was just before he left. He touched the monolith, and it presented him with a view of a valley on Sarpeidon—just that view, and no other—which is in complete contrast to the portal's customary *modus operandi.* I believe he communicated mentally, giving the Guardian a silent command—which it obeyed."

"I see . . ." Morrow shook his head. "Too bad he can't help us this time. But there are other telepaths—"

"Admiral Morrow," the vid-screen brightened into life. "We're within hailing distance of Kent."

"Can we talk to them?"

"We can talk to the group that is controlling the evacuation on the planet's nightside. The dayside blocks off the EMP."

"Get me whoever is coordinating the evacuation."

Moments later, an older woman's face filled the screen. Spock had never seen anyone look more exhausted, yet her eyes, though bloodshot, met Morrow's steadily, and her speech was clear. "Martha Hardesty, Coordinator for Planetary Civil Defense, Admiral Morrow."

"How many left to come aboard?"

"Just the remainder of the evacuation team, now. About two hundred and fifty of us."

"That'll be tight." Morrow glanced over at Spock. "How's Alpha B holding out?"

The Vulcan shook his head. "I checked status with Lieutenant Washington before we began this briefing, Admiral, and she informed me that the star was already beginning to swell."

"Damn it . . . how much time do you think we have?"

"Insufficient data to speculate, sir."

Morrow opened a channel to the bridge. "Lieutenant Washington, how long do we have to get those people out of here?"

"Admiral," Washington sounded extremely nervous, "the sooner we're at least another A.U. from that thing, the happier I'll be. I can *see* it growing, sir."

"We've run out of time," Morrow told Hardesty. "Send your people up in whatever shuttles you've got, and we'll keep a steady flow through the transporter. Are all civilians gone?"

"No." Hardesty's gray features took on even grimmer lines. "There are 184 idiots who refused to leave."

"Damn! Stubborn fools—"

"We couldn't force them. Some of them were old, said they were ready to go anyway. Some wouldn't believe us, no matter what we told them. A few—" she fought down a surge of hysterical laughter, "said they wanted to *watch,* if you can picture *that.*"

"Oh, I can believe it," Morrow said bitterly. "Never mind, Hardesty. You did what you could. Send your people up."

"We're coming."

An hour later, Spock stood with Kirk, Martha Hardesty, Dr. McCoy, and Admiral Morrow on the bridge as *Cochise* pulled out of orbit. When the ship emerged from behind the planet's bulk, he blinked in dismay.

Alpha B was swelling even as they watched. The star was already twice its normal size. Spock stared at it, riveted by the sense that here was something out of control, something malignant, growing without reason, against nature.

The screens wavered as Alpha B took on new, even larger contours. The star was still orange-yellow, but Spock knew that would not last. Soon it would cool even as it ballooned, wantonly consuming its inner fires. Eventually it would become a red giant, so huge that, four years and four months from now, when its light reached Earth, it would dominate the skies of the southern latitudes, visible even during daylight hours.

Cochise headed out and away at impulse power. "Olson's gone," Lisa Washington said calmly, referring to Alpha B's innermost planet.

The consumption of the little, dead world, similar in size and makeup to Mercury in the Sol System, hadn't even caused a flicker on their screens. As *Cochise* backed away from the burgeoning star, slowly, recording the event, Washington stoically reeled off the names of its planets as they died. "Perry is gone . . ." Then, minutes later, "That was Lang, it's gone."

And, finally, "Kent . . ." Her voice broke, and Spock knew she was thinking, even as he was, of the 184 sentient beings and the wildlife seared into nothingness.

Martha Hardesty began sobbing. "My home . . . I'll never see it again . . . my home, my home . . ."

Kirk patted her shoulder, and the old woman broke down completely. The admiral held her, patting her back gently, whispering comfortingly. Watching Kirk's face, Spock realized, with a sudden surge of empathy, that the old woman's words had brought back memories of Winona Kirk's last days, of her anguished pleas to her son to take her home.

Jim's mother had forgotten that her home had been destroyed when lightning struck the 350-year-old farmhouse, burning it to the ground. Had it not been for young

Peter Kirk, home on vacation from Starfleet Academy, Winona would have perished, but her grandson had carried her, unconscious from the smoke, to safety. The accident had provided a setback she never recovered from, either physically or mentally. She died six months later, of pneumonia.

"Well, guess I'd better go see if I can help out the doctor," McCoy's voice broke into Spock's musings. "Some of those refugees are undoubtedly going to need sedatives. We're too crowded to afford mass hysteria."

"The medical staff aboard *Cochise,* unlike the rest of the crew, is at full strength, Doctor," Spock told him. "Admiral Morrow anticipated this situation. I believe your time, and Jim's, would be better spent in rest. We will need to be alert when we reach Starfleet Headquarters."

McCoy paused, considering. "I hate like hell to say it, but you're right, Spock. But only if *you* rest, too. And I don't want to hear any crap about Vulcans and how long they can postpone sleep. Deal?"

Having won this round, the Vulcan could afford to be gracious. Spock inclined his head. "Very well, Doctor."

The three officers wound up bunking in a three-bed room with three other officers—and, due to their importance to the mission, they had been given favored status. Little *Cochise* nearly bulged with people. Refugees cluttered the hallways and filled the small rec deck. There were long lines to use the lavatories. Sobbing became part of the background noise, mingling with the faint vibration of the warp engines.

Spock had decided he would lie down until Kirk and McCoy drifted off, then get up and offer his services to the medical teams, but the events of the past two days had tired him more than he'd realized. Within minutes, he felt himself sinking toward sleep, and, with a sigh, gave in and let it take him.

The Vulcan dreamed he was standing in a featureless void, extending to infinity in all directions—and yet, somehow, he could *see* infinity, and knew that nowhere was there anything else. No stars, no planets—no dust, no atoms

. . . nothing. Nothing, nothing, *nothing*. He shivered, realizing that this was what they had all feared—the end of the universe.

He had never felt so alone.

There must be something, he thought, glancing carefully around. *Something . . . someone . . .* He twisted, turning completely around. *There must be someone . . .*

And there was. For a moment, he thought he was looking into a mirror, then realized he was seeing Zar, though his son was considerably older than when he'd last seen him. They stared at each other, and Zar spoke, but no sound emerged. *Of course not,* Spock thought. *We are in vacuum. Sound does not travel through vacuum.*

"Zar," he tried to say. "Son—"

But he could make no sound, either.

We cannot be alive in vacuum without spacesuits, Spock realized, then. *I must be dreaming.*

And awoke.

Somewhere one of the refugees was shrieking with pain and despair. The engines had changed their barely perceptible vibrations. *Impulse drive,* the Vulcan thought. *We are nearing Earth orbit.*

"You could've knocked me over with a feather, Jim," Leonard McCoy said irritably, picking up his drink. He glowered at the collection of ancient weapons hanging on the wall of Kirk's San Francisco apartment. "I swear, every time I think I've got that pointy-eared sonofagun figured out, he does an about-face like the one he pulled yesterday. It's pure cussedness on his part."

"Forgive me for sounding skeptical," Kirk said mildly, "but don't you think a desire to help in the face of such a potential threat might be part of what triggered Spock's revelation?"

McCoy shot him an *Et tu, Jim?* look, then sighed and shrugged. "Well, you can't blame me for getting sore. I was in the middle of lying like a rug for him, only to have him yank it out from under me." He shook his head, a smile touching his blue eyes. "Wish I'd gotten a holo of Morrow's face. I don't think he'd have looked any more poleaxed if both the Romulan Praetor and the Klingon Emperor had toe-danced into his conference room wearing pink tutus."

Kirk couldn't repress a grin. "He *was* pretty surprised."

"I guess he never saw that report you filed with Admiral Komack."

"Why should he? The commander, Starfleet, has too many responsibilities to sit around reading old reports." Kirk sipped his brandy. "Besides, I'm not sure I ever got around to stating Zar's *exact* relationship to Spock. I may have left it a little . . . vague."

"I see."

"Don't give me that 'holier than thou' look, Bones. *You* were the one who never mentioned the fact that our estimable Vulcan and Zarabeth discovered the pleasure of each other's company back in ice-age Sarpeidon. From your report, nobody could have guessed they ever got past the handshake stage."

McCoy's glance was sardonic. "Reports are supposed to be composed of *facts,* Admiral. All I had until we found out about Zar's existence were speculations." He took a quick, nervous sip of his drink. "After all, it's not as though I was *there* when . . . I mean . . ." he trailed off, staring fixedly down at his bourbon.

Kirk took pity on his friend and rescued him by changing the subject. "This whole business with the Guardian has me stumped," he said. "After untold millennia of operation —if we take what it has told us as truth—what could be wrong?"

"A loose connection?" McCoy hazarded, grinning.

Kirk got up and went into the kitchen. "You've got a warped sense of humor, Bones. Have I ever told you that?"

"Constantly, for the past nineteen years or so."

"We might as well eat." The admiral began scanning menus on his kitchen terminal. "What would you like?"

"Fried chicken and mashed potatoes."

Kirk's fingers skipped over the keyboard. "Coming up."

The doctor hooked a leg over the stool at the breakfast bar and sat down, watching as Kirk tossed salad with quick, expert motions. The food preparation unit beeped, and the admiral withdrew two steaming plates. "Here you go, Bones."

"Thanks. At least the condemned will have time for a few hearty last meals." McCoy scooped up a forkful of mashed potato.

"The whole notion is so . . . incomprehensible." Kirk picked at his own greens. "I mean, for all the years I've been in Starfleet, I've traveled maybe . . . I don't know . . . one tenth of a percent of space as far as we've been able to see or measure it? One one-hundredth of a percent? One millionth? What's one millionth of infinity, Bones? If I can't imagine it, then how the hell is the end of it going to seem real to me, either?"

"Yeah, I know what you mean. I've always been more comfortable poking around in *inner* space—inside the human body, that is—than I ever felt thinking about *out there.*" McCoy sighed. "But after watching Alpha B, I find that I can now imagine Sol swelling up and steaming off San Francisco Bay out there—not to mention the rest of the oceans."

"I dreamed about just that last night," Kirk admitted.

"If only we had more time!" McCoy stabbed savagely at a slice of tomato.

Ninety days, the little mantra repeated itself in Kirk's mind, as it had been doing ever since yesterday. *Ninety days. If we can't change what's happening, at least that's enough time to get out to that research station to see Carol and David . . . maybe I ought to tell David, this time . . .*

Spock's reference to Zar had made the admiral think even more about his own son, David Marcus. At least the Vulcan had met his adult son, had gotten to know him, even if only for a few weeks. In the face of this new threat, the admiral felt his own mortality weighing on him again, more strongly than ever before.

I always thought there'd be time . . . years, decades . . . but now . . . ninety days . . . Kirk shook his head, frowning. *That's it,* he decided. *No matter how this turns out, I'm going to arrange a meeting. I'm going to tell him . . . no*

matter what Carol and I agreed long ago, it's past time.
Maybe we can spend some time together, get to know each
other . . .

The communications system flashed, interrupting his
thoughts. "Admiral Kirk here. Go ahead."

The screen filled with Morrow's dark, handsome features.
"We've found one, Jim," the admiral said, without preamble.

"One what?"

"A telepath. She's got one of the highest sensitivity
ratings around—not surprising, considering that she's a
Marishal. Spock helped me interview candidates."

"Where is Spock?"

"On his way over to your place now. Can you leave
tomorrow?"

Kirk reached over and began programming a vegetarian
meal. "You mean for Gateway?"

Morrow nodded. "I want you to take charge of getting
that telepath out there as quickly as possible. Can you leave
tomorrow?"

"Of course," Kirk said, then smiled. "Harry . . . ?" he
began.

"What, Jim?"

"Do I get the *Enterprise?*"

Morrow shook his head bemusedly. "I should have
known. Can she be readied in time?"

"She can. Scotty's never failed me yet."

Morrow sighed. "You want Chief Engineer Scott, too?"

"Along with Commander Uhura and Commander Sulu
—has he gotten that promotion to captain yet?"

"It's in the works."

"Tell him I need him. He'll come." Kirk turned to
McCoy. "And . . . let's see, where's Dr. Chapel?"

"Researching Hephaestus fever on Vulcan."

"Too far. And *Reliant's* been assigned to a long-term
mission, so Chekov's out. But at least Scotty, Uhura, and
Sulu, Harry. And anyone they request for their depart-
ments."

"Yanking that many key people off their jobs is going to disrupt half of Starfleet!" the admiral protested.

Kirk smiled serenely.

Morrow scowled. "But you've got me over a barrel, and you know it. Okay, you've got them." He smiled with grim amusement. "Will there be anything else, O Hero of Starfleet?"

"That ought to do it," Kirk said, blandly.

"And you'll leave tomorrow?"

"You bet."

"All right, I'll have my aide contact your crew immediately," Morrow said.

"Tell them to meet me aboard ship. Bones, Spock and I will beam up as soon as he gets here."

"Right." Morrow broke the connection.

McCoy surveyed his former captain in amazement as Kirk calmly resumed his interrupted dinner. "Harry Morrow wasn't kidding when he said half of Starfleet is going to be in turmoil because of this! Not to mention the academy having to find other berths for all those cadets. I'm surprised Morrow didn't tell you to go to hell, Jim."

"Nope," Kirk said, complacently, around a last mouthful of eggplant parmesan. "He needs us. This mission is too important to settle for less than the best."

The door signal chimed. "That's Spock," Kirk said, triggering the unlocking mechanism and wiping his mouth. "I'm going to get into uniform. Tell him his dinner's ready."

Kirk's bedroom door closed even as the Vulcan walked in. "Hello, Spock. Here's your dinner," McCoy told the Vulcan, taking the plate out of the unit. "Jim's getting dressed. We're beaming up to the ship right away, so don't dawdle."

Spock sat down and picked up his fork. "The *Enterprise,* I presume?"

McCoy grinned. "How'd you guess?"

"Vulcans never guess. Knowing the admiral, it was the only logical response."

* * *

Enterprise! Just to be back aboard his ship lifted James Kirk's spirits. He stood in the turbo-elevator and could barely restrain himself from touching her. *You're acting like an ensign with his first assignment,* he chided himself.

But why not? He was alone; there was no one to see. Kirk put out a hand and patted the olive-gold padding inset into the walls. "It's good to be back," he whispered. "I've missed you."

He grinned, feeling foolish, but not caring. The turbo-elevator decelerated, then stopped.

"Bridge," the destination readout flashed.

Ever since the *Enterprise* had been refitted prior to their encounter with Vejur, Kirk had felt a bit disconcerted by the redesign of the bridge. He missed the red doors, his feet didn't automatically know the number of strides it would take to reach the command seat . . . some of the consoles were in the wrong places. Little things, but it always took him a few minutes to adjust.

Most of the crew was now aboard; Commander Nyota Uhura swung to face him as he entered, a warm smile brightening her dark, tired features—he knew she'd been working without relief so she could personally double-check all of communications, and he silently blessed her for it.

Spock was there, too, bent over the science station beside Lieutenant-Commander Naraht, the Horta science officer.

"Sulu?" Kirk asked, looking around.

"He and his staff just beamed aboard," Spock responded.

Kirk sank into the command seat, then signaled the engineering deck. "This is Admiral Kirk. Mr. Scott, are you there?"

"Aye, sir," came the familiar Scot's burr.

"Estimated time till departure?"

"I've just completed m'systems checks, sir. We'll be ready whenever you give the word."

"I knew I could count on you, Scotty. We'll be heading out as soon as our passenger is beamed aboard."

"Verra good, Admiral."

"Admiral," Uhura said, "transporter chief reports the

54

Marishal is safely aboard, sir, and that Dr. McCoy will escort her to her assigned quarters."

Behind Kirk the bridge doors opened, and a moment later Commander Hikaru Sulu walked by, pausing with a brief salute and smile for his commanding officer. At Kirk's signal, he slipped into the helmsman's seat that a junior officer hastily vacated.

"We have clearance, Admiral," he said, as a light on his console flashed green.

"Stand by to depart spacedock, Mr. Sulu," Kirk said. "Uhura, signal Admiral Morrow, please."

"Go ahead, sir."

"Harry, we're on our way. Good luck keeping things together here."

Morrow's voice was warm. "Good luck to you and your crew, Jim. We'll be keeping our fingers crossed for you."

"A few prayers might not hurt, either," Kirk muttered under his breath as Uhura terminated the transmission.

Slowly, cautiously, the *Enterprise* drifted through the cavernous maw of the Starfleet spacedock. The doors slid back, then they were free, in temporary orbit. "Beneath" them Earth turned, the Pacific uppermost, clouds gleaming white over azure water. The brownish-green landmass of North America was still visible on the far right.

"Lieutenant s'Bysh," Kirk said, to the green-skinned navigator, "compute our course and best speed to Sector 90.4."

"Aye, sir."

Kirk sat gazing around the bridge, mentally rehearsing the "all crew" speech he would give as soon as they were underway. He'd barely gotten past "vital," when the Orion woman turned around from her navigation console. "Course computed and laid in, sir."

"Mr. Sulu, prepare to implement course."

"Aye, sir." Sulu's long fingers danced over his helm console surely, without a moment's hesitation.

The admiral's mouth quirked as he watched the helmsman. "I'm grateful that you consented to join us, Mr. Sulu.

I'd have given a lot for your skills a couple of days ago, when I found myself trying to handle a tricky piloting job."

The helmsman looked deliberately inscrutable, but the dark almond eyes twinkled. "May I respectfully inquire whether the admiral's ship successfully reached its intended destination?"

Kirk chuckled. "Eventually, Hikaru. After a few wrong turns. Are we ready?"

"Course laid in, sir."

"Then take us out, Commander. Impulse power."

"Aye, sir!" Sulu's voice betrayed excitement, and Kirk knew just how he felt.

The helmsman increased speed to full impulse power, and suddenly the stars blurred ahead of them and Sol was gone. Within minutes they were nearing the gas giants.

Still watching Saturn as it receded into the blackness, Kirk pressed the button for the all-ship intercom. "This is—" the captain, he almost said, but corrected himself in time, "Admiral Kirk, commanding. First, let me congratulate all crew members on the speed and dispatch they've shown in readying the *Enterprise* for a deep-space mission. I am unable to reveal the details of our assignment, but it is vital to the safety of the Federation. I know you will continue to give one hundred percent of yourselves." He paused for a second, realizing there was nothing more to say except 'thank you.'

"Thank you. Kirk out."

He leaned back in his seat, gazing at the viewscreen. Ahead of them lay nothing but innumerable stars, blazing with all colors, all hues. *So beautiful,* he thought. *I've come home again.*

He found himself wondering—for the hundredth time—why he'd ever accepted the promotion that had turned him into a desk-bound, planet-bound administrator. Part of it had been that he knew Starfleet needed competent people for high command slots; at the time it had seemed like his duty. But more and more often, he wondered whether his duty really lay in doing what he now knew he did best

—commanding a starship. Exploring. Solving problems. Averting threats.

If only we can handle this one, he thought, feeling the fear stir again. For all her speed, *Enterprise* could not transport him fast enough. *Ninety days . . .*

If only, he found himself thinking, he could figure out some way to stay aboard his ship, even after the mission to Gateway was finished—one way or the other. If the universe were going to run down, James Kirk knew where he wanted to spend his last months or years—in space. Was there a way to gain that freedom? Could he manage to talk Morrow into returning him to space duty?

I could always do something to make them demote me, he thought. *Disobey orders, or go AWOL.* He grinned sourly. *Sure, that'll be the day.*

"Admiral, we're nearing the orbit of Pluto," Sulu said.

Kirk opened the channel to Engineering. "Scotty, are we clear for warp drive?"

"Any time, Admiral."

"Thank you, Mr. Scott. Ahead warp factor seven, Mr. Sulu."

Enterprise quivered for a split second, then flung herself into infinity. Kirk felt the change immediately, throughout his body, as he watched the stars blur, sliding past, leaving their afterimages to shimmer, rainbow-colored, in his eyes.

He stood up. "Mr. Sulu, you have the con. I'll be in the VIP cabin. Mr. Spock, let's go welcome our guest."

Kirk walked into the rightmost turbo-elevator, remembering the days when there had been only one exit from the bridge. They'd all had occasion to regret that fact more than once—the new design was infinitely better.

But he still missed the red doors.

Spock joined him in seconds and Kirk keyed their destination into the turbo-lift. The doors closed. "Ten days to reach Gateway," the Vulcan said.

Kirk nodded. "And no doubt Scotty's going to be pulling his hair out by the time we reach there. Sustained high-speed cruising puts a strain on his beloved 'bairns.'"

His former First Officer's mouth curved infinitesimally. "I well remember."

"So do I," Kirk admitted, diffidently. "I miss it, Spock. Do you?"

The Vulcan's gaze was level. "At times, Jim. But I also value my current assignment; teaching the young carries its own rewards."

"I agree. I wish I could spend more time doing just that." Kirk frowned, ruefully. "Harry keeps promising me that soon I'll be able to teach at least half-time, but every time I make plans to do just that, there's another brushfire to put out." He sighed. "Well, I've almost cleared away my current projects. After that, I swear, if anyone waves another memo to initial at me, I'm going to run off and join the space marines."

The Vulcan's eyebrow rose, but he only said, "You know how much we value your experience, Jim. Your record as a starship commander has never been equalled—much less excelled. The cadets learn a great deal from you."

Kirk smiled. "And when I'm teaching, we get to see each other more often."

The turbo-lift slowed and stopped, and the two officers stepped out. "Before we meet our guest, refresh my mind on the Marishal, Spock. I've seen references to Marish, but I know very little about its people."

"The Marishal," the Vulcan said, "are a race of nontechnological bipeds from a planet located near the Procyon sector. They are gentle, prolific herbivores, completely nonaggressive. Their discovery by the Federation nearly two decades ago came as a fortunate occurrence in their history; they had seriously overpopulated their world, to the point where only strict reproductive control would save them from starvation. Vulcan teams were brought in to teach them biofeedback techniques of population limitation."

"Have you ever met one?"

"No, they seldom travel off-world. I will be interested to discover why this D'berahan chose to do so."

"What else do you know about them?"

"They are a nocturnal people, and possess no ears or other auditory organs. Instead, they appear to have developed telepathy as a survival characteristic against the many predators on their world. Current research indicates they developed the telepathy first, then, later, sentience, which is unusual. Most known telepathic species developed sentience first."

"And they're powerful telepaths," Kirk said.

"Very. So powerful that they never developed any form of spoken or written language. Physically, they are small and furred. The Marishal have three sexes: females, that produce ova, males, that produce sperm, and *carriers*—who receive fertilized ova, nurture them until birthing, then suckle them for the first months of their lives. From that point on, the young become part of the herd, and the responsibility of all. Marishal mature very fast, and their lifespans are comparatively short—fifteen years from birth to death."

"That *is* short," Kirk said. "This D'berahan . . . is it male, female or a carrier?"

"Unknown, Jim. All Marishal sexual organs are concealed in a pouch near the being's abdomen. Since all the Federation's contacts have been with Marishal who identified themselves as female—once they understood the concept of a mere two sexes, which reportedly amused them—I would hypothesize that perhaps D'berahan is female. Admiral Morrow did say 'she,' did he not?"

"Yes, you're right. Okay, then, 'she' it is."

Kirk stopped before the VIP suite and raised a finger to press the intercom, but he never completed the action. Instead, a "voice" filled his mind.

[Enter, welcome you both.]

Kirk had no trouble understanding the nonverbal concepts filling his mind with a soft, somehow *furry* warmth.

The portal slid aside, and Kirk walked in, blinking. The cabin illumination had been darkened to considerably less than normal ship's lighting. Doctor McCoy was seated on the couch, and a creature crouched near him. As the two officers entered, the being—*she*, Kirk reminded himself

—scrambled down and drew herself up to her full height. The top of her head came to just above Kirk's belt.

The Marishal vaguely resembled a wallaby, in that she balanced herself on a stubby tail and two powerful hind legs, and had two arms extending from almost nonexistent shoulders. She wore no clothing; her fur was short and plushy, a mottled brown and green, shading to palest amber on the belly and whiskered face. Her head was narrow, with a domed forehead rising above a blunt muzzle. A topknot of brownish fluff began just above her huge, wide-pupiled amber eyes.

"Ma'am." McCoy's Georgia drawl was in full force, as was his "old-time Southern gentleman" charm. "May I present James T. Kirk and Mr. Spock. This is D'berahan, from Marish."

"How do you do," Kirk said, bowing slightly, and on his right, Spock gave the Vulcan salute and murmured his greeting in his native tongue. *Of course,* Kirk realized. *Languages are almost extraneous when communicating with a being possessing this level of telepathy.*

He tried clumsily to phrase his greeting mentally, without verbalizing, but the furry warmth was in his mind again.

[Vocalize, Admiral, please, for your comfort. This one]—an image of the Marishal sprang into his mind, vibrant and individual—[comprehends your good wishes delivered in your normal manner. Comfort is best between those who must strive together for the good of the All.]

Kirk nodded, noting that Spock was doing the same. *What message did she send him?* he wondered. *The same? A different one?*

The Marishal waved a graceful, fully opposing "hand" —the digits moved so fast Kirk hadn't yet counted them —toward the seats. [Rest/comfort yourselves. Tell this one more of our shared peril.]

Kirk looked over at Spock. "As our science expert, I'll turn this one over to you."

The Vulcan nodded, then, after a moment of staring into the Marishal's enormous eyes, put out a hand to lightly touch her forehead. Several seconds later, he broke contact, and D'berahan turned back to Kirk.

[This one fully comprehends, gratitude to]—Spock's saturnine features flashed across Kirk's mind—[Be assured, this one will utmostly strive to contact]—the Guardian of Forever's bagel-shape flickered—[so that harmony/continuity of the blessed All may be preserved to its natural conclusion. But, truth to tell, this one's extremities tremble with flight-urge whenever the thought occurs that failure may prove disaster of such completeness.]

"That you try 'utmostly' is all anyone can ask," Kirk said, liking the being for her honesty. "And I've been having some of those 'flight-urge' feelings, too."

"As have we all," Spock agreed, gravely.

Spock had little free time during the voyage to Sector 90.4, and ordinarily would have spent it in solitary meditation in his quarters, but instead, he chose to spend it visiting D'berahan. He liked the Marishal; she was a gentle, sensitive creature with a quiet sense of humor. Her religious belief in the "All" reminded him of the Vulcan philosophy of NOME. Best of all, she did not demand emotion from him the way Humans often did; he knew she accepted him for the way he was.

D'berahan benefited even more than Spock from their friendship. The Vulcan was the only officer aboard who was telepathic; only with him could she freely discuss her mission.

And telepathic contact, Spock realized almost immediately, was essential to the alien's mental well-being. She explained that the Marishal were very social beings, with every waking hour (and much of their dream time) given to telepathic interaction. Mental solitude, to D'berahan, was nearly as painful as the presence of a shipful of non-telepaths, most of whom were unable to "shield" their thoughts.

He also learned her personal history. D'berahan was eight years old, and, compared to the rest of her rather insular species, she had an adventurous, unconventional turn of mind—which explained her presence on Earth. She had been attending college, studying literature, drama, and art. Despite her people's lack of a written language, D'berahan wanted to record some of their mentally told legends and images so non-telepaths could read, see, and appreciate her people's art and myth.

[This one has learned to distill words from thoughts], she told him, [and the method of inscribing such words by keying them into your electronic think-machines]—an image of a computer terminal flashed into the Vulcan's mind. [This one will use words and visuals to render an approximation of]—she hesitated, searching for a concept—[our "mind-plays," "mind-dances," and mind-paintings."]

I am pleased to know that, Spock responded. *The ones you have shown me are indeed beautiful and worthy of preservation.*

[If only this one may prove worthy of her ambition. This one has but little talent for the arts in the eyes of her people], D'berahan admitted.

I do not agree with their perception, Spock reassured her. *Perhaps you, like many artistic pioneers, will need time to make you honored on your own world, but your work will certainly be lauded in the Federation, if what I have seen is representative.*

[You are kind to tell me thus]—her mental projection carried extra warmth, the telepathic equivalent of a smile —[This one hopes she may prove worthy of your confidence.]

During their visits, the Vulcan discovered that D'berahan was actually a carrier, not a female. *But you refer to yourself as "she,"* he told her. *Please, teach me the correct term in your language.*

[The thought/concept/word you have grasped is correct] came the amused reply. [Among my people, we have but one way of expressing all gender . . . as "life-giver." Your universal translators rendered this as "she," and so we are all known . . . males, females, and carriers. Are we not all givers-of-life?]

Indeed, Spock responded. *I had not thought of it in that way before.*

[And you, my friend? Are you not a life-giver?]

Spock had a sudden memory of Zar, as he had glimpsed him in his dream, and knew the Marishal shared the image. *Yes, I am,* he answered. *Though I have not seen my son for years. We are separated by*—death, he started to say, then, for some reason he did not analyze, said instead—*time as well as space.*

[Nevertheless], the Marishal told him, [in the immensity of the All, you are forever his father.]

I find that thought, Spock told her, seriously, *to be a singularly comforting one. You are wise, D'berahan.*

[But I am not logical, as you have told me many times already] her thought was gently teasing. [Can there then be wisdom beyond logic?]

There have been times I have found that to be true, the Vulcan admitted. *But do not tell Doctor McCoy I said so, please. I would never hear the end of it.*

"Entering Sector 90.4, Admiral," Sulu announced.

Here we go, Kirk thought. He took a deep breath; he'd made his peace with the cosmos last night, sharing a Saurian brandy with Spock and McCoy in his quarters. They'd talked a little, but mostly they'd just sat, companions for so long that words were no longer necessary at such a moment.

Kirk saw that the Vulcan was watching him, waiting for his signal. "Prepare for full sensor monitoring, Mr. Spock."

"Ready, Admiral," Spock said, and turned to his board. Commander Uhura sat on his right, and a Ryjhahx lieutenant on his left; their task was to monitor the newly installed auxiliary sensors that would give the *Enterprise* additional sensor range.

"Decrease to sublight, helm."

The star-rainbows blurred, ran, then darkened into the inky blackness of normal space-time. Everyone aboard felt the translation into sublight velocity, as their bodies gave a brief, nonphysical *twitch*.

Sector 90.4 lay around them, dark with the remains of burned-out and exploded suns. The star residue glowed faintly once they were inside it; it was only when viewed from outside the system that it appeared as a dark blot against the normal, luminous stars.

"Time wave!" Uhura called. "Bearing four-three-six mark two-eight!"

"Evasive, Mr. Sulu!"

Enterprise heeled over so fast that her internal gravity systems lagged half a second behind—everything lurched for a moment, then steadied. Kirk slapped his restraint system button, and felt the field grip his torso, while the clamps settled over his thighs. *Guess we made it,* he thought dazedly, a moment later. *Since we're still here.*

"Mr. Spock, can you give us a schematic showing the waves, so s'Bysh and Mr. Sulu can plot a course in?"

"Difficult, Admiral." Spock sounded abstracted, and even his calm tones held an edge of tension. "They spread out after they are emitted . . . in some places they even overlap."

Great, just great. "Well, do your best. We need guidance, we can't just go on leapfrogging over them—we'll plunge into another one."

Spock was programming so fast he didn't even respond. Kirk waited until he paused after transferring the requested data to the navigation and helm consoles. "Well? Can we get in?"

"Yes, though doing so will require pinpoint navigational and helm accuracy."

"Lieutenant s'Bysh? Mr. Sulu?"

The Asian's tone was abstracted. "Still working, Admiral."

Kirk leaned over and saw the glowing schematic on the navigational console, showing the time disturbances in violet. They coiled around the small red sphere that was Gateway like a nest of cobras, and the many places where they overlapped gleamed yellow. Kirk wet his lips. "s'Bysh,

Sulu, if you can get us through that labyrinth, I'll . . ." he trailed off, unable to think of a reward or incentive wonderful enough. "I'll be very glad," he finished anti-climactically.

"I'm trying, Admiral," s'Bysh murmured, in her soft, throaty voice. Sulu gave his commanding officer a quick nod that said he understood, without ever looking up from his board. Tense moments crawled by as they drifted, monitoring the time waves, waiting.

Finally the helmsman turned back. "Course plotted and laid in, sir."

"Very good, Mr. Sulu, s'Bysh. Stand by to implement." Kirk keyed his intercom. "Mr. Scott, prepare for a rough ride."

"Aye, Admiral. M'engines won't let you down."

"Take us through, Mr. Sulu."

Enterprise gained speed slowly, until they were traveling at half impulse power. The heavy cruiser swung back and forth, up and down, as it followed the wildly looping course through a menace they couldn't even see. Kirk forgot to breathe as Sulu's fingers made minute course corrections and changes.

"Time wave dead ahead, seven-six-nine mark oh-four!" the Ryjhahx's voder shrilled.

Sulu's hands were there, and the *Enterprise's* brilliant green blob on the schematic sailed over the undulating violet coil that was the computer's representation of the time wave.

The admiral let out his breath after ten more seconds had gone by, and they were still there, growing ever closer to the little red sphere. He just sat there, feeling helpless, wishing there was something he could *do* as the minutes dragged by. And then, when his uniform felt clammy with sweat and his heart was tired of jumping with fear, just when he thought he couldn't stand it a moment longer, the red sphere wasn't little anymore—and there was a small planet in their viewscreen.

"We made it," Sulu mumbled, wonderingly. "Hey, we made it!"

"We did," Kirk said. "Congratulations on a difficult job well done, everyone. That was one hell of a course you plotted, Lieutenant."

s'Bysh gave him a grateful smile as she pushed sweat-damp black curls off her forehead. "Thank you, Admiral."

Kirk turned to his helmsman. "Sulu, words are inadequate. I'm convinced nobody else in this entire galaxy could have accomplished what I've just seen you do today."

Sulu tried, without much success, to look suitably modest.

Kirk turned to the Vulcan. "Mr. Spock, are we safe here?"

"As long as we hug the side of the planet opposite to our destination, we can remain *beneath* the trajectory of the waves, Admiral. Unless, of course," the Vulcan's voice was very level, "that trajectory changes."

"Will we be able to get within range of our target?"

"We should be able to take the shuttlecraft down in safety. On the surface, I will be able to continue monitoring using my tricorder tied into the ship's computers."

"Commander Uhura, can you raise the archeological expedition? Any response from the *El Nath?*"

She tried for several minutes, then shook her head. "No response on any frequency, sir."

"Spock, what do your sensors indicate?"

"No life forms at all, Admiral."

Kirk sighed. "I guess that comes as no surprise. Two starships, now . . ." He gave himself a mental shake and keyed the intercom. "Mr. Scott, you have the con. If you don't hear from us in an hour, assume the worst, and get the *Enterprise* out of here. Understood?"

"Aye, Admiral," Scotty said, resignedly. "Good luck."

Chapter Four

Spock piloted the shuttlecraft through Gateway's erratic winds, rolling and pitching, cruising only a hundred meters above the jumbled, grayish-white ruins that covered the entire surface of the ancient little world.

Nobody spoke aboard the craft, though the Vulcan was conscious of a subliminal mental "hum" from D'berahan —the telepathic equivalent of nervous pacing, perhaps.

Finally, after a last buffeting by the constant wind, Spock swooped them toward a relatively level space, setting them down onto what might have once been a courtyard, or street. He powered down the shuttlecraft automatically, hardly daring to take his eyes off his sensors.

They were only 137 meters from the Guardian, and, though his instruments told the Vulcan this particular spot was not in the line-of-sight of the time waves, they would be directly in their path as they approached on foot. If a time wave erupted, there would be no time to escape . . .

Spock frowned as he adjusted his tricorder. There would be no time, period.

"We must hurry," he told the others as they climbed out of the craft. The Vulcan glanced over at the alien, who moved with her customary half-hop, half-shuffle. "D'berahan, if you would permit . . . ?" He made a mental picture for the Marishal.

[Certainly. This one's feet are unused to heaped stone for footing.]

Bending down, Spock picked up the little alien, cradling her as he would a child, and began picking his way across the buckled stone. The Vulcan glanced over at the site where the archeologists' camp had stood, but saw no sign of it. *Logically, it crumbled to nothingness when the first time wave hit,* he thought, remembering the informal concert he had attended there long ago with a twinge of sadness. *I wonder why Gateway itself is seemingly immune to the time waves. There must be something unique about this world and these ruins. If we succeed, I must ask the Guardian . . .*

Kirk and McCoy followed them, all three men scrambling a little as the broken rock underfoot shifted with their weight. As they drew closer to the massive stone monolith that was the Guardian, the ruins became more intact. The three officers were forced to detour around crumbling walls, duck beneath half-fallen columns. The sky overhead remained black and star-filled, unchanged for millennia, and the same wind moaned among the stones, forlorn.

Spock felt something move against his chest, and glanced down to see a bulge ripple beneath the Marishal's abdominal fur. Even as he looked, another small bulge heaved and subsided. *D'berahan!* Spock thought, his mental voice the equivalent of a groan. *You are carrying?*

[Of course. I am a carrier, after all. Do not be concerned, Spock,] the Marishal's mental "voice" was tranquil. [Think, my friend. This threat we face is too great to let individual concerns affect our actions.]

You should have told us, he protested.

[Why? Doctor McCoy has some very odd ideas about life-giving . . . almost, he regards it as an illness. He would have forbidden this one to try what she must. And when this one is carrying, she is at the height of her thought-sensitivity. It is always so, for protection of the unborn. So this one could have no better chance at success.]

But—

[Besides, it is too late to turn back.]

68

Spock was reluctantly forced to concede the logic of her statements. He stumbled on, his jaw set, his eyes grim.

They reached the Guardian, and Spock put the Marishal down. She stood next to it, looking doubly small and fragile against its enormous stone bulk. [Does it have a name that I may call?]

"It calls itself the Guardian of Forever," McCoy answered.

She motioned them all to step back. [Very well. Please do not interrupt this one's concentration.]

The Marishal's presence was abruptly gone from Spock's mind as she turned to face the monolith, closing her eyes. He glanced over at Kirk and McCoy and could see the anxiety in their expressions. He tried, without much success, to regain his customary inner calm.

Gradually, Spock became conscious of a strong telepathic calling. It was not aimed at him, so he caught only the fringes, and, glancing at Kirk and McCoy, the Vulcan realized they felt nothing. But the sheer summoning *force* behind it left him awed. D'berahan's mental cry went on, and on . . .

He sensed that she was concentrating her entire being on picking up the mental emanations from the Guardian, trying to track them, to follow them through a vast, trackless void . . . and she was succeeding! He glimpsed her triumph as she touched—

—then D'berahan stiffened and gave a small shrill cry (the first audible sound he had heard her make). Her huge eyes opened, wide and blind, and Spock leaped toward her, seeing, sensing, *agony*—both physical and mental. "Doctor!" he cried.

McCoy was already moving.

D'berahan crumpled where she stood. Spock and McCoy barely reached her in time to keep her head from striking the rocky ground as she fell.

"What *happened?*" Kirk crouched over Spock and McCoy as they eased the Marishal to the ground.

McCoy ran his medical scanner over the small form.

"Cardiac arrhythmia! Damn!" He began scrabbling through his belt medikit.

Spock clamped his fingers against the fluffy topknot on the alien's skull. *D'berahan?*

Her consciousness was only a fading spark in a rush of darkness, like the light of a single candle trying to stand against a hurricane. Spock lost contact with his surroundings, his own body, as he sent his mind racing after hers. It was like being in space, out of control, speeding through darkness shot through with images that were totally alien —for a moment Spock remembered his journey through Vejur.

But Vejur had been a machine, sterile, devoid of all passion except a programmed compulsion to ingest data. D'berahan was a *person*, lively, whimsical, humorous—to realize that she was dying filled the Vulcan with grief, and an iron determination to save her. He launched himself after her with every bit of will he possessed.

Even though his consciousness no longer responded to external stimuli, his ears automatically picked up and recorded the sounds of concerned voices:

"Can I help, Bones?"

"Hold her arms. She keeps trying to curl up. I've got to get some cordrazine into her."

"Won't that hurt her? She's an alien."

"Dying's gonna hurt her a lot worse. There." The hiss of the hypo followed. "I've been studying Marishal physiology ever since I knew there'd be one aboard, Jim. Give me a little credit!"

"Sorry, Bones."

Spock was gaining on the tiny spark. He increased his speed, ignoring the alien images assaulting his mind. Flashes of Marishal faces, of a world he'd never seen. A total absence of sound. Telepathic "voices" in such profusion that they jumbled into a single mental scream.

"She's stabilizing a little, Jim."

"Spock's trying a mind-meld."

"We'll have to monitor him, too. If she goes, she could drag him with her."

"Should we try to separate them, Bones?"

"I don't know, Jim. He might be able to save her."

Spock caught the flickering life-spark and thrust his consciousness into it. There was no time for finesse.

D'berahan! This is Spock. Use my strength to regain yourself. Link with me!

There was no response.

Only then did Spock become aware of the reason for the alien's collapse and imminent demise. If he'd thought D'berahan's mind alien, it was as nothing to the mental chaos surrounding him now. The Vulcan was jolted as though he had been struck by a massive electrical shock.

The Guardian. The force of the time-entity's consciousness enveloped him—vast, ancient, powerful. All-encompassing.

He was linked with an awareness that made all of Vejur's knowledge and logic seem infantile. And yet that awareness, while it was fundamentally artificial in nature, was not passionless. The Guardian *loved,* it *hungered,* it was *lonely* —all on a level that made Spock feel that, by comparison, he had always been the happiest of beings.

Words/concepts took shape in his mind:

SUMMONING . . . SEARCHING . . . LONGING. FULFILL PRIMARY PROGRAMMING. BUT WHERE? SO MANY UNIVERSES . . . INFINITY. INFINITE LOOP? SURELY NOT . . . BUT . . . THE LONELINESS. THE SUMMONING. THE SEARCHING . . .

The intensity of that communication nearly blasted Spock's mind into gibbering withdrawal—now he understood why D'berahan had collapsed. The little alien had absorbed the full force of that questing, anguished superconsciousness, absorbed it at a far greater level than the Vulcan, with his lesser telepathic abilities, ever could.

He wrenched his attention away from the Guardian and cast about for the Marishal. She *must* be here—or had that minuscule spark been engulfed? Had it gone out forever?

"This isn't good, Jim. Now Spock's heartbeat is becoming irregular."

"Damn it, Bones, he's going to kill himself! We've got to get him away from her!"

"D'berahan will die if we do."

"She'll die anyway. I—we—can't lose Spock."

"His muscles are spasmed, Jim. Can't . . . budge . . . them . . ."

"Let me try, Bones. Oh, no. We'll have to break his fingers."

D'berahan? Spock thought, casting about, feeling desperation for the second time in his life. *D'berahan?*

CANNOT NEGLECT SECONDARY PROGRAMMING. MANY SUCH JOURNEYS ARE POSSIBLE. LET ME BE YOUR GATEWAY. ACTIVATE SECONDARY INTELLIGENCE PERIPHERAL TO REINSTATE TEMPORAL PROGRAMMING FUNCTION.

D'berahan? Spock began withdrawing his consciousness, suddenly convinced she was gone, and he was in terrible danger.

But even as he started his retreat, he became aware of a faint presence.

[?]

D'berahan!

There was no concrete response, but Spock knew that as much of her mind as remained was with him. He fled, "towing" the Marishal.

"Wait a minute, Jim! His heartbeat's evening out and getting stronger."

"What about the Marishal?"

"She's not dead, Jim—but I'm not sure whether she's really alive."

"Catatonia?"

"Similar, I think. I'll need to do brainwave scans."

Spock came back to his body like a swimmer who has been submerged far past the lung-bursting point. He gasped, all his muscles jerking, then sagged, exhausted, darkness threatening to engulf him. Only Kirk's supporting arm kept him from collapsing. "Spock! Are you all right?"

The Vulcan shut his eyes, concentrating on slowing his breathing, controlling his muscles. "I am . . . well." Painfully he sat up, then steadied himself, and Kirk let him go. "D'berahan?"

"She's still alive," McCoy said grimly, "physically, at least. Mentally . . . I don't know."

Spock wavered to his feet. D'berahan was limp, eyes closed, her chest rising and falling. The Vulcan hesitantly touched her, but could detect only a faint echo of her mental presence. "She has withdrawn," he said. "The force of the Guardian's communication was too intense for her to withstand it and remain sane. And I haven't the mental strength to reach her."

"Will she recover?" Kirk anxiously asked both officers.

"Unknown," Spock said.

"I have no idea," McCoy admitted. "All I can do is make sure she's given all possible supportive treatment. She may pull out of it by herself. We'd better get her back to the shuttlecraft." The doctor moved to pick up the Marishal. As he touched her body, it stiffened.

"Another seizure?" Kirk dropped to his knees beside the medical officer.

"Nooooo . . ." McCoy ran his scanner over the little alien. "More like—" He broke off, running the instrument over her belly again. His eyes were blazing furiously when he raised them to meet the Vulcan's. "Did you know about this?"

Spock placed a gentle hand on the Marishal's abdomen. "Not until we landed. She would not allow me to tell you, Doctor. She is experiencing contractions?"

"Apparently." McCoy's mouth twisted bitterly. "Damn you, Spock! I would never have let her . . ." He began palpating the Marishal's midsection with cautious, capable fingers.

"That is what she said," Spock replied, levelly. "She considered this mission worth the risk to herself and her unborn."

"Oh, no!" Horror replaced confusion on Kirk's features. "Are you trying to tell me she's going to have a *baby?*"

"Three," McCoy said. "Either the shock or the cordrazine has acted to induce labor. I only hope they're full-term. It'd be hell trying to rig an incubator."

"Can't we get her back to the shuttlecraft?"

"Let's try. Jim, you go ahead, and collapse the rear seats onto the floor in the cargo space. Activate the emergency sterile field."

"Okay—and then I'll have to check in with the ship," Kirk responded, already moving. "If Scotty doesn't hear from me by the end of the hour, we'll wind up marooned here."

With infinite gentleness, McCoy scooped the little alien into his arms. "Hell! The whole goddamn universe is falling apart and *I* get to play midwife!"

"You have done so before, successfully," Spock reminded him, as they picked their way across the rock-strewn ground.

"Yeah, and a fat lot of help you and Jim were, too," the doctor snarled. "As I told Jim, I've been studying Marishal physiology, but I doubt I'm ready for this. You'll have to assist, Spock. I read that with Marishal, immediate telepathic contact is essential. And if you faint on me, those pointed ears will never hear the end of it, I swear by all that's holy."

"I will not faint," Spock promised, for once too concerned to take umbrage at the gibe.

When they reached the shuttlecraft, Kirk anxiously helped McCoy lift the Marishal into the cargo section, where he had arranged the seats to make a makeshift bed. "Is it safe to remain here, Spock?" the admiral asked. "Or should we take off and try and make it back before the next time wave?"

"My projected time for the next one to occur passed while I was linked with D'berahan," the Vulcan said. "That we are still here tells us that it did not happen. Also, I chose this location because my sensors indicated that this area is located on a sufficient angle to protect us from the wave-path."

The Marishal gasped sharply. "I'd rather not move her, Jim," McCoy said. "This is apt to be tricky enough, without any roller-coaster rides like we went through to get here."

"Okay," Kirk said. "We'll stay. I'll go tell Scotty."

The first infant was born forty-five minutes after they reached the shuttlecraft. McCoy carefully picked up the tiny creature to suction its nose and mouth, then dried it off. Under his ministrations, it squeaked faintly, opening its eyes wide.

"Dim the lights," McCoy instructed Spock.

When its fur dried, the baby resembled a fuzzy copy of D'berahan, so tiny that McCoy could hold it cupped in his palm. The doctor quickly checked the heartbeat and respiration, then handed it to Spock.

The Vulcan concentrated for long moments, his features all angles and shadows in the dimness. Finally he nodded, handing the baby back to McCoy. "My mental contact cannot, of course, match what D'berahan would have given, but the child's mind is now telepathically 'awake.' It can begin to develop."

"Good," McCoy said, placing the infant back near the now-distended opening of the Marishal's abdominal pouch.

As soon as the minuscule body encountered its parent's warmth, the infant Marishal began crawling upward, toward the pouch. "Where's it going?" Kirk demanded.

"The Marishal pouch conceals the mammaries as well as the sexual organs," Spock explained, as the infant burrowed under the loosened folds and disappeared. "Their young nurse and sleep inside the carrier's pouch for the first few months of life."

"Like kangaroos?"

"Not really," McCoy said. "The Marishal resemble mammals more than they do marsupials, in that the young are born furred and capable of spending time away from the parent's pouch immediately after birth. My reading says that as soon as the first infant is safely nursing, the next one will probably arrive, so be ready."

Within ten minutes the birth opening located just inside the lower end of the pouch dilated again, and a second baby emerged. The third followed about forty minutes later.

As Spock finished establishing mental contact with the last-born baby, Kirk hesitantly reached over to gently stroke the top of the downy little head, grinning as it blinked its huge eyes at him in the dimness. "You're going to be all right, little guy, or girl—or carrier—as the case may be. We'll take care of you, till your mom's better." The baby Marishal opened its mouth, nuzzling inquiringly at his finger.

"Nope, there's nothing for you there," McCoy said, placing it near the pouch opening. "Go find the real stuff."

The infant crawled unhesitatingly into the pouch.

"We'd better get underway," McCoy said. "I want to get D'berahan onto a diagnostic couch as soon as possible."

Kirk glanced around at the never-changing landscape. "We've been down here"—he checked the chrono—"nearly three hours."

Spock nodded as he settled into the pilot's seat. The little craft quivered, then rose and banked.

Kirk activated his seat restraints absently. "And so far, no time waves."

"Does that mean D'berahan succeeded?" McCoy called, from the rear of the craft where he monitored his patient.

"My impression is that her mental summons may have caused the time entity to recall some of its responsibilities to our universe," Spock said, as the shuttlecraft swooped low over the time portal. "But I have insufficient data to speculate whether the waves will resume."

"I'm ordering you to speculate, Spock," Kirk told the Vulcan. "Were you able to get any sense of what's happened to the Guardian from D'berahan's memories of her contact with it?"

Spock hesitated. "Nothing concrete. I did gain a strong impression that the time portal is . . . preoccupied. That its attention is elsewhere. *Literally* elsewhere. In another universe, or dimension. Searching."

"For what?"

"I do not know. Something very important to it. Something it longs for, and has missed for eons."

"And this . . . preoccupation . . . is causing the time waves?"

"It seems likely that it is in some manner related."

Kirk sighed. "Now what? We're back to square one. Or negative one, really."

"I could attempt—"

"No," Kirk said. "I can't afford to have you out of commission, too. And the time waves *have* stopped."

"For the moment. But it is entirely possible—even likely—that they will resume. The impression I gained from linking with D'berahan's fading consciousness is that the Guardian will require all its unique resources of mental and physical energy to complete its search successfully. The moment it returns its complete 'attention'—for want of a better term—to its goal, the time waves will resume."

"What makes you think that?"

"I am beginning to believe that the Guardian gives off time waves much as most entities breathe. But that when it is conscious, *aware*, it deliberately controls those waves so they will not prove harmful to the space-time continuum."

"I see . . ." Kirk thought for a moment. "So there is nothing malicious in what it is doing."

"Not malicious, no. Merely . . . negligent."

McCoy snorted disgustedly from the cargo area. "I'd hate to think what it could do to us if it *intentionally* got nasty."

Commander Nyota Uhura was sound asleep when her intercom buzzed. *Huh?* she thought fuzzily, automatically checking the chronometer. *Still six hours before I go back on duty. What's going on?* The 'com buzzed again, insistently. Uhura pushed her hair out of her eyes and swung her legs out of the bunk. *This had better be good.*

She activated the voice-only circuit with a vicious poke. "Uhura here."

"Commander Uhura, this is Spock. I apologize for disturbing you while you are off-duty, but I have an urgent request to make of you."

Uhura blinked. "Mr. *Spock?* Is anything wrong? Am I needed on the bridge?"

"No, no, Commander. The ship is fine."

Uhura activated the 'com for one-way viewing only, and

the Vulcan's familiar features coalesced before her. He cleared his throat, then swallowed. *He only does that when he's really upset or nervous*, she thought. "What is it?" she asked, gently.

"I have a . . . personal . . . request."

"Anything I can do, Mr. Spock, I will," she assured him, completely baffled now. *A personal request? From Spock?*

"I can best explain in sickbay. Can you meet me there in ten minutes?"

"Give me twelve," she said. "I was asleep."

Even through the habitual Vulcan control, she could read his dismay. "Of course. I apologize again for disturbing you."

"No problem, Mr. Spock. I want to help."

With a puzzled frown, she cut the circuit, rose, and pulled on an off-duty caftan. After splashing water on her face, she slid a pick through her hair, fluffed it, then grimaced at her reflection. *Good thing it's only Spock I'll be seeing—if I shaved my head and painted it green, I doubt he'd notice.*

With a rueful chuckle, she hurried out into the corridor.

The Vulcan was waiting for her in the lab next to McCoy's office, pacing, hands clasped behind his back.

"Commander," he said, inclining his head in a brief but formal salutation. "Come with me, please."

Spock led her into one of the infirmaries, dimly lighted. Uhura paused in the doorway, blinking, but Spock never hesitated as he made his way over to one of the beds that was surrounded by a waist-high, rectangular enclosure.

A Coridian duty-nurse looked up as they approached, and the Vulcan, pitching his voice low, requested that they be allowed to see the Marishal in private. The huge, red-skinned creature nodded. "Doctor McCoy has given orders that you be allowed to visit, sir. I will be in the next room should you need me." He saluted and withdrew.

Uhura stood staring down into the bed-enclosure. "It's D'berahan," she said, recognizing the small, furred figure. "I was on duty when you docked, and I relayed Doctor McCoy's order for a stretcher unit. What happened?"

"She attempted mental contact with the Guardian of Forever," Spock said, his usual calm tones bleak-edged. "But the time entity's mental energy overwhelmed her —she has withdrawn from the here-and-now. She is buried deep inside herself, and I do not know whether she will recover."

"The poor thing," Uhura murmured. "I wish I could help."

"You can. That is why I asked you to come here."

She was startled. "Me? How?"

"While she was unconscious, D'berahan gave birth to three infants. They are currently inside her pouch, but they will emerge several times each day. It is vital that they not be mentally isolated—just as it is important for D'berahan to receive mental warmth and reassurance."

"But I'm not a telepath . . ." Uhura began.

"I know. But you are the most empathic person I know. Your warmth and sensitivity to others, including nonhuman beings, is well-documented. The Taygetians, the Eeiauoans . . . even"—did his mouth quirk upward a fraction? In the dimness Uhura could not be sure—"even the tribbles."

Uhura felt herself blushing for the first time in years. "Why . . . thank you, Mr. Spock. How can I help D'berahan?"

"Spend a few minutes with her and her children, as many times a day as you can spare. Sit beside them and create positive mental images of strength and health. Reflect on your own most pleasant memories, those you feel comfortable sharing. Or read your favorite poetry or stories. The benefit comes from having warm and gentle thoughts in close proximity, where the Marishal will sense them easily."

"It's a pity they're deaf," Uhura mused. "I could sing to them."

"Please do so. They cannot hear the sounds, true, but they may well sense the vibrations, and they will understand the lyrics as you think them. Positive images will—"

"*Oh!* What's happening?" Uhura broke in, watching fascinated as one of the infants burrowed out from beneath the edge of the unconscious carrier's pouch. "That's one of the babies . . . it's adorable!"

The tiny creature blinked solemnly up at her. It was soon joined by its two siblings, and all three stared inquiringly at the Vulcan and the human. "Mental companionship is essential to Marishal," Spock explained. "They need it as urgently as they require their carrier's pouch for food and shelter. Since their parent cannot supply it, we must."

Uhura nodded. "I understand, Mr. Spock. I'll come as often as I can."

"Thank you, Commander. I will so inform Dr. McCoy."

They left the infirmary together, but when they reached the waiting lounge, Uhura stopped suddenly. "Mr. Spock," she said, hearing the urgency in her own voice, "why *me?*"

He raised one eyebrow in surprise. "I already explained about the Marishal's need for mental contact—"

"No, I understand that," Uhura broke in, shaking her head, troubled. "What I meant was, why me as opposed to *you?* You're the telepath, therefore you are the," she gave a small, ironic shrug, "*logical* choice for the job. What's preventing you from maintaining contact with D'berahan and her children?"

The Vulcan was clearly uncomfortable with her perception, and for a moment Uhura thought he was going to tell her to mind her own business (*though he'd never put it like that,* she thought. *He'd find some incredibly stuffy, civil way to say it*).

But after a second's hesitation, the calm mask of the Vulcan's features relaxed slightly. "A logical deduction, Commander. One I should have foreseen you would make. There is a . . . possibility that I may not be able to continue visiting the Marishal, therefore I have asked you to do so, in the event of my . . . inability."

"You mean, your . . . absence?" Uhura guessed.

"I did not say that," Spock said, stiffly.

But that's what you meant, Uhura thought. *What's going on? Where are you going?* She gasped softly as realization dawned. *He's going back down to Gateway to mind-meld with the Guardian!*

She knew by the flicker of the dark eyes that he had seen and catalogued her reaction, and knew what it meant. "Mr. Spock . . ." She cast about for words. "I've served under you for a long time now. You're one of the best commanding officers I've ever had—you and Admiral Kirk. I'd hate to lose you."

He relaxed slightly when he saw that she was not going to put the truth they both knew into words. "We all have our duty, Commander. There are times when each of us must . . . interpret . . . the nature of that duty according to our individual consciences. I believe that the exigency of our current situation makes this one of those times."

"I understand," she said, but she could not keep the slight tremor from her voice. *What is* my *duty here? He'd hardly call me down here for a "personal request" if Kirk had authorized him to do this—therefore the admiral doesn't know. But, on the other hand, I don't know for certain that Spock is planning to act against orders . . .*

"But, Mr. Spock . . ." she bit her lip, then plunged on, "I don't know much about the Marishal, but from what I've heard, they're powerful telepaths. More so than Vulcans. And if D'berahan failed . . ." She hesitated, not wanting to put the rest of it into words.

"It may be, Commander, that D'berahan failed precisely *because* of her telepathic strength. It is possible that a being of lesser mental power and sensitivity—one with stronger mental shields—would not be similarly overcome."

"Anything's possible, but it's terribly dangerous. Nobody's ever done it."

"There is no logic in denying the danger of such a mental link," Spock admitted. "However, you are wrong, it *has* been done. The only person to accomplish a successful telepathic contact with the Guardian was trained in Vulcan mental disciplines. He possessed considerably more esper abilities than I, but he"—Spock's dark eyes were opaque, unreadable—"is no longer available."

"Who was that?" she asked, intrigued.

"Zar," Spock said. "I believe you would remember him."

"Of course I do," Uhura whispered, her throat tightening at the memory of the young man she'd known so briefly. "How could I forget? I was in command of the landing party that day on Gateway. It was I who sent him to create a diversion so we could rescue you and Captain Kirk"—she took a deep breath, then finished, softly—"and that diversion, of course, was the explosion that killed him. I . . . sent him to his death."

Spock was staring down at her, obviously troubled. "Commander," he said, after a long pause, "there is something you must know. Zar did *not* die during that explosion. Instead, he chose to use the Guardian to return to his own world, which exists only in the past. Admiral Komack ordered the tightest security surrounding the entire Gateway incident, so then-Captain Kirk and I were under orders not to discuss it. But if I had known . . ." He swallowed. "I would have found some way to let you know. I did not realize that you . . . felt responsible."

The Communications Officer blinked. "Zar didn't die?" She felt a huge sense of relief sweep over her, followed almost immediately by anger. "And all these years I thought . . ." She bit her lip. *How could they have kept silent! Surely they had to have known how I'd feel!*

Spock had obviously sensed the direction of her thoughts —the Vulcan's dark gaze held undisguised regret. "I apologize, Commander. I deeply regret that you were forced to carry such a burden."

"There's no need to apologize, sir," Uhura said, her tone formal. "As a Starfleet officer, I understand about security directives."

"I know that, Commander. Nevertheless, I should have realized that you would feel responsible, and entrusted you with the truth. But after Zar left, I was somewhat . . . distracted. That is no excuse, I know, but . . ." the Vulcan trailed off, shaking his head slightly.

Distracted? I've never heard Spock admit to such a thing! He must've cared more about Zar than he ever let on . . . of course, Zar was a member of his family . . . though we never

*found out just how they were related . . . though they looked
so much alike . . .*

Nyota gazed up at the angular, alien features, remembering Zar, and experienced a sudden, startling revelation of her own. *Dear God . . . of course he was distracted! Who was she? When did it happen? It can't be true . . .*

But, instinctively, she knew it was.

"Zar was your son, wasn't he?" she asked softly, her eyes never leaving his.

He blinked, startled, then the grim mouth relaxed, ever so slightly. "Yes," Spock said, his voice becoming deeper, rougher. "He decided that to protect the integrity of the time-stream, he must return to his own world. I often wonder how he fared in the past."

"I want to thank you for telling me the truth, Mr. Spock," Uhura said. "It's such a relief to me to know that Zar was able to live out his life, instead of dying violently in battle. He was a fine person . . . we all liked him."

The dark-velvet voice held a hint of wry amusement. "You are correct, as usual, Nyota."

It took Uhura a second to puzzle that one out, and when she did, she smiled. "It's a pity you can't activate the Guardian and use it to contact him again. You said that he was able to mind-link with it. Perhaps he could discover what's gone wrong with it."

Spock stared at her intently. "Yes, it is unfortunate that he is . . . unavailable." The dark eyes grew suddenly distant. "But I was his teacher, so perhaps there *is* a chance . . ."

"A chance for what, Mr. Spock?"

Even though his features retained their usual impassivity, the Vulcan couldn't hide the hope in his eyes. "A chance for all of us," he told her. "Thank you again, Nyota."

Before Uhura could question him further, the Vulcan was gone.

Fifteen minutes later, as she was sitting by D'berahan's bed, singing softly to her wide-eyed children, Uhura was jerked out of her musical reverie by the sound of the ship's intercom, paging the Vulcan.

The voice of her communications duty officer went on for nearly a minute, then fell silent. Uhura lowered her head, knowing there would be no answer to the summons. Fighting tears, she offered up a silent prayer for the Vulcan's safety to anyone who might be listening.

Chapter Five

THERE WERE ONLY two things Spock, son of Sarek, son of Skon, citizen of the planet Vulcan, feared. Death was not one of them. While he would prefer to continue living, Spock knew that if logic or duty demanded it, he was fully capable of risking his life, or even choosing his own demise, without regret or fear.

But now as he stood on Gateway, facing the Guardian of Forever, Spock knew that he was confronting his worst nightmare . . . and the Vulcan could not deny that he was afraid.

Afraid of mental disability—either through insanity, or brain damage. Spock could visualize nothing worse than existing with a crippled or irrational mind.

He cleared his throat and turned on the recording unit in his tricorder. "This is Spock," he said, evenly, without preamble. He did not have much time. "In the event of my physical or mental death, I wish it understood that I am . . . was . . . in full possession of my faculties at the time of this recording. Admiral Kirk is in no way responsible for my decision to make this attempt—as a matter of fact, he has expressly forbidden such an action."

The Vulcan hesitated, then continued. "I find the idea of life without full mental awareness and acuity abhorrent, and, in the event that this attempted contact disables my mind, I hereby remind the finder of this record of the terms of my will . . . that no life support measures whatsoever —including liquid or solid sustenance—are to be used to preserve my existence."

And, he thought, *since I am alone, and there is no one to whom I can entrust my katra, my living spirit, the absence of physical existence will mean true death. So be it.*

He took a deep breath. "To my shipmates . . . my *friends* . . . aboard the *Enterprise,* farewell. It has been a privilege to serve with you. May you live long and prosper."

He touched the pause control and considered leaving Kirk a more personal message, but such a communication was already appended to his will; duplication here was illogical. Jim would understand. He flicked the tricorder back on. "Endit."

Spock laid the tricorder atop a nearby fallen column, then set its homing signal to activate after a twenty-minute delay. A gust of wind struck him and he shivered, wishing he had donned his uniform exploration jacket; but wearing it would have advertised his intention to beam down to Gateway. He moved into the shelter of the stone monolith, out of the wind.

The Vulcan raised his hands and, taking a deep breath, touched the Guardian.

Harsh stone beneath his palms, but not cold . . . warm. Like something living. A faint glow flickered within the rock, making it nearly translucent. Spock concentrated, thrusting his consciousness outward, seeking to link his mind with that of the ancient entity.

He had the sense of balancing on the edge of a limitless black abyss. The Guardian's "mind" was far, far removed from Gateway, even though its physical existence remained tied to the planetoid. Spock concentrated harder, trying to probe that darkness . . .

Faint echoes of contact tantalized him, but he could not break through . . . his mental ability was not strong enough to establish the meld. Spock tried again, but it was like trying to grasp a handful of gas—too diffuse, too all-encompassing. He sagged against the Guardian's bulk, exhausted.

The entity is . . . occupied, he thought, remembering the impressions he had gained while trying to save D'berahan. *With what? Why?*

Slowly he began pacing before the time portal, hands clasped behind his back, thinking. Zar's success at communicating with the time entity fourteen years ago had given him hope that he, too, might be able to forge a link. But no; he was not a strong enough telepath to break through and follow the entity's trail.

D'berahan's telepathic abilities had been powerful enough, but her personal mental shielding had not been —the force of the Guardian's mind had enveloped hers, smothering her sense of identity. Spock sighed. *There is some way to make contact, there must be. There are always possibilities.*

The Vulcan tried to remember exactly what the time portal had "said" while his mind had been linked with the Marishal's. At the time he had been concentrating all his mental and physical energies on breaking the alien's mental link with the Guardian. Something about initiating . . . no, activating . . .

Suddenly it was there. *Activate . . . activate secondary intelligence peripheral . . . reinstate temporal programming.*

Spock looked up at the Guardian, experiencing a renewed flare of excitement, of hope. "Guardian," he said, saluting the time entity. "This is Spock, of Vulcan. I have traveled with you before. May I again make use of your temporal relocation properties?"

After a long pause, the stone shape spoke—but it was not the deep, warm, welcoming voice Spock had heard before. This was a high-pitched, jerky, artificially generated sound. "Request acknowledged. Destination?"

"The planet Sarpeidon, which formerly orbited the star Beta Niobe before that sun exploded 16.4 Terran Solar years ago."

Again that long pause. *System response is far too slow,* Spock thought, concerned. *It is possible that the entity's temporal transportation abilities are similarly circumscribed . . . but there is, of course, no way to ascertain that, short of attempting to use them.* His mouth tightened as he waited, counting seconds.

"Location reference unacceptable," the portal said, finally. "Access to primary memory limited. Please specify location."

Spock sighed and requested the entity to project star maps of the Sagittarius Arm. Once the time entity understood which portion of what galaxy Spock was referring to (*Does that mean the Guardian could actually transport me to a location in another* galaxy? the Vulcan wondered. *Fascinating!*), its central hole began filling with three-dimensional images. The starfields slowly took shape before the Vulcan, one after another. Spock shivered as he watched, wishing again that he had worn his jacket. Finally—

"Stop."

The projected starfield held steady.

"Eliminate all but top right quadrant."

"Magnifying specified quadrant."

"Eliminate all but lower right quadrant."

"Magnifying."

"Eliminate all but top left quadrant."

"Magnifying."

"Stop. Beta Niobe is the diffuse cloud third down and fourth over from upper left."

The indicated stellar object began to pulse. "This one?"

"That is correct. 16.4 Terran Solar years ago that nebula was Beta Niobe, a red giant orbited by seven planets. Sarpeidon, located fourth from that sun, was the only moonless world."

"Acknowledged and located."

Spock hastily retrieved his tricorder, setting it to record at maximum speed. "Initiate history of Sarpeidon."

Images began swirling within the central opening. Spock watched as the tricorder whirred, and saw, for the fourth time in the presentation, massive ice rivers flooding the northern continent. *Zar is there, alive, on the other side of this portal*, he thought, remembering his conversation with

D'berahan. *Time is the true barrier between life and death . . .*

Forcing his gaze away, he concentrated on monitoring his tricorder. After a minute or so he glanced up again to see sophisticated buildings and transportation systems, and, knowing what was coming, shut his eyes. The searing flash that marked the end of this world came only a second later, so bright that he could see it even through both sets of closed eyelids.

"History of Sarpeidon concluded," the Guardian stated. "End of request?"

"For the moment," Spock told the entity. "As soon as I complete my analysis of requested data, I would like temporal transport. Is that also within your programming?"

"Yes. Many such journeys are possible. Let me be your gateway," the time portal responded, parroting its customary phrase in its new, mechanical voice.

"Acknowledged," Spock said. Behind him he heard the faint whirr of a transporter beam, and turned to find Commander Beranardi al Auriga's massive, two-meter-plus form materializing beside the column. Two of his Security people accompanied him: Lieutenant-Commanders Snnanagfashtalli, a ruby-fanged felinoid being, and Max Arrunja, a past-middle-aged gray-haired human, with a unique talent for remaining unnoticed—unless he wanted to be. Then Arrunja's eyes were colder than the snows on Europa.

A formidable force, indeed, the Vulcan thought, amused. *More than enough to subdue one erring Vulcan officer.*

"Commander al Auriga," Spock nodded politely at the black-skinned Commander of Security, while slinging his tricorder over his shoulder.

"Sir," al Auriga saluted him dispassionately, his scarlet eyes carefully expressionless, "Admiral Kirk has requested that we escort you back to the *Enterprise*. If you will accompany us, sir?"

"Certainly, Commander," Spock said, and walked over to take his place in their midst. *To make such a public display*, he thought with a rueful sigh, *the admiral must, indeed, be in a rare temper.*

The transporter beam shimmered the air before his eyes.

"Damn it, Spock!" Kirk, pacing, confronted the seated Vulcan across the length of the briefing room. "This is the *second* time you've pulled this stunt! First Vejur, now the Guardian! I swear, if you *ever* sneak off to try mind-melding with an alien intelligence again, I'm going to boot you out the nearest airlock without a suit! We'll see if keelhauling is possible in space! *Understand?"*

Spock raised an eyebrow. "Keelhauling? The term is unfamiliar to me, Jim."

"Well, look it up in your unabridged file," Kirk snapped. "Don't try to change the subject. I *ordered* you to leave the Guardian alone!"

Spock swallowed. "I apologize, Admiral. I believed I saw a chance to establish communications with the entity, and I took it. I *was* successful," he finished, hearing a faint defensive note creep into his voice and hoping Kirk hadn't noticed.

The admiral grimaced. "That doesn't excuse your action, Spock, and you know it. The whole ship knows you went off without orders! How does that make me look?"

The Vulcan said nothing, only sat waiting. Finally Kirk sighed gustily, then sank into a seat opposite his former First Officer. "All right. I'll court-martial you later. What did you find out?"

"I discovered that we can now utilize the Guardian. Apparently D'berahan's attempted contact triggered a reminder of its responsibilities in the time portal, for it has set up a secondary 'brain' to handle its temporal functions."

"How does that help us?"

"It means that, although I was unable to establish a mind-meld with the Guardian, we now have access to someone who has done so."

Kirk looked startled. "You mean . . . *Zar?"*

"Yes. His telepathic abilities exceeded mine considerably, though they were overshadowed by his empathic skills.

With the *vedra-prah* disciplines I taught him, he may be capable of not only contacting the Guardian, but also protecting his mind from being overwhelmed, as D'berahan's was."

"But can we pinpoint his time precisely enough to locate him?"

Spock tapped his tricorder with a lean forefinger. "Given the technological improvements of the past decade, this instrument was able to record at sufficient speed to have scanned all of Sarpeidon's history when the Guardian showed it to me. If Zar's presence 5,000 years ago was of any historical significance, I should be able to actually *see* him. Then I can calculate—"

Kirk was holding up a hand. "Wait a minute, hold that thought. I want McCoy in on this."

Spock nodded, then sat back as the admiral talked to the doctor on the intercom. The Vulcan began scanning the tricorder's images, searching for his son's presence in the planet's history. Zar's painting of the *Enterprise* had appeared on the wall of an ancient stronghold in the Lakreo Valley; thus it was probable that he had gone back to become someone of at least minor historical note . . . court painter, teacher, or perhaps a councilor to the ruler of the city called New Araen . . .

Spock scarcely heard McCoy enter and Kirk's briefing of the doctor; he was intent on the tiny screen of his tricorder.

"Well, it's a helluva time for a social call, but I'll be glad to see Zar again, no matter what the circumstances," McCoy said, warmly. "I've missed him."

Spock stiffened, then his forefinger stabbed hard at the pause control. Carefully, his face an impassive mask, he backed up the battle sequence he'd found and focused in on one figure on a small hilltop. He played it through again —seeing the armed warrior's stained weapon rise, then descend—

Watching the spray of blood, and the crumpling, lifeless body . . .

"Spock?" Distantly, he heard Kirk's voice, realizing this was the second time the admiral had called him. "Spock, what is it? Did you find him?" Worry sharpened his friend's tone.

"Are you all right?" McCoy demanded anxiously.

The Vulcan realized he must have paled; both Kirk and McCoy were staring at him. He cleared his throat. "Yes, I found him," he said, not quite steadily. "Zar evidently became some kind of ruler in Sarpeidon's past. He reigned successfully for nearly two decades, then fell in battle. I just . . ." The Vulcan drew a deep, shaky breath. "I just watched him die."

McCoy uttered a sound that was half-protest. "Are you sure?" He shook his head, dazedly, and his eyes, usually a vivid blue, were faded and old. "Stupid question . . . I'm sorry, Spock, of course you're sure . . ." He slumped, rubbing his face wearily.

"I knew, of course, that he had died . . ." the Vulcan muttered, half to himself. "But it was . . . unsettling . . . to witness." Struggling to regain his composure, he looked back up to meet Kirk's eyes, seeing the sympathy there, and for once not rejecting it.

But then, as Spock watched, the admiral's gaze sharpened suddenly. "Spock!" Kirk said, urgently. "Has it occurred to you that this may be our chance? Why couldn't we go back in time and yank him out of that battle just before that final moment? If Zar died anyway, then there would be no reason he couldn't just come back with us and finish out his life here, right?"

"It is possible," the Vulcan admitted, feeling hope stir within him. "I would have to study the ramifications of his death on the time-stream to determine whether it could be done. Also, we cannot simply 'yank' him out of his time without his permission. That would not be ethical."

"So, we just go back in time to a couple of days *before* the battle!" McCoy's eyes lit up with excitement. "And we *ask* him! We'll explain that he's done his duty to history, and now he's free. He didn't really want to go back, remember?"

"Yes," Spock said. "But it would be best if I went back alone. Anyone using the Guardian in its present condition will be running a considerable risk."

"No way!" McCoy protested. "I'm going!"

"So am I," Kirk said, grimly. "And don't tell me about risks. We're in terrible danger just being in this system. The three of us will probably be much safer in Sarpeidon's past."

Spock's eyebrow went up. "In the middle of a war?"

"Compared to the way the Guardian's time waves could blink us out of existence like *that*," McCoy snapped his capable surgeon's fingers, then deliberately broadened his Southern accent, "why, shucks, a little native fracas on Sarpeidon sounds downright friendly by comparison, doesn't it, Jimmy?"

Kirk rolled his eyes at the doctor, then sobered. "Seriously, this mission is too important to take the chance of sending someone in solo . . . and the three of us have been there before. We *know* Zar. We have the best chance of convincing him to help us."

"But, Admiral," Scotty protested, "I knew th' laddie, too. He'd listen to me."

"I'll volunteer to go, too, sir," Uhura said.

"So will I," Sulu put in.

"There's no need for you and th' doctor and Mr. Spock t'risk yourselves," the Chief Engineer said.

Kirk sighed. "I appreciate your offer, Scotty, but you can't be spared here. If those time waves resume, you're the only one who can get the *Enterprise* out of here. Ditto for you, Hikaru. It was hard enough getting in, remember?"

Privately, Kirk was also thinking that the Chief Engineer was getting along in years, and that Sarpeidon was a cold, higher-than-Earth-gee planet, with some *very* unfriendly natives.

"But out here you don't need communications, Admiral," Uhura said in her most persuasive tones. "So I can be spared. Lieutenant-Commander Riley and I could accompany Mr. Spock."

I wonder why she, of all my officers, automatically accepts Spock's presence as a given, Kirk thought, glancing at his communications officer. *Does she know? How could she?*

The admiral considered for a moment. The idea was tempting . . . but of all of them, Bones had had the best relationship with Zar, and he wasn't about to send the doctor anywhere he wasn't willing to go himself.

And, let's be frank, Jim, he admitted to himself, *it's been too long since you've set your feet on alien soil. You've been pining for a chance to do fieldwork.*

"Thank you, Nyota, but no," he said. "I've got a hunch about this one."

"We all know about your hunches, sir," she said, nodding. "Good luck, then, Admiral."

The rest of that "day" went by in a blur as the three officers prepared for their venture, studying the available data on Sarpeidon's history, then trying on the native clothing the computer produced—"hide" breeches, homespun "woolen" tunics and jerkins, knee-high "leather" moccasins, rough-knit caps and hooded "fur" cloaks. ("I'm getting a rash already," McCoy mumbled darkly, trying to scratch discreetly. "Can't I even keep my damn synthetic skivvies, for heaven's sake?" "Oh, go ahead," Kirk told him, disgustedly. "It's a good thing you're a doctor, not an actor. You'd never have made it in costume drama.")

While the admiral gave Scotty his final instructions, Spock finished his calculations for their jump into the past.

Finally, dressed as poor herdsmen, weaponless save for belt knives, the three officers assembled in the transporter room, and Scotty beamed them back down to Gateway's surface.

McCoy checked the medikit he wore strapped against his body, then the miniature tricorder in his belt pouch. He shivered as the wind poked chilly fingers beneath his cloak. *I hate this place. Always have. Ever since that first time, when I was so high, so crazy, thinking my friends were trying to kill me. Their faces kept shifting and dripping . . . running like candlewax . . . horrible . . .* Resolutely, the doctor forced his attention back to the present. *Concentrate on not screwing up this mission, Leonard. Too much depends on it, remember?*

The doctor watched as Spock strode over to the Guardian. "This is Spock," he said. "If we make use of your temporal displacement abilities, will you perform standard monitoring and subject-volitional return programming?"

"All programming will be executed correctly," the portal replied, after a pause.

"Acknowledged. Implement temporal displacement sequence. History of the planet Sarpeidon."

"Acknowledged," said the Guardian tonelessly. Its central portion filled with a hellish view of a newborn planet, molten and turbulent. Even as they watched, it began visibly cooling.

"What happened to its voice?" McCoy asked. "It used to sound like a tour guide I once had on Altair VI, but now . . ." He cast a worried glance at Kirk. "This thing isn't firin' on all thrusters, Jim."

The admiral shrugged. "We don't have a lot of choice, do we, Bones?"

Spock never took his eyes off his tricorder. "The Guardian has activated what it refers to as a 'secondary intelligence peripheral' to handle its primary temporal functions, Doctor."

"I'm so glad I asked."

"Be ready," Spock said, watching the tricorder and ignoring McCoy. "Only a few thousand years to go."

"The mere wink of an eye," McCoy muttered under his breath.

The three officers gathered closer, shoulders almost touching. McCoy crouched, ready for the leap, feeling the adrenaline course through his body, making him tremble.

"On my count of three," came Spock's voice, on his left. "One. Two . . ."

Time hung suspended.

"Three!"

McCoy jumped—

(whitestars on black, blackstars on white, his body expanding to infinity and contracting to a single atom at one and the same moment)

—and found himself falling nearly a meter to the ground. Rain spattered him. He landed in black mud with a huge, one-and-a-half-gee *splat*, knocking his wind out. Icy water needled his hair (his cap had fallen off) and ran down his face as he gasped like a landed fish. He could see little beyond the end of his nose—only patches of mossy aqua ground cover, torn and trampled into the inky muck.

Finally, after long seconds of struggle, the doctor was able to force air back into his straining lungs. It seemed to him that nothing would ever feel so good again as that first sweet gulp of oxygen. He levered himself up onto his arms, spat filth, and blinked, trying to see . . .

Feet.

A circle of feet and legs surrounded him. The feet wore tall hide moccasins like his own, plus a thick coating of the ubiquitous mud.

A brutal hand seized his shoulder and rolled him onto his back. McCoy blinked rain out of his eyes and squinted upward. Overhead was an aqua-tinged sky filled with swollen-bellied purple clouds, and silhouetted against them, nearly a score of bearded, scowling faces. The men staring at him were dressed much as he was, except that they also wore helmets and armor of layered leather reinforced with crude bronze scales. "What the hell . . ." the doctor muttered. He tried to sit up.

Immediately, all of the warriors raised wickedly barbed lances with unmistakable menace. The medical officer let himself sink back onto the soaked ground. "Okay, I get your point," he said, lying perfectly still.

He heard a groan from somewhere to his right. "Damn it, Bones, we're in enough trouble without you making bad puns!"

"Jim! Are you okay?"

"Just muddy and bruised. And surrounded. Where's Spock?"

"I don't know."

"I am undamaged," came the Vulcan's voice. It seemed to be emanating from the doctor's left, but his view was blocked by the tribesmen.

"Did we make it?" asked Kirk. "Is this Sarpeidon?"

"I believe so, Admiral," Spock said. "The ground cover appears to be the correct color."

"Then who are these people?"

"Unknown."

Two of the tribesmen guarding McCoy jabbered at each other. The doctor expected the universal translator imbedded in his arm to translate, and was surprised when it didn't. *Why isn't it working?* he wondered. Then the light dawned. *Of course. The U.T.'s hooked into the* Enterprise's *computer—parsecs away in space, and nearly 5,000 years in the future. Damn.*

One of the men pointed at McCoy, gesturing him to get up. Every muscle protesting, *I'm getting too old for this stuff,* the doctor obeyed. He could see Kirk and Spock now, their caps still in place, each surrounded by a group similar to his own.

They were standing on a small sloping plain enclosed on all sides by foothills. Beyond their forested slopes, a white-crowned mountain towered ragged and rocky against the lowering sky. *No sign of the sun,* McCoy thought, *but the light does seem to be on the reddish side, which would be right for Beta Niobe.* The unfamiliar scents of woodsmoke, animals, and crowded, unwashed people made the doctor wish for nose filters.

The smells came from some kind of camp—hide tents squatted around them like malevolent ochre mushrooms, and there were animals on tether lines. The dun-colored creatures resembled Terran moose, but their heads were more like those of an elk, slender-horned and graceful. They had bristly manes and short, bushy tails.

"This is a war camp," Kirk called. "An invasionary force, if I'm not mistaken."

"Great," McCoy said. "Just where we wanted to end up."

The tribesmen gabbled among themselves for another moment, then one of them (evidently an officer by his more elaborately scaled bronze breastplate and helmet) left the group.

McCoy essayed his best "let's be friends" smile at the

warrior nearest him. "Hello," he said. "Terrible weather you're having, isn't it?"

The man he addressed scowled, spat out words that sounded like "dioti-gick'nuf," then pointedly looked away.

"So much for that," muttered the doctor. Even if the words were incomprehensible, it didn't take a genius to realize that they weren't an endearment.

All the warriors turned at a hail, and then, in response to another shout, they roughly pushed the three Starfleet officers together, until they stood within a large circle of armed men.

"I *knew* I should've brought my phaser," McCoy muttered, to nobody in particular.

"The presence of phasers when contacting a non-technological society is in direct opposition to the Prime Directive, Doctor," Spock said. "You are fully aware of that."

"Tell it to my corpse," the doctor snapped.

"Knock it off, Bones."

The bronze-armored officer was approaching them again, accompanied now by a shorter, cloaked and hooded figure. The circle of tribesmen parted to let them through. Finally, they stood before the three Federation officers.

McCoy found himself facing the cloaked person, who was nearly on his eye level. It was only when she raised roughened hands to push back her hood that he realized the newcomer was a woman.

A beaten gold coronal studded with cabochon rubies held her thick, bronze-colored hair off her forehead, and the doctor glimpsed a matching necklet at her throat. *Some kind of ruler, obviously.* He bowed slightly, and Kirk and Spock echoed him.

She stood studying the three of them for nearly a minute, her eyes penetrating and chilly. They were unusual eyes, the clearest, palest green the doctor had ever encountered, and her lashes were thick and dark.

The remainder of her face was arresting, but hardly beautiful. Her mouth was too large, her jaw too square and heavy, and her skin, though naturally fair, had been darkened by exposure, until the freckles across her cheeks and nose barely showed. Her front teeth were slightly crooked. She was perhaps in her mid-twenties . . . not young, as non-technological peoples reckoned youth. But hardship and responsibility, not age, had graven the lines around her mouth and eyes.

When she concluded her appraisal of the three prisoners, she spoke to them in the language of the tribesmen. McCoy shook his head and shrugged eloquently.

Kirk bowed again and spoke aloud. "I'm sorry, I'm afraid we don't speak your language."

The woman turned to the officer escorting her and addressed him. He nodded, then she turned back and spoke in slightly accented Standard English: "I am Wynn, High Priestess of the Danreg. How did you come here? Who are you?"

Kirk, though obviously surprised, recovered quickly. "I am James T. Kirk, your Highness, and these are my friends, Leonard McCoy" —the doctor bowed—"and Mr. Spock." The Vulcan inclined his head as he saluted the woman in the ceremonial fashion of his people.

"We came here from a faraway place," Kirk continued cautiously.

"Kirk . . . Spock . . . McCoy. Strange names. And you speak the tongue of our enemies." Wynn's eyes were cold. "Commander Madon told me and my father that you dropped into our midst from the sky. Is that true?"

"Uh . . ." Kirk hesitated. McCoy knew that he was weighing the pros and cons of telling the truth. *Don't do it, Jim*, he wanted to say. *In a culture this primitive, they'll think you're talking about witchcraft, and I'd rather be hanged as a spy than burned as a sorcerer.* "Your Highness," Kirk said, finally, "I can't tell you how we got here, because I really do not understand it myself."

She eyed him measuringly. "Your . . . words . . . are true, but the spirit behind them is a lie, Kirk. I do not like being summoned out of a war council with our allies only to listen to lies."

McCoy didn't miss the admiral's tiny start of surprise

—and neither did Wynn. "You are wise, your Highness," Kirk said, trying to recover, turning his most charming smile on the High Priestess. "I wish I could tell you everything, but that is impossible. But we are not enemies, I assure you. We will not harm you or your people."

She also smiled, but not pleasantly. "Of that I have no doubt, Kirk. From this moment on, you will not be free to do us any harm. Tomorrow, before I pronounce the battle oracle, I will give you one more chance to tell me the truth, and if you do not, then you will find yourself speaking to the Goddess Ashmara, and *She* will tell me what I must know about you. I warn you, She does not like liars, and there is no falsehood or equivocation allowed on the Other Side."

Turning away, she snapped out an order to Commander Madon, and the three officers were quickly and thoroughly trussed hand and foot. One tug at his bonds was enough to convince McCoy that he was going to stay tied until someone saw fit to release him—or until Beta Niobe went nova, whichever came first.

Then they were dragged over to several unoccupied hitching posts near the largest of the tents and tethered to them. The tribesmen had removed their knives (with much exclamation and wrangling over possession of the steel blades) but, beyond a cursory search for concealed weapons, they had not been harmed. McCoy and Spock still had their tricorders in their belt pouches, and the Danreg had not discovered the doctor's medikit.

As soon as their captors left, McCoy slumped down, huddling under his cloak as much as possible, trying to escape the rain. "'Thou wert better in a grave than to answer with thy uncovered body this extremity of the skies,'" he growled.

"*King Lear*, Act Three, scene four," Spock responded automatically, but his heart obviously wasn't in the game.

"We're all going to drown, damn it. Whose bright idea was this, anyway?" McCoy complained, hoping someone would rise to the bait.

"Yours," Kirk said, but there was no amusement in his

tone. He rubbed water off his nose on the shoulder of his cloak, then sneezed. "Damn."

The hours crept by as the three Starfleet officers tried to conserve their energy, to rest, to keep the bone-gnawing damp from sapping their strength. They were tied too far apart to reach each other; they could share no physical warmth. They talked a little, at first, but conversation soon lagged. Their captors ignored them, except for one time when Commander Madon and two heavyset guards took each of them for a visit to the midden.

They were neither fed, nor given any water.

"You think they just don't care, or that this is designed to break us down, Jim?" McCoy asked, as night darkened around them. With the setting of the sun, chill gusts of wind had sprung up, lashing the rain before them. The only light came from the sullen torches and protected campfires.

"Break us down," Kirk said. "Wynn wants the truth about what we're doing here. I don't blame her, I'd want to know myself." He stretched, trying to relieve cramped muscles across his back.

"What do you think she meant, that if we didn't talk, tomorrow we could tell it to her Goddess on the Other Side?" McCoy asked uneasily.

"It seems likely that she meant we would be executed . . . or, possibly, sacrificed in some ritual, Doctor."

McCoy swallowed. "Great."

"I wonder how far away from New Araen we are?" Kirk said, breaking into the bleak silence that had fallen.

"It is unfortunate that we cannot reach our tricorders," Spock said. "By scanning the surrounding area, I could determine the location of the nearest population center. That should be New Araen."

"Don't count on it," McCoy growled. "Remember how messed up the Guardian was. It could have dropped us anywhere—not to mention any*when.*"

"Let's hope you're wrong, Bones," Kirk said. "Spock, was there any mention of the Danreg in the Atoz library records?" He raised his head just long enough to speak, then immediately burrowed his reddened nose back into the warmth of his cloak.

"Just of one Heldeon of Danreg Ford, apparently one of the legendary warrior-rulers."

"Did it say where these Danreg were camped, in relation to New Araen?"

"No. It mentioned only that the forces of four great leaders met in battle on Moorgate Plain at the foot of a mountain called Big Snowy: Heldeon of Danreg Ford, Laol the War Queen of Clan Kerren, Rorgan Death-Hand of the Asyri, and the Sovren of the Lakreo Valley. The records are understandably vague and overwritten with legend. It is as though you attempted to piece together a factual history of the Trojan Wars by reading Homer—only the details that constituted 'high drama' are mentioned, and there is considerable doubt as to their accuracy."

"If we don't get out of this damned camp, the whole question of where we are is gonna prove moot," McCoy pointed out. "And if we delay our escape much longer, we'll all be too chilled to move even if the opportunity comes up. The natives may be acclimated to this cold, but we're not."

"You are correct, Doctor. I have been using biofeedback techniques for the past hour to ward off hypothermia, but I cannot do so indefinitely . . . especially if the temperature drops below freezing."

"So what's the plan?" McCoy asked.

Kirk thought for a long moment. "If we make enough noise to attract Wynn's attention, maybe we can get her to talk with us again. If so, I guarantee I'll tell her something that will at least keep her interested enough in us to make her give us some food and shelter."

"What are you going to say to her, Jim?" McCoy grinned suddenly. "Don't tell me . . . you're going to point to the stars in the sky and say we fell from the biggest one—and then you'll gaze deep into her eyes, and soon all our troubles will be over, right?"

Kirk's response was short and to the point.

McCoy's eyebrow went up. "That's anatomically impossible, you know, Jim. Anyway, can't you take a joke?"

"Not when I'm this cold and hungry," the admiral retorted, but, after a moment, his expression softened. "Sorry, Bones. At least getting mad got my blood moving again. I'll think up a good story while we wait for the camp to fall asleep. If we start hollering now, Commander Madon will just gag us."

"It's a good thing we're tied up beside what appears to be the VIP tent," McCoy said. "With all three of us yelling, she'll be sure to hear us."

"Looks like some of the troops are bedding down," Kirk observed. "Let's hope it won't be too much longer."

"Yeah, and as long as we're hoping, let's hope that Wynn doesn't decide to just cut her losses and have Madon slit our throats," McCoy punned, gloomily. "In a culture like this, life isn't just cheap, it's practically worthless."

"We've got to chance it, Bones, since the alternative is to stay tied up here and die of exposure."

"You're right," the doctor sighed. "It's a safe bet we can't survive a night in the open."

Kirk sneezed explosively. "Damn! I wish that once, just once, I could command a mission where everything goes perfectly. *Everything*. The transporter functions without a hitch . . ."

"Amen," interjected McCoy.

". . . both the warp drive and the impulse engines stay on-line for the duration . . . nobody from Security suffers so much as a hangnail . . ." Kirk's voice grew stronger as he warmed to his subject, ". . . and the ship's computer doesn't even hiccup. Not to mention avoiding power-mad tyrants, megalomanic computers, tribbles, or, God forbid, Harry Mudd!" He took a deep breath, only to have it turn into another sneeze. "Just *once*, is that too much to ask?"

"Jim," Spock said, into the ensuing silence, "there have been a number of such missions since we have served together. The time we were dispatched to contact the wave-dancers of Bellatrix V, for example. The incident with the Giant Rat of Tamuras. The deathday celebration for the Arch-Duchess sa'Gliszppkk of Rumon Alpha III. The investiture of the Neo-Pope of Ecatholos, which resulted in the peace treaty between the Ecatholans and the phlyrinigi of—"

"Okay, Spock, I concede your point," the admiral broke in, evidently realizing that the Vulcan would no doubt go on cataloguing successful missions *ad infinitum*. "There have been some . . . I just wish that this could be one of them." He coughed, then the doctor heard him mutter in a plaintive undertone, "So much for the adventure of fieldwork . . ."

McCoy peered at the lines of rain visible against the light of the closest campfire. "Rain's turning to snow," he observed.

"I'm not surprised," Kirk grumbled. He sniffled again, then added plaintively, "And to top it all off, I think I'm catching a cold."

Chapter Six

"BONES . . . HSSSSST! BONES!"

Sleep . . . and warmth. They were the only important things. The urgent whisper was not. Leonard McCoy buried himself in the warmth, refusing to hear.

"Damn it, Bones! Wake *up*, that's an order!"

"Doctor McCoy! Wake up!"

Despite his wishes, the warmth began to fade. McCoy turned over, seeking it, then gasped when a clump of wet snow slid off the edge of his cloak and onto his face. *"Mmmmph!* Huh?"

"Bones, sit up! This minute, understand?"

Groggily, the doctor shook the wet slush off his nose and mouth, then levered himself up. "I'm up," he mumbled, unhappily. "Wha's happening?"

"You nearly froze to death, that's what happened. Move your arms! Stamp your feet!"

"Breathe deeply, in and out," Spock admonished. "Do not lie down again."

Clumsily, the doctor tried to obey. As his brain began functioning again, he was frightened to realize how close he'd come to freezing to death. "How long was I asleep?"

"I don't know," Kirk said, grimly. "I dozed off, too. If it hadn't been for Spock, we'd have been a pair of ice cream bars by morning. You all right, Bones?"

"Better. Is it time?"

"We can't afford to wait. Yell as loud as you can," Kirk instructed, then bellowed, "Lady Wynn! I have to talk to you!"

"High Priestess Wynn, we must speak to you!"

"Your Highness, hey!" McCoy's lips pulled back from his teeth and a piercing wolf whistle blasted the sleety air. He grinned, irrationally pleased to find he could still do that . . . it must've been forty years since he'd had the occasion (or the immaturity) to whistle at a woman.

"Bones!"

"Jim, she's not gonna know what that means back on Earth!"

"Don't count on it. Just yell."

"Wynn! Lady Wynn!"

Before the doctor could draw another breath, they were surrounded by grim sentries. Commander Madon, carrying a torch, joined them a second later. "You!" He aimed a kick at Spock, who was nearest. "What you do?"

"I want to speak to her Highness," Kirk babbled. "I'm so cold, I can't stand it anymore! I'll tell her the truth, *please!* Just give me some food, and a blanket!"

The painted hide curtaining the opening of the largest tent opened and Wynn, her cloak pulled around her, emerged. Behind her was a massive, aging man with a shock of faded red hair and a bristling beard and moustache. *Heldeon*, the doctor guessed.

"What is all this noise?" the High Priestess demanded, in English.

Commander Madon bowed, then jammed his hissing torch into a bracket. He jerked a thumb at the prisoners in silent explanation.

"We're gonna freeze to death out here!" Kirk nearly sobbed, "And I'm so *hungry!* Please, I'll tell you the truth!"

His portrayal of a broken man was perfect. McCoy had to smother an admiring grin.

Wynn wasn't taken in easily. She glared suspiciously at the admiral. "So I should bring you to shelter and give you food, just to listen to more lies, is that it?"

"No, no, no lies, I swear by the Goddess! We're spies, all right. But please," his teeth chattered audibly, "I'm so cold I can't think, your Highness——"

Kirk broke off as a clamor of shouting reached them from the left side of the camp. Even as they all turned to look, two distant tents burst into flames. Commander Madon beckoned to the sentries, all but two of them, and he and the main group took off toward the disturbance, swords drawn.

Wynn and Heldeon shouted something (*probably "Fire!"* McCoy thought), and more troops began staggering out of their tents, buckling on weapons as they ran, bare-chested and barefoot, into the night.

"Kirk! Are you responsible for this?" Wynn was furious.

"How could I be?" Kirk retorted, indignantly. "I was tied up here, under guard!"

Heldeon muttered something to his daughter, and she whispered back. Then the High Priestess demanded, "Who are you working for? The truth, or my father swears he'll send you to the Goddess right now!"

The admiral hesitated for a moment, then, with the air of a man speaking against his will, continued, "Rorgan Death-Hand sent us, but I don't know anything about this——"

"Quiet!" Wynn interrupted, listening.

After several moments, McCoy heard it, too. A rhythmic dull pounding . . . and it was growing louder.

What is that? wondered the doctor. *It sounds vaguely familiar . . .*

The thud of racing hoofbeats suddenly filled the night. As the High Priestess and her father turned to run, a group of riders mounted on the horned creatures galloped into the camp from McCoy's right—the opposite side from the burning tents. They made no outcry as their mounts skidded to a halt in the icy mud, surrounding Wynn and Heldeon, cutting off any escape.

Heldeon stopped, howling with rage, and drew his sword.

Wynn shouted, dragging her father away from the foremost rider, just as the two sentries attacked. McCoy saw the lead rider's arm move, heard the *thunk* of a blade as it bit deep into living flesh. The sentry fell, shrieking, sounds of such agony that the doctor fought his bonds again, trying without success to break free so he could tend the man. The rider's mount dealt with the second sentry, swinging its horned head, sending the man flying through the air, to land unmoving.

Heldeon slipped in the slush, then struggled to get up, roaring orders at his distant warriors. The High Priestess dropped to her knees, reached beneath the wounded man, and came up with his sword. As McCoy watched (*where in hell did these guys come from?*), she dragged her cloak off, wrapping it hastily around her left forearm, to use as a crude shield. She dropped into a half-crouch, the blade weaving expertly before her. In the flickering torchlight she looked like a drowned wraith in her damp white shift, her long hair spilling down her back.

McCoy heard the yells of the warriors, and knew the tribesmen were finally aroused to their chieftain's danger. The lead rider glanced at the oncoming horde, and his mount skittered, leaving his left leg unguarded for a critical second. Wynn's backhanded sword-slash was smooth, economical, and only the battle-trained mount's reactions saved its rider.

But even as the High Priestess moved, a loop of rope flicked out from one of the other riders, dropping over her head. She flailed wildly, trying to bat it aside, but it jerked tight over her shoulders, pulling her off her feet.

Heldeon lunged to help her, but another noose pulled him down.

In a moment the lead rider had dismounted and bent over Wynn, binding her arms to her sides, then he threw her thrashing body across the saddle of his now-kneeling beast. He pointed at the three prisoners. "Bring the spies, too!"

Before McCoy could do more than blink, one of the riders swooped down on him and severed the rope tethering him to the post. The man caught the free end, dragged the doctor over to his mount, then, one-handed, he grabbed the back of McCoy's jerkin and hauled him up across the animal's withers. The beast surged forward with a leap, sending the doctor's breath whooshing from his lungs as they went galloping into the darkness.

McCoy was terrified. He lay head-down, his face grinding into the straining shoulder of the mount. His hands were still bound behind him, and the only thing holding him on was the angle of his body and the rider's one-handed grip on his belt. The racing animal twisted and turned to avoid boulders and trees, but bushes whipped the doctor's head and legs. McCoy froze; if he struggled, his captor might loosen his hold, sending the doctor crashing, face-down, onto the rocky ground.

Finally the nightmare race slowed gradually, until the beast was cantering, then trotting. With every stride, its bony withers jabbed the doctor's midsection. McCoy's abused stomach protested, but it was too empty and too constricted to rid itself of its scanty contents. He could only gag and retch dryly.

That broke his captor's silence. "Puke on my leg and I swear that I'll drop you off this cliff, spy." The only plea for mercy the doctor could muster emerged as a groan, but moments later the man slowed his panting beast to a walk.

Did they bring Jim and Spock? McCoy wondered, dully. *Will I ever see them again?* He tried to raise his face to look around him, but his head whirled so badly that he dropped it back against the animal's sweaty shoulder.

The ride went on, until it seemed to McCoy that they had been riding forever, and would continue riding until the end of time. He slipped in and out of consciousness, but there was never any relief from his discomfort.

Most of the time they were descending, because the man had to hold him across the saddlebow to keep him from sliding down his mount's neck. *Dear God, let this be over,* the doctor prayed. *I don't care how, just let it end, please . . .*

Finally, the doctor roused again from his stupor, only to realize they had stopped. He opened his eyes to see the gray light of predawn, and tried to raise his head, look around him, but his muscles refused to obey. After a moment, the rider slung him down—fortunately, not head-first—onto a hard surface. McCoy collapsed immediately, almost beneath the hooves of the horned beast, but he could not move, not even when one of its feet brushed his shoulder.

"Steady, there," came the voice of his captor, soothing his nervous mount. The creature moved away, then the doctor was half-lifted, and after a second, his arms swung free and his legs were no longer bound. They buckled immediately, and with a curse, the man pulled the doctor's limp arm over his shoulder and began dragging him.

McCoy glanced groggily around him, and glimpsed a stone-walled courtyard. Beyond its walls rose a short tower that was part of a two- or three-story stone fortress. His captor hauled the doctor through a massive, barred door. Yellow light and black darkness came in blurred flashes, and finally McCoy realized they were traveling through a torchlit corridor. His captor cursed again beneath the doctor's dead weight, then, as they reached a stairway, he halted, easily boosted his prisoner over his shoulder, and started down.

A wave of dank, smelly air engulfed them. McCoy retched again at the odor of open privies and sweat-rancid bodies, fighting to stay conscious. He felt his captor stop, heard a muttered exchange he couldn't catch, then a grating noise. The man began moving again, but halted in a few strides and lowered the doctor onto a slightly yielding surface. Hands fumbled at his foot, and he heard something *clink*, then *click*. His ankle felt suddenly heavy.

"Here, you'd better fetch him a blanket," his captor said. "The Second wants to question all of them when they come around. We don't want this one dying on us."

"Right," came a different voice, and a moment later something rough but warm settled over the doctor's body. He made a desperate effort.

"Jim?" he whispered, pawing feebly at the man's arm. "Spock?"

"What's he want?" the man demanded of McCoy's captor.

"No idea. He kept mumbling that all the way down the

mountain. Probably praying . . . he's sure in enough trouble to need all the help he can get."

"You're right about that." Both men turned away and the doctor heard their footsteps. *Don't go!* he wanted to scream, but could only manage a moan. "I wouldn't want to be wearing their helmets. Cletas doesn't deal soft with enemy spies."

The door slammed behind them, and McCoy discovered that he could fight the encroaching darkness no longer . . .

The doctor awoke to the sound of gentle snoring, and to a body so bruised and stiff that just sitting up on his pallet was raw agony. He saw sunlight streaming in through a narrow, barred window near the ceiling of the cell—for cell it was, stone-walled, with a huge, timbered door inset with a barred opening. His leg was shackled to the wall with a long iron chain.

There were two other narrow pallets with humped shapes in them, and from one of those recumbent forms the somnolent buzzing sounds emanated. Despite his pain, McCoy grinned with relief; he recognized those snores. *"Jim!"*

The noises ceased abruptly and a tousled head appeared from beneath the blanket. "Bones . . ." Kirk croaked, "is that you?"

"You look just about as terrible as I feel. Is that Spock over there?"

"Affirmative, Doctor McCoy," said the Vulcan. He emerged also. He was the only one of them who had not lost his cap.

Carefully, not troubling to repress his groans, the doctor managed to swing his legs over the side of his pallet. "I thought I'd never see you two again. Are you all right?"

"Even my hair hurts," Kirk said, also sitting up, "but I guess I'll live." He straightened his back with a hiss of pain. "I just won't be happy about it for awhile. Spock . . . you okay?"

"I am bruised and stiff from such an unorthodox means

of transportation, but otherwise undamaged," the Vulcan allowed, cautiously stretching the kinks out of his lanky frame.

"Here," the doctor said, fumbling beneath his jerkin, "I've still got my medical kit. These should help." He held out two pills, while popping the third into his own mouth.

Spock took his with a raised eyebrow, but swallowed it meekly enough.

"How do you feel, Jim? Feverish? Do you need something for that cold?"

Kirk took a deep, experimental breath, then looked surprised. "I guess I was wrong about getting one. I'm all right. Maybe the snow last night froze all the germs."

Spock raised an eyebrow at him. "Admiral, that speculation is totally—"

Kirk grimaced. "Spare me the scientific lecture, Spock. Say, is there any water in here? I'm so thirsty!"

The three officers found a bucket of cold water near the door. After each had drunk his fill, they used the remaining liquid to sluice their faces and hands. By then the painkiller had taken effect, and they were moving almost normally.

"The question is," Kirk paced, dragging his chain, "where are we? In the fire, as opposed to the frying pan?"

"How the hell should I know?" McCoy snapped peevishly, trying to knead a cramp out of his calf. "For God's sake, sit down, Jim! You look like Marley's ghost, dragging that thing!"

"Ah." Spock looked up from his tricorder. "Dickens. *A Christmas Carol.*"

Just then the bolts on their cell door *skreeked* back, and a stocky little man with greasy hair entered. From the keys hanging from his belt, McCoy guessed he was their jailer. He was accompanied by two armed guards, and carried bowls on a tray, plus a fresh bucket of water. At his gesture, one of the guards dumped the remains of the first bucket down the midden hole. "So everyone's awake, now," he said, eyeing them. "Lookin' a little livelier than you was, all right. Eat up, now."

He passed out spoons and bowls of warm porridge, each accompanied by a twist of dried meat jerky. Spock gravely handed his meat over to the admiral, who divided it between himself and the doctor. In return, they both spooned some of their porridge into the Vulcan's dish. The jailer and his guards watched as they ate.

McCoy tasted the brownish stuff tentatively, expecting to find it repulsive, but, though coarsely ground, it was good, with a sweetish, nutty flavor. He scooped it into his mouth eagerly, scraping the last out of the bowl with regret.

When they were finished, the jailer collected the bowls and spoons. "Thank you, sir," Spock said. "May I ask whether we have reached New Araen?"

"I'm under orders to tell you nothin'," the little man said, brusquely. "The Second will be down to talk with you himself. Though," he grinned and winked at them jovially, "it's my guess he'll have you *answerin'* questions 'stead of *askin'* 'em!"

"Great," muttered McCoy as the door banged shut behind them. "We get a comedian for a warden. Who is this Second?"

"No idea," Kirk said. "But at least these people speak English. *And* they fed us." He began gnawing on his jerky.

"Yes, they did," Spock said. "I have noted a number of significant facts since we awoke. First, my tricorder readings indicate this to be a sizable population center. Secondly, the condition of this cell: while damp, it does seem to have been designed with some regard for its occupants' comfort. The window provides adequate ventilation. The blankets —rough, but uninfested. The food—plain, but edible. The edges of these shackles have been filed smooth so as to avoid abrading the skin of the wearer. And—"

"So?" McCoy broke in. "We can nominate this place for our list of top-ten favorite jails. Heaven knows we've been thrown in enough of them to be connoisseurs. What's your point, Spock?"

"That this dungeon seems to be run along rather . . . enlightened . . . lines, in comparison to its time." The Vulcan thoughtfully fingered the links of his chain. "Thirdly, this is made from wrought iron, a substance requiring higher technological advancement than the bronze weapons and armor we witnessed in Heldeon's camp."

"Conclusion: we've reached New Araen," Kirk said. "I think so, too."

"I don't care whether this is New Araen or the Emerald City, sitting here on our butts isn't doing anyone a helluva lot of good," McCoy protested. "Zar's battle could be today! We can't just do nothing, we've gotta break out!"

"I calculated our jump to bring us here several days before that conflict, Doctor."

"Yeah, but don't forget you calculated our *last* visit to Sarpeidon so we'd find a cute little pointy-eared tyke!"

"I concede your point, but nevertheless, I do not feel that an escape would be our most logical course of action at this time," Spock said, leaning back against the wall and arranging his blanket over his legs. "I believe we should wait until someone in higher authority turns up and make our case at that time. If it then proves necessary, I can always rewire my tricorder to disintegrate the cell door bolt, but doing so would render it useless for sensoring, and we may need it."

"I agree with Spock," Kirk said. "We all took a beating yesterday. We can use this chance to get our strength back. Let's wait a couple of hours and see what happens."

McCoy shrugged. "You're the boss." Idly he took out his medical tricorder and amused himself taking readings of the life forms within range. "This is strange," he said, presently.

"What?" asked Kirk.

"This is the first opportunity I've had to get readings from the natives of Sarpeidon—Zar didn't count, of course, because of his mixed parentage—and my tricorder shows that these people probably did not evolve on this world. There's little correlation between their basic body chemistry and that of their animals—at least from an evolutionary standpoint."

"Fascinating." Spock looked up. "That observation ties

in with an anomaly which puzzled me from the beginning. My studies of Sarpeidon's ecology showed that it has no animals analogous to primates at all. I had speculated that perhaps all the missing primate-analogues had become extinct due to some disease, but if the sentient life forms were transplanted here from someplace else, that would explain this lack."

"Transplanted? From where?"

"I don't know, Jim." McCoy scanned the readings again. "Not Earth. Their makeup is closer to Rigellian, closer still to Vulcan. No wonder they're so strong."

Kirk looked doubtful. "Vulcan? But what about their . . ." He tapped his ear.

"This world is much colder than Vulcan, Jim. If what Dr. McCoy speculates is true, then the transplanters would know that the Vulcan ear, evolved to cup sound waves in a thin, desert atmosphere, would not prove a survival characteristic here. They made suitable alterations in the basic genetic material."

" 'They' who?"

Spock shook his head. "Impossible to say. We know that there were a number of now-vanished races that 'seeded' intelligent life throughout the explored portion of the galaxy. The Preservers and Sargon's people, to name two."

"Then if your people and the Sarpeids came from the same genetic stock, that would explain why you and Zarabeth could, uh . . ." Kirk's voice trailed off as he searched for words.

The admiral was rescued by the sound of the cell door bolt. The three officers hastily climbed to their feet as the door opened, this time admitting a middle-aged man of medium height who wore a chain-mail shirt, but whose head was bare, revealing a shock of graying brown hair. He was heavily tanned, and his eyes were blue. At least, McCoy assumed both eyes were blue . . . his right eye was swollen nearly shut and sported a magnificent shiner. His lower lip was split and puffy.

He was unarmed except for a dagger, but the two guards

flanking him made up for it. They fairly bristled with steel weapons . . . swords, halberds, and knives.

What Jim wouldn't give to have some of those beauties to hang on his wall back home, McCoy thought, wryly.

"I am Second-in-War Cletas," the officer said. "Who are you?"

"Before we answer that," Kirk said, "where are we?"

"This is the trade city of New Araen," the man answered, scornfully amused. "Don't pretend you don't know that."

Kirk grinned at his companions. "We did it!"

"Did what?" asked the Second, his eyes hard and wary. "Who are you? They told me that the Danreg had captured spies, but you are none of mine. Who are you working for?"

"Listen, we don't have time for that," Kirk said, impatiently. "We're *not* spies. I'm Kirk, he's Spock, and that's McCoy. We need to see your ruler . . . the Sovren . . . immediately. There's not much time to lose. The battle hasn't started yet, has it?"

Cletas's hand went to the hilt of his dagger. "What do you know about when the attack will begin?"

"Nothing!" Kirk made an exasperated gesture. "That is, we know there's going to be one, but nothing about the exact time of the attack. We're not with your enemies, we're friends. We *must* see the Sovren before the battle begins, or it'll be too late!"

"We've come to deliver a warning," McCoy put in. "He knows us, just ask him."

Cletas gave the three of them a long, up-and-down look, his eyes taking in every detail of their bruised faces, their torn and muddy clothes. "You do, eh? You expect me to believe that?" He shook his head. "You're not spies, you're lunatics."

"It's true!" Kirk insisted, a little wildly. "Just tell him our names. He'll be down here so fast . . ."

One of the guards snickered under his breath. Cletas shot him a glance and the man stiffened back to attention. "I may be able to arrange an interview," the Second told them, *"if* you will tell me who you're working for."

"Rorgan Death-Hand," Kirk said, evidently deciding that this was the best way to handle the situation. "He sent us to spy on the Danreg and they caught us. Then your people captured us, in turn, during a raid last night . . ." He peered closely at the Second's face. "You were the one leading that attack!"

The man shrugged, as though he had no reason to deny Kirk's statement. "All right, so Rorgan Death-Hand sent you?"

"Yes!" Kirk was as frustrated as the doctor had ever seen him. "Now take us to see your Sovren!"

"First, tell me why he's called 'Death-Hand,'" Cletas said, hooking his thumbs in his belt and rocking back on his heels.

"Uh . . ." Kirk gave Spock an imploring glance, but the Vulcan gave his head a tiny, negative shake. "Because he's killed so many men?"

The guard's mouth twitched. "Because," said the Second levelly, "he wears a spiked bronze mace where his severed right hand used to be. You never saw him in your life. Maybe a couple of days on bread and water will convince you that I'm serious."

Cletas turned to leave. *"Wait!"* McCoy yelled, seized by sudden inspiration. His chain clashed wildly as the doctor shuffled rapidly over to Spock and snatched the Vulcan's cap off. *"Now* will you believe we know Zar?"

The Second stared for a long moment, his good eye narrowing, then he turned to the guards. "Stay here," he snapped. "See that nothing happens to them. I will return."

McCoy slumped back down onto his cot, limp with relief. *Is it really going to be all right, after all this?* He was afraid to hope.

Kirk sat down next to him. "Good going, Bones. I should've thought of that."

McCoy lowered his voice. "I almost didn't. I'd nearly forgotten he was present, he was so quiet."

They both glanced up at the Vulcan, who was standing, hands behind his back in his accustomed pose, his expression completely serene. McCoy grimaced and whispered, "He's as nervous as a long-tailed cat in a room full of rocking chairs, Jim."

"I know," Kirk returned, also whispering. "I can imagine how he feels."

McCoy noticed a certain wistfulness in the admiral's expression, and was puzzled by it. But now hardly seemed an appropriate time to pursue the matter.

Time dragged by. Even the guards shifted their weight. "How long has it been, Spock?" Kirk asked, finally.

"Seventeen minutes, fourteen seconds, Admiral."

What's going on? McCoy wondered, fidgeting. *Has New Araen been attacked? Is Cletas dead, his message undelivered?*

He passed more time by taking readings of the guards with his tricorder. They showed neither fear nor interest at the sight of the instrument.

Finally, the doctor slumped back onto the bunk. "I can't stand this," he said, his voice doubly loud in the stillness. "Spock, how much time now?"

"Thirty-six minutes, ten sec—" The Vulcan stopped, listening.

Nearly a full minute later, McCoy heard the footsteps, too.

Faintly, Cletas's voice reached them. "The Lady Wynn will wait a little longer, sire. I believe you need to see these prisoners for yourself."

The steps halted outside the cell door, and they heard a different voice say, "Cletas, there is something you're not telling me. What's going on here?" Even before the guards snapped to attention, saluting, McCoy recognized the voice. A sudden rush of feeling made him bite his lip hard.

The bolt screeched, and the door opened. Kirk and McCoy rose to their feet as a tall, broad-shouldered man who moved with a noticeable limp entered. He carried a red-plumed steel helmet and wore a scarlet cloak over his mail.

118

Zar.

He stood on the threshold, staring, one-by-one, at the three of them for a moment that stretched almost beyond endurance. Nobody spoke.

Finally, Zar blinked. His voice eluded him for a moment, but when it finally emerged, it was admirably calm. "I *am* awake, therefore this must be real."

McCoy's eyes were stinging as he grinned foolishly. "Hello, Zar. Long time no see."

Kirk groaned. "If you don't quit making horrible puns, I'm going to leave you in the dungeon, Bones. Zar, I'm glad to see you."

"And I you," the Sovren said, then his eyes turned back to Spock and his fingers moved into the Vulcan salute. "Sir . . ." he began formally, "welcome to New Araen."

A faint half-smile softened the stern mouth as the Vulcan returned the gesture. "Greetings, son. It is good to see you again. It has been too long."

The younger man's gray eyes began to shine, his voice was no longer completely steady. "Obviously longer for me than it was for you, Father. It has been almost twenty years."

"For us 14.5 years have passed." Concern touched Spock's voice. "Are you well? You were limping."

"An old wound. It's worse when it's damp." Zar had regained most of his control with an effort. "I missed you, Father." He glanced over at Kirk and McCoy. "I've missed all of you. I never expected to see you again. This was a complete surprise."

"You mean Cletas didn't tell you who was waiting?" Kirk asked, with a twinkle.

"If you told Cletas your names, he didn't see fit to tell me." The Sovren turned back to his officer, who by now was grinning broadly. "I see you're enjoying your little joke."

"I am, sire," the Second admitted. "And to think I almost left them down here on bread and water . . ." He nodded at Spock. "I kept thinking there was something familiar about the tall one, but it wasn't until McCoy pulled his cap off that I realized who he must be."

Zar's gray eyes took on a hard, fatalistic expression the doctor had never seen in them before. "Ah, yes, my doppelgänger." He glanced back at Spock, deadpan. "This means that one of us is fated to die, you know."

Cletas's grin vanished; the man looked stricken. "Doppelgänger, my liege?"

"An old legend from another . . . land," Zar explained. "If a person meets an apparition who is his double, it's supposedly a sure sign of impending death."

He knows he's going to die in the coming battle! McCoy thought. *But how?* Zar had claimed that the empathic/clairvoyant abilities he had demonstrated during his time aboard the *Enterprise* didn't apply to himself, only to those he cared for . . .

Trying to break the sudden tension, the doctor said, over-heartily, "I don't know anything about ancient legends, but for a moment when you first walked in I thought we were back in a parallel universe we visited once. A mirror universe, where we all had ruthless twins, Zar. I told Spock I liked him with a beard. He looked like a pirate."

Kirk chuckled, only to have it turn into a cough.

Zar made a "what am I doing?" gesture. "I'm sorry, Captain, by all means let's get out of this dampness so you can get cleaned up. Cletas, they'll want hot baths, clean clothes, and food." He waved Kirk toward the door.

"By the way," McCoy jerked a thumb at Kirk's back, "it's Admiral, now."

"I should have realized," Zar said. "Congratulations, Admiral."

"Make it Jim," Kirk said, as the group started along the corridor toward the stairs. "We've all come up in the world, it seems. We didn't expect to come back here and find you running the whole show."

"That condition," Zar said grimly, lines of pain deepening around his mouth as he limped up the stairs, "may well be temporary. But I can at least see to your comfort while you explain how you ended up in my dungeon."

"I will oversee their care, sire," Cletas said. "And bring them to you as soon as you are free to talk."

"What do you mean? I'm going to personally—" Zar began, then he broke off and sighed. "Oh. The Lady Wynn. I must speak to her."

"Yes, my liege. She is awaiting you in your study, under guard. Be careful, sire."

Zar's mouth quirked. "I'll be sure to keep the table between us, seeing what she did to you. By the way, McCoy is a healer. I'll wager he could fix that eye of yours."

They left the stairs and went out into an upper corridor, stone-walled and stone-floored, as before, but narrow, room-high leaded windows provided light, and occasional tapestries and rugs broke the gray monotony with bright colors. Zar paused and faced them. "Much as I wish I could stay, I must go. Cletas will bring you to me when I'm free again."

"Doesn't sound like he's very eager to talk to her," McCoy said, watching him walk away, thinking that, despite the limp, he still moved with a measure of his old feral grace and quickness.

"He is not," Cletas said. "But I believe that the Council and I have convinced him to go against his personal wishes, to do what he must."

"What's that?" asked McCoy, thinking uneasily about hostages and examples-of-war.

"Persuade her to marry him, thus either removing Heldeon's troops from the coming battle, or causing them to change their allegiance so they will fight on our side. The High Priestess is of limited use as a hostage; most likely the Danreg have already added her name to the Death Scrolls for vengeance and are preparing to attack as soon as the waters of the Redbank subside enough to allow them to cross it. Although," the Second added, "their lack of a Battle Oracle is bound to make them hesitate."

"And if they attack?" McCoy asked, with an uneasy premonition that he wasn't going to like the answer.

"We are outnumbered nearly four to one," Cletas said grimly.

The doctor frowned. "I hadn't realized it was that bad. He's only got this afternoon to gain her consent?"

"Yes," the Second said. "If the Lady Wynn does not agree to the handfasting today, then by tomorrow night we will all probably be dead."

Chapter Seven

THE HALL SEEMED ENDLESS, barred with shadows that crouched, waiting and patient . . . hunters ready to pull down a maimed prey. Zar gritted his teeth as he limped through them. His leg hurt, the once-severed muscles sending dull stabs throughout his body.

In a way the pain was a relief, for it distracted him from the darkness growing within him. "Depression," McCoy might call it. Or, more likely, "battle fatigue." But the Danreg had a term, "d'arkeh n'esth," meaning "death-shadowed," and to Zar that described it better.

For years he had held it at bay, throwing himself into his work, ignoring the aching void inside. But lately, when he realized that everything he had come back to Sarpeidon to achieve was crumbling—that his valley could not escape the invaders—the shadows had overtaken him.

Zar left the long gallery with its high windows, and the unlit corridor beyond seemed a reflection of what waited inside him. *Not today,* he told the darkness, silently. *You'll have to wait. Not long now, though.*

Long enough, he reminded himself, feeling again the small spark of warmth his father's words had kindled down in the dungeon. It fought the cold darkness threatening to engulf him, fought it as he'd no longer had the strength, the will, to fight. *Long enough to hear him call me "son," to see*

123

the light in his eyes. He came back for me, it doesn't matter why.

Zar smiled inwardly. *It's almost as though he knew this would be his last chance. The last bit of unfinished business, and now it's done, over.*

A sense of peace swept him, peace and acceptance.

At first he had tried to fight the despair, the feeling of being "d'arkeh n'esth," but recently he had given in, let it take him. He was tired of struggling, he had been tired for years; but, like a warrior too battle-hardened to feel the pain, to let his wounds stop him, he had refused to acknowledge it until these last few days. Wynn's prophecy had plucked a shadowed minor chord within him, and now all his being vibrated in tune to it.

It was done. Over. Soon, he could rest.

That was why he had agreed to do as Cletas and the Council wanted. What difference did it make, if he took the High Priestess of the Danreg as his consort? That counterfeit of a marriage would last only a day or two at most, then he would be gone, and she could use her influence as his successor to beg clemency from the Kerren and the Asyri. The State handfasting would save bloodshed, would spare lives. His people might still be conquered, but they would not be massacred.

With all his being, he hoped that was true. It all depended on what kind of person the High Priestess was, on whether she truly served her Goddess, Ashmara who espoused life, or whether Wynn only gave lip-service to her beliefs. From everything Zar had been able to discover about her, the former was true. But he'd *know* after he spoke with her; it was impossible to deceive an empath.

He reached the door to his bedchamber and turned to enter the room, nodding at the saluting guard. Once inside, he limped past the high, curtained bed, past his portrait of Araen, to the washstand. Voba was already there, pouring warm water from the ewer into the basin, a clean towel flung over his shoulder. *Somehow he always knows what I'm going to do before I know it myself,* Zar thought wryly.

After stripping to his black leather breeches, he began washing. Mud and sweat from the parade ground had dried in streaks on his arms; his nails were black-rimmed. The soap Voba handed him smelled faintly of herbs.

Finally he was clean and dry. Zar shrugged into the open-necked gray tunic the aide held out, then cinched it around his waist with a plain black-leather belt that supported only a sheath for Zarabeth's knife. He shook his head at the silver and jet Medallion-of-State Voba held out. "Nothing official, Voba. That would only anger her worse than she already is."

Zar combed his hair, smoothed his beard, then, with a sigh, turned back toward the door. "Has she calmed down? Eaten?"

"Yes, sire," the little man said, bobbing his wiry red head. "I thought she might pitch the food at me, but she didn't."

So, she can control her temper, as well as unleash it, Zar thought. *A valuable trait in a leader.*

"Incidentally, my father and two of his comrades just arrived for a visit. Cletas is escorting them to the guest chambers. Please see to their comfort, Voba."

"Your *father,* my Sovren?" It was the first time in years Zar had seen his aide-de-camp surprised.

"Yes. You'll know him when you see him. His name is Spock. The others with him are Doctor McCoy and Admiral Kirk. McCoy is the one with the blue eyes."

Voba bowed slightly. "I shall attend them personally, sire."

Zar nodded absently, his eyes on the portrait he had painted twenty years ago. The pictured features were small and oval beneath the masses of black hair. Huge dark eyes dominated the pale, fine-boned face. "Araen was beautiful, wasn't she, Voba?" he murmured.

"She was, sire," the little man agreed, and Zar caught his sidelong glance. *He's surprised that I spoke her name, after all these years.*

"Is this Wynn beautiful?"

The aide considered. "Well, she's not ill-favored, my

liege, but it's my guess nobody'd call her a beauty. Tall and sturdy-built, strong-looking. Eyes that go right through you."

"What color are they? Not dark?" Zar didn't know why he cared, but it was important, somehow.

"Oh, no, sire. They're green. And her hair's kind of a light chestnut."

Zar nodded absently, his momentary interest fading. *What does it matter?* He turned abruptly and went out into the hall, then halted before the guarded door to his study. *Let her listen to me, please.*

Taking a deep breath, he unlatched it and went in.

Wynn sat gracefully in the big padded seat, her spine barely touching its back. She was scared, but it would not do for Heldeon's daughter to show fear, so her eyes as they surveyed the room (for the hundredth time) were cool, and her hands lay quietly on the chair arms.

It was a large room, with thick, colorful hangings on the stone walls, except for the one facing her, where a picture was painted. It was an odd picture. Wynn sat staring at those strangely colored stars, trying to unravel its meaning. It *had* meaning, she was sure of that . . . but she knew suddenly, intuitively, that it depicted a time and a place completely outside her frame of reference, something she might not comprehend even if it were explained to her.

The picture added to her unease.

True, she had been well-treated so far, offered a tub of hot, herb-scented water so she could bathe, and a selection of finely woven gowns for her wearing. They had given her food; fruit, bread, cheese, and meats, plus flagons of water and wine.

The ugly little man who had served her had even ceremoniously taken a sip from each vessel to demonstrate that their contents were neither poisoned nor drugged. (Though Wynn could envision several ways to administer additives that would get around ceremonial tasting by a servant . . . drying the substance on the lip of a goblet, or placing it on the corners of the napkins, for example. She was a chieftain's daughter and intrigues were nothing new to her.)

But the High Priestess had already *known* the food and drink were untainted, because she could *feel* the little servant's lack of duplicity. So she had eaten and drunk without worrying . . . after all, if they had simply wanted her dead, they could have riven her with a spear when she was first captured, or tossed her off a cliff during the ride down-mountain.

Even under extreme provocation, her abductors had not harmed her. When they had first ridden into the courtyard in New Araen, her captor, the leader of the raiding band, had reached up to lift her down from the saddle of his vykar. True to her father's training, Wynn had seized her chance—first, with a kick to the chin that staggered the officer, then she'd leaped down and followed up with a hard left before the guards could grab her.

She'd stood laughing down at him as he sprawled unconscious on the sodden stones of the courtyard . . . and the stony-faced guards had only escorted her inside. Wynn rubbed her bruised knuckles, smiling grimly. She shouldn't have lost her temper, but it had felt good to lash out. Since that incident the guards and servants had treated her with a wary respect.

No, they definitely wanted her alive. But why?

Wynn got up to pace over to the room's only window and looked out on the marketplace of New Araen, surrounded by the city that was nestled into the Lakreo Valley. Before her, so distant that she could not see them, massed on the other side of the raging river, the Kerren and Asyri troops were waiting.

Could it be that the Sovren of New Araen wanted to discuss terms of surrender? They said he was strange, not as other men, but nobody had ever implied that he was a fool. If the Sovren wanted to surrender, he had only to send a party up-mountain with their swords bound into their scabbards with blue peace-thongs, and Heldeon would receive them under a banner of truce. There was no need for a dangerous raid and a kidnapping that would be guaranteed to leave her father spoiling for every drop of her abductors' blood.

Perhaps the Sovren wanted to plead for amnesty for his people. That was far more likely, Wynn decided, studying the stone and timbered houses, each with its own garden plot. New Araen seemed a well-tended, prosperous place. If it were possible to capture it without more than a token bloodshedding, she would do her best to convince her father to do so.

That would please the Goddess. Ashmara was a woman's deity, and Life was her concern, not death—except death through natural causes, always a part of Life.

Even though she had been lessoned in the arts of war, and had led her father's troops during battle, Wynn *hated* the looting, killing, raping sprees that were a conquered city's lot. The wails of the children, the shrieks of the men and women—whenever Heldeon would listen (and he usually valued her counsel), she had interceded with her father to prevent the sacking of enemy towns. The shared pain she felt sickened her; in the screams of the vanquished she heard echoes of her own cries when she'd discovered the hacked bodies of Nahral and little Lelinos, two years ago.

Despite her control, Wynn's fingers clenched spasmodically on the stone windowsill. She still missed them, with an ache like a cold fist within her breast. Big, laughing, blond Nahral, with his broad, gentle hands . . . and her baby, Lelinos, barely five, his chubby features slack and aged with death, his huge-pupiled eyes staring at nothing. The Asyri had not left Nahral his eyes . . .

Wynn hated Rorgan Death-Hand, despising the lies the Asyri leader had told Heldeon to forge the current alliance. He had smoothly explained that the raiding party which had attacked the Danreg camp was composed of cashiered soldiers and outlaws who had been acting on their own, not as his warriors.

It was so plausible it might even have been true . . . except Wynn *knew*—as soon as the man's gaze met hers —that his words were false. She had no evidence, beyond those strange flashes of shared emotion that came to her, and her "power" made Heldeon uneasy—it was a gift from the Goddess, he said, but she knew he did not trust or understand it.

Besides, the Danreg needed the troops and supplies the Asyri alliance had brought, thus Wynn had kept her silence. Ashmara knew the truth, and the Goddess had no love for liars. Rorgan would pay, eventually. Wynn trusted Her.

Footsteps sounded outside the door.

Hastily, Wynn returned to her chair and sat down, smoothing her gown and composing her face as she heard the latch rattle. A moment later the door swung open, and a man entered.

He was tall, taller even than Nahral had been, though not as heavily built. But his shoulders were muscled and broad, his waist lean. Obviously a warrior—except that he was crippled.

Absently, he shut the door behind him, then stood gazing at her. Wynn unflinchingly returned his stare.

His face was . . . strange. Lean and weathered as any warrior's, but . . . different. Long and sharp-angled in its planes, hollow-cheeked and austere. Lines scored it, crossing the brow, running downward from the nose to bracket the unsmiling, steady mouth. Thick, slightly curling black hair tumbled across his forehead and grew shaggily down the back of his neck. He went bearded, a close-cropped beard such as soldiers favored. No silver mingled in hair or beard, but he was not young.

His eyes were gray, the color of distant storm clouds, and above them his brows slanted upward. They were cool, aloof eyes, but somewhere behind them Wynn sensed despair.

The High Priestess was troubled by those eyes, troubled also by the sense that she had seen him before, though she was equally positive they had never met.

He was the first to break the silence. "Greetings, my lady," he said, giving her a formal bow. His voice was pleasant, not as deep as Nahral's massive-chested rumble, but a hardness beneath the courtesy told Wynn that he was accustomed to command.

Wynn inclined her head, as to a near-equal. "My lord."

His mouth twitched slightly. "May I sit? I am not comfortable standing."

She indicated the seat opposite her. "Please do. I suspect it's your chair."

After he was seated, he gazed across the table at her, and she picked up the first faint touch of emotion from him . . . he was nervous, which left Wynn feeling almost cheerful. "You are the one they call the Sovren?"

"Yes," he replied. "I should offer my apologies for bringing you here so . . . precipitously."

She smiled grimly. "You should. Don't you?"

"No," he said flatly, his tone bitter. "I don't. You were my last chance, and my people were instructed to keep you safe at all costs, even at the expense of their own lives. My Second, Cletas, paid the price for those orders. Believe me, if there had been any other way I could have arranged to talk to you, I would have employed it."

Wynn lounged back in her seat, expertly feigning an ease she didn't feel. "I see . . . why did you wish to speak to me?"

"Because you are Ashmara's priestess, and thus sworn to Her service, yes?" One of the slanting black brows rose. Wynn nodded. "And She is a Goddess who loves life. I hoped that I might persuade you to join me in an effort to spare many lives. The lives of my people and yours. Are lives important to you?"

So, she had been right. Wynn nodded. "Yes, they are."

"If the battle is joined tomorrow, or the day after tomorrow, not only the lives of soldiers will be lost," he said. "As things now stand, the lives of the people of New Araen —including the children—will be forfeit if we lose."

Wynn met his eyes levelly—again feeling that haunting stab of recognition. With an effort she shook it off. "You are right. Our forces are overwhelming . . . you will be overrun. Obviously, the fate of conquered cities is familiar to you."

He nodded, his eyes bleak. "I know what happens."

"I will be truthful with you," she began, for something about this man compelled honesty from her. "I am outraged at the way I was captured and brought here . . . but . . . I am also in sympathy with your efforts on behalf of your people."

Even though his expression did not change, Wynn felt his relief at her words and raised a warning hand. "It may not help, though. I have some influence with my father, and I will attempt to intercede with him for the safety of the noncombatant citizens of New Araen. The city and its skilled tradespeople will be worth more to us intact, anyway."

She sighed. "But, frankly, Heldeon may be so angry at my abduction that he will not listen to anything I have to say. And I have no sway at all over Laol, Rorgan, or their respective troops. Our alliance has been an uneasy one."

His disappointment reached her clearly. "I see," he said heavily, steepling his fingers before him. Wynn looked at his hands . . . long-fingered like those of a scribe, but sword-callused and capable, also. Two scars, old sword slashes by the look of them, crossed the back of the right hand and disappeared beneath his sleeve.

"I am truly sorry," she said softly.

"I know," he said. "I can tell. What if I could suggest a tactic that would diffuse much of your father's anger, *and* give him a strong incentive to spare the lives of my people?"

Something about his voice made Wynn's heart begin to pound, though she had no idea what he was talking about. She found she could not look away from his eyes. Her own voice sounded muffled, because of the blood thrumming in her ears. "What tactic? What are you proposing?"

A faint smile touched his mouth as the eyebrow went back up. "Coincidental that you should use that particular word. I am talking, my lady, about marriage."

It took Wynn a moment to find her voice, but when it finally emerged, it was completely level. "You mean between you and me." It was not a question, but he nodded. "How interesting. It's certainly the best offer I've had all day." She laughed, genuinely amused. "State your terms, my lord."

He took a deep breath. "I am talking about a State

handfasting, my lady. They tell me bride-raiding is an accepted custom among the Danreg, so Heldeon's anger will be lessened when he hears the reason for your abduction, if you freely consent to wed me. And then the Danreg would be my kin-by-marriage, thus unable to march against me."

He shrugged one shoulder. "I will almost certainly still have to face the Asyri and Clan Kerren—and I will still be gravely outnumbered. But then there may be a slim chance. As matters stand now, there is none—although," his voice grew colder and harder than the walls around them, "our conquerors will pay dearly for their victory, I assure you."

Wynn leaned back in her chair. "Very well-reasoned, my lord. You are right, Heldeon would never sin by attacking one who stands blood-by-marriage. He might even ally with you . . . which would still leave your forces outnumbered, by our latest intelligence, but . . ."—she shrugged, and gave him a wry smile—"you might have a fighting chance, then—wordplay intended. But tell me, since you seem to have thought of everything, what is *my* inducement to enter such an alliance?"

He leaned forward. "I am prepared to declare you my co-regent and successor. I have no heir. You are accustomed to command, and you possess both wisdom and compassion. You will rule the Lakreo Valley well."

"But your people—" she began.

"The Council will uphold my chosen successor, as will the army. My people worship Ashmara and you are Her priestess, so that will make them well-disposed toward you —especially if this alliance spares their lives and property. The Valley is wide and prosperous, you have seen that for yourself. You will possess a tidy little domain."

"Providing Rorgan and Laol do not snatch it."

"That is a risk you must take," the Sovren admitted. "But Heldeon will surely support you with troops, even if he will not aid me. And there is a chance that they would, instead, make an alliance with you, even as they did with your father."

"You are right," she conceded, finding to her surprise that she was actually considering his offer.

This man was correct in thinking she would be tempted by this prosperous valley; she was her father's daughter, born to rule. An alliance between the Lakreo Valley and Danreg Ford would be of immense benefit to her nomadic people, giving them a new market for their herd animals. And the foothills held sheltered steppes that would provide excellent winter grazing.

Leaguing with these people would benefit us more than our current alliance with Rorgan and Laol—there we are committed only to war, and then only so long as the actual fighting lasts. As soon as the smoke of battle clears, it is likely we will be at each other's throats . . .

Wynn covertly studied the man sitting opposite her. Despite the strange cast to his features, he was not ill-formed or ugly. She glanced down again at his hands, hard and scarred, and wondered for a fleeting second if there could be any pleasure to be had in his touch. The High Priestess sighed; she had been fortunate with Nahral . . . Ashmara had blessed her. That was too much to expect twice in a lifetime.

When she looked back up he was staring at her with a tight-reined eagerness, and for a startled second Wynn wondered if he had somehow sensed the direction of her thoughts. Her cheeks grew warm. "Your offer is tempting, if risky," she admitted.

He leaned forward, his gray eyes intense. "If you are willing, we must act *now.* A message from you to your father this afternoon, then a private meeting tonight to settle terms, followed by the ceremony. A public announcement tomorrow."

Wynn hesitated, thinking of what it would be like to sleep tonight beside a stranger, then she smiled wryly. *State marriages are always so . . . you know that.*

"There is one thing . . ." she began.

"What?"

"They say you are not as other men, and I can see with my own eyes that you are like no one else I have ever met. They say . . ." She broke off, embarrassed, fighting not to blush.

"That I am demon-spawned?" Wynn sensed his scornful

133

amusement, though his expression remained unchanged. "And you believe that?"

"No," she snapped, "of course not. But I think I am justified in asking precisely *how* you are different. Believe me, I have no illusions about State marriages. I am not a girl, someone who demands soft words and wooing. I am years past that, and glad of it. But I have the right to know what I contract to bed this night."

He stared at her, speechless. Finally he cleared his throat. "My lady . . . you have mistaken my meaning. I did not intend that this alliance should be an actual *marriage* . . . in any physical sense, that is. I am sorry if I gave you that impression."

"Is that your difference, then?" Wynn asked coolly. "You aren't capable?"

He gaped at her, then stammered, "No! Well, perhaps . . . it's been a long time . . ." He faltered to a halt, took a deep breath, then his expression hardened. "My lady, my virility is not the issue here. I was married, once. She died in childbirth. I . . . cared . . . for her, very much. I have no wish for that kind of relationship again."

"Nor do I," Wynn admitted, thinking of her husband and son. They'd had to drag her away from the bodies. She had wanted to die herself. "I know what it is to lose those dearest to you."

"As to my . . . differences," the Sovren continued, "they are minor and internal, with one—or, rather, two exceptions." He ran his hands through his hair, then turned his head from side to side, so the High Priestess could see both ears.

Wynn studied him with narrowed eyes for several moments, then shrugged. "Thank you for satisfying my curiosity. They are natural to your kind?"

"Yes," he said, seeming relieved at her unruffled acceptance. "So, now that you understand the terms of my offer, what do you say? Would you like time to consider it?"

"I was almost convinced," Wynn said, slowly. "But now that you have . . . clarified . . . matters, I do not believe I can reconcile your kind of marriage with my service to Ashmara."

"Why not?"

"What you offer is not true marriage, but only an imitation for the outside world to view. Ashmara would not look with favor upon such a hollow sham, or those who lent themselves to it."

She straightened her skirt, not looking up. "Besides, if I were to marry again, I would pray the Goddess to bless me with children—for the succession." She kept her voice casual, not wanting him to know how much she missed Lelinos, how greatly she longed to hold a child of her own again . . . even as she feared to love that much again.

"You speak as though we are talking about a lifelong deceit here," he said. "You would soon be free to select a true consort, have children by him, if that is your wish."

Wynn blinked. "I would?"

"Of course. We are speaking of a union lasting no more than a day . . . possibly two. Then you will rule New Araen alone."

"Why do you say that?"

"Have you forgotten? You yourself declared me *d'arkeh n'esth*. I will not survive the coming battle."

The High Priestess stared at him in shock, and there was a roaring in her ears like the sound of a great storm. *Now* she knew why she had experienced that haunting sense of familiarity—only yesterday she had "seen" this man die in a gush of blood and shattered bone.

Wynn seldom retained clear memories of the visions Ashmara sent her—her priestesses had to repeat for her any prophecies she'd made during the sacred trance. Her throat grew suddenly, absurdly tight. *Are you mad?* she demanded of herself. *You barely know him! Why should the thought of his death trouble you?*

But it did—the vision of his body was mixed up somehow with her memories of Nahral and Lelinos, and for an instant Wynn relived the shrieking agony of the moment when she'd first found them in the ruins of the camp.

A second later the haze before her eyes cleared slightly, and Wynn realized she was clinging to the arms of her chair with both hands, trembling violently. The Sovren was on his feet, staring at her anxiously. With a muttered exclamation, he limped around the table and splashed some water into a goblet. "Are you all right? You're pale as death."

Wynn nodded as she tried clumsily to take the goblet, but her hands shook so that she sloshed the liquid onto the tabletop. "Easy," he said, helping her. With his aid she was able to swallow a few sips, and that steadied her.

"I'm sorry," she whispered, finally. "I *had* forgotten. The visions come, and I speak them, but when the Goddess talks through me, I am only the mouthpiece. I remember little of what happens in them, or of what I say."

He nodded. "I know what it is like." He relaxed slightly, hitching his bad leg up so that he half-leaned, half-sat on the tabletop before her. Arms folded across his chest, he stared down at her intently. "Do they always come true?"

"In one form or another," Wynn said. She felt drained and wondered why, then remembered confusedly that she'd had almost no sleep the previous night. "The words are right, but sometimes what I see happens in a different form, or in a different place."

"But when you see death, death is what comes." He did not sound particularly concerned. Wynn raised her face and studied him. The cool remoteness was back in his eyes. They might have been discussing the best soil for planting grain.

"Yes," she admitted.

He gave a curiously satisfied nod. "Well, then," he said. "Now you know. Will you do it?"

Wynn's back stiffened, and she could not contain her anger. "Don't you *care? You ought to care!*"

A one-sided smile touched the stern mouth for a moment. " 'Do not go gentle into that good night . . . rage, rage, against the dying of the light.' "

"Yes," she said, her eyes never leaving his. "That's exactly what I meant. Are those your words?"

"No, a man named Dylan Thomas wrote them." He

shook his head. "You're right, I ought to care. But it's just not there anymore. And what good would it do if I did? You said it yourself, your visions are always true."

"But you are warned!" she cried. "I was never able to warn anyone before . . . I can tell you how it will happen, and perhaps you can guard against it!"

His eyes never left hers, and Wynn felt the color wash into her cheeks again. "Thank you," he said, finally. "For caring, when you don't even know me, after what I've done to you. You are a good person."

"So are you," she said. "I can tell about people . . . what's inside them. What they are feeling." Up to now she'd told only her father and Nahral her secret. Wynn did not know why she'd confided in this man . . . but she did not regret her decision.

"Empathy as well as precognition," he said. "I suspected it. I can tell about people, too."

Wynn had no idea what the two strange words meant, but she couldn't hide her skepticism. "How could you? It's a gift from the Goddess, and you're a man."

"I'll prove it," he said. "Take my hand."

Wynn hesitated, then slipped her fingers into his. His sword-callused palm was hot against her skin, and—

—and she could *feel* what was inside him, despair, aching loneliness, bitter determination. The sharing went deeper than it ever had, and after a moment, Wynn realized that was because he was reading her, too—her loneliness, her pain, her unflinching refusal to give up, her love for life despite its agonies. They were like mirrors of one another, but his was the shadowed reflection.

Fight, she shouted silently at him. *Rage!*

Wynn experienced his startled, unwilling response to her emotion—for a moment something vital and alive flared within him, in answer to her passionate demand.

Then the contact between them lessened, withdrew, and she was back in her own mind, alone again. After a minute she realized she was still clutching his hand like a lifeline. Her fingers felt cramped as she loosened them.

He was staring at her, eyes wide with surprise, but even as

Wynn watched, the shuttered, blank expression closed down over his features again. But with the brief rapport had come knowledge, and Wynn knew suddenly that this time his remoteness was a mask, that behind the impassivity his thoughts were racing. She wondered what they were. "I believe you, now," she said.

"I'll leave you to consider my offer," he straightened, coming out of his musings abruptly. "When shall I come back?"

Wynn took a deep breath and rose from her seat. "You don't need to come back. I've made my decision. I accept your proposal." *I must be mad,* she thought, but her mind was made up. "I'll write a message to my father telling him we'll ride there tonight, under a truce flag."

The Sovren took her hand and bowed deeply over it. "My Lady Wynn . . . thank you. Thank you." Straightening, he looked down at her, and the sudden light in his eyes was echoed by the rush of hope Wynn experienced.

"You know my name," she said, after a moment. "May I have yours? I'd feel foolish wedding a man—for however brief a time—that I could not call by name."

He smiled, a real smile this time. "Haven't you heard the old stories that anyone you honor with your name has power over you thereafter?"

"And you believe that?" she retorted, using his own words.

The smile faded and he solemnly raised her hand to kiss her fingers. She could feel the warmth of his breath against her skin. "My name is Zar. I would be honored if you would use it."

Chapter Eight

"NO, THANK YOU, VOBA, I couldn't eat another bite," James Kirk said with an appreciative sigh, waving the red-haired aide-de-camp's offer of another honey roll away. "Matter of fact, I could almost go to sleep right here, it feels so good to be warm, clean, and full." He yawned so widely his jaws cracked.

Leonard McCoy hesitated over the proffered platter in his turn, then succumbed. "I shouldn't, but I'm going to anyway." He busied himself spreading jam on the roll. "Do you realize we've been here less than a day? Seems more like a week."

Spock left the table, pacing slowly over to the window. The three officers had been given individual sleeping chambers that opened into this large, high-vaulted living area.

Hand-woven rugs, in bright colors and patterns that reminded Kirk of Zuni designs he'd seen, hung on the walls and were scattered over the stone floors, and two monstrous fireplaces crouched at either end of the room. Three big unglassed windows stood with their shutters open, giving a view of a large, flat plain behind the fortress. It was evidently the parade ground, for cavalry and foot soldiers were drilling there. The northern mountains lay in the distance.

The Vulcan stood staring out at the parade ground, hands clasped behind his back. "You might find this interesting,

Jim. Zar is using a variation on the ancient Roman manipular system, which in turn was derived from the Greek phalanx. However, he is using archers with longbows as flankers . . . which should prove effective against enemy chariots."

Spock glanced at the other side of the field. "His cavalry is well-drilled and armed with lances. I would theorize that he is using them as a mobile strike force to harry the rear lines of the enemy at their weakest points."

"But Cletas said they were outnumbered four to one," McCoy said. "What difference can increased mobility make?"

"You'd be surprised, Bones," Kirk said, rubbing his eyes. If he sat there a moment longer, he *would* fall asleep. Reluctantly, he got up to join Spock. "Three thousand trained soldiers can inflict a lot of damage against a disorganized force that fights like twelve thousand individuals, instead of as a unit." He squinted against the sunlight. "Is the cavalry using stirrups? I can't see from here."

"Yes," Spock said, without hesitation. "They are."

"Were those saddles we saw yesterday in Heldeon's camp equipped with stirrups?" Kirk asked.

"No, I believe not," Spock said. "That is definitely another asset."

"Stirrups?" McCoy raised an eyebrow.

"The invention of the stirrup was a vital one in the history of mounted warfare, Doctor," Spock said. "Stirrups allowed cavalrymen to more effectively hurl lances, since the riders were able to brace their feet. They also gave the riders increased stability, so they could better engage in swordplay. It was the development of the stirrup by the Goths that allowed them to overcome the Roman legions."

"You learn something new every day. Do you think Zar's 'innovations' could possibly outweigh the sheer numbers of the opposing forces?" McCoy asked, skeptically.

"They will certainly help. Whether they will help enough is impossible to predict without more data."

Kirk frowned. "I'm not sanguine about their chances,

Bones. At least the ground is drying out a little—" He broke off at a tap on the door. Voba moved quickly to open it.

Second-in-War Cletas entered and saluted. "The Sovren is free now. If you will please follow me?"

Kirk caught up the reddish-brown cloak he'd been given, then followed the officer; the sun might have been shining outside, but the stone walls retained the cold dampness, and standing at the open window had raised goose-bumps on his bare arms.

I'll have to remember this, the next time I sit looking at my weapons collection, feeling nostalgic for romantic bygone eras, he thought, tossing the warm folds around his shoulders and pinning the garment at his throat with a red-gold brooch. *Living at the mercy of the elements . . . no modern plumbing . . .*

The Second led them down the halls until they came to a guarded doorway. Kirk followed Cletas into the room, Spock and McCoy just behind him.

Zar sat on the edge of a massive inlaid table made of varying shades of golden-colored wood. Sitting in the chair before him was the High Priestess, wearing a pale amber gown two shades lighter than her hair. The heavy bronze mass was braided and coiled behind her head, and her small gold earrings sparked fire in the candleglow. She appeared perfectly at ease.

Kirk glanced quickly around the room, deciding it was Zar's private office. A desk sat beneath the room's only window, which gave a view of the southern exposure, and New Araen.

On the opposite wall of the room, the admiral saw a familiar sight—Zar's mural of the *Enterprise*, its colors still vivid.

As the three Federation officers entered, Zar stood, his hand reaching down for Wynn's. She let him draw her up to face them, standing with her head held proudly, her expression impassive, but the admiral was sure that for a second he had glimpsed surprised recognition.

"My lady," Zar said, formally, "may I present Admiral

Kirk, Dr. McCoy, and Mr. Spock. The High Priestess of Danreg Ford, the Lady Wynn."

"Pleased to meet you, ma'am," McCoy said, bowing.

Kirk also bowed, summoning his best smile. "My pleasure, Lady Wynn."

This time, she smiled back at him. "My charming spy," she said. "So you *were* working for New Araen."

"Actually, no," Zar corrected. "It was pure coincidence that they arrived where they did, when they did."

Wynn's eyes widened as they fixed on Spock. The Vulcan gravely inclined his head. She glanced up at Zar. "Your brother, my lord?"

Kirk didn't miss the gleam of amusement in the gray eyes. "No, my father."

She looked startled and skeptical all at once, but said nothing. Zar gave her that faint half-smile. "It is true. A long story, but if we have time, I shall tell it to you."

"I shall be most interested to hear it, my lord," she said, "but now I fear I must withdraw to prepare that message for *my* father." She smiled at Spock. "How fortunate that you chose this time to visit, sir. By custom, blood-kin *should* be present at a handfasting."

Zar nodded to Cletas, who came forward. "This is my Second-in-War, Cletas, who will escort you and see that your message to Heldeon is dispatched."

The officer bowed deeply. "My lady."

She regarded him for a moment, and Kirk watched the color rise in her cheeks before she spoke. "I took advantage of you this morning, which was an unworthy thing to do, Cletas. I am sorry for it."

The Second, though obviously surprised, recovered quickly. "Doubtless I deserved far worse, my lady, for the rough handling you were forced to endure. I can only offer my sincerest apologies—belated though they are. And now, my lady, if you will permit me to escort you?"

"Certainly," she said, and accompanied him from the room.

Kirk looked over at Zar, even as the younger man dropped wearily into a chair, signaling for them to join him around the big table. "Congratulations," the admiral said dryly, as he found a seat. "Talk about whirlwind romances . . . how did you manage it?"

The Sovren's voice held rueful amusement. "I promised to make her my co-regent and successor. She wants New Araen."

"When will the marriage take place?" Spock asked.

"As soon as possible," Zar said, resignedly. "Tonight. The ceremony will take place after the alliance negotiations are completed." He sighed and looked over at the Vulcan. "Would you . . . would you stand with me, Father?"

"It would be an honor," Spock said, gravely.

The exchange gave Kirk a sudden flash of *déjà vu*, but the memory eluded him. Zar turned to him and McCoy. "I would be pleased if you would attend, also . . ."

Kirk glanced over at McCoy. "We'd like to, Zar. But before you go through with this . . . arrangement, we should discuss the reason we came. I'm afraid this wasn't purely a social call."

"I suspected that, knowing the restrictions placed on the Guardian of Forever. What is the problem?"

"You just named it. The Guardian of Forever," Kirk said. He nodded at Spock, who launched into a concise summary of the Guardian's erratic behavior, and the danger it posed to the universe 5,000 years in the future. Zar listened intently, frowning a little, automatically scribbling notes on a sheet of vellum. Kirk watched his face, noting how he had changed over the years—aged more by responsibility and power than by time. Jim knew only too well how those things burdened an individual.

". . . with some difficulty, I was able to establish partial communication with a strictly mechanical portion of the Guardian," Spock was concluding. "Enough to ask it to transport us back here and monitor us until we are ready to return. It is our . . ." the Vulcan hesitated, then went on quite deliberately, "our hope that you, with your greater telepathic ability, will be able to fully link with the entity, discover its problem, and convince it to resume its normal functioning."

Zar gazed at his father, his expression closed, shuttered, then slowly shook his head. "I haven't done a full mind-meld since that day on Gateway, twenty years ago. I doubt if I'm capable of contacting a nonhuman entity anymore."

"I can help you. We can review——" Spock began, only to break off as the Vulcan took in Zar's bleak expression.

"Even if I *could* perform the meld, I cannot leave. I'm sorry, but I have a battle to fight."

Kirk cleared his throat. "Yes, we understand that. And we also know something you don't, something that may influence your decision." He held the gray eyes with his own. "You won't survive that battle, Zar."

The Sovren made a faint sound somewhere between a derisive snort and a wry chuckle. "I know."

Kirk gave Spock a startled glance. *Does he really know? How could he?* "Perhaps I haven't made myself clear," the admiral said. "Spock watched that battle in his tricorder. I saw it. We both saw what's going to happen to you. Unless you come with us, Zar, you'll *die.*"

"Yes, I know."

"How could you know?" Spock asked.

"Because my bride-to-be prophesied my death in the coming battle yesterday afternoon. Wynn is an esper. An empath, as I am, but also precognitive. What she regards as sendings from the Goddess are actually precognitive visions. I think—no, I *know*—that part of her reason for agreeing to this marriage was that she felt sorry for me. Her way of honoring a last request, I suppose. At any rate, it will happen; there's no help for it."

"But, Zar," McCoy spoke for the first time, "there *is.* You can come back with us. You've accomplished what you set out to do here. You've guided your people into civilization . . . now you can stop. Come back to *stay*, this time."

"And do what?" Zar demanded, bitterly. "I doubt the Federation has much demand for unemployed rulers. Don't tempt me, Leonard!"

Pushing his chair back, Zar rose and began pacing, his words coming with increasing urgency. "You have no idea how much I'd like to escape from all of this, but if I did, I'd be condemning my people to be massacred! No, I have to stay. If I stay and marry Wynn, at least New Araen will have a chance to survive after I'm gone and she succeeds me."

He turned to face them again. "Heldeon has over seven thousand warriors. If I can persuade him to ally them with my forces, they would bring our strength up to within five thousand of those Laol and Rorgan command. With odds like those, my people might stand a chance of winning!"

"All right," McCoy said, "suppose you go ahead and marry her, then disappear during the first charge of the battle—what's the difference between that and becoming a casualty later on? You've given your life to these people —you don't owe them your death, too! As for what you could do in our time, don't give me that—competent people who can get things done are always in the minority. You're young enough to—"

McCoy broke off as Zar's lip curled. "You're wrong, Len. Soon I'll have forty-five summers, as I used to put it. That's . . . I've forgotten the conversion factor for Terran Standard."

"Forty-nine point four years," Spock said.

"Don't you realize that in my culture anything over forty is *old*? Although thanks to those immunizations you gave me, and to my . . . parentage"—Zar glanced over at Spock —"I'd probably have quite a few years left—if it weren't for this battle." Wearily, he dropped back into his chair. "But, damn it, I *feel* old . . . too old to change. Better to go down fighting."

"That's a lot of bull, and you know it!" snapped McCoy, visibly upset. "You could go to school—you'd have time to learn a whole new profession, Zar! You could even join Starfleet, if you wanted. The exploration teams are begging for espers, or a man with your survival experience could write his own ticket on the colony worlds."

"Bones . . ." Kirk reached over and put a hand on his friend's shoulder. "Take it easy. It's Zar's decision to make."

But McCoy shrugged off Kirk's grip. He rose and strode over to face the Sovren, eyes blazing. "Damn it, Zar, I never figured you for a coward, but that's how you're acting! In my book it takes more courage to keep living than to give in and die!"

The doctor's voice cracked on the last word, and he paused to regain control. "Twenty years ago you gave up the stars, to do what you thought was right. Though I knew I'd miss you, I had to applaud that decision. Now that duty has been fulfilled, and you've got a second chance—something most people never get—and you're telling me you're just going to *throw it away?*"

Zar stared at him, obviously moved by the doctor's words. When he spoke again, he sounded wistful. "If only I could, Leonard. But you don't understand . . . morale is a powerful factor in war. My troops know about this prophecy, but they know I'll lead them despite it—and thus they'll be prepared to fight to the last, too. Determination like that *might* mean the difference between victory and defeat for them. I can't desert them."

"And if you don't contact the Guardian," McCoy said, softly, "it's going to mean *our* lives. Not to mention the population of the Milky Way galaxy—and, from what Spock tells us, eventually *every* galaxy."

Zar leaned his elbows on the table with an exhausted sigh, then began rubbing his temples. "I'll think about it, Len. Maybe there's some way . . . that's all I can promise at the moment."

McCoy cast a cautiously triumphant glance at Kirk before turning back to Zar. "Headache, son?"

"That is an understatement."

"Here." The doctor took a small packet out of his medikit. "Swallow these. With water, not wine."

Zar obediently poured a goblet and downed the medication. "Thanks. The wine was for Wynn. For some reason my stomach can't tolerate ethanol . . . it makes me violently ill."

"I remember," Kirk said. "Zar, as I was about to say," he shot a warning glance at McCoy, "this is *your* decision, and we will *all* respect it. Frankly, it's a choice I wouldn't want to have to make."

"Well, whatever I decide, I'm still going through with that ceremony," Zar said. "One way or another, I've got to declare Wynn my successor." After a moment, he pulled a platter of bread and cheese over. "I just remembered, I forgot to eat today. No wonder my head is pounding. Anyone want a sandwich?"

"Not after the way Voba stuffed us," Kirk said.

Zar poured himself another goblet of water. "I'm starting to feel better. That medicine of yours works quickly, Doc." He hesitated. "I see that you brought your medikit. Will you do something for me?"

"Depends," McCoy said, cautiously. "If you want me to stop trying to convince you to return with us, I won't."

"No, it's not that. I need your services as a physician."

"Of course. I've been meaning to talk to you about that leg." The doctor broke off at Zar's headshake. "What, then?"

"I'd like you to immunize Wynn against disease, the way you did me twenty years ago. That's no guarantee of an extended life in this society, but anything that might help her stay healthy enough to rule New Araen for a long time . . ."

McCoy nodded. "I can do it, but are you sure you want her running things? Her people are pretty barbaric, from what I saw."

"She has a conscience, and compassion," Zar said. "Compared to Laol and Rorgan and the rest of their ilk, she's the soul of civilization. Don't forget, Wynn is an empath . . . which makes it extremely difficult to be cruel. I believe she'll do well."

The Sovren busied himself slicing bread and cheese for a moment, then glanced over at the others. "Please, help yourselves. There's wine in that flagon . . . or I can send someone down to the cellar for something stronger, if anyone wants it."

"This will be fine," the admiral said, filling a goblet for himself and the doctor. "Spock?"

"Thank you, no."

Zar finished putting together a massive sandwich. "While I eat, why don't you tell what you've all been doing for the past 14.5 years?"

Starting with Spock, the three officers briefly sketched in the major events of their lives. Kirk was last, and, when he mentioned Winona's death, he was surprised to realize that it had been several days since he'd even thought about his mother. He felt a twinge of guilt, but shook it off, knowing Winona would have been the last one to demand protracted mourning. *Matter of fact, if she were here, she'd probably give me a swift kick and tell me to get on with my life,* he thought, smiling a little.

By the time Zar had downed two cheese sandwiches and several pieces of fruit, they were finished with their accounts. "Your turn, now," Kirk said. "Tell us how all this"—he gestured around him—"came about."

"Obviously, it's a long story." Zar put his silver goblet down, then began twirling its stem absently in his fingers. "When I left you that day, the Guardian deposited me on the other side of the mountains from where New Araen now stands. I hiked my way up to the nearest pass, and that night I encountered a group of herdsmen.

"I couldn't speak their language, of course, and once they got a good look at me, they pronounced me demonspawned, and were going to impale me." Zar raised an eyebrow at his father, who returned the favor, a glint of amusement in his dark eyes.

"I managed to temporarily dissuade them by broadcasting goodwill with all the intensity I could, so they merely tied me up—rather poorly—and went off to have a long council about it. I sat there until it was dark, and used telepathy to pick up some of what they were talking about. They were worried about a rogue vitha that had come down out of the mountains to ravage their herds. I began working on the thongs binding me to my post . . .

"The next afternoon they were surprised when I walked back into the camp, dragging the carcass of the creature

. . . but the gesture worked. They accepted me. I lived with them until I learned their language, then accompanied them over-mountain when they brought their herds to market. New Araen was then a small, nameless settlement . . . a quarter its present size. Most of the buildings were wattle-and-daub, instead of the way they are now."

Zar took a sip of his water. "The current ruler of this territory was a man named Tekolin. When he heard about the helpful demon, he sent for me. We talked. He was a good man, intelligent and something of a visionary. I stayed with him, serving as a guardsman, and within a few months he made me his Captain of the Guards.

"That was ideal, as I got to do a lot of traveling out on patrol. I began gathering a following of young people, mostly men, a few women—those who weren't already tied down with babies—and educating them, teaching them my language, all with Tekolin's blessing. You've met two of them—Cletas and Voba.

"During the next two years they and the others helped me gather all the available technological advances on this continent. Sometimes they'd travel hundreds of kilometers to bring back new inventions, new techniques . . . expert stonecutters, for example. Breeding stock for the taller, more slender-legged vykar that were suitable for riding."

Zar paused for a moment, then took a deep breath. His mouth tightened, and when he continued, his voice was edged with pain. "Araen, Tekolin's daughter—his only child—was one of my group. A season after we met, she begged her father to let us marry. Tekolin agreed. Not quite ten months later, she died."

Zar fell silent, turning, turning the goblet.

"I'm sorry," Kirk said. The words felt as clumsy and inadequate as they usually made him feel, but, as always, he felt compelled to say *something. Nine months . . . it probably was in childbirth.*

The admiral remembered Miramanee, who had died without ever feeling their baby quicken, then he thought of his living child again. *Why didn't Carol tell me about David before I accepted the five-year mission? I must contact him, he's old enough now to understand when I explain . . . at least I hope he is . . .*

"I'm sorry, too. But then what happened?" McCoy prompted, gently.

"Tekolin declared me his successor, then he died a year and a half later. I ruled as Sovren, but I also continued gathering the advances of my world, educating my group, developing technologies . . . writing books. In the first five years, I wrote ten or twelve texts . . . reading primers, math, grammar, science, physics, even a dictionary. I kept a staff of clerks busy just copying them, as I had neither the time nor the underlying technology to build a printing press or develop paper—yet. I've almost got it now, but . . ." he sighed.

"All these books were on a very elementary level, you understand. My people weren't ready for quantum mechanics—they still aren't. I've barely gotten the most educated of them to accept the idea that everything is composed of atoms. And then it's just an intellectual conceit."

"Developing technologies?" Spock asked. "Such as mining iron ore and smelting it into steel?"

"Among other things."

"I have seen the chain-link armor and swords worn by your guards," the Vulcan said. "Is your entire army so equipped?"

"Only two-thirds have chain mail," Zar answered, "but they all have steel swords, helmets, and breastplates. Production of weapons has, sadly, taken precedence over everything else for the past four years. At the moment I have more blacksmiths than teachers here in New Araen."

Spock nodded thoughtfully. "Considering the merits of steel over bronze, those weapons and armor provide a major asset."

"That's what I'm hoping Rorgan and Laol won't suspect. They may be careless because their numbers are so huge."

"But, Zar . . ." Kirk was puzzled. "How could you master all those subjects? It seems impossible for one individual

—no matter how intelligent or comparatively sophisticated —to accomplish so much."

The Sovren nodded, half-smiling. "You're right, it is impossible. The answer is simple . . . I cheated, Jim."

"Cheated?"

"You never saw what I had in that pack I took with me," Zar said, rising. He limped over to his desk, to return a moment later with an object he placed on the table before them—a very familiar object.

Kirk grinned admiringly. "You sly sonofagun! A tricorder!"

"Equipped with solar-powered batteries," Spock said, the eyebrow rising. "I wondered at the time where my spare unit had gone. I assumed you had borrowed it, and that it had been lost during the fighting on Gateway."

Zar shrugged, looking not at all repentant. "When I first saw my painting in the Atoz records," he nodded at the mural on the stone wall, "I knew I must be going to go back—"

He broke off, shaking his head. "Nothing like time travel to confuse your verb tenses, is there? At any rate, I 'borrowed' spare cassettes from sickbay—sorry, Doc—and ordered the library computer aboard the *Enterprise* to copy all files under certain subjects, especially those dealing with colonization and survival on primitive worlds. By the time I left, I had cassettes on everything from making soap to smelting iron, battle tactics to candle-making and glass-blowing. They're so small, I was able to fit nearly a hundred into that pack. And I had them copied at the highest possible data density."

He pressed a button on the machine and the unmistakable opening notes of Beethoven's Fifth Symphony resounded. Zar flicked it off again. "I brought music, and literature, too." His voice dropped to a near-whisper. "There were times when I think the music was all that kept me sane."

"Classical buff, eh?" McCoy said.

Zar nodded. "A complete reactionary, I'm afraid. Nothing more recent than T'Nira, and she's been dead for two hundred—" He paused, then sighed. "I mean, she will have been dead for two hundred years, five thousand years from now."

"Finish your story," Kirk said.

"There's not much more to tell. At first I tried to instill concepts like democracy, hoping that eventually I could step aside in favor of the Council, but that's something my people just weren't ready for . . . frankly, I barely managed to get the idea of the Council accepted. The best I could do was to function as a fairly benevolent despot."

He wiped a speck of dust off the tricorder, frowning a little. "I've accomplished less than half the things I'd hoped to by now. And, to make it even more frustrating, just when the valley began to really prosper, *they* came—and all they wanted was to obliterate everything we'd worked for all these years . . . destroy it in the space of a single, bloody day.

"For the first ten years we had peace, but we've been fighting since that. Small bands, at first. This little valley must've seemed like an easy mark, but within a few years, they'd learned to respect us. Then, finally, came this alliance between the Danreg, Clan Kerren, and the Asyri . . . and I began to realize that it was probably all over."

"'It was the season of Light, it was the season of Darkness,'" McCoy quoted.

"That sounds familiar, but I can't place it, Bones," Kirk said. "What is it from?"

McCoy smiled, nodding at the Vulcan. "Be my guest, Spock."

"A Tale of Two Cities, by Charles Dickens."

"I'm ashamed to say I haven't read it since the Academy," the admiral admitted. He looked over at Zar and sighed. "But the quotation fits. Even with all your advances, your troops are going to have a hard time of it."

"I know." The lines around Zar's mouth grew deeper. "Every time I pass a dungheap I'm tempted to 'discover' gunpowder. Three or four blasts, and it would be all over."

"Dungheap?" McCoy looked blank.

"Chemical reactions within middens produce potassium

152

nitrate—saltpeter—which, along with sulfur and carbon, is a component of black powder, Doctor," Spock explained.

The medical officer raised an eyebrow. "Well . . . why don't you? Just for this once?"

"Gunpowder won't be invented for another hundred years," Zar said. "I'd demolish the integrity of the timestream. And, from what you've been telling me about the Guardian, that action might have repercussions extending beyond this one planet."

"You've made the right decision, Zar, but I know that's got to be cold comfort," Kirk said. "It hasn't been easy, has it?"

Restlessly, the admiral got up and paced around the chamber, finally stopping by the massive fireplace. "Is this your sword?" he asked, pointing to a sheathed object hanging over the mantel. Zar nodded. "May I?"

"Go ahead."

Grasping the scarred leather-and-wire-bound hilt, the admiral lifted the blade down, then, careful not to touch the steel, slowly slid it out of its plain black scabbard. "Beautiful," he murmured, giving it a small exploratory swing.

The sword was two-edged, pointed, and slightly over a meter long. The spherical steel pommel was lead-filled to help balance the heavy blade. Hilt, cross-guard, and pommel were all plain and unornamented.

"Your smith did a wonderful job," Kirk said, admiringly. "Though he obviously had no use for decorations."

"Thank you," Zar said. "They seemed superfluous to me."

Kirk glanced at the other, surprised. "*You* forged this?"

"Yes. I made it when I became Captain of the Guards. Took me countless tries to get it right, even though I had a cassette on ancient weapons-making." Zar smiled faintly. "I suspect that file was one of Hikaru's additions to the library."

Kirk struck an *en garde* position, but the weapon was much too heavy for his wrist—the point sagged immediately. "Surely you don't fence with this?"

"No," Zar said. "It's too heavy, though it's suprisingly

well-balanced. But in fencing you have to parry, and with a weapon this long and heavy, there's a major problem. Even carbon-tempered steel can break. So you need to carry a shield or buckler for parrying. But I *have* introduced the use of the point to my troops. They had learned the use of the edge only . . . most bronze swords don't even have points."

The admiral nodded. "This is what they call a hand-and-a-half sword, isn't it? You can swing it either one- or two-handed?" He knew that it was also called a "bastard sword"—an ironic designation, considering the circumstances of Zar's birth.

"Yes . . . that's one of its names," Zar said, giving him a wry smile and a raised eyebrow.

The admiral cleared his throat and changed the subject. "By the way, what *is* its name?"

"Name?" Zar looked puzzled for a moment, then understanding dawned. "Oh, you mean a name like 'Excalibur,' or 'Fred'—something like that?" The gray eyes were bleak. "It doesn't have one, Jim. 'Killer,' maybe, because that's what I use it for. Frankly, I *hate* what I do with it, but I've learned to be damned good at it. Lately, none of us has had much choice."

Slightly daunted—*there goes another of my romantic illusions*—Kirk cautiously slid the sword back into its scabbard and hung it back up.

"Now what?" he asked, turning to face the others.

Zar glanced at the chronometer on his tricorder. "Now I'd better check to see if Heldeon's responded to Wynn's message. We ought to start for the Danreg camp before sunset. I'll order mounts for you three." He stood up, steadying himself on the edge of the table, his mouth tightening as his game leg took his weight. "I get stiff if I sit too long."

"I'd really like to look at that, son," McCoy said. "Might be something I could do to help. What happened?"

"Took a lance through the thigh, nearly ten years ago," Zar told him. "It killed my vykar, and I was pinned beneath the body until Cletas found me. I suspect nerve damage —that's not something you can repair, if I recall correctly."

"There have been advances since you were with us," the medical officer said. "A doctor named Corrigan, working with a Vulcan healer, Sorel, perfected a nerve-regeneration technique over a decade ago. I have a unit aboard the *Enterprise* . . . but, of course, you'd have to come back with us."

Zar gazed at him for a long moment. "I see . . . still the expert gambler. You really know how to raise the stakes, don't you?"

Chapter Nine

RIDING A VYKAR wasn't much like riding a horse, McCoy discovered. The beasts moved with a side-to-side motion that reminded him more of a camel. They wore bitless bridles, and were controlled more by the legs and voiced commands than by tugs on the reins. Still, sitting upright on the creature's back was infinitely preferable to being thrown across its withers.

Darkness had fallen over the slopes of Big Snowy as their little band pressed onward, up the mountainside. The guards, their weapons bound with the blue peace-thongs, carried lit torches, but their light did not reach the center of the group, where the doctor rode.

McCoy hoped uneasily that his mount possessed better night vision than he did. Even though tonight was clear, Sarpeidon's lack of a moon made the darkness seem endless and looming. The doctor glanced up, seeing stars that were only vaguely familiar from his previous trip here, when they had brought Zar back for—he hoped—the *first* time.

McCoy experienced a sudden, aching nostalgia for the clear-eyed youth with the shy smile whom he had known for those seven weeks aboard the *Enterprise*. He'd virtually adopted Zar, becoming the young man's confidant and adviser. In a way, as Kirk had observed at the time, it was as though Zar were *his* son, rather than Spock's. When Zar had returned to the past, McCoy had grieved for weeks

. . . almost as he would have mourned his daughter, Joanna, if anything had happened to her.

The vykar lurched its way up the rocky path and stumbled, sending a rock spinning away from its cloven hoof. The doctor sensed, rather than saw, the stone pitch over a cliff two meters to his left. He listened for the clatter of its landing, but no sound came. McCoy swallowed. "Be careful, buddy," he admonished the vykar, patting the beast's warm shoulder in front of the saddle and catching a whiff of its musky odor borne on the dark breeze. "It's a long way down."

His mount snorted, unimpressed, as it plodded on. McCoy returned to his musings.

He was worried about Zar. The man he'd seen today was so different from the eager, impetuous youth he'd known fourteen years ago, that, except for brief flashes of familiarity, he could have been a different person altogether. The Zar he'd known before had been passionate and intense, quick-tempered and proud (at times, arrogant), yet touchingly vulnerable in his loneliness.

The man McCoy had met today seemed little more than a hollow shell filled only by a bitter determination to do his duty. All the passion, the intensity, the pride, were gone. Only the loneliness was still there—greater than ever. *What happened to him?* McCoy wondered, trying to dig deeper than the bare-bones recital Zar had given them, to unearth the old sorrows.

Obviously, the death of his wife is a good part of it . . . he loved her very much, if I'm any judge. It must have been childbirth. Not surprising, in a society this primitive. Rather, it's a wonder that any of them survive . . .

McCoy's thoughts turned to Wynn, remembering the tension in her tough-muscled biceps when he'd given her the immunizations Zar had requested. She'd been afraid of the hypospray, flinching involuntarily every time it hissed, but she had obviously trusted Zar enough to accept his reassurances that McCoy was a healer, that the doctor's actions would benefit her.

That's a lot of trust to place in a man you've only met

today, he decided, *even if you are planning to marry him tonight. A State marriage, at that, which I gather from Zar will be strictly one of convenience. A lot of trust . . . still, don't forget that she's an empath also . . . she'd know, surely, if someone meant her harm . . .*

McCoy sighed, shifting position in the narrow saddle. He had always been thin, and had lost weight the last few days, leaving his rump even less padded than usual. Added to the stiffness from yesterday's alarums and excursions, he was undoubtedly going to be saddle-sore.

Damn. But it'll be worth it all, if Zar comes back with us. Maybe I'll take some of that leave I've got coming, and the two of us can borrow Jim's cabin in Garrovick Valley for a couple of weeks. Just take it easy, maybe fish a little . . . he needs it, he's been under unbelievable stress for years, trying to keep those wolves from ripping the throat out of New Araen . . . no wonder he looks haunted . . .

Not to mention the sheer pressures of leadership. Sword of Damocles, and all that. He'd counseled James Kirk too many times to have any illusions about how agonizing some command choices could prove. The "if only I'd—" syndrome was a killer.

The trail (at least McCoy presumed they were still following a trail) beneath them seemed to be leveling out, and the doctor glanced up to see campfires and torchlight glimmering from a plateau ahead. At the same moment he heard an incomprehensible demand from a shadowy figure, obviously a sentry's challenge. Cletas, who was riding point, answered in the same tongue.

Suddenly the torches waved wildly as the lead riders increased speed. McCoy's vykar snorted and gathered itself, breaking into a rough canter. The doctor clung unashamedly to the pommel as they thundered over the meadow and into the center of Heldeon's camp.

"Whoa, damn you!" he yelled, sawing at the reins. "Stop!"

With a lurch that nearly sent the doctor flying spread-eagled onto its antlers, the vykar halted.

"Bones, you okay?" McCoy heard a familiar shout. He

turned, pushing himself upright, to see Kirk expertly threading his galloping mount through the melee, then bringing it to a neat-footed halt.

McCoy grimaced as he nodded. *It's positively disgusting how all Jim has to do is try something once, and he masters it. Why couldn't I have been born with balance and reflexes like that? Ten to one he isn't even sore tomorrow.*

The admiral swung effortlessly off his vykar without signaling for it to kneel. "Good girl," he said, scratching the beast's neck while she grunted with pleasure. "Need some help getting down, Bones?"

"No, actually I thought I'd just sit up here and pose for a quasi-equestrian statue," the doctor snapped peevishly. "Damn it, I've forgotten the command to make these critters kneel."

In the torchlight, Kirk's mouth quirked. He tethered his mount, then approached McCoy's. Reaching out, he tapped the middle of the beast's shoulder. *"Down,"* he said, firmly.

Grunting, the vykar ponderously knelt.

"Smart-ass," McCoy growled, swinging off in high dudgeon—only to have his knees buckle when his feet touched the ground.

"Steady, Bones," Kirk said, grabbing the doctor's arm.

"I'm all right . . . or I would be after a good night's sleep, a soak in a hot tub, a massage, and a stiff drink," the doctor said, fighting back a yawn as they moved toward a torchlit circle that had been arranged beside the tent where they'd been tied the previous night. "I feel like I've been awake half my life."

"Well, try to look alive. You don't want to disgrace Zar by dozing off during his wedding."

"Where is he?"

"He's off talking with Heldeon and Wynn. The ceremony will start as soon as they can get the succession rights, the property settlements, and the battle negotiations worked out."

"Where's Spock?"

"As the groom's closest relative, he went with them. From what Cletas told me as we rode, the connubial couple isn't supposed to talk—their representatives do it for them. Zar was briefing him on what to ask for the whole way up here."

McCoy chuckled wearily. "Old Heldeon had better look out. Spock has negotiated with everyone from the Romulans to the Talosians. Zar's apt to wind up owning the whole planet."

As she sat in her father's tent, pretending to drink a goblet of wine, Wynn realized that she was nervous, which surprised her. She had been nervous eight years before, the night she had married Nahral . . . but that had been a true marriage, and she a maid, which was only natural. So why, now, did her stomach knot within her, and her hands shake so badly she was afraid to put the goblet down on the low table, for fear she would spill it and someone would see?

The High Priestess swallowed a fraction of the dryness from her mouth and forcibly turned her attention back to Heldeon and Spock. Their nods told her that they had come to an acceptable compromise on the grazing rights. They were almost done, then. *Soon it will be time for the ceremony,* she thought, with a stab of real fear.

Vellum rustled as the scribes produced the completed papers, then each negotiator signed. "And now," Spock said, "about the approaching battle. What support can we expect from you, most honored chieftain?"

Heldeon sneezed, then sniffled; he'd taken a rheum from the wetting he'd received the night before. The older man mopped his nose on his sleeve before answering. "Support? You speak of troops? You ask me to go foresworn and fight against my allies?"

"But they are neither blood-kin, nor kin-by-marriage," Spock pointed out, his voice and words so calmly reasonable that Wynn smothered a smile. "Surely the greater transgression would be to allow kin-by-marriage to come to harm through your inaction."

Heldeon blinked reddened eyes, then scratched his graying hair. "Hmmmmm."

At first the High Priestess had wondered about her new

lord-to-be's wisdom in replacing the senior member of his Council, old Davon, with his father as his marriage-terms negotiator. But now she realized why Zar had done it. Zar's sire was neither intimidated nor overawed by the Chieftain of Danreg Ford . . . an attitude Heldeon was not used to encountering. Spock's unruffled demeanor put her father off-balance, as no amount of aggression or attempted bravado could have.

"Of course, I *will* withdraw from my alliance," Heldeon said, finally. "The blood of our Lakreo brethren will not stain Danreg hands." He smothered a cough.

Spock raised a disdainful eyebrow. "Forgive me, but is it not true that he who stands back and allows his brother to be attacked and murdered, sins fully as much as the hand that guides the killing blade? Without your strength, great chieftain, all the Lakreo efforts will likely come to naught . . . your daughter will rule a city blooded, gutted, and hung for butchering at Laol and Rorgan's leisure. Is that what you wish for her?"

Heldeon shifted uncomfortably. "You make your point well, man-from-distant-places, but . . . there is the matter of being foresworn. Ashmara does not look with favor upon oath-breakers."

"Ah." Spock glanced quickly over at Wynn. "That is undoubtedly so. Yet, this is perhaps a matter of degree. Which sin does Ashmara repudiate more—the sin of oath-breaking, or the sin of kin-killing?"

Wynn considered for several minutes. *Ashmara,* she thought, *Great Mother. Lend my tongue your wisdom, so that I may correctly express Your will.* Finally she looked back up and met her father's eyes. "Honor is a two-edged blade," she said slowly. "At times it is impossible to wield it without injury. Yet it seems to me that the sharper wound to a spirit arises from kin-killing, than it does from oath-breaking. And, after all," her voice hardened, "it is not as though Rorgan has not already broken faith with us."

"What do you mean?" her father demanded, speaking in Danrei.

"He ordered that attack on our camp the time Nahral and Lelinos were butchered," Wynn replied, in the same tongue. "The Goddess sent me certain knowledge of this the first time I looked into his eyes. He is already foresworn, Father."

Heldeon snuffled again, looking very grave. "I see. Why did you not tell me this before, daughter?"

"Because I knew that my Sendings from Ashmara make you ill-at-ease with me . . . and, we needed that alliance. Now, I believe, we are offered a better one. My counsel is to accept my lord-to-be's offer and lend him all the support we can muster. I myself will lead our troops, if your rheum worsens, and you cannot."

Heldeon coughed, the sound coming from deep in his huge chest. "I will do as you advise," he said. "But, believe me, I shall not miss the opportunity to ride against the double-tongued liar who murdered my grandson. Before you leave to lie with your new lord tonight, you must use your healer's skill to concoct a tisane to lift this fever and lighten the weight in my chest."

"I will, Father," Wynn said. "And my lord has with him one whom he says is a powerful healer. If you wish, I will ask him also to aid you. His name is McCoy."

Heldeon shivered with a chill. "Perhaps. Is this McCoy a sorcerer?"

"No," Wynn said. "But my lord says his healing powers are little short of magic."

"Very well." The chieftain dropped back into the Lakreo speech. "As always, my daughter counsels me wisely. To-morrow I will advise Laol that I cannot hold to an alliance made with that liar and child-killer, Rorgan Death-Hand. Then, after she has been fairly warned as to my intentions, Danreg and Lakreo troops will march together to rout these invaders. I, Heldeon, Chieftain of Danreg Ford, will pronounce sword-oath on it."

The grizzled warrior rose to his feet and raised both hands, palm out. Commander Madon hastily placed the old chieftain's bronze blade across them. "May my own weapon smite me in this, if I be foresworn," Heldeon intoned the formal words, his voice hoarse, but still impressive.

"And I, also, offer sword-oath that I will abide by all the covenants made here between us today," Zar said, speaking for the first time since the formal greetings. "My lady?" he asked, also standing and holding out his hands.

Wynn hastily tugged the Sovren's weapon out of its scabbard, thinking the moment she felt its weight that she had never encountered its like before. *Such a strange color. What is it made from?*

Carefully, she laid the sword across the younger man's palms. "May my own steel smite me in this, if I be foresworn," Zar said, his eyes intent on Heldeon's.

Wynn heard Spock give a faint sigh of relief.

"And now, for the ceremony," Heldeon boomed. "Tell our people to make ready, Madon."

Wynn found herself hustled off to her sleeping tent by her Under-Priestesses. There she washed, cleansing and purifying herself as she would for any ritual. Her women loosened her hair and brushed it until it shone in the lamplight, leaving it to fall free over her shoulders and spill down her back.

The gown they brought for her was Ashmara's traditional green, the color of blood, of life. Wynn slipped it on, then fastened her ruby necklace around her throat. Finally, she placed the coronal on her head, and was ready.

Escorted by her Under-Priestesses, she walked out of the tent, into the torchlit circle. She could feel the pulse in her throat hammering until she thought it might choke her. She tried to swallow, but her mouth had turned to dust.

What am I doing? she wondered, dazedly. *Great Mother, why did I agree to this? Am I ensorceled?*

She stepped into the center of the circle and stood waiting, her chief Under-Priestess, Lylla, on her right, her father on her left. *I can't do this,* Wynn thought. *I don't even know this man. Why am I doing this?*

After several minutes the circle of watchers rippled, and she saw him approaching, his sire on his right, Cletas on his left. He went unmailed and carried no weapons, for war had no place in one of Ashmara's rites.

Instead of the traditional green, he still wore black . . . breeches, boots, and a sleeveless leather tunic that left his arms bare to the night breeze. A silver-and-jet medallion swung against his chest, matched by his wrist-guards, but he wore no coronal or other symbol of rank. As Wynn watched, Cletas unfolded and shook out a red cloak and draped it over his Sovren's shoulders. Zar tossed the folds back as he approached.

He halted, facing her, then bowed formally. Wynn inclined her head in the greeting-to-equals, and lifted her hand, palm outward. *I could still stop this. One word, and my will would be obeyed. I could stop . . .*

The Sovren moved toward her, his hand also raised. When he stopped, he was so close she could see the pulse beating beneath his jaw. Slowly, formally, he met her flesh with his own, so they stood palm to palm and forearm to forearm.

As before, his skin was warm, warmer than hers . . . as if he were fevered. As soon as they touched, the contact between them came alive again. Wynn drew a deep breath, fighting that link. *Why do I feel like this? Why am I doing this?*

She willed herself to resist that mental and emotional merging, refusing to look at him, staring fixedly at the medallion he wore, struggling to keep her thoughts and feelings barriered within her . . . and realized that Zar was having the same difficulty.

From the crowd came a slow drumbeat, then a low, insistent chanting. Lylla was speaking an invocation to Ashmara. Wynn's mind automatically supplied the words, since she had officiated at many handfastings before, but to another part of her, they were only gibberish.

I could stop . . . I should stop . . . my will . . . this is too fast . . .

Lylla moved forward, still chanting, carrying heavy thongs that had been dyed green. The Under-Priestess began winding the leather strips, wrapping their arms together, until they stood bound, fingertip to elbow, past any breaking free.

Wynn's heart hammered so hard that she was shaking. *It is almost too late. If I am going to stop this, it will have to be now, it must be now . . . Lady Goddess, can this be Your will?*

Gasping, she raised her head to shout out the words of denial, but her eyes met his, and they died unspoken on her lips. Zar was gazing at her anxiously, she could feel his concern, and she suddenly realized—with the sureness of a Sending—that she was doing what she must. This man meant her no harm, she knew it, had always known it.

She stood there silent, still trembling, but her fear was now mixed with another emotion.

Lylla stood back, leaving them bound together. "The binding is complete. They can only be separated by death —Ashmara has witnessed it!"

The High Priestess felt her wrist seized from behind, and knew without looking that Heldeon was playing his part. At the same moment Spock, at a signal from Cletas, also stepped forward and grabbed Zar's wrist. Both men tugged sharply, and Wynn stumbled back, away from her lord, even as he was pulled away from her.

Chanting filled her ears now, along with the sound of drums, as she was stretched bodily, her arms spread-eagled by her father's great strength—three hard pulls—*once . . . twice . . . thrice*—but Lylla knew her business, and the green thongs, though not knotted, had been bound correctly. They held through all three ceremonial tugs.

Having demonstrated that Ashmara blessed this handfasting by making it proof against family attempts to separate the handfasted couple, both fathers were supposed to release their respective wrists. But Heldeon, with a ribald guffaw, spun Wynn even as he let her go, sending her staggering back into Zar's involuntary embrace. The High Priestess would have fallen if he hadn't thrown his free arm around her shoulders, steadying her.

Wynn colored, silently cursing her father, as she directed a scathing glance at the chieftain. As she straightened in her new husband's hold, she was acutely conscious of his body against hers. She looked up, only to find him staring down at her, his eyes wide with surprise . . . and something else she couldn't read.

"Kiss her, son-by-marriage!" Heldeon whooped. "She won't bite—much!"

"Is that necessary to complete the rite?" Zar asked softly. She could barely hear him over the cheering.

"It is traditional, but the handfasting is complete, my lord," Wynn said, trying to pull away. "Most of those who enter the circle can barely restrain themselves, but we are different, you and I."

"Yes, we are," he agreed, but, bending his head, he brushed her mouth with his own. She felt the soft roughness of his moustache on her upper lip. "There," he said, drawing back and finally releasing her. "Traditions should be preserved, don't you agree?"

"Of course," she said automatically, and was angry to realize that she was slightly breathless. *Don't be a fool,* she thought. *He meant nothing by that, nothing! He was only answering Father's challenge. Any man would have done the same.*

Then they were surrounded by well-wishers, and it was time to undo the thongs.

Zar was sitting alone in his bedchamber, finishing a late supper (he'd been too queasy from nerves to eat at the wedding feast), when he heard the tap on the door. He frowned as he pushed himself up from his chair by the hearth; if the guard had permitted his visitor to knock, both the visitor and the reason must be important.

"Come," he called out.

The door opened and Spock stood there, his blue cloak pulled close around his shoulders. "I thought you might be awake."

"Too tired to sleep." Zar let himself sink back into his seat, then waved at the chair facing his. "Sit down. I'm pleased you came by. Can I get you anything?"

The Vulcan shook his head as he sat, stretching his booted

legs out to the fire. "Cletas told us it is nearly summer, yet even here in this valley there is still frost at night. I confess I am grateful for the fire's warmth."

"I rarely feel the cold," Zar admitted. "After living on the tundra all those years, this southern climate still seems warm by comparison. I doubt I could have managed Vulcan's heat."

"It is not too late to find out," Spock said, glancing over at him. Zar didn't miss the unspoken appeal in his father's eyes, though his expression never altered.

The younger man sighed. "We've been through that. There's no way I can come back with you. My people need me. Besides, Sarpeidon, for better or worse, is my world. Vulcan isn't . . . I don't know anyone there."

"You have family there," Spock reminded him.

Zar raised an eyebrow, the movement coming so naturally that for a moment he forgot that it might seem as if he were mocking his father. "You mean T'Pau?"

"She died some years ago. No, I was speaking of your grandparents."

"Amanda and Sarek? They know about me? How?"

"I told them," Spock said, flatly. "While I was on Vulcan preparing to study for Kolinahr, I hung two of your paintings in my room. When my mother saw them, she inquired as to the identity of the artist." He paused for a beat. "I had been planning to inform them anyway."

Zar caught his breath, remembering vividly how shamed the Vulcan had felt by his "krenath" offspring—living proof of his own fallibility. *And he told his father about me? Sarek, the person he wanted most to impress?* He cleared his throat, searching for words. "How did they take it?"

"They wished they had had the opportunity to meet you. If you will come back with us, they still can. Dr. McCoy is correct . . . your duty to this world does not demand your death. I have scanned the events following the battle in question, and the time-stream is free of any complications or repercussions relating to your demise. It will not matter whether you die, or are listed as 'missing in action.'"

"What happens to New Araen?"

"Peace descends. The Lakreo Valley continues to prosper."

It's possible that Wynn succeeds in holding off the invaders, then, Zar thought. "That's wonderful," he said, without irony. "I'm glad you told me. It makes it easier."

The Vulcan's mouth hardened, and for a second the Sovren sensed his father's frustration. "'It' does *not* have to happen." Spock's dark eyes were very serious. "Zar, if you return with me, I will take several months' leave to see you settled—more, if it is needed. We could visit Earth, Vulcan —anywhere you wish. The explored universe—and it is very wide—would truly be yours, son."

Spock drew a deep breath. "And for Amanda it would mean—" He swallowed. "Understand that for years, my mother has studied Vulcan mental disciplines, including the control of her human emotions. She has made considerable progress in this regard. Yet, when I spoke of you, and she told me that she wished she could have met you, there were tears in her eyes."

You're fighting dirty, Father, Zar thought, glancing down, refusing to meet the other's gaze. He cast awkwardly about for a change of subject. "Which two paintings were they?"

"The Beta Niobe ice-scape, and an enlargement of your self-portrait from the cave. It was the only image I had of you. But an image is not what I want . . ."

He is letting me know how much I matter to him, something that never happened when we were together before—except once, in the privacy of a meld, Zar thought. *But to actually hear him say it . . .* His mouth thinned. *I can't let it matter. I can't let him sway me.*

"You've changed," Zar said, bluntly.

"So have you."

"You're right about that," the younger man said. "Twenty years ago I was about a century younger—or, at least, that's how it feels. And now," he cocked his head, the eyebrow going back up, "thanks to the paradoxes of time travel, you're less than a decade older than I am."

"I know." Spock glanced around the room, with its big curtained bed, and tapestry-hung walls. There were only a few pieces of massive furniture . . . a wardrobe, and the cabinet where Voba stored the armor and weapons. The Vulcan's gaze stopped on the portrait. "Your work?" he asked, as though he already knew the answer.

"Yes. That was Araen," Zar said. "My wife . . . that is," he corrected himself with a touch of bitterness, "my *first* wife."

"She was lovely," Spock said, gently.

"She was," Zar agreed, keeping his voice steady with an effort. "Fine-boned and so delicate . . . intelligent, but *kind*. She never used her wit to hurt, only to make others happy. When she was in a room, people would gravitate toward her just as they do toward a fire in winter." He sighed, realizing he couldn't afford to let himself sink into *those* memories. "May I ask you a personal question?"

Spock considered. "You may ask. I do not promise to answer."

"Fair enough. Why haven't *you* ever married?"

It was the Vulcan's turn to raise an eyebrow. "There is no single reason. Once the liaison the family arranged for me was terminated by divorce, there was no reason to enter another immediately . . . so I elected not to do so. Time went by . . . my contemporaries were all partnered. Then our five-year mission was over, and I began the study of the Kolinahr disciplines. When one is an acolyte in pursuit of Kolinahr, one must give up . . . external . . . links." He steepled his fingers. "By the time I left Kolinahr, I also left Vulcan. I have not been home since."

"So, you just haven't met the right woman," Zar said, deadpan.

Shared amusement touched his father's eyes. "You could put it that way."

"I thought you had a duty to 'the family' to keep the bloodline going."

Spock nodded. "So I have been told. Considering the Vulcan lifespan, I still have time, even if you choose not to return with me. Although I do not feel as bound by family traditions as I once did. As one grows older, one's perspectives and priorities alter."

"The understatement of the evening."

Spock's eyebrow rose again. "And what about you? I gather that the Council has been urging you to remarry for years. Why has it taken you this long to do so?"

Zar hesitated for nearly a minute before speaking. "What took place tonight between Wynn and me won't be a true marriage," he said finally, deliberately hedging the question and hoping Spock wouldn't notice. *He's the last person I want to discuss* that *subject with . . .*

"I see," his father said. "An in-name-only arrangement, then, contracted for political reasons." The dark Vulcan eyes held his, and the Sovren knew then that Spock had not missed his evasion. "Why not an actual marriage?" he asked. "I do not wish to pry, but . . ."

Zar swallowed. "I don't know . . . I never met the right woman either, I suppose. Or, if I did, I never let myself know it. To tell you the truth, Father, McCoy was right. I'm a coward."

"Not by any measure of the term as I comprehend it. If I may offer an opinion, you have acquitted yourself well in an admittedly difficult situation, Zar."

The younger man blinked in surprised pleasure. "Why . . . thank you. It means a lot to me to hear you say that." He mused for a moment. "You know what's been hardest, in some ways, about my 'situation'? I came back here fired up with determination to save the world. But it didn't take long before I realized that just because something is the 'right' thing to do, doesn't necessarily make it enjoyable. I really don't *like* 'running the show.' And a sense of duty and obligation can take you only so far. I've regretted not staying with you more times . . ."

"You don't enjoy command?"

"No, not the way Jim Kirk does. He was born for it, he thrives on it, you can look at him and tell. When he's in charge, even when he's wrong—he's right, somehow. It's hard to put into words."

"I know what you mean," Spock told him.

"I suppose you do, more than anyone."

"But surely your work here must have had some compensations."

"Years ago, when we had peace, it did, yes. I'd visit the classrooms and know that the people of my valley would one day be literate. I'd watch the farmers using their new steel plows, and it would all seem worth it, then. No matter how much I disliked levying taxes, or judging criminals, any of the day-to-day work of 'running the show'—I was accomplishing what I had set myself to do, and that *meant* something."

He shook his head. "Even though to do it, I had to give up my personal freedom—and, if you think about it, my entire life before, I'd been about as free as anyone could be. No one to answer to but myself. But when I came here, I was responsible for thousands of lives—nobody is more constrained than a ruler of a territory this size—" Zar broke off, gazing down at the table between them. His sword, which Voba had cleaned and placed there for his inspection, lay gleaming bluely, unsheathed.

His mouth twisted as he stared at it. "And then the wars started . . ."

"I understand," Spock said. "But why do you say that you lack courage?"

Zar flexed his hands, absently rubbing one of the old scars. "I've lost so many people, through the years . . . Araen, and Tekolin . . . Alyn, one of my best tacticians, Matric, who was with me from the first . . . others . . . and, of course, my mother. With each death I've received the warning that something terrible was happening, or was going to happen to them . . . just the way I knew that time when Commander Tal was going to execute you. Sick, dizzy, disoriented . . . the greater the danger, the worse it was."

"I remember."

"It's hard to let yourself care, when you know you're going to be there—mentally and emotionally, at least —when they die." Zar's voice faltered on the last syllable. "I've spent a lot of years now, trying to care as little as possible. And yet, it still happens to me. Tomorrow I may wake up sick, and realize that Cletas or Voba will be the next. That's hell to live with."

"Yes," Spock agreed. "But the alternative is to live without friendship or warmth . . . in a sterile, joyless environment. I experienced such a barren existence during my mind-meld with Vejur."

"Vejur?"

"A gargantuan computer-generated spaceship we encountered. It had come to Earth searching for its creator, for something to give purpose to its arid existence. It had accumulated so much data, had achieved such perfect logic—and yet it had no concept of compassion, of friendship, and so remained . . . empty. Barren. It came very close to destroying Terra before we could prompt it to search for a higher purpose."

Zar listened intently. "So, what's the moral here?" he asked, when Spock had finished. "Logic isn't everything? I'm *shocked*, Father!" he said with a half-smile.

Unabashed, Spock returned it. "Some things do transcend logic." He sobered, steepling his fingers together as he stared into the fire. "Actually, the inherent limitations of logic were only part of 'the moral,' as you term it. More important, I believe, is the lesson that anything—or anyone —who ceases to grow, to reach outward, even at great risk or cost . . . is spiritually dying."

As he listened to the Vulcan's words, Zar had lost his air of casual amusement; now he leaned forward, his eyes as hard and intent as the blade resting between them. "So you're saying that I should take the risk of caring, no matter who dies, and what it does to me when it happens? You're saying I should fight to stay alive, even when I have it on the best authority that I'm a corpse just waiting to fall down? You're saying I should—" His voice cracked, and he rubbed his forehead, fighting for control.

After a moment, a hand rested on his shoulder, gently, then was gone. Zar took a deep, shuddering breath and looked back up at Spock. "I apologize for that outburst. Just when I think I'm completely resigned, something wells up, and I realize that part of me is still scared and doesn't want to die."

"I am vastly relieved to hear you say that," the Vulcan said, his dark eyes intent. "Ever since we met this time, I have been concerned that you were, indeed, resigned past the need for all striving. The thought . . . distressed . . . me more than I can easily tell you."

Zar heard the roughness in his father's voice, even as he sensed the other's emotion . . . even without reaching out, it was there, close to the surface. Ever since he had watched that bloody little scene in his tricorder viewer, the Vulcan had been haunted by it . . . his pain and sorrow were profound.

"Oh, Father . . ." Zar searched for words. "I didn't realize . . . I didn't think what it would be like for you, to see me . . ." He stumbled to a halt. "I'm sorry."

"It is hardly logical for you to apologize for what I saw in my tricorder," Spock said, gently. "Obviously, if the event had been something under your control, it would not have happened. Or be going to happen." He frowned at the tangle of tenses.

"No, but if I hadn't been so self-obsessed, I'd have realized what effect all this would have on the people who care about me. I'd have tried to summon a little rage."

"Rage?"

"Something Wynn said on the same subject earlier today."

"For her milieu, she is truly an admirable person," Spock said, thoughtfully. "Intelligent, compassionate . . . I find myself liking her."

"So do I," the Sovren admitted, then remembered, for no reason, the expression in Wynn's eyes just after he had kissed her, there in the firelit circle. *As though she thought I was mocking her, when actually it was just an . . . impulse. I hope I have time to explain that to her. She deserves to know . . .*

The Vulcan stirred. "It is very late," he said. "I expect you need your rest."

And so do you, Zar thought, seeing the deep lines etched

around his father's mouth. "You're right." As Spock got up to leave, he cleared his throat. "Father?"

"Yes?"

"You've given me a lot to think about. About whether I should remain here, or go with you . . . whether I should stay still, or risk growing . . . whether I should . . . rage. Thank you."

"You are very welcome," Spock said, then added in slow, deliberate Vulcan, "Rest well and peacefully, my son. Remember that on any world the wind eventually wears away the stone, because the stone can only crumble; the wind can change."

Then the door closed with a soft click, and he was gone.

Zar sat for several minutes, thinking about those final words. Finally he sighed, grasping the arms of his chair as he prepared to rise. It was then that he heard the faint, cautious *click* from behind the tapestry at his back. A soft rustle, as of fabric, followed . . .

Soundlessly, he was out of his chair, and his sword was in his hand. Shifting his weight cautiously, he crept toward the arras, fighting a wild impulse to shout, " 'Dead for a ducat, dead!' " as he plunged his blade through it.

Control yourself, he admonished himself sternly. *Whoever this is, it isn't Polonius.* A second before Zar swept the heavy folds aside, he knew the identity of the intruder.

"My lady wife," he said, giving Wynn an ironic bow, then holding out his hand, "wouldn't you be more comfortable near the fire?"

Chapter Ten

I SHOULD HAVE REALIZED, Zar thought, *that Cletas would put her in the room adjoining mine. State marriage or no, she is my wife and co-regent, and therefore entitled to all the privileges and honors of her rank. Including the consort's bedchamber.* Since Araen's death, he had never entered the room . . . he'd bolted the connecting door and had it covered with the tapestry, and nearly succeeded in forgetting it was there.

Wynn hesitated for a second, then her chin came up in a way he was beginning to recognize. "Thank you, my lord," she said, coolly. "I *am* somewhat chilled."

The fingers she placed in his felt like icicles; she wore only a thin linen shift, her cloak thrown over it. Her hair was loosely braided down her back. Zar led her over to the chair and seated her, then he busied himself poking the fire up, adding several logs until it was snapping comfortably.

When he turned back to Wynn, she was staring at him, her eyes defiant. "I don't suppose you will believe me, my lord, but I never intended what happened just now. I had fallen asleep, and suddenly . . ." she bit her lip distractedly, "suddenly I was awake, thinking someone had called my name. So I approached the door—Cletas showed it to me tonight, when he unbolted it. It was open a crack, and I heard your voice . . ."

She shrugged, tiredly. "I stepped through, intending to

call out, but then I heard your father speak, and knew that you were both here. I realized then that no one had summoned me.

"When I heard what you were talking about, I was ashamed to admit that I had listened to such a personal conversation, and turned to leave. But the door had closed behind me; I could not get it open without making some sound, so I waited, intending to turn and leave as soon as I could do so without discovery. When you were sitting there so quietly, after Spock left, I thought you had fallen asleep and my chance had come . . ."

Her mortification was genuine; Zar could pick it up without even trying. He nodded, resting an arm against the high back of her chair. "I understand. These things happen, don't worry about it. And we *were* speaking of you, so it is entirely possible you did hear your name."

"But that is not all," she continued, not looking up. "While I was standing there, trying not to listen—though of course that was impossible—it was as though I were receiving a Sending. No vision, no words—but a strong conviction, my lord, that you should do as your father wishes. You need to go . . . wherever it is he wants to take you. You *must* help him. Helping him may be your only means of saving yourself. I *feel* this, so strongly . . . I am sure Ashmara wills it."

"You don't understand what they want me to do," Zar said.

"You are right, I don't. They are not of this world, are they?" She hesitated, lacing her fingers in her lap. "I don't mean spirits or demons, either. I'm not sure what I *do* mean . . . except that Kirk told me when first I saw him that he could not explain how they had traveled here. They come from . . . someplace else. But that's not altogether it, is it?"

"No. They come from a place—actually, a world, or worlds—that is different, not only in location, but in *time*. They come from a time that has yet to be."

Wynn sighed. "Perhaps you had better give me that explanation you promised me earlier, my lord. It is important that I know all I am capable of understanding about you . . . and them. Please trust me about this."

The Sovren shrugged one shoulder. *What difference can it make? She probably won't believe me anyway* . . . "Very well."

Choosing his words carefully, he outlined the truth in the simplest terms he could. The High Priestess listened, never interrupting, frowning a little as she concentrated.

When Zar finished, she looked up at him. "All my life I have sensed that there are things in this world . . . in this *universe* . . . that I might not understand. Now I *know* that there are many, *many* things beyond my comprehension. You tell me that there are worlds beyond worlds, and stars beyond stars . . . and that distance and time can somehow be one and the same thing. But I *do* know that no one would undertake the journey those three did without good reason. You are the one they need to help them."

Zar frowned. "Just because I contacted the Guardian once . . ."

"I sense that they are right. If anyone can make this—this God of Time—resume its duties, you are that one."

"They hope I can. Nobody knows."

She leaned forward, her green eyes shining with excitement—and hope. "You *must*," she said. "You must do as they ask."

"Leave and never return?" Zar raised an eyebrow. "You will indeed inherit quickly, my lady."

"I do not mean that," she said, brushing his cynicism aside impatiently. "This Guardian—to it Time is nothing, a roll of fabric folded or discarded as it wills, yes?"

Zar nodded.

"Then it can return you to *before* the battle begins. You will be there to lead our troops. You will fight, and, perhaps, you will *not* fall. The Sending is strong, but there is no picture to guide me . . . just the impression! But if I am right . . . if you could be *saved* . . ."

"Yes?" he prompted, as she trailed off. "What then?"

She bit her lip, all animation vanishing from her features.

"Why . . . nothing, my lord. Except that a good man would not die."

"*Can* such a fate be averted?" Zar mused, half-aloud. "Wouldn't that cause a paradox? I wonder . . ." He considered for a moment, then abandoned the effort. He was too tired to ponder problems in theoretical physics.

But there was something else bothering him, something to do with Wynn herself, and *that* mystery he felt compelled to understand. He gazed back down at her, his eyes very direct. "I also wonder why it should matter so much to you."

"It matters," she said brusquely, plainly nervous. "It's none of your concern *why* it matters."

His hand clenched on the chairback; suddenly he was furious. *What's going on here? Why is she being so secretive?* His voice became soft, deadly, and very mocking. "If it concerns me, I have a right to know, my lady. Why would you wish to delay your succession? What is all this to you? *Why* do you care?" He leaned over and tipped up her chin, so she was forced to look at him. *"How* do you care?"

Stung, Wynn surged to her feet, anger written in every line of her face. "Does everything have to have a *reason*? Can't people do things just because they *feel* like doing them? You *think* too much, my lord!" She whirled away from him, heading for the connecting door.

Exasperated, he grabbed her arm and halted her, turning her to face him. "If you had experienced what I have," he gritted, so angry he was trembling—*First McCoy, then Spock, now you! Why can't everyone leave me alone!*—"then you wouldn't be so sure that feelings were such a great idea, my lady. I learned a long time ago to *think*, not to feel. Feeling . . . *hurts."*

She glared back at him. "You imagine you have some monopoly on pain? Your sire was too easy on you. You're right, you *are* a coward!"

He gripped both her arms, ignoring her attempt to wrench away. "You think so? I'll show you and you can judge, then!"

"Very well," she snapped. "Show me."

Zar released the barriers between them, so that his mind, his memories, surged into hers. Wynn ceased struggling, stiffening as the intensity of the meld claimed her. After a moment, Zar touched the side of her face, his fingers slipping naturally into the old contact points.

In the meld, years rushed past with the speed of heartbeats:

Growing up with only Zarabeth for a companion. The loneliness, the longing . . . for a playmate, for a friend . . . for his father . . . the loneliness which had seemed terrible —until he discovered the true meaning of the word, the day of his mother's death. Zar felt again the heaviness of her body as he carried her into the ice-cavern. His only companion, gone . . .

And then, Araen, screaming in hoarse delirium as she tried to rid her body of the death his child had become to her. He had waited, delaying long past the time when he had known it was hopeless, hoping still for some miracle, something . . . and then it was over, his hands and the knife were slippery wet and hot with new-shed blood, Araen was dead, and his daughter was trying feebly to cry . . .

Little Araen had lived for six hours. More than long enough for him to forgive her for her mother's death . . . to establish an emotional bond that shattered him as he stood holding her, willing her to breathe. He had waited too long to take her. Twice he had succeeded in breathing life into her when her tiny lungs failed, but not the third time . . .

All the deaths, down the years, all the pain . . . all the loss. And never the solace of tears. He had tried, but they weren't in him . . . why, he didn't know. Instead of healing, the wounds had drawn and puckered into a festering knot of grief and anger . . .

But even as the last of his memories flowed into Wynn, Zar became aware that the meld was changing, becoming two-way. He began to experience things out of Wynn's past . . . her mother's death, of a lengthy, wasting illness. Wynn had nursed her tenderly, had closed her eyes when she finally found peace.

Then a short time of joy with Nahral, the birth of Lelinos,

her son . . . a happiness which only worsened the agonizing shock of finding their brutalized bodies in the ruins of her home . . .

Zar swallowed, his throat aching. Wynn was right. He had no monopoly on suffering. But, unlike him, she had been strong enough to keep risking herself, to allow herself to continue caring. She had faced her own grief and learned to live with it, not shut it away unhealed.

He realized, then, dimly, that her face was buried against his shoulder; she was shaking violently. And, as the meld between them lessened, he heard her sobbing, deep, racking sounds that seemed to tear themselves from her chest.

"Shhhhh," he whispered, drawing her closer. "Shhhhh."

I am sorry, Wynn was repeating without words, in his mind. *I grieve for you.*

And I for you, he told her. *I wish I had your strength.*

He never knew how much time went by before her weeping lessened, then subsided, but his bad leg was throbbing. Inside, though, where the knot had been drawn so agonizingly tight, there was a loosening. Through their meld, he had experienced her expression of grief and had finally gained some inner release. He sighed, feeling drained, yet calm . . . as though the bleeding from some invisible yet mortal wound had finally been stanched, allowing healing to begin.

Wynn stirred and sniffled. "Do you have a handkerchief?"

Zar dug into a pocket in his jerkin and managed to locate one. "Here."

"Thank you." She stepped back, away from him, and he let his arms drop, trying not to notice how empty they felt.

He stood watching her dry her eyes, feeling awkward. "Are you all right now?"

"Yes," she said. "I regret having called you a coward. I was wrong."

"No, you weren't. And I apologize for my behavior," Zar said, stiffly. "I don't know what made me act like that . . . you obviously have your own reasons for wanting to help me . . . but whatever they are, they are none of my concern. I am sorry."

Wynn sighed, turning to leave. She took a step in the direction of her chamber, then halted suddenly, her chin coming up. She faced him again, her eyes holding his. Her expression reflected an odd mixture of emotions . . . tenderness, amusement, and frustration, all at once.

He watched as she drew a deep breath. "My dear lord, of course my reasons concern you . . . and are your concern. These things happen, though never before to me. Denying how I feel—as I've been trying to do for hours—won't make it go away. I should have known better than to lie to myself . . . or to you."

Zar stared down at her, eyes widening. *Don't be an idiot, she can't mean what you're thinking . . .* He swallowed, then tried to summon words. "It almost sounds as though you're saying that you . . . that you . . ." He faltered into silence.

She flushed, stepping back another pace, but her eyes remained steady. "I know what it sounds like. You want it in plain speech? All right, then. Sometime during this day past—and a truly mad day it has been—I found myself loving you. Wanting you. I didn't want to admit it, even to myself, but it's true . . . and I'm not ashamed of it." For the first time she hesitated, glancing away, her next words coming in a whisper. "I don't expect you to share my feelings."

Zar's heart was hammering now, and without realizing he'd moved, he found himself close enough to put his hands on her shoulders. Even as they touched, the link flared to life again, and he could feel her emotions . . . her immediate response to his nearness. His own reaction was so strong and urgent that his breath caught in his throat.

"Wynn . . ." he began, haltingly. "I'm not good with words at times like this, but ever since we met, I felt . . . something, I don't know . . ." He reached up and gently touched her face, blindly tracing the coutours of her cheeks, her brows, her lips. "I don't know what to think . . . what to say . . . or do . . ."

"I think," she said quietly, "that *you* should stop thinking."

Through the link came the knowledge that she very much wanted him to kiss her . . .

So he did.

Her mouth was cool and soft beneath his, and after a few seconds he pulled her against him, holding her tightly. As the kiss deepened, Wynn's hands slid up, caressing his shoulders, the back of his neck. The link between them flared up again, then grew steadily . . . he experienced her pleasure at the feel of his body against hers, and it intensified his own.

No, don't! The danger . . . a small voice in his mind warned, but was drowned in the dizzying wave of sensation. He drew back slightly, began kissing her cheek, her hair, her small, rounded ears. She murmured his name, softly, on a shaken breath. Zar ran his lips along the line of her jaw, then down her throat, feeling her pulse leap beneath them like a startled animal.

As he did so the link between them deepened into a meld, stifling the little voice that cried danger, submerging his identity, his very sense of self, until there was no room for anything but the feel of her in his arms.

"Wynn . . ." he whispered.

I love you. The words were not spoken, and Zar had no idea which of them had thought them first. When he raised his head, staring at her with a silent question in his eyes, she answered him wordlessly by pulling his mouth back down to hers. Her kiss filled them both with a starving intensity that blotted out everything except the blind, instinctive need to unite—mind and body, completely.

The covers on the huge curtained bed were like sheets of ice, but Zar scarcely felt the shock of them on his flesh; there was only Wynn. Their lovemaking shook and consumed him, their passion seared away the last of the death-shadow . . . leaving only physical exhaustion, and, finally, sleep . . .

When Wynn awoke, she had no trouble remembering where she was . . . even in sleep, the new-forged link she shared with Zar had not disappeared, only faded until it was now just a comfortably glowing ember in the back of her mind. She yawned, stretching her arms above her head, then hastily yanked the comforter back up to her chin—neither of them had thought to draw the bedcurtains, the fire had died out, and the chamber was freezing.

But beneath the covers, next to him, it was warm. Smiling, Wynn rolled over.

Zar was lying curled on his side, arms folded neatly against his chest, his breathing soft and regular. She studied him, remembering Nahral, how he had appeared younger when he slept, but Zar looked the same as he did awake, frowning a little, intent—as though he were concentrating on a problem.

She wondered what time it was . . . late, certainly. The window curtain was drawn, but bright sunlight seeped around its edges. Dimly, she remembered seeing the gray of early dawn just as she had fallen asleep. *It must be close to noon,* she thought, realizing with a slight shock that not even a full day had passed since she had first met the man now lying beside her.

Memories of yesterday—the raid, their first meeting, the council, the handfasting ceremony—jumbled together in her mind, leaving her dizzy. *It's as though I leapt through that time gate he told me of, and years passed in a heartbeat.*

Wynn thought about a world—a universe—where people could travel from star to star inside great space-wagons. The painting in the study that had troubled her so was of a space-wagon named *Enterprise*. Zar had told her that the *Enterprise* was capable of traveling so fast that it could circle this entire world (which he had told her was *round*, of all things!) in less time than it would take to blink an eye. He was her husband, she had been inside his mind where it was impossible to lie, so she must perforce believe him . . . but it was difficult.

He stirred slightly, then relaxed again with a sound that was not quite a snore. Wynn could see the sharp tip of one ear through the rumpled black hair. *He is so strange, at times, so alien . . . and yet, last night it was as though we were truly one being . . .* The memory sent a surge of desire throughout her.

Cautiously, she moved one hand until it rested within a fingertip's width of his shoulder. Even without touching him, she could feel the heat of his body—warmer than hers, as though he were fevered, but she knew now that was normal for him.

What will happen today? she wondered. *Will he leave, to try and heal this God of Time, the Guardian? If he leaves, will he come back to me? Should I even want him to return, when it may mean his death?*

The gruesome vision that Ashmara had sent her flashed across her mind's eye, and Wynn blinked back tears. *Lady, protect him, I beg you. You brought us together for a reason . . . I know you did. If only I could be sure that last night was a true Sending! That if he goes with Spock and the others, he will live!*

She wondered whether last night's Sending meant that Zar would live only if he remained in his sire's time. *Perhaps I should convince him to go, and not return. But to never see him again . . .*

Wynn's throat tightened painfully. *I must be strong,* she resolved. *If Ashmara sends me knowledge that he'll be safe only if he does not come back, then that is what I will beg him to do.*

As if her decision had been a silent signal, Zar woke. He lay staring at her for several moments, his gray eyes shadowed and still weary, then he smiled and reached over to gently touch her hair. "I hardly know what to say, my lady. The customary formal greetings to a visiting envoy just don't seem to apply."

Wynn chuckled. "Then we'll be informal. Fair morning to you, my lord—assuming it is still morning, which I doubt."

"Fair morning," he replied, obediently. "Did you sleep well?"

"Very," she said, straight-faced. "I had little choice. You tired me out."

He propped his head up on one hand, and his eyebrow

disappeared beneath his hair. *"I* tired *you* out? I thought Ashmara didn't like liars."

"That's what I told James Kirk, anyway," she said, grinning, then stretched, enjoying the way his eyes traced her body beneath the comforter. "Is it today that you go back with them?"

"If I go back. I haven't decided yet."

"You should go. You *must* go."

"But they told me one esper—that's what they call people like you and me, in my father's time—has already been injured, almost to the point of death. What if I go, but cannot return?"

Wynn drew a deep breath, feeling actual pain knife through her, but somehow she managed to keep her expression unchanged. "Then I will rule New Araen for both of us, as well as I am able, my lord." She glanced down at her midsection. "And, if I am lucky, our daughter or son will rule after me."

Zar's features froze, and she felt his shock through the link between them, even though they were not touching. *"Our* . . . child? Is that possible?"

She gave him a mock-incredulous look. "You've forgotten so soon? I'm hurt."

He sat bolt upright, his cheekbones like stone, his mouth a grim slash. "I mean, is it the right time for you?"

Wynn gazed up at him, startled and worried. *What can be wrong?* "Yes, it is," she replied. "And I have taken no herbs to prevent conception. If Ashmara chooses to bless me, there is a good chance." She sat up, too, pulling the comforter up over one shoulder, her hair tumbling around her. "Why do you look like that, Zar?"

She could feel the fear that sent his heart pounding even before she put out a hand and touched his arm—with the physical contact between them, it was so strong it made her gasp. "Tell me, please! What is wrong?"

He swallowed, and she could feel the effort he was making to control his reaction. "Araen . . ." he said, in a low voice. "I was thinking of how she died . . ."

Wynn shook her head. "As I saw her in your mind last night, my lord, she was a small, delicately boned woman, was she not? Tiny and not strong?"

He nodded. "Her head barely reached the middle of my chest."

"And that was her first babe, yes?"

He nodded again, refusing to turn toward her.

"My dear," she said, caressing the line of his jaw, *"look* at me. My people are taller and bigger-boned than your Valley-dwellers. *I* am tall, even for my people. As tall as Cletas, or McCoy. And no one could call me frail. I have borne one healthy child already . . . my entire labor took less than half a day. Trust me, as a healer and midwife, I know about these things. I understand your fear, but I do not share it. Any risk is nothing compared to the joy our child will bring me."

"But . . ." he began, then stopped and shrugged one shoulder. "Perhaps you are right."

Wynn was sure, however, that she had not convinced him. She considered pursuing the subject, but decided against it. He would see. She would be fine.

She studied him in the dimness, remembering the way his lean, muscled body had felt in her arms, smooth skin and scars . . . so many scars. Few warriors lived long enough to collect that many.

Hesitantly, she touched his right shoulder, running her forefinger down it, feeling the hard sinew beneath the flesh, tracing the jagged ridge marring it. "How did you get this one?"

He glanced down at himself and raised an eyebrow. "Those toothmarks?" he said, deadpan. "Obviously, somebody bit me."

She smothered a grin and glared at him in pretended indignation. "No, I meant *this* one."

"An outlaw's lance. That's the one that made me decide that I couldn't put off inventing chain mail." At her look of incomprehension, he explained, "Armor made from links of steel—the metal my sword is made of. Much stronger than boiled leather, even with scale reinforcement. It can turn a cut from a bronze weapon."

Wynn's mind was off and running. "Do you have more of this metal? It would give our forces an advantage."

"I can equip perhaps two hundred of your soldiers with steel swords," he said. "And three hundred with steel lance-heads. But no more than that. My smiths have been working night and day for months, just to forge armor and weapons for my own troops."

"We have smiths, too," she said. "Can your people teach ours to smelt this new metal?"

"If we make it through the battle, nothing would please me more," he said. "When do you think they will attack?"

"As soon as the waters of the Redbank subside enough for them to cross with the chariots, they will come," she said. "My guess is that it will be tomorrow or the day after—no later."

"That agrees with my latest intelligence," Zar said. "I want to meet them on Moorgate Plain. My battle plan calls for room to maneuver."

She gave him a mock-disgusted look, then nipped his shoulder. "Tactics, battle strategies . . . fine talk for two people in bed on the morning after their handfasting."

He smiled his half-smile, smoothing her unbound hair back from her face, then bent to kiss her neck where it joined her shoulder. "Wynn . . . just this time yesterday, I was making you that crazy proposal. Why did you accept?"

Wynn nestled close to him, resting her cheek against his chest. "I don't know . . . not for your looks, certainly."

She heard and felt his breath release in what she recognized as a chuckle. "Seriously," she said, "it's hard to put into words. From those first moments in your study, I knew there was something binding us together . . . as though we were pieces cut from the same hide. Very different in the way we were formed, and shaped, but created from the same material. I didn't let myself realize it, at first . . . but it was always there."

He drew her closer. "I know. But I only began to

recognize it for what it was, when your father goaded me into that kiss."

"I was furious with him," Wynn said, smiling reminiscently.

"I could tell."

"Are you going to help your father, my lord?"

He sighed deeply, his arms tightening around her. "Yes. I have no choice, now."

"I'm glad."

Wynn shut her eyes, thinking that soon—too soon—they would have to get up, that he would have to leave, that she might never see him again. *Stop thinking,* she told herself fiercely, concentrating on feeling only warm skin and the soft prickle of black hair beneath her cheek. She gave herself up to the moment, trying to convince herself (and almost . . . *almost* . . . succeeding) that it would never end.

Zar was sitting at his desk in his study, checking supply requisitions, when Cletas entered and saluted. "Here are the latest intelligence reports, my liege."

"Good. I've ordered a meeting of all troop commanders in two hours. Commander Madon, Heldeon, the Lady Wynn and the rest of the Danreg commanders will be joining us." He took the vellum sheets and studied them. "So, the Redbank will not permit a crossing today . . . how did Rorgan and Laol take the news that Heldeon is now allied with us?"

The Second-in-War smiled. "About as we expected. They were heard quarreling long into the night."

"Good. If they're fighting each other, they're not planning for this battle. Status on the catapults?"

"We've moved two, and will move two more this afternoon. Two more tonight."

"The footing?"

"Drying fast. The cavalry will drill late this afternoon."

Zar let out a long breath. "Then I guess we'll be as prepared as possible. I want you to break out all the extra steel weapons and distribute them to the Lady Wynn's selected troops, on her orders."

"Yes, sire." Cletas hesitated. "By the way, I haven't encountered the lady yet today. Heldeon sent her waiting women down this morning, but when they went to her chamber, they said she wasn't there. Have you . . . seen her?"

The Sovren glanced up quickly, suddenly remembering just who it had been that had unbolted the connecting door. "She's taking a bath," he said, levelly. "In my chamber."

"I . . . see," Cletas said, his tone carefully neutral.

Zar raised an inquiring eyebrow. "You see *what*, Cletas?"

"Nothing, my liege," the Second said, fervently. "Just a figure of speech."

A rap on the study door saved the Second. Zar gave Cletas an "I'll deal with *you* later" look. "That will be Zaylenz, Yarlev, Ingev, Reydel, and Trebor Damas," he said. "I asked them to assemble before the briefing. I have something important to tell all of you."

Doctor McCoy grinned exultantly. "You'll come! This is great! I knew you'd see reason . . . wait'll I tell Jim and Spock."

Zar raised a cautioning hand. "Not so fast, Leonard. As soon as I meet with the Danreg officers, I'll go with you and try to contact the Guardian. But then I'm returning for the battle."

McCoy felt as though he'd been punched in the stomach. He sat blinking, then finally took a deep breath, searching for his voice. "Why, Zar? You know what's going to happen . . ."

The Sovren's mouth was set. "Maybe. On the other hand, now that I know about it, maybe I can do something to prevent it. Wynn thinks there's a chance."

"And you're telling me you're planning on staking your *life* on a barbarian priestess's superstitious mumbo-jumbo?" the doctor asked, using his most cutting tone.

The gray eyes opposite his were nearly colorless in the sunlight. "I have to come back here," Zar repeated. "And don't forget you're talking about my wife, Leonard."

"God*damn* it, you're as stubborn as your old man!"

McCoy raged, slamming his fist on the table. "What's keeping you here? Or do you just have a martyr complex?"

Zar's mouth tightened. "What's keeping me is why I had to see you . . . why I told you first. Doc, I need your help. *Please.*"

The medical officer drew a long, slow breath, held it, then let it out. Then another. "All right," he said, finally. "What can I do?"

"While I'm aboard the *Enterprise,* I want you to sterilize me."

"Sterilize?" McCoy repeated blankly. For one wild moment all he could think of was Nomad, that weird little robot that had wiped out an entire system of sentient beings, following its programming directive to "sterilize." The thing had nearly killed them all. "What do you mean, 'sterilize'?"

"What do you think I mean?" Zar demanded, his control visibly slipping. "I never had the chance to learn Vulcan bio-control. So I want you to do whatever it takes to render me infertile . . . incapable of fathering children. How much more explicit do I have to be?"

"Okay, okay, I understand *what* you want. But *why?*"

The Sovren didn't meet his eyes. "I'm afraid for Wynn."

McCoy sat back in his chair and raised an eyebrow. "Oho. I begin to see. So much for the marriage of convenience."

"I also want you to take a tricorder reading on her today," Zar said, his face schooled to an impassive mask. "And, if necessary, give her something."

"Like what?"

"Something to prevent conception, damn it!" Zar's voice cracked. "You have to!"

The doctor sat up. "The hell I do. You're the one who has a right to decide about your body, and the same goes for Wynn. I gather you . . . have cause to worry?"

The Sovren nodded, tight-lipped.

"Well, how does Wynn feel about it? Does she want a baby?"

"Yes. And she can have them—but not by me. She can

choose anyone she wants, but I'm . . . there's something . . . wrong . . . with me. Genetically."

"When I examined you twenty years ago there wasn't."

"There must've been an error in your tests. Araen . . ." Zar swallowed, fighting for calm. "Araen died as a result of childbirth."

"I figured."

"And my daughter, too. She lived only a few hours. It must have been my mixed parentage. My genes are defective somehow . . ."

"For a number of reasons, I doubt that," the doctor said, gently. "First of all, did Araen have a normal pregnancy?"

"As far as I knew . . . I mean, as far as I could determine from what the midwives said, and from reading the medical texts I brought. But she was never strong. Her father told me she'd always been frail. But she was so *happy,* so full of life, you didn't notice it."

"What about the delivery?"

"She couldn't," Zar told him, unsteadily. "She was in labor for two days. The moment the contractions started, I began to feel sick, you remember how, and I *knew—*" He took a deep breath, then cleared his throat. "The midwives tried everything, but she never dilated more than a few centimeters. Finally, when she was comatose, and I knew she would die no matter what, I did what she'd been begging me to do for hours . . . I took my knife, and performed a Caesarean. I—I—it was hard to cut deep enough . . . at first. And I thought I'd seen blood in battles, but—"

"I understand. Take it easy, son," McCoy broke in, feeling his heart go out to the other. "But what makes you think it was *your* fault? Was the child deformed?"

Zar had leaned his head in his hands, and didn't look up. "No, outwardly she was perfect. She just never breathed properly."

"Tiny? Premature?"

"No, the midwives told me she was a good-sized baby."

"Well . . . it's impossible for me to give a completely accurate diagnosis in a case like this, of course, but it sounds to me as though the infant was too large for the birth canal.

It's not an uncommon problem, especially considering that Araen was a small woman. And after such a prolonged labor, the baby simply didn't have the strength to survive."

Zar looked up at him, wordlessly.

"Are you listening to me?" McCoy held the younger man's eyes with his own. "I found out something this trip that I didn't know before. The people of this world probably evolved from the same basic stock as the Vulcans and the Rigellians." Briefly, the doctor went on to outline Spock's theory.

Zar looked thoughtful. "That explains a lot of things that have puzzled me since I first met you. I was really surprised, for example, to discover that human blood was red. I'd never seen it that color before . . ."

"But the most important thing is that there's no reason to think you and Wynn couldn't have healthy offspring," McCoy said. "What happened to Araen wasn't caused by some defect in your chromosomes. It was a tragedy, yes, but *nobody's* fault. If you want, I'll give you a complete genetic workup in sickbay, but I know that's what I'm going to find. And," he finished grimly, "if you still want me to, I'll do what you're asking at that time. All it takes is one hypo."

"And Wynn? What if she's already . . ."

"If she's pregnant, and wants the baby, then that's her risk . . . and her decision. But, frankly, from my tricorder readings of her yesterday, I'd say don't worry. She's strong and healthy." He smiled reassuringly.

Zar nodded, though McCoy knew he hadn't convinced him. "All right, Leonard. Thanks."

"You're welcome, son." The doctor stood up. "I'll tell Kirk and Spock that we've got a date with an ailing time portal."

James T. Kirk entered the common room to find Spock standing, hands clasped behind his back, staring out the window. "Bones says that Zar has agreed to return with us and attempt to contact the Guardian."

The Vulcan turned, the reddish light from the westering

sun highlighting his features into a satanic mask. "Did he indicate whether he will remain in our time?"

Kirk nodded, reluctantly. "He says he's coming back to New Araen in time for the battle. He won't budge on that."

Spock looked away, his mouth tightening. "That is his right."

Kirk nodded. "But maybe we can still get him to change his mind. If we can convince him to spend a day or so aboard the *Enterprise* . . . remember how he loved the ship?"

"Yes. But I also recall that Zar is a remarkably stubborn individual."

Kirk cleared his throat. "Well . . . 'the fruit don't fall far from the tree,' as the saying goes." At the Vulcan's raised eyebrow, he translated, "I'd say he comes by that honestly."

"Are you by any chance intimating that *I* am stubborn, Jim?"

"Uh . . . well, yes. Not that that isn't a good character trait at times," Kirk added, hastily. "It's saved my hide more than once."

The Vulcan's mouth twitched fractionally. "You are right. I *am* stubborn. So are you, by the way."

"Who, *me?*" Kirk's hazel eyes widened innocently, then the admiral gave in with a chuckle. "You're right, as usual."

They stood together, watching the swollen crimson disk of Beta Niobe sink toward the peak of Big Snowy. "Bones tells me he's worried about whether Zar is up to this . . . he's been under a lot of pressure, trying to hold things together here. Are we doing the right thing, asking him to tackle the Guardian? What if he cracks wide open?"

"The same concern has been on my mind," Spock conceded. "Especially in view of what happened to D'berahan. Zar has not had an easy time of it here."

"So I gathered."

The Vulcan's voice was grim. "But our duty is to restore the time portal using any means possible. Zar has agreed to try, therefore we have no choice but to let him."

"I suppose so," Kirk agreed, reluctantly. He hesitated,

and then on impulse asked, "Spock . . . have you ever thought about whether you did the right thing, contacting Zar?"

The Vulcan raised a surprised eyebrow, and the admiral impatiently shook his head. "No, that's not what I meant, of *course* you did the right thing! Zar was alone in that frozen wilderness, with no chance at a normal life. But . . . suppose he *had* had a normal life. School, a job, friends, relatives . . ."

Kirk turned to stare fixedly out the window, watching the first fingers of darkness crawl down the mountain slopes. "In a case like that, do you think it's . . . fair . . . for a father to contact an adult child? Someone he's seen a few times, but who was never told who his father was?"

The admiral felt the Vulcan's concerned gaze, but did not turn away from the window . . . could not turn away. "I do not know, Jim," Spock said, finally.

"Neither do I," Kirk whispered.

After a long moment, he felt a light touch on his shoulder. "Jim . . . is there anything I can do to help?"

The admiral took a deep breath, then turned back to face his friend. He squared his shoulders. "I don't think so, Spock. Let's find Zar and get on with it."

The Sovren had obviously just concluded his briefing session when the two officers reached his study. Heldeon was halfway through the door, his arm around Wynn, Commander Madon beside him. The rest of the Danreg and Lakreo officers followed. Kirk and Spock nodded to the Danreg chieftain, then went in.

McCoy was sitting on the big inlaid table, talking to Zar, who was surrounded by orderly piles of tactical diagrams, maps, and lists. Spock immediately walked over and immersed himself in studying the battle plans.

"Ready to leave?" Kirk asked the Sovren.

"As soon as I say good-bye to Wynn," Zar said. He rose and left the room, reappearing a moment later with the High Priestess. Kirk's gaze sharpened as he watched them. Neither Zar nor Wynn touched or even looked at each other as they entered the room, but something had changed about the atmosphere between them . . .

Uh-oh, the admiral realized. *I suspect this marriage no longer belongs in the 'in name only' category. This really complicates things.* Kirk gave McCoy an inquiring glance over Spock's oblivious head, and the doctor, guessing his thoughts, nodded silent agreement.

"Are you leaving now?" Wynn was asking, softly.

"In a few minutes," Zar told her.

"Can I watch you go?"

Her husband shook his head. "I don't think that would be a good idea. The Guardian isn't working properly. There is a chance you'd be pulled through with us."

Her chin came up. "All right." She hesitated, then went on, her voice carefully controlled, "My lord, I had hoped that Ashmara would give me knowledge as to whether you should try to return, or not. But She has remained silent, so I have no way of knowing what is best . . . for you, that is. So you must decide."

"Don't worry," Zar said, softly. "I will come back." He raised a hand to brush her cheek, and, turning her head, she kissed his palm.

"I know," she said, steadily. Then she turned and walked out of the room, head high.

Zar stood watching her until the guard closed the door, before he turned to look at Kirk. "All right, let's go."

The admiral glanced down at his former First Officer, who was still intent on the battle plans. He cleared his throat ostentatiously, then, when the other did not respond, bumped the chairleg with his booted toe. "Spock?"

The Vulcan looked up. "Yes, Admiral?"

"Time to go. We've got a universe to save."

Chapter Eleven

EVEN AS HIS FEET felt the shock of landing on Gateway's ashy soil, Zar's mind filled with a terrible, echoing emptiness. He staggered, his bad leg gave way, then he found himself on his hands and knees, gasping.

Wynn! No!

She was gone, erased, as though she had never been. Black oblivion flickered at the edge of his vision, and he had no strength to fight it.

"Zar!" he heard McCoy yell, then, "Grab him, Jim!"

Hands clamped on his shoulders, and Kirk's voice, hoarse with alarm, filled his ears: "Spock—what's wrong with him? The same thing as D'berahan?"

"I do not know—"

"Spock, Jim, turn him over so I can get an airway—"

Vulcan fingers brushed the side of his face, then Spock's voice, tersely: "I should have realized. Suddenly, he has lost contact with Wynn . . . in this time and place, she is dead. You know what a shock that is for the survivor of a bonding, Jim."

The blackness was flooding over him in waves, each stronger than the other. With a final sigh, Zar let it claim him.

But even as he did so, light blossomed in his mind, and a familiar presence grew, filling the void. *Wynn is waiting for you,* it told him, wordlessly. *She is not dead . . . she is just on the other side of this portal. You promised to return to her . . .*

Yes, he thought, remembering. *I did promise . . .*

Breathe, instructed Spock's presence. *I will help.*

With an effort Zar drew a long breath, then another, and as he did so the darkness ebbed and was gone. He still felt Wynn's absence, but now that he understood what had happened, he could stave off the despairing emptiness. Then, with a rush that left him sick and dizzy, he was back in his body, hearing the moan of Gateway's desolate wind, feeling the ground cold beneath him.

Zar opened his eyes to find Spock bending over him.

"You okay now, son?" McCoy's voice asked, and Zar turned his head to see the doctor, with Kirk crouched beside him.

"I'm all right," he tried to say, but his tongue was numb and would not cooperate. He nodded, instead.

After a moment he tried to sit up, and they let him. Spock studied his face intently, his own face still pale from the strain of the mind-link. "I am sorry," Spock said. "I should have warned you. But I did not realize that you and Wynn were bonded."

"Not your fault," Zar said, his voice still a little slurred. "I didn't know, either. Is that what you call it, when someone's mind is always there, in the back of yours? Araen was not esper, so my . . . contact . . . with her was different."

His father nodded. "Yes. On Vulcan when one partner in a bonding dies, the family links mentally to offer support until the remaining partner can adjust to the loss."

Zar shook his head, trying to clear it, then his eyes widened with alarm. "Wynn!" he said. "Did the same thing happen to her? There's nobody to link with her!"

"I do not know," Spock said. "But the solution is for you to return only a heartbeat after you left. In that case, she would barely have time to realize your absence."

"If the Guardian will cooperate," Zar muttered, turning to look over at the time portal. "Let me up."

Still shaky, he climbed to his feet and brushed himself off.

Slowly he limped back and forth, feeling his legs gradually steady. His mind cleared, grew calm. The lack of Wynn was still an aching void within him, but now he was able to shut the pain away, ignore it, so he could concentrate on the task at hand.

Finally, he stopped before the portal and stood braced against the desolate wind, his scarlet cloak whipping behind him, staring up at the stars through its central opening. Memories of his last time on Gateway ran through his mind.

Off to his right he could see the outcropping of rock where he and Spock had hidden from the Romulans, cramped into a tiny space for hours. Over there was the place where he had struggled with Tal, the Romulan leader. And where he stood now was the place where Spock had joined minds with him, to tell his son the truth about the Vulcan's encounter with Zarabeth . . . that they had shared something very special. That Spock had, in that time, in his own way, loved her.

That was when he told me he was proud of me . . .

Zar turned at the sound of a familiar *wheep.* "Kirk to *Enterprise,*" the admiral was saying. The younger man wondered where he'd gotten the communicator, then decided Kirk must have cached it against their return.

"Enterprise. Scott here."

"How long were we gone, Scotty?"

"About fifteen minutes, Admiral. Did ye find the laddie?"

Kirk looked over at Zar with a wry grin. "You couldn't call him a 'laddie' anymore, but yes, we found him."

"Good. Shall I order you beamed up, sir?"

"No, as long as we're here, we'll make the attempt now. If I don't check back in an hour, or if the time waves reappear, get the *Enterprise* out of this system and contact Admiral Morrow for further instructions, Scotty. Understand?"

"Aye, Admiral. Good luck, sir."

"Thanks, Scotty. Out."

Zar moved closer to the monolithic stone structure; he was now within touching distance of the Guardian. He heard the soft slither of rock beneath bootheels and turned to find Spock at his side. He tried to smile at his father, but his mouth was so dry it felt more like a rictus. "It's embarrassing to admit, but I'm scared," he muttered.

"Logical, under the circumstances. So was I," Spock said.

Quickly, before he could change his mind, Zar placed both hands on the stone.

It was like handling his tricorder—nothing sentient responded to his cautious mental probe. Nothing at all.

This isn't right, Zar thought, probing harder. *When I touched it before, it was alive—even if artificially constructed, it was self-aware.*

He leaned his forehead against the portal, between his spread fingertips, and tried again, putting all his effort into breaking through. The external world faded, grew dim and remote, then was gone altogether.

It was as though he stood (but he had no physical body) within a near-infinite black cavern, where occasional streaks of light brightened, then dimmed, with no pattern that he could see. His mind was only a tiny dart of white light, trying to find its way through an immense invisible maze.

The real Guardian must be here somewhere, he thought. *After all, it is tied to its physical being, even as I am. Or is it?*

Flashes of light exploded beside him, or through him, but the "thoughts" they represented were sterile and artificial —machine-generated, reminding Zar of Spock's description of Vejur.

Where is it? he wondered, sending his little dart of light faster, moving deeper into the illimitable labyrinth. *Where?*

Zar bounced off barriers, careened into dead ends, hurtled down blind alleys, searching . . .

He was now so deep into the machine-generated portion of the entity that he was in danger of being lost—the link between his physical body and his mental self stretched perilously thin. *Can't go much farther . . . have to find it soon. Where?*

He wished he had asked Spock to link with him. The Vulcan could have amplified the connection between his mind and his body . . . too late now.

Can't . . . go . . . much farther—

—What's that?

In the distance, he "saw" something different—rapid-fire pulses of golden light stretching into infinity. They dimmed even as Zar watched. He threw himself toward them, praying his own mind-body link would hold.

Made it!

The moment he "touched" the gold light, Zar knew he had reached his goal. The warmth, the sentience, even the humor belonged to a living, self-aware being—he had located the Guardian.

Chaotic images danced in his mind, assaulting him with their alienness—he had to pull back, shielding his consciousness, lest he be pulled under, his own identity submerged by the vast, ancient mentality he now touched.

Guardian? he projected the thought. *There is a problem. Time is not running correctly. Come back with me. You must resume your duties.*

No response.

The flashes of aurulent light stretched thinner. . . thinner . . .

Alarmed, Zar realized that even the Guardian itself was in grave danger of being lost in this . . . dimension? Plane? There were no words to describe this immensity—and he knew he could not follow the time entity any farther. His own mind-body link was too fragile . . .

Guardian! he demanded, thrusting the thought as he would have aimed a sword-stroke. *Link with me! I know the way back!*

A slight flicker of awareness . . .

Yes! he insisted. *I know the way back. I have been seeking you. Come with me, before you are lost!*

IMPLEMENTING PRIMARY PROGRAMMING SUBROUTINE 'UNIVERSE/DIMENSION/CONTINUUM OF ORIGIN—RETURN' TO FACILITATE RETURN OF SELF AND ORIGINATORS TO TEMPORAL DISPLACEMENT LOCATION. GUIDE IS NOW AVAILABLE.

Zar caught only fragments of the Guardian's thought processes, but he understood enough to know that it was accepting his offer. As swiftly as he could, he reversed "direction" and headed back.

Almost immediately, he knew he was in trouble. The energy he had expended to reach the Guardian had left him with little in reserve. It was like trying to swim against a violent current . . . he kept going, but his mind-body link was now so weak that tracing it back was difficult. Zar struggled, trying not to panic, using the Vulcan mental disciplines Spock had taught him long ago to help him focus his energy and calm his mind.

Serenity . . . peace . . .

Starlight, cool water, shadows on sand . . .

Strive without anxiety, focus effort, harness energy . . . the mind rules . . . the mind rules . . .

He was making progress, but so slowly! And the link was fading, even as he tried to summon the power to renew it . . . fading . . .

Suddenly the strength was there, his for the using—not his own energy, but another's. For a wild moment Zar thought that the Guardian had recognized his danger and was aiding him, but as he drew on that other power, he recognized it for Spock's.

Of course he'd monitor . . . I should have realized . . .

He was moving again, faster and faster, as his mind-body link was renewed. Moving—and the Guardian was still following him.

The surrounding darkness grew lighter . . .

He was—back!

Gradually, Zar grew aware of the roughness of stone against his hands and cheek, and the pressure of Vulcan fingers against his temple. He could hear the wind, feel its cold touch. Opening his eyes, he saw the bluish-gray rock, and the ruins through the central opening.

The Sovren caught his breath with relief, even as his legs threatened to buckle under him. Bracing himself against the Guardian, he levered himself up off the stone monolith. As he did so, Spock dropped his hands. Zar turned his head, met his father's eyes, dark and exhausted in a haggard, drawn countenance. *He looks like I feel.*

Zar swallowed some of the dryness in his mouth, then opened it to thank the Vulcan for rescuing him—

—just as the fabric of the universe around them exploded into a million insane pieces.

I'm going mad, was his first thought as he lurched back, closing his eyes, flinging his arms over his face, trying to hide from the searing barrage of color now erupting from the time portal. Color and sound—taste and smell—they all jumbled together, mixed and ran like water-soluble pigments on a palette held beneath a waterfall.

Several times Zar had been wounded so badly that he'd become delirious before he had regained consciousness . . . this was a little like that, but infinitely worse. He grunted with pain, heard Spock's agonized gasp, then stole a glance and saw the Vulcan reel and go to his knees, evidently blinded by the shrieking flashes of color.

Still shielding his eyes, Zar staggered forward, made a wild grab for his father's arm, and dragged him up. Ten weaving, stumbling steps, all the while praying his leg would hold out, then he thrust Spock into the shelter of a crumbling wall and followed him.

Once out of sight of the Guardian, the assault changed, invading Zar's mind with callous disregard for his individuality, his sanity—not to mention his privacy. He struggled to remain conscious, but couldn't tell whether or not he succeeded . . . it was like being thrust, awake, into an unending nightmare:

Thunder boomed and insect wings whispered, dissolving into splashes of acid vermilion and icy aquamarine . . . leaving the bitter coppery taste of blood in his mouth to send mocking kisses trailing down his skin . . .

. . . even as the cosmos formed around him, ballooning outward from a single mathematical point containing near-infinite mass to spawn a seething vortex of embryonic galaxies, fleeing each other at terrible velocities . . .

. . . and he was born and died in a single instant, his mind simultaneously crushed and expanded, sifted and tossed aside, all that he was, that he had striven for, recognized and rejected by intellects as far above his own as his was above an insect's—leaving him hollow, drained and shamed . . .

. . . to stare, helplessly mesmerized, at an orange one-

dimensional universe filled with jade green dots, which began to shimmer and waver, looming and receding—then he was rushing at warp-speed down a black, contracting hole in space, toward a radiant, welcoming Light. I'm dead, he thought, with unshakable certainty. The twentieth century metaphysicists were right . . .

. . . but just as he reached the Light, and realized that it was actually a portal to Somewhere Else, it slammed shut with a bang that made him wince, leaving him in the dark, eternally alone and abandoned, lost now beyond any finding, lost, lost . . .

Zar returned to awareness slowly. He realized he was sprawled face-down, his head and upper chest resting across something warm and living, his belly and legs on something cold and unyielding. Harsh breathing and low, moaning gasps mixed with the sound of the wind. Zar's teeth fastened in his lower lip as he tried to move his arms, and the moans stopped. Only then did he realize he had been making them.

The harsh, pain-filled breaths were coming from Spock, who was crumpled beneath him. Zar quickly pushed himself up, realizing he must have shoved the Vulcan down and then fallen on him when the worst of the—the whatever it was—hit.

Kneeling, he carefully turned the other over, gently brushed some of the ashy dirt from the austere features. "Father?" he whispered hoarsely. "Are you all right?"

It was nearly a minute before Spock slowly opened his eyes, and it was another before they became rational. He coughed, trying to stifle the sound, and Zar supported him. "Jim? McCoy?" he asked finally, his voice low and rough.

"I don't know," Zar replied. "They were farther away than we were . . ." For a moment he was tempted to shout for the admiral and the doctor, but he reconsidered. It might not be a good idea to advertise their position, and the fact that they were still alive. "I don't like the sound of that cough," he continued, keeping his voice low. "Is your chest all right?"

The Vulcan nodded, wiping his mouth. "Only dust." His

voice was a husky wheeze. "I . . . inhaled it when you fell on me. Knocked my wind out."

"I'm sorry. Can you move your arms and legs?"

Spock tried, stiffly. "Yes," he said, his voice growing stronger. "I am essentially undamaged. And don't apologize. I suspect you may have saved my life. Although," he repressed a groan as he struggled to sit up, and only succeeded with Zar's help, "I would not care to repeat the experience. What happened?"

"I don't know. I was just getting ready to thank you for bringing me back—thus saving *my* life—when something erupted out of the portal. I remember stumbling back, and yanking you out of range, and—that's all. Except for a lot of . . . hallucinations. Rather . . . unsettling . . . ones."

Spock nodded. "You, too?"

Zar frowned. "The question is, what do we do now?"

"Locate Jim and McCoy. Have you seen my tricorder?"

"No." The younger man crawled over to peer out at the time portal. "Yes. It's lying beside the Guardian."

"Do you see any sign of our attackers?"

"Nothing visible out there. But that may not mean anything. I don't believe those . . . things . . . had physical bodies."

"Can you reach the tricorder?"

"I . . . think . . . so . . ." As he spoke, Zar dropped to his belly and wriggled closer to the time portal. Finally, when he had run out of cover, he made a long arm, a quick rush, and then beat a hasty retreat to their hideout. "Got it."

The Vulcan took the instrument and studied its readouts for a moment, then nodded, obviously relieved. "I pick up two live humans. Jim and McCoy."

"What about the others? The ones from inside the Guardian?"

"Readings are fluctuating . . . at times it seems as though there are energy surges near the portal . . . but it is not a type of energy I have encountered before. At other times, the readings are closer to that of matter . . . but there are differences." His eyebrow climbed. "Fascinating. Now I am getting readings that show a strange ambiguity somewhere between the two states."

"Where are Jim and Leonard?"

"That way," the Vulcan nodded over at a heaped pile of ruins. "We should—" He broke off, listening.

"Zar," a warm, feminine voice was calling. "Spock? I'm sorry that happened, it wasn't intentional. Come out, please."

I am *dead,* Zar thought, feeling the blood drain out of his face. *Or mad.*

He bit his lip fiercely, telling himself that he *couldn't* be hearing that particular voice. Then he saw Spock's expression, and realized that the Vulcan heard it, too. *Collective hallucination? Or are we* both *dead?*

"That sounds like . . ." Spock began, then shook his head, frowning. "I must be mistaken."

"You're not," Zar assured him. "I don't know how this could happen, or why, but that voice was the only other one I ever heard for the first nineteen years of my life. I *couldn't* mistake it."

Heart pounding with a wild mixture of hope and apprehension, he edged over to peer out again.

Zarabeth.

She was standing about twenty paces from the Guardian of Forever, her pale hair brushing the shoulders of her fur jacket, her blue eyes eagerly scanning the area around her. With a gesture so familiar that it hurt Zar to watch, she raised a hand to push back a strand of wind-tossed hair. "Zar?" she called, anxiously. "Son?"

The Sovren sagged back against the stone, his palms pressed against his eyes. "Oh, Goddess," his voice emerged as an agonized whisper. "It *is*. It's Mother. Zarabeth is standing right in front of the portal."

In a moment Spock moved past him, stared for a long moment, then turned back, propping himself up against the wall as though he, too, needed its support. The Vulcan rubbed his temples wearily. It was nearly a minute before he spoke, and when he did, there was a trace of old pain in his voice. "Zar, you know as well as I do that cannot be Zarabeth out there."

Anger flared. "Why not?" Zar demanded. "She came out of the Guardian, didn't she? Maybe it went back and got her before she . . . before." The Sovren glared at his father, stubbornly refusing to acknowledge what he already subconsciously knew was the truth.

Spock just stared back at him, wordlessly.

Finally Zar broke their locked gaze and sighed. "You're right, damn you. But she looks so *real*. Just as I remember her, on her last dawn, when she stood in the cave mouth waving—I had left her asleep, and my mind was on the hunt, so I didn't go back to say a proper good-bye . . . you can imagine how much I regretted *that* later . . ."

The Vulcan's gaze sharpened. "More proof that we are presented with an illusion. I saw her as she was when *I* said farewell to her—when she was some twenty years younger than the Zarabeth you just saw."

"Spock? Zar? Please, we need to talk."

The Sovren winced and resisted the urge to clamp his hands over his ears. "You're saying that the image we both saw was extracted from our minds. That the . . . beings . . . who came out of the time portal gave us an illusion we would both recognize."

"Yes."

"To lure us out so they can finish us?"

The Vulcan shook his head. "I think not. If they had wanted us dead, we would indeed be dead. Their mental power was . . . beyond anything I have ever encountered. I believe instead that we may have fallen prey to some kind of unintentional backlash caused by their arrival through the Guardian, and that one of them has taken Zarabeth's form to reassure us."

"So, what are you suggesting?" Zar asked, raising an eyebrow. "That we just walk right out there?"

"Yes, I believe that would be our wisest course," Spock said, unruffled.

"Zar? Spock? Please . . ."

"And I worried that *I* was crazy," Zar muttered.

"They can find us, even if we attempt to hide," his father pointed out. "Whereas a demonstration of trust and goodwill may improve our situation." Spock stood up and began brushing himself off. "I only hope that Jim still has his communicator and has checked in with Mr. Scott. His hour time-limit passed nine minutes and thirty-five seconds ago, and I have no desire to be marooned here on Gateway."

"We could go back to Sarpeidon through the Guardian," Zar remarked, shaking the dust out of his cloak. He looked over at the Vulcan, deadpan. "I'm always in need of good officers. Want a job? Can you handle a sword?"

Spock's mouth quirked. "I have, although I am better with other ancient Vulcan weapons. Let's go."

Together, they stepped out from behind the wall, and headed toward the woman standing before the time entity.

"Zar! Darling, oh, I've missed you so!" She ran toward them. "Spock, I've found you again!"

Despite his resolution to hang back, Zar found himself a step or so in the forefront. As 'Zarabeth' reached him, he moved forward, determined to grab her, thus brutally shattering the illusion—and then berate the creatures that had given him that one moment of cruel hope.

His hands encountered living flesh, and a moment later she was in his arms, hugging him frantically. "Oh, Zar! Son!"

Zar's mouth dropped open with blank astonishment—he had convinced himself that he would embrace only air. Over her shoulder he saw Jim Kirk and Leonard McCoy step out of the ruins and walk over to stand beside the Vulcan. All of them—even Spock—wore expressions similar to his own.

She was so *perfect*—the color of her hair (white strands liberally mixed with the gold, a pale, silken helmet); the feel of her fur parka (white fur from a *bardok*, he had made it for her himself, as a present); even her scent (oilsmoke and sweet herbs).

Zar permitted himself a last hug, then he kissed the smooth cheek gently, and stepped back. "Thank you," he said, holding his voice steady with an effort. "I never got to say a proper farewell to her, but now I feel that somehow I have. Now, please . . . who are you?"

'Zarabeth' looked up at him, then over at the others.

"I—well, I am not an 'I,' strictly speaking . . . but sometimes, yes, I can be . . ." she seemed to be arguing with herself, "but suppose I just say 'I,' all right?"

Zar cast a sidelong glance at Kirk and Spock, then shrugged. "Certainly."

"I created this world . . ." the being said, looking around, as if noticing for the first time the heaped ruins, the desolation, and the perpetual night. "My, it's gotten rundown, hasn't it? Where was I—we? Oh, yes . . . my—our—creation, all of it. Including the . . ." It frowned, looking over at the time portal. "What do you call yourself?"

"The Guardian of Forever," the time entity responded, its voice deep, reverberating, and somehow . . . *content.*

"You built the Guardian?" Kirk asked, trying to keep the skepticism out of his voice.

"Oh, yes . . . that is, well . . . it built itself, really. We just defined the parameters and provided the initial . . . there are no words in your language . . . 'programming' comes closest, I suppose."

As the alien spoke, Zar had stepped back to stand with the others. "Are you all right?" he whispered to McCoy.

"Fine," the doctor answered, *sotto voce.* "We weren't as close to it as you two. The minute those crazy colors burst out, we took cover. And apparently, from what Spock just told us, that mental contact was much more devastating to anyone with esper abilities than it was to us."

"Didn't it knock you out?"

"Nope. Just shook us up a little. Jim called Scotty and asked him to stand by. We were just coming to find you when you two stepped out of the ruins."

"Why did you create the Guardian?" Kirk was asking. "And *when* did you create it?"

"When?" 'Zarabeth' looked around vaguely. "When did we? I can't say . . . but *I* can . . . yes, tell them . . . why should we bother telling them anything!" The creature frowned. "Don't confuse me, please. You're *always* confused!"

Zar listened to the alien bickering with itself, and realized that it had meant the "we" quite literally. They were conversing with a number of vastly different personalities.

"Now, what did they want?" the creature asked, helplessly.

It seemed to listen. "Oh, yes. Well, we made the—what was it?—the Guardian—because this universe had just gotten so *small,* you know. No challenges left at all, nothing to see or do. There were a lot more of us in those days . . . back when there weren't nearly so many stars and galaxies as there are now, Admiral, but I'm afraid I can't tell you *when* more precisely than that . . . it's been too long."

The entity began to blur slightly around the edges, as though it were dissolving. "So we needed something to do, somewhere new to go. First we used it to journey in Time, but we ran out of that pretty quickly, because there wasn't a whole lot of it yet . . . only a couple of . . . billion, what's your word . . . 'years'? Yes. But then we decided to sample other *dimensions,* each of which was its own complete universe . . . layered and overlapping, like the pages in one of those old-fashioned books you're so fond of, Admiral."

The alien was just a soft glob of shimmering white light, now, but 'Zarabeth's' voice continued unchanged. Zar wondered for a moment whether he were actually hearing it with his ears at all, but there was no way to judge. Whatever form of communication these creatures were using, his mind was *perceiving* it as speech.

"And the Guardian transported you there?" Spock asked.

"Yes . . . but we kept getting farther *away.* Finally we found a continuum we rather liked . . . such lovely bridges between the stars, all of it laced together with tachyons, and so *compact* . . . and we stayed there for awhile . . . I guess perhaps a long time? Yes, a long time. Long, long, it was long."

"And you just now returned to this universe?" Kirk gave Spock an uneasy glance. Zar could sympathize with the admiral's concern. These creatures were so powerful

. . . but so confused. There was no way to predict what their next whim might be.

"Yes, and it's wonderful to be back," the alien creature was saying. "We wanted—It was *my* idea first!—Some of us who were left, that is, wanted to come home. Sentimental, yes, but isn't that one of the traits of old folks in your species, too, Admiral Kirk?"

"Uh, yes," Kirk said, glancing at the light-glob, then quickly away again, blinking. The creature was now an eye-searing violet patch. Gazing at it, Zar had the uncanny feeling that if he were to step into it, he'd fall through it to . . . somewhere else.

"Look," the alien voice chided itself, "you've let your form slip. It's painful for them to look at you. That's *very* rude." The light began drawing in on itself, coalescing. "My apologies," it said. "It's been so long since we were here, I'm a little rusty on the physics in your—our—universe. Perhaps something larger? Yes, a bit larger might be easier to maintain . . . that's better."

Suddenly, a pale yellow house stood before them.

Kirk gasped, visibly paling. "That's—that's my home! The farmhouse in Iowa. But it burned down . . ." Dazedly, the admiral walked forward, laid a hand on the neatly painted porch railing, shook it. *"Solid—*I can't believe it!"

He bounded up the steps, raced inside. Faintly, they heard his voice. "Spock, Bones! It's all here! The old piano, the rugs Winona's great-great-grandmother wove! The dent in the stair railing from that time Sam and I tacked up the carpet runner and tried to ski down the steps!"

A moment later he was back outside, flushed and wide-eyed. "How did you *do* that? It's perfect!"

"Thank you, but the credit is yours, Admiral," Zarabeth's voice answered him. "Your mind is most detailed."

"With all due respect," Spock addressed the alien, "I venture to remind you that we have been exposed to many different shapes and varieties of sentient life over the years. I see no reason why you cannot assume and remain in your natural form to speak with us. I seriously doubt we would find it shocking or repugnant."

"That's a good idea!" the creature said, enthusiastically, but then its voice became filled with regret. "We—I—forgot. If only we *could* appear as ourselves again, Mr. Spock . . . but it's been so long, I'm afraid we've forgotten what our natural forms *are.*"

"*I* remember!" came a different voice, a hostile, slightly mad voice from behind them, and, turning, they saw a flame-colored shadow wavering atop a fallen column. "But nobody ever listens to me, so I'm not going to tell you!"

"*That's* where you've been," said the voice from the house. "We—I—thought you had been lost during the transition."

"No, you didn't," objected the flame-shadow. "You just don't want to admit that you forgot me!"

"My programming would not permit that," the Guardian of Forever interjected, sounding a bit miffed. "I returned all of you safely."

"At *any* rate," the house-alien continued loudly, in the tone of one who has been interrupted one time too many, "it's much easier for us to borrow shapes from your minds."

"How many of you are there?" Kirk asked. "Do you have names?"

"There are—eight—is that all?—of us," the creature said. "And our names for ourselves are . . . not translatable into verbal speech."

"I call them the Originators," rumbled the Guardian. "If I may interject a comment?"

"Very well," said the house-alien in the careless tone of one speaking to a moderately valuable servant.

"Admiral Kirk," the time portal said, "I very much regret having neglected my duties in this continuum. I am functioning normally again."

"I am glad to hear that," Kirk said.

"However," the time entity continued, "I had no choice in the matter. I had to respond to my primary programming when my Originators contacted me with instructions to locate them and transport them home. Searching a nearly infinite number of dimensions was not an easy task, and required almost all of my capabilities."

"I see," Kirk said, his tone carefully neutral. Zar knew the admiral was thinking about all the deaths the Guardian's absence had caused. "Of course. But, uh, Originator, with so many possible dimensions to choose from, *why* did you wish to return to this one?"

The house began to waver, lose solidity. The alien did not answer immediately. Finally it said, "To everything there is a season, James, as it says in a book sacred to one of your human religions. It was a sentimental whim for the eight of us to wish to end our existence in the same universe we began it."

The house vanished into a pillar of rainbow light. "In other words, Admiral, we have come home to die."

Chapter Twelve

JAMES KIRK WATCHED the farmhouse where he had spent his childhood vanish, and felt fear growing inside him like something with a life of its own. His sixth sense (which he'd come to trust as fully as the conscious, rational part of his mind) told him that these creatures posed a considerable danger. *Calm down, Jim,* he ordered himself silently. *They've done nothing threatening, unless you count the backlash of their arrival, but I believe them when they say that was not intentional.*

But all his instincts still whispered a warning. "I see," he said, finally, to the rainbow shimmer. "Are you speaking of something imminent? You, uh . . . don't seem ill to me . . . but . . ." He spread his hands.

"He's insulting us!" flame-shadow said, indignantly. "Illness, indeed! Speaking as if we were mere matter!"

"As we may indeed have been." The voice emanating from the farmhouse sounded stern. "Does any of you truly remember?"

Apparently none of them did, for there was silence except for the wind.

"No, Admiral," the stern, distant voice (the one Kirk was coming to think of as "the rational one") continued finally, "we are not sick, but even for creatures such as ourselves, entropy catches up eventually. We are . . . tired. Winding down . . ."

"Your form's lapsed again," flame-shadow pointed out rudely.

"So it has . . ." The shimmer elongated, shifted, and then a man stood there before the admiral, a slightly taller, broad-shouldered man with dark blond hair and hazel eyes the same shade as Kirk's own. He was grinning—that same "give 'em hell" impish grin Jim recalled from the stair-skiing attempt.

"Sam . . ." Kirk whispered, his throat tight as he remembered those even white teeth bared in the grimace of agony etched on his brother's features the last time he'd seen them. George Samuel Kirk, Jr., had died years ago on Deneva, one of the victims of an infestation of insanity-producing parasites.

A moment later Kirk felt Spock's hand grip his shoulder, steadying him. "Are you all right, Jim?" The Vulcan glanced over at the Originator. "The image you are projecting is causing him pain," he protested.

"But it is a true image," flame-shadow protested mockingly. "How can the truth be harmful?"

Kirk straightened his shoulders. "It's all right, Spock. Thanks." He forced himself to look directly at 'Sam.' "I gather you intend to make this world your final resting place?"

"Well, no, Admiral," the creature said. It shifted, its horizontal outline wavering, and then another handsome, broad-shouldered young man stood beside the image of Kirk's brother. *Gary!* Kirk recognized the image of his best friend from his Academy days.

Commander Gary Mitchell had met his death soon after Kirk had assumed command of the *Enterprise*. He had been the victim of a dangerous "god-complex" Mitchell had developed shortly after they had tried to take the ship through the energy "barrier" at the edge of the galaxy. As the strange syndrome developed, Gary grew more and more powerful, even as his humanity diminished; finally, he had become such a threat that his best friend had been forced to hunt him down.

Oddly, seeing Gary's image steadied Kirk. *These are alien beings,* he reminded himself. *This is not Sam, this is not Gary! No matter how perfect these images seem, this is no different than looking at a holo of my brother or Gary.*

Now 'Mitchell' spoke with the querulous, uncertain manner they had heard before from one of the Originators. "We want—at least *I* want—to find our planet of origin again. A beautiful place . . . at least, I think it was . . ."

"You mean *this* isn't your home world?" McCoy gestured at the ruins around them.

"Fools! Why are we bothering with them?" snapped flame-shadow.

"You maundering ancient," said a different voice from any they had yet heard, a cold, contemptuous voice that made the hairs at the back of Kirk's neck stir. Before their eyes another form coalesced. An ancient Vulcan woman, with an ascetic, implacable face, and two broad streaks of white running through her black hair. *T'Pau!* Kirk identified the image of the Vulcan head-of-state. "You no more remember our world of origin than *I* do," she said to 'Gary.' "But we will recognize it when we find it, if we must search for a millennium."

"No, Dr. McCoy," came the measured, distant tones of the rational one, "this is not our home world. We only created this one as a base of operations for our servant, the Guardian."

"And it's gotten so *rundown,*" complained a new voice, and suddenly a slender woman was there, wearing modern clothing, with salt-and-pepper hair and an intelligent, disdainful face. *Jocelyn,* Kirk identified the image, even though he hadn't seen Leonard McCoy's ex-wife in nearly twenty years. "Of course we can't stay *here,*" she said, scornfully.

McCoy had gone pale, his lips thinned, his eyes narrowed. The doctor's divorce had not been an amicable one. "Bones," Kirk said, in a warning undertone. "That's *not* Jocelyn, remember."

McCoy nodded, slowly relaxing. "Would you really search for a thousand years?" he asked the rational one.

The image of Sam Kirk smiled faintly. "If necessary."

"But you said you were dying. Doesn't seem like it to me."

"Time," said the rational one, "is one of the most relative things in this universe, or hadn't you realized that yet, Doctor? Death does indeed seem imminent when you compare a possible thousand years with billions, wouldn't you agree?"

"Why bother to explain to them?" snarled flame-shadow. "I can't believe how much time you are wasting talking to them!"

"But . . . that is, perhaps . . . talking to them is . . . is . . . not a waste," the Gary Mitchell image stammered. "It would be easier, you know . . . more ethical . . . that is, more comfortable, if they want to help . . . if they agree to assist us . . ."

"Assist you with what?" Kirk demanded.

"Yes, with what?" Zarabeth said, reappearing. *That's six of the eight,* Kirk thought. "Are the non-sentients still here?" She turned to regard the four of them. "Oh. I thought they were gone. Or did I forget again?"

"We don't need them," T'Pau stated. "Or, considering the physical laws of this continuum . . ." she trailed off, uncertainly.

"Yes, we do," said the rational one wearing Sam's image. "Expending the energy necessary for travel would greatly shorten our remaining time."

"But the indignity!" protested Jocelyn. "Depending on non-sentients? I won't do it."

"Perhaps the, uh . . ." Mitchell waved tentatively at the Guardian. "You know . . . maybe it could . . ."

"The distances between stars have altered too much for us to provide coordinates," said the rational one.

"But travel in that orbiting vehicle?" T'Pau asked, doubtfully. "How primitive. Suppose the non-sentients don't agree to transport us?"

"Then we take it," flame-shadow said. "They can't stop us."

The Enterprise . . . *they're talking about commandeering my ship for their insane search for a world that may not even exist anymore!* Kirk realized, feeling the cold lump of fear congeal in his stomach. "Now, just a minute," he said. "I can sympathize with your desire to reach your ancient home, and it may be that the Federation will choose to assist you in your search. But my ship is on a mission—"

"You may have no choice, Admiral," the Sam image quietly warned him. "My . . . comrades . . . can be a trifle . . . capricious."

I'll bet, Kirk thought, bitterly. *What the hell am I going to do?*

Something nudged his elbow. The admiral glanced sideways at Zar, only to see him raise an eyebrow and jerk his head at the other side of the clearing.

"Will you excuse us for a moment?" Kirk said. "We . . . uh, we need to discuss the best way of handling your request."

"Why are we *bothering* with them at all?" flame-shadow whirled on Sam. "Let's go!"

Kirk felt *something* brush the edges of his mind. Whatever it was, it made flame-shadow shrink into itself, silent. "Certainly, Admiral," the rational one said. "By all means."

When they reached the other side of the clearing, Zar sat down, rubbing his left thigh with a grimace. "We've got to talk," he said.

"But they'll 'hear' us," McCoy said, tapping the side of his head. He sank down beside the younger man with a sigh.

"That cannot be helped," Zar said. "Besides, I doubt they will bother listening in. They're very sure of themselves."

"Yes, they are," Kirk agreed, grimly. "What's up?"

"I've been picking up the mental and emotional emanations from the two non-physical Originators—the ones we haven't yet seen." Zar's voice was a strained whisper. "If several of the ones we've been speaking with appear irrational or senile, by humanoid standards, then these two are completely deranged. They're mad, viciously so, and far more dangerous than the other six put together. They *can't* be allowed to stay here."

"Well, what do you suggest we do, Zar?" McCoy asked sarcastically. "Politely ask the entire lot to leave this continuum? Damn it, they could erase us all with a single impulse! Those things can generate matter and wipe it out as easily as I could trigger a phaser!"

"Zar's right," Kirk said. "I'm certainly not going to tamely hand the *Enterprise* over to them so they can warp off through an unsuspecting galaxy!"

"Maybe we can convince 'em that the world they're looking for is Klinzhai and dump them off there," McCoy suggested, cynically. "Give the Klingons something to worry about besides making trouble for us."

Kirk ignored the doctor. "We can't threaten, bribe, or coerce them," he said, slowly. "Could we influence them? Appeal to their better natures?"

"What makes you think they have any?" McCoy growled.

"Because if they didn't, they wouldn't have bothered to speak to us at all. They'd have just forced us to do as they wished."

"Well-reasoned, Jim," Spock said. "It is clear that some of them, at least, wish us to help them willingly. They do not want to mentally compel us."

"I agree," Zar said. "By the way, it would help in discussing them if I knew whose images they've assumed."

Kirk briefly identified the four Originators.

"Sam is the most rational of them, and seems to have considerable influence over the others," Spock pointed out.

"Gary, also," Zar said.

"You should begin your appeal with those two, Jim," Spock said.

"So I'm elected to do the talking?" Kirk smiled humorlessly. "I don't recall volunteering."

"R.H.I.P.," McCoy pointed out. "Besides, you're the best Starfleet's got at this kind of thing."

"All right." Kirk got to his feet and shivered, pulling his

cloak around him. "I only hope my best is good enough, this time."

As they walked back toward the waiting Originators, a rock shifted under Zar's boot, throwing his weight onto his bad leg. He grunted with the pain, then cursed under his breath. McCoy caught his arm as he staggered. "You okay?"

"That meld took a lot out of me," the Sovren admitted. "And even the peripheral contact with those two Originators . . ." He shuddered at the memory.

"You look terrible."

"I don't doubt it. I've ridden home from a day on the battlefield in better shape than I am now."

As Kirk, Spock, and McCoy moved to stand shoulder to shoulder before the rational one, Zar limped around to the side, stopping next to the time portal. He felt drained, both physically and mentally. He was near exhaustion, and his leg ached savagely.

Feels as though I've been awake for two days . . . not five or six hours, he thought. He remembered waking that morning, to find Wynn lying beside him, watching him as he slept. *Will I ever see her again?*

If only I could get back, he thought wearily, *and make it through alive, things would be different. Damn it, I want to live, now. Talk about irony . . .*

To take some of the strain off his leg, he dared to lean his shoulder against the time portal.

"Have you decided whether you will help us, Admiral?" the Sam Kirk image said, finally.

Kirk's eyes narrowed. "I don't think you realize what you're asking," he said, evenly. "Or that you comprehend the ramifications of your return."

Sam's image frowned uncertainly. "Ramifications?"

"The effects of your return on this universe. More than a thousand beings have already died because the Guardian was searching for you. Your people are so powerful, and so easily angered, that they pose a grave threat to this continuum. If you take my ship and begin searching for your home planet, things will only get worse. More will die. Is that what you want?"

"A thousand are dead?" The rational one was obviously disturbed. "Because of us? How can that be?"

"Four hundred and thirty beings on the *Constellation,* swallowed forever by a black hole. Four hundred and thirty more on the *El Nath,* vanished to dust in far less than the blink of an eye. A hundred and eighty-four people—and an entire world of plant and wildlife—on a planet called Kent, incinerated, vaporized, when their sun became a red giant. Twelve scientists who used to live right over *there"*—Kirk spun on his heel and pointed—"are no more, because you forced the Guardian to concentrate its energies on *you,* instead of on its responsibilities to this universe."

Sam and Gary glanced quickly at each other, obviously taken aback. "We . . . did not know that our summons . . . would produce such havoc," Mitchell's image stammered.

"Oh, I'm not finished, yet," Kirk said, inexorably. "What about the people of Kent? You say you want to find your home? What about *their* homes? Obliterated! They'll spend the next months or years crowded into refugee camps —damn it, they've lost everything they had in the world, *plus* the world itself! The morning we left on this mission, there had already been over forty suicides among the survivors."

"There's another death to add to your total, Jim," McCoy put in. "Did you hear that woman screaming that night we spent aboard *Cochise?* She was pregnant, but stayed on the job during the evacuation—went into early labor, and delivered a stillborn boy, right in the corridor, because the infirmary was overflowing with patients in even worse shape—strokes, catatonia, coronaries, and such. The medical staff did all they could, but . . ." The doctor shrugged. "Add that baby's death to your total, Originators."

Zar, picturing the scene, swallowed.

"There is also," Spock said, "D'berahan to consider. She risked her life to contact the Guardian, and now she lies in a coma, with three newborn infants. She may well die, and her children with her."

Zar felt the Guardian of Forever's reaction to Kirk's, Spock's, and McCoy's words through the physical contact between them. Sorrow flowed through the stone, and a question formed in his mind: *Is all this true?*

Yes, he answered, sadly.

I am sorry. The time portal's regret was profound and genuine. *I never wished harm to anyone.*

Zar projected understanding. *You had no choice but to obey them when they summoned you. We know that you could not supersede your programming.*

The image of Sam Kirk considered silently for several minutes before it spoke again. "We did not return to cause death. And we are sorry. But what has happened, has happened. Why do you say that our continued presence will be harmful?"

"Because of your power," Kirk said, his hazel eyes never leaving the ones so like his own. "There is a saying among my people that 'absolute power corrupts absolutely.' You two, who wear the bodies of two men who were honest and decent—tell me the truth. Can you control the others so well that their whims will not cause tragedy before you can stop them? Be honest—*can* you?"

"Why are you listening to this one?" flame-shadow spat. "We are beyond his dim level of understanding! You cannot allow a non-sentient creature to dictate to you!"

The image of Kirk's brother swung to regard the others. "Just because they cannot match our mentality, does not mean they—and others like them—have no right to live out their brief lives in such peace as their squabbling allows them to enjoy."

"Rights?" T'Pau's image was openly scornful. "They may well owe us their very lives! Didn't we seed thousands of those barren, steaming worlds with life-generating molecules? Don't they owe us help now?"

Zarabeth roused herself for a moment. "I think I remember doing that, long ago," she said. "It was like a game, watching to see what life-forms might evolve . . ."

"What are you saying?" Jocelyn was horrified. "That we may be responsible for *them?* What an odious thought!" She

221

glared at McCoy. "They aren't even civilized. You should hear what this one said to his wife the last time they encountered one another!"

"Why, you—" The doctor started forward, blood in his eye, but halted with a jerk when Spock grabbed his arm. "Doctor—"

"Bones—"

McCoy subsided, rubbing his arm and casting a resentful glance at the Vulcan. "Okay, okay . . . but if you Originators think *we're* so uncivilized, you ought to try listening to *yourselves* for a while. You sound like a pack of five-year-olds."

"We don't have to stand for this," flame-shadow hissed. "Let's abandon these four here and re-form aboard their ship. We don't need the crew to run the vessel."

"So what would you do with them?" Sam Kirk asked, heavily. "Toss the crew outside to perish? Leave these four on this decaying worldlet without sustenance? Add another 435 lives to our grim total? I am beginning to believe that the admiral is right. We *would* endanger this continuum and the beings inhabiting it."

"No! You cannot say that!" Jocelyn's image began to blur with her rage. "Think of how long we have waited to come back!"

"Admiral Kirk is lying about those 'thousands of deaths,'" flame-shadow said.

"No, he is not," Gary said, suddenly. "I have touched his mind, and he speaks the truth. He is right. Our presence *has* proved harmful."

"At any rate," T'Pau said, "any casualties were not our fault. Our servant is responsible."

Zar experienced the ripple of sadness that passed through the Guardian at the Originator's words. *You didn't know,* he comforted the time-entity. *All of us have unknowingly done things that we have later regretted . . .*

"And it is now clear to me that our presence may continue to harm this continuum," the rational one said, regretfully. "James Kirk speaks the truth. Search his mind for yourselves," the alien entity invited the others. "You will see that I am right."

"Yes," agreed Gary, speaking in its new tone of certainty, "you know that his mind cannot hide the truth from us. Search it, and see. Search *all* of them, as I did, and you will find the same thing."

All the Originators were silent, then, for several minutes.

Zar felt several minds brush his, sensed unspoken communication passing between the aliens, but it was not on a mental level that he could tap. He received an impression of bitter conflict.

At last the rational one turned to regard Kirk. "We are attempting to convince our comrades to depart."

"Never!" Jocelyn stamped a foot. "I want to go home!"

"If we go home, we will destroy the inhabitants of this universe," Gary said. "Is that what you want? They are, in a way, our children."

"I am beginning to think we should leave, also," T'Pau said, haughtily. "If only to put an end to this tedious bickering."

"Why are we still here?" Zarabeth asked, vaguely. "If we aren't wanted, let's go somewhere else. This place is so dull . . . so drab . . ."

"How can *you* side with these . . . vermin?" flameshadow raged. It began to swell threateningly toward the humans, but Gary quickly stepped between them. Mitchell's shape began to waver, lose form, and then there were two insubstantial shapes, flickering at each other.

Suddenly, as Zar watched, all of the Originators winked out. The air was again filled with a mixed barrage of color, sound, taste, and feeling—hastily, he squeezed his eyes shut.

Moments later, he opened them again, to see three of the amorphous shadows—*Gary, Sam, and which of the others?* —surrounding, enclosing, the remaining Originators. Then the shapes coalesced, merging into one entity.

The single alien form pulsed wildly, and the Sovren caught the fringes of the mental communication passing between the rational one and the Guardian, and an impression of the time-entity's search to obey the Originator's command. The portal came to life, glowing blue-white.

As he watched, the central portion filled with an image —Zar turned away after a single, stomach-wrenching glance. It was not that the new universe the Guardian displayed was in any way *ugly*—it was just that its shapes, colors, and angles were so mind-blastingly *alien* to everything he'd learned to accept as normal and sane . . .

Even the physical laws of that universe, he thought, would be different. Zar tried to picture a continuum where dropped objects never fell, parallel lines quickly crossed, and the inhabitants could perceive and build in four dimensions. He shook his head with a grimace. *It's hard enough managing in this universe.*

"We leave you to your own destiny," the voice of the rational one echoed in his mind. "Farewell, children."

Then, with a final whirl of swirling, prismatic color, the Originators dissolved and flowed through the Guardian's opening like fractured rainbows.

Kirk stood staring after them as the Guardian's central opening flickered back into its normal view of fallen columns and tumbled buildings. "They're gone," he said, as if trying to convince himself. "Damn . . . that was a close one." He fumbled at his belt-pouch and withdrew his communicator. "Kirk to *Enterprise.*"

"*Enterprise* . . . Uhura here."

The admiral grinned affectionately at the little instrument. "Commander, have I ever told you what a lovely voice you have?"

"Sir?" The soft contralto sounded understandably confused. "Uh, no, sir."

"Well, you do. There were times during this past hour when I seriously doubted that I'd ever hear it again."

"Are you all right, Admiral?"

"We're fine, Uhura. Four to beam—"

"No, Jim!" Zar cried suddenly. *"Don't."* He glanced quickly around him, trying to *see* what he had dimly sensed a moment before. *Maybe I am crazy—was it really there?*

"Huh?" Kirk hesitated, then: "Stand by, Commander." He shut the communicator. "Zar, what the hell is it?"

"I don't—" Zar frowned. "Just a moment—" He closed his eyes, sending his awareness spinning out, searching—

—and felt again that brush of non-rationality, of skewed, warped thinking . . . of intense, psychotic paranoia.

Zar swore a barracks oath in Danrei, and saw Spock raise an eyebrow as his universal translator rendered the obscenity. "They're not all gone," he told the others. "I felt them, just now. Two of them stayed behind. I don't think I have to tell you *which* two."

Kirk glanced around, uneasily. "Are you sure?"

"Yes."

"From the frying pan to the fire," McCoy, shivering, whispered. "What the hell are we going to do?"

"Ask them to appear, and find out what they want," Spock replied. He raised his voice. "Originators, we sense your presence. Please materialize, so we may speak with you. What do you want?"

Silence.

Kirk cleared his throat. "Zar . . . are you *sure?*"

The Sovren nodded. "I don't feel anything now, but a minute ago, I am positive I did. Do you think they're still here? Or could they already be aboard the ship?"

The admiral's mouth tightened. "And in what form? Standard procedure dictates I should order red alert, but what good would it do?"

A shape swirled and materialized in front of Kirk. "Absolutely none, Admiral."

As he surveyed the new arrival, James Kirk made an inarticulate sound of pain and closed his eyes. This Originator had appeared as a young woman with black hair, dark, vital eyes, high cheekbones—no classical beauty, but possessed of a vibrant, discerning loveliness. Zar heard the unspoken word "Mom!" echo in the admiral's mind, and realized the alien had taken the form of Winona Kirk.

Even as he watched, the image altered, shrinking into that of a withered, sad shadow of the same woman. She stretched out a blue-veined claw toward Kirk, and spoke in a halting whisper. "Please, Jim . . . let me go home, son. Take me home . . ."

Kirk paled.

"Stop it!" Spock stepped protectively between the alien and his commanding officer, his dark eyes flashing with anger. "I insist that you assume another form. This is cruel. Why should you wish to cause pain? He has done you no harm."

"Oh, but he has," the alien said, its image altering into that of the young Winona Kirk again. "He drove our people away with his lies. He refused to help us reach our home, just as he refused his own mother."

The image crumpled inward, until the aged woman stood there. "Jim? You'll take me home today, won't you?" The alien laughed suddenly, horribly. "You know, Admiral, if you'd had the house rebuilt, and taken her home, she'd still be alive today . . ."

"Shut *up!*" Leonard McCoy surged forward. "This is monstrous!"

Kirk took a deep, shaky breath. "Easy, Bones. Thanks. But I'm . . . all right. I did everything I could for my mother, and, wherever she is now, she understands that. This . . . *thing* . . . doesn't know anything about it." He looked straight at the image of his mother. "Why are you trying to hurt us?"

"Because . . ." The alien shrugged. "Why not?"

"Tell us what we can do to help you," Kirk said. "Do you want us to try and find the planet you originally came from?"

"I don't know . . ." Winona's image said indifferently. "Perhaps . . . or, perhaps not." The creature paused, and the malicious, mocking tone crept back into its voice. "You caused her death, you know."

"No, I did not," Kirk said, his voice filled with conviction, though still harsh with pain.

"Leave him alone!" Zar demanded. "He offered to help you—what more do you want?"

Slowly, the image of Winona Kirk turned to look at him,

and Zar flinched from the soulless depths reflected in its eyes.

"Perhaps we shouldn't talk to the brave admiral, but to you . . . you can't argue about whom you've killed, can you, Sovren?"

The air in front of Zar swirled, and suddenly Araen stood there before him.

It's only the second Originator—just an image, just an image—not real! he told himself, biting his lip against the pain of seeing her there, so much the way he remembered her. The brunette, wavy hair ruffled by the wind, her eyes, lovely, dark, a little wistful . . . she wore only a pale blue shift that left her slender arms bare to the shoulder. Beneath it he could see the tiny points of her breasts . . .

"Stop it," he said, stonily. "I know you're not real."

"Would you like to see the reality?" the alien asked. "Do you want to see her as she was the moment *you* killed her? Swollen and agonized and bloody . . . gasping because she had no strength left to scream?"

Zar shook his head, closing his eyes. "No!"

The being's mind brushed him then, and the picture it described formed behind his closed eyelids. He flinched away from it, instinctively tightening his mental shield against any deeper contact with the Originator. These creatures were decayed and demented beyond the ability of anyone or anything to reason with them. The irrationality of the alien's mind shocked and sickened him, as though he had plunged a hand into something rotting and putrid.

The wave of vertigo came again, gagging him, and he had to clench his teeth to keep from vomiting. *They're going to kill us,* he realized, suddenly comprehending what was happening to him. *This is the way I feel when people I care about are in danger of dying. Spock, Jim . . . Leonard . . . there's no way they'll let any of us go. They'll take the* Enterprise *and do as they please . . .*

He glanced over at the others, saw that they had reached the same conclusion. *If only we could fight them!*

But how could you fight an opponent that had no more

physical reality than a soap bubble—that could exist as matter or energy, as it chose?

"Let's talk about this," Kirk suggested, keeping his voice soothing, conciliatory.

"There is nothing to talk about," the Originator's voices echoed, though neither Winona's nor Araen's lips moved. "You have all betrayed us."

"Why do you say that?" McCoy said.

"We say it because it is true. You envy our powers, you have tried to thwart us. But all of that will be over soon. We have been patient long enough."

Zar shuddered, struggling against the nausea and the growing pain in his head. His vision was blurring, and he had to fight to remain conscious. Dizzily, he braced one hand against the Guardian's stone bulk, knowing that the end could not be far off because his sickness was so intense. Fear warred with the nausea, and he began shuddering.

Fear . . .

As he looked out across the desolate waste that was Gateway, Zar had a sudden memory of crouching beside Spock while they watched two Romulan guards pace slowly back and forth. He had empathically projected his own fear of death at the pair, with such force that it had killed both soldiers. The effort had nearly killed him, too . . .

Would it work with these aliens? he wondered, glancing at the silent, motionless forms of the Originators. *They're already crazy with paranoia—projecting fear at them might be enough to drive them into the equivalent of catatonia, or even death . . .*

But he also knew that the backlash from the aliens' fear would almost certainly kill him—and Spock, Kirk, and McCoy, too.

The bodies of the Originators began to glow.

This is it, Zar knew, instinctively. *What should I do? Have to decide . . .*

He wished that he had time to consult Kirk and the others, but there was no more time. *If I can stop them, I must. I can't let them kill everyone aboard the* Enterprise— *and who knows where else.*

Silently, Zar apologized to the others, then he started breathing faster, deliberately triggering the fight-or-flight reflex in his body. Seconds later, the blood was rushing through his veins and he was shaking, no longer from sickness, but from adrenaline rush.

The Originators began to lose their human shapes, as they shone brighter and brighter—pulsing red, pulsing yellow, pulsing blue-white . . .

Zar shut his eyes, summoning images of death.

Don't, said a voice in his mind. *I will help you against them.*

Startled, Zar focused his attention on the stone beneath his hand. Even through the growing heat from the now-formless aliens, he felt its warmth. *Guardian?* he thought, incredulously.

Yes, the time-entity replied. *They are my creators, but I cannot allow them to become a force of wanton destruction in the universe I have protected for so long. Lend me all your mental strength—this will not be easy.*

You have it, Zar replied, soundlessly. Aloud he yelled, "Spock!" as he reached out toward his father.

By now the two aliens had merged into one livid mass of light and heat—it was like standing near the raw heart of a nova.

He'll never make it, Zar thought desperately, as he gathered his energy, preparing to mind-link with the time portal. *Nobody could get past that inferno now . . . nobody could—*

A hand clamped onto his own, held hard.

Father and son had become one consciousness even as the Originators began to expand, reaching out to obliterate them. In another heartbeat, Zar launched his mind into a link with the time portal, and began channeling all of their combined mental energy into the ancient entity.

They were one with the Guardian as it gathered their combined power to create a physical and mental vortex that lashed out from the time portal's central opening, catching the two aliens off-guard. For a moment both were drawn helplessly toward that churning void—then they began to resist.

As the Originators fought back, the Guardian used more and more power, widening the path of the maelstrom it had created. Zar found himself "pulling" mentally, using all his and Spock's united strength; it was as though the two of them were mentally digging their heels into the ground and trying by main force to haul a mountain toward them.

There was room for neither thought nor fear—only for the effort they were expending. Everything was channeled into the struggle to drag the aliens into the heart of the vortex.

Zar was dimly aware through the mind-link of the sheer magnitude and power of the Guardian—and the ancient time portal was using every scrap of that power.

But it was not . . . going . . . to . . . be . . . enough . . .

Without warning, a tiny measure of additional strength entered the meld—only a thread, but it was enough to tip the balance. Zar felt, rather than saw, the Originators drawn into the very heart of that whirling, writhing nothingness—

—and then they were gone.

The Guardian released his mind, and he withdrew, dissolving the meld. He could hear the time-entity speaking aloud:

"They have joined the others now, so many continua away that they will never find their way back. Please accept my gratitude, Admiral Kirk, Dr. McCoy, Mr. Spock . . . and especially Zar, who helped me realize where my duty lay. I assure you that from now on I will fulfill my responsibilities to this universe to the best of my ability. Again, I thank you."

Chapter Thirteen

As THE ECHOES of the Guardian's voice died away, Zar opened his eyes to find himself slumped against the time portal. Spock, Kirk, and McCoy crouched beside him, their faces filthy and scraped from wind-blown pebbles and grit. The fabric of Kirk's cloak and jerkin was ripped, baring his arm and shoulder. Spock's sleeve was charred and torn, and there was a slash along his right cheekbone; a green trickle slowly welled and dripped. McCoy had torn both knees out of his breeches.

"You all right?" McCoy asked, his question for all of them.

They all nodded.

"You joined the meld," Zar said to McCoy. He shook his head, still dazed. "You and Jim. You were the ones who supplied that last bit of mental energy, weren't you?"

"Don't pin any medals on me," McCoy growled. "I was frozen with terror. If it hadn't been for Jim hauling me over to join you, I'd still be standing there."

"Bull," Kirk said. "I was the one who was immobile, when Bones shook me so hard my teeth rattled, and yelled, 'Don't just *stand* there, we've got to help! Grab Spock's hand!' "

Kirk, Spock, and McCoy climbed slowly to their feet. All three were stumbling with exhaustion.

Zar hesitated, wondering if he could stand. His left leg

was doubled beneath him, and felt like one massive cramp. Spock reached down a hand without comment, and his son grasped it, then painfully pulled himself up, swaying slightly as he waited for the pins-and-needles of returning circulation to cease.

Kirk was speaking with the *Enterprise,* reassuring a worried Commander Scott. "It's *really* over this time, Scotty," he concluded. "And the Guardian is back to normal."

"Thank heaven, sir! Will that be four t' beam up?"

"Yes. Ener—" Kirk broke off at Zar's emphatic headshake. "Stand by, Scotty." He flipped the communicator shut. "You're coming back with us, Zar."

"No, I have to return to New Araen," the Sovren said, then glanced sideways at McCoy. "All I need is that hypo, Doc."

"You'll have to come to sickbay," McCoy said. At Zar's wary expression, he snarled, "Okay! I've accepted the fact that you won't stay, damn your stubborn hide! I just want to take a look at that leg and see if I can't help you. The Guardian is working normally again, it'll send you back a moment after you left, whether you leave now or a year from now!"

Zar shook his head, wondering why he felt so lightheaded. "I appreciate it, Leonard, but—"

McCoy's temper snapped. *"Shut up!* You can't go back like this, you idiot, you can barely stay on your feet! You're in no shape to march off to a battle!" His hand darted up to the younger man's temple, carefully pushing back the hair. "Superficial," he grunted, after a glance, "but it still needs closing." His fingers came away slick with greenish blood. Zar stared at them in surprise, then realized the side of his jaw did feel cold and sticky. Perhaps that was why he was so dizzy . . .

"Didn't even feel it, did you?" the doctor asked. "You're out on your feet, Zar. Now, you're coming back to the *Enterprise* and let me patch you up—even if Spock has to nerve-pinch you and carry you. Right, Spock?"

The Vulcan nodded. "Extraordinary as it may sound, the good doctor and I are in full agreement." A faint curve touched the stern mouth. "However, I would prefer not to have to carry you, son. I am not in the best of shape myself."

Zar managed a weak smile. "All right, you win. Who am I to ruin an historic occasion?"

Kirk, grinning, reactivated the communicator. "Mr. Scott?" he said, then paused as Zar extended a hand.

"May I?"

Puzzled, the admiral handed the little instrument over. "I've always wanted to do this," Zar confided, *sotto voce.* Then he spoke into the communicator. "Mr. Scott, this is Zar."

"Well, hello, laddie. It's good to hear your voice! Are you coming up t' see us?"

"They twisted my arm," Zar said, and grinned. "So please beam us up, Scotty."

When the soft chime of the intercom roused Zar the following morning, all he wanted to do was burrow back under the covers (*I'd forgotten how comfortable these low-gee mattresses are* . . .) and drift back to sleep. *I'm so tired* . . . Instead he sat up and rubbed his eyes gingerly. They ached.

The ache flowed, spreading over him like sweat under armor, dull and unfocused. *Goddess, so tired* . . .

The intercom sounded again. Zar swore and swung his legs out of the bed.

It took him a moment to recall how to activate the intercom. "Yes?" he grunted, not using the visual circuit.

"Sorry to wake you, Zar," came McCoy's voice, "but we ought to get started on those tests. When can you get down here?"

"Uh . . ." he said, trying to consider, his mind fogged like the cloud-shrouded summit of Big Snowy. "Can I have breakfast? And *coffee?* I haven't had coffee in twenty years."

"I'll put in the order. Cream and sugar?"

"Black."

Zar sank down on the edge of the bunk, glancing around the luxurious senior officer's cabin. His leather breeches and woven shirt were still piled on the chair, but on the bureau was a plain black jumpsuit that had not been there. *Spock,* Zar realized. *Nobody else could have come in without waking me.* He dimly remembered Kirk telling him last night that he'd been assigned quarters next door to the Vulcan.

He stretched, every muscle in his body protesting, then padded naked into the head. He spent a few minutes renewing his acquaintance with the controls. *Sonic or water?* he wondered, and, in the end, took both.

Back in paradise . . . he thought, leaning against the softly gleaming wall, while the hot water pelted him. *I'd forgotten how clean it is . . . everything smells so good.*

Memories of standing barefoot on a stone floor, breaking the ice skim on a basin of water so he could bathe, and of outdoor privies in midsummer, assailed him. He glanced longingly over at the Jacuzzi and promised himself a long soak.

But I'd trade it all to see Wynn . . . Zar probed the void in his mind, delicately, the way a tongue is irresistibly drawn to a missing tooth. In this time and place she was dead, and while he was here, part of him was dead, too.

In sickbay, he grimly endured McCoy's seemingly endless tests. When the doctor finally released him, Kirk announced that he was ready to take their visitor on a tour of the *Enterprise.*

Their first stop was, of course, the bridge. Zar glanced around in wonderment. "You weren't kidding when you warned me that things have changed, Jim," he said.

"The entire ship was overhauled and rebuilt several years ago," Kirk said. "It does look a lot different."

"New viewscreens, new uniforms, different control stations . . ." Zar turned around to look at the twin sets of turbo-lift doors. "Even the doors are different."

"The new design is much more efficient," Spock said,

glancing up from the science station, where he was conferring with Lieutenant-Commanders Maybri and Naraht. (Zar still couldn't get over the presence of a living, thinking *rock*—especially one with a sense of humor!)

"Aye, that it is," Scotty said. "Wait'll you see m'engine room, lad. Two stories high, with an elevator in the middle of it."

"It all looks incredibly streamlined," Zar said, "but you know, I miss those red doors."

Kirk grinned wryly. "So do I, now that you mention it. But progress is a necessary evil, I suppose." He gestured at Scotty. "I'll see you later tonight, at dinner. I'm hosting a party for you and the senior officers, Zar. But right now, Mr. Scott is dying to show you his engine room."

"I propose a toast," Dr. McCoy announced, raising his glass. "To the Guardian of Forever. If it hadn't been for it siding with us against its creators, we wouldn't be here tonight."

The rest of the assembled company nodded gravely and drank. Zar sipped the fruit juice Spock had suggested he try—though its orange color had given him pause. It was good, just tart enough to be pleasing.

Thank you for the acknowledgment, a familiar voice echoed inside his mind. *I appreciate it very much.*

Zar hastily swallowed the mouthful of orange juice before he choked on it. *Guardian?* he asked silently. *But we are in orbit, hundreds of kilometers away . . . how can you reach me?*

I have many abilities, the time-entity told him, ambiguously. *But I can cease contact, if you would prefer.*

That's all right. I enjoy conversing with you.

You do? A wash of genuine pleasure colored the ancient creation's thought-pattern. *Then . . . I wonder . . .*

Yes?

Would you consent to 'talk' with me sometimes? There are innumerable worlds and times that I can scan for diversion and learning, but I discovered yesterday that communication with another sentient being is also valuable. My search for my creators made me realize—or, perhaps, remember—that I have been lonely for a very long time.

Zar thought about what it might be like to exist in isolation for millennia and felt a rush of empathy for the time portal. *I would be pleased to 'talk' with you,* he told the Guardian, *but I don't believe you will be able to reach me for long. Soon I will be returning to my home in the past.*

I will be able to reach you, came the confident reply. *And I am grateful for your compassion.*

As suddenly as it had come, the contact was withdrawn.

Zar came back to himself to realize that Uhura, who was sitting beside him, had just repeated his name. He blinked. "I beg your pardon, but I didn't catch what you were saying."

She smiled. "I'm not surprised. You were parsecs away."

"No, only about 400 kilometers."

She looked startled. "Beg pardon?"

Zar shook his head and smiled ruefully at her. "I am sorry, Nyota. I had a lot on my mind, but that is no excuse for boorish behavior. Forgive me, please."

She chuckled, a rich, throaty sound. "I was saying that you've changed," she said. "I remember when we first met . . . you were such a quiet, sweet boy. So earnest . . . and so naive."

"Don't remind me." Zar shook his head reminiscently. "I got tongue-tied every time I looked at you. It took me a whole week to even manage an intelligible response when you said hello to me."

"Will you be staying, this time?"

He shook his head, half-regretfully. "I can't, I'm afraid."

She gave him a quick, knowing glance. "Someone's waiting for you."

He nodded. "My wife, Wynn."

"And you miss her."

The remark was a statement, not a question, but Zar answered it anyway. "More than I thought possible."

Later, they adjourned to the chairs and couches on the other side of the officers' lounge, and talked. Zar was deep in a conversation with Sulu about fencing lunges and parries, when he noticed Uhura's expression as she spoke with his father beside the doorway. He concentrated, and picked up her anxiety, her distress . . . she was terribly concerned about something.

As he watched, she turned away from the departing Spock, then, picking up the skirt of the flowing white gown she wore, hurried toward the door.

"Will you please excuse me, Hikaru?" Zar said, hastily. "I must see Nyota before she goes."

The helmsman nodded. "Sure. Meet me in the gym tomorrow about 0900, and I'll demonstrate that lunge I was speaking of."

"I'll be there."

Uhura moved quickly down the hall, wondering whether she ought to change out of her long dress and evening slippers before going down to sickbay. "Darn shoes," she muttered, and stopped to pull off the opalescent sandals.

"Nyota!"

She turned to see Zar limping after her, concern in his gray eyes. "What's wrong? I sense that you're very upset."

"It's D'berahan," Uhura admitted. "I was just talking with Spock, and he told me that the three babies' telepathic capabilities are becoming arrested. He thinks it's because their mother is not communicating with them. This could end up making them outcasts among their own people."

"What are you going to do?"

"The only thing I can . . . spend more time with them, letting them pick up my thoughts. I'm just afraid that won't be enough." She signaled the lift. "Want to come with me to see them?"

"All right."

"It's so tragic," she said, as they stepped into the turbolift. "I've been trying to provide a sort of mental 'anchor' for the children, but they really need their mother."

They entered sickbay, moving quietly through the hushed quiet and the shadows cast by the nighttime lighting.

D'berahan lay curled in a different position than Uhura had last seen her, but she knew by now that the nurses regularly shifted her limbs and turned the little alien, so this was not unusual. The communications officer smiled as the three infants wriggled out of their mother's pouch in response to her presence. "Hi, kids," she whispered.

The small faces, with their enormous eyes, blinked solemnly up at her. "Can you sense their thoughts?" she asked Zar.

"At this stage, they're really too young to have coherent thoughts, but I can pick up their emotions . . . their appreciation of warmth, and full stomachs, and companionship."

Uhura bent over the enclosure and gently stroked the tiny domed heads, humming softly. "What about D'berahan?"

"She's a complete blank."

"If only someone could help her," she said, smoothing the unconscious alien's fur. She glanced up at her companion as a sudden thought struck her. "Could *you* help her, Zar? Spock told me your esper abilities are much stronger than his."

He hesitated, and Uhura immediately regretted her impulsive question. *He looks so exhausted,* she thought, studying the lines of fatigue in his face, the tightly held mouth and dark-shadowed eyes. "I'm sorry," she said. "I shouldn't have asked that. I know mind-melding is supposed to be very difficult . . . an intensely personal invasion. Especially with a complete stranger."

Zar glanced over at the little alien and her babies, and his eyes softened. "I'd like to help her . . ." he said, slowly.

"Do you think you could?"

"I don't know. Probing a non-humanoid stranger's mind could prove risky . . . for both of us."

Nyota watched D'berahan's chest rise almost imperceptibly as she breathed. "What if you had a guide? Somebody who had been in mental contact with her before?"

"That would help considerably. I could let the other handle the deepest, most personal part of the meld. Is there another Marishal on board?"

"No . . ." Uhura said, straightening up and going over to the intercom. "But if you're sure you'd be willing to try, I think I know the next best thing."

He nodded. "Go ahead."

As Uhura punched codes from memory, Zar moved over to stand beside her. "Who are you calling?"

"Your father," she told him, as she completed the connection. "I hope he's in his quarters. He could be up on the bridge." She gave him an impish grin. "I owe him a late-night call."

Zar's eyes widened with surprise, but before he could say anything, a familiar voice emerged: "Spock here."

"Sir, this is Uhura. Would it be possible for you to meet me in sickbay? I have a personal request for you."

"On my way."

Uhura switched off the intercom. Zar was watching her intently. "How did you know he's my father?"

"Guessed," she replied matter-of-factly. "Then, when I asked him, he confirmed it."

"Oh." He was about to say more, when they heard the outer door *whoosh* open.

That can't be Spock, Uhura realized. *He hasn't even had time to reach the turbo-lift.*

Leonard McCoy entered and stood blinking at them. He was still wearing his dress uniform trousers, but had changed his jacket for a medical tunic. "Hello," he said, finally. "What are you two doing here? The party isn't over yet."

"We came down to see D'berahan," Nyota answered, feeling absurdly like a kid who has been caught raiding the cookie jar.

"What are *you* doing here?" Zar asked. "Weren't you enjoying yourself?"

"Yeah, but I'm the only doctor aboard this trip. I came down to check on Ensign Weinberger—boy broke his shoulder when a gravity flux down in Engineering tossed him against a bulkhead this afternoon." He peered at them suspiciously. "Nyota, you look guilty as hell. Zar, don't pull that Vulcan poker-face on me . . . I can tell something's going on. What are you up to?"

Uhura looked over at Zar, who raised an eyebrow at her. She shrugged. "I asked Zar to try and reach D'berahan.

He thinks if Spock directs the probe, it may be possible."

"I see." McCoy took a deep breath, puffing out his cheeks a little, then slowly released it. "When Spock tried it, both he and the Marishal almost died."

"I know it is potentially dangerous," Zar said.

"Do you think it's worth the risk?"

Zar hesitated, then said, slowly, "Yes, I do. Life is full of risks . . . you can't shut yourself away from them, just because you're afraid you'll be hurt."

McCoy eyed him narrowly. "You must've been talking to Jim. That sounds like something he'd say."

"It wasn't Jim," Zar said, dryly.

"Who, then?"

"You wouldn't believe me if I told you."

The doctor frowned. "Would you be able to monitor the effects of the link on D'berahan, so you could get out if it was causing her any harm?"

"I think so."

"All right," McCoy said. "But you'd better get the hell out of there if you get into trouble, hear? It's not as though there are no other telepaths . . . we even have to bypass Vulcan on our way home. Maybe it would be better to wait for—"

He broke off as Zar turned toward the door. "Spock's here."

A moment later, Uhura heard the outer door to sickbay slide open. As Nyota explained why she had called him, Spock stood looking down at the motionless form of the little alien.

Finally, when she was finished, the Vulcan nodded. "Despite her fear, she risked everything to help us complete our mission. If there is a chance to help her, it is my duty to do so." He glanced over at Zar. "But you . . . she is a stranger to you . . ."

"I'll just be supporting you and monitoring," Zar pointed out. "If you're willing, I am, too."

Spock hesitated. "Do not underestimate the danger," he

warned his son. "She may have withdrawn so far that she cannot be reached. And I know from experience that you will be supplying most of the energy for the search."

Zar regarded him levelly. "If our positions were reversed, would D'berahan try to reach me?"

"Yes, I believe she would," Spock said.

Zar shrugged, a "there you have it" gesture. "Let's begin."

Uhura watched as McCoy lowered one side of the enclosure. At the sight of the newcomers, D'berahan's babies tried to make a crawling beeline back inside their mother's pouch, but the communications officer, at a nod from McCoy, gently prevented them. "What are we going to do with the children, Mr. Spock?"

The Vulcan considered. "They cannot be in physical contact with D'berahan while we do this. Doctor, can you rig a temporary partition to separate them from her?"

McCoy hastily complied. "Now what?" he asked.

Zar studied the three infants. "There is no way to discover whether they are in mental contact with their mother, since their minds are so alien. Nyota, would you be willing to link with me, then remain on the outskirts of the meld so you could warn us if they experience any distress?"

Uhura hesitated, trying to hide her initial reaction to the suggestion. She had never been part of a mind-meld before, and the idea of letting anyone else touch her thoughts made her mouth dry and her palms grow wet. *But I have no choice,* she realized. *D'berahan's children need her.*

"All right," she said, steadily.

"Good. You'll sense things, probably, but you'll still be conscious, able to see. And," Zar slanted a look at her, "I'll do all I can to stay out of the deeper levels of your mind."

She flashed him a shaky smile. "I trust you."

"Ready," Spock said, and, leaning forward, touched his fingers to the domed forehead with its now-ragged topknot of fur. He extended his right hand to Zar, who took it in his left. Uhura looked at their hands. How alike they were— even though Zar's were weathered and scarred.

Both closed their eyes, their faces becoming expression-less masks. Uhura could almost feel them withdraw from the here-and-now. Then Zar reached out with his right hand.

Taking a deep breath, she touched the outstretched fingers, feeling them grasp hers gently. Even so, she was fully aware of a potential strength that could have crushed bone. Stronger still was the mental link that sprang up between them.

Suddenly it was as though she were part of Zar's body, inside his skin—seeing with his eyes, breathing with his lungs. Her heart lurched, trying to beat at an impossibly high rate, and for a second she felt its throbbing, not beneath her left breast, but lower down, on her right side.

There was nothing overtly sexual about the experience, but for a moment, Uhura felt more intimately aware of a man's body than she had ever been before. Then the contact between them changed, settling into her mind. She could still see, but was conscious of a strange double vision—with one set of eyes (her own) she watched the three Marishal babies, with the other she experienced only darkness . . . a darkness shot with alien images.

Are you all right? The words entered her mind as though they had been sketched in fire.

Yes, she thought back, marshaling her strength to form the words mentally. *Tell Spock to proceed.*

Zar's consciousness withdrew, but she was still aware of the link between them, alive and pulsing, bringing her snatched bits and pieces of the search he and Spock were making. Too quickly to grasp, scattered memories and images that were not her own flashed by—of Sarpeidon (*so that's where Zar is from! I'd give a lot to know how that happened!*), of Vulcan, and of Marish.

Uhura kept the physical part of her vision on the Marishal infants, watching them for any sign of distress, snatching an occasional glance at her partners in the meld. Their faces remained blank, but she knew the strain they were under by their bone-white knuckles, the faint sheen of moisture on their foreheads.

242

I've never seen Spock perspire, she thought. *I didn't know he could.*

Finally, the trickle of transmitted memories were mostly of Marish, and Nyota realized they must be reaching their goal.

A sudden brush of terror, then a wild torrent of denial
—[No! Must escape! Hide!]

Uhura realized, with a surge of excitement, that Spock had located the Marishal's identity.

D'berahan, this is Spock. You are safe now. Come back with us. The wordless reassurance was strong, bringing images of comfort, of friends, of safety.

[Denial, fear]

You are safe, D'berahan, safe. Come with us. We are your friends . . .

[No, no—Hide!]

Without any conscious decision on her part, Uhura suddenly found herself forming words, projecting an image: *D'berahan, see your children? I am looking at them . . . see them, through my eyes. They need you. They might die without you! You must come back, for their sake. Look at your babies!*

After a moment she felt her words, her projected vision, picked up, amplified, and thrust at the Marishal with all the force of two expertly honed minds.

[My children?]

Yes!

[My children!]

Suddenly, Uhura "heard" a fourth "voice" in the meld, and she was aware of a telepathic presence so strong that it eclipsed the others. The presence "spoke":

[Friends . . . you have risked much for this one. This one expresses utmost thanks to all . . . but especially to you, new-friend Nyota Uhura, who loved this one's children when this one could not . . .]

The little Marishal concluded her speech by broadcasting such a wave of gratitude and affection that Uhura came out of the dissolving meld with tears on her cheeks. She gulped back a sob as she saw D'berahan stir. McCoy released the partition, and the Marishal babies crawled over to their mother, who raised her head to look at them, her hands to touch them.

"We did it!" Nyota whispered, on a ragged breath. She stepped back, her legs trembling with reaction, then turned to Zar, knowing she was grinning like a fool. "We *did* it!" She flung her arms around him in a fierce hug, feeling both ecstatic and shaken.

"No, *you* did it, Nyota," Zar said, giving her a return squeeze that lifted her clear off the deck. "If you hadn't projected the image of the children . . ."

"Zar is right," Spock said, and for a second Uhura was sure she felt the Vulcan's hand brush her shoulder.

"You *all* did it," McCoy said gruffly. He cleared his throat. "Thanks from me, too."

"But—"

Leonard McCoy leaned over his desk and shook an admonishing finger at his patient. "Quiet! You promised to hear me out."

"But *five weeks* is out of the question! I can't afford that much time!" Zar protested.

"You ungrateful—" McCoy began, then took a deep breath, obviously struggling to keep his temper. "Listen, Zar. You're damned lucky that I can do anything at all about that injury, it's so old. I'm a doctor, not a wizard. I'm telling you that after a week in suspension therapy, then three to four more of rehabilitation, you'll walk almost normally again. No more pain. For the love of Mike, isn't that worth a little time?"

Zar slouched back in his seat, arms crossed over his chest. "You're right, I am an ungrateful bastard . . . no pun intended. I *do* appreciate your attempt to help, I really do."

He rubbed a hand across his forehead, sighing. "It's just that . . . every minute I'm gone, I can't help thinking that things are happening without me. Intellectually, I know that isn't so, but the sense of *urgency* . . . it gnaws at me."

His voice dropped to a whisper. "And there's this . . . this empty place, inside me, where Wynn was. It's as though I have lost an arm, or am going blind . . . I'm able to shut it away, so I can function, but I can't forget it, not for a second."

"I understand how you must feel, and it's completely natural, under the circumstances," the doctor admitted. "However, you'd be crazy to pass up this chance—and you know it."

"So I'm supposed to just lie around and take it easy for over a *month?*"

"Why the hell not?" McCoy glared at the younger man. "Listen, my stubborn friend, do you know what those tests showed me? Besides the condition of your leg, I mean?"

"What?"

"A man on the brink of a physical and emotional breakdown. A man who has been under too much stress for way too long. If Jim showed readings like that, I'd declare him unfit for command. Your muscle tone is slipping, your reaction time is off, your stamina is shot—you're in no shape for a strenuous hike, let alone the fight of your life!"

McCoy drummed his fingers on the top of his desk. "You know I'm right, and if you're honest, you'll admit it. You're *tired,* Zar. Bone-tired. Extreme stress and fatigue can cause metabolic imbalances that impair judgment, did you know that?"

Zar sighed. "I know that tired people make mistakes, which is something any commander learns very quickly."

"How long have you been having stomach pains?"

The gray eyes widened. "How did you—" He broke off, shrugging. "I've always had a sensitive stomach, you know that."

"I know that if you don't quit driving yourself so hard, and don't quit skipping meals, you're going to develop the Vulcan version of a full-blown ulcer. And you won't like *that,* at all."

"Can't you repair the damage?"

"Sure. But if you go back and subject yourself to the same

stresses in the same way, it'll come back. You need to take better care of yourself. Start meditating again, every day. How long has it been since you painted?"

"Probably ten years."

"Paint, too. Or, if you don't want to do that, go for a quiet ride in the woods—anything to let your body and mind take some time off, understand?"

"Yes. But I can't stay here for five—"

"How long has it been since you had a vacation? Be honest."

Zar looked down. "Two years ago, when I got this." He tapped his midsection. "I was confined to quarters for a week from a spear thrust. My mail kept it from penetrating, but the impact broke a rib."

"It broke two," said McCoy, shortly. "And cracked another. It's a miracle you didn't get a punctured lung from getting up too soon, you fool. That's no vacation. You *need* a month off, son. You need to eat nutritious meals, catch up on your sleep, and exercise sensibly."

"I suppose I do. But Wynn—"

"Listen to me, Zar. You told me that Wynn *wanted* you to accompany us, right? That she was very insistent about it?"

"Yes, she was."

"And that she told you the reason she wanted you to come back with us was that she had received a . . . whatever she called it—a Sending—that it was vital for you—for your life—to do so, right?"

"Yes."

"Well," McCoy sat back confidently, "hasn't it occurred to you that perhaps the reason she was so set on your coming back to help us was that your getting back into shape and my fixing your leg would turn out to be essential to your survival?"

Zar glanced up at the doctor, startled. *In top condition, with two good legs, I might be able to dodge or parry a blow that otherwise would land,* he thought. Slowly, reluctantly, he nodded. "That does make sense."

"You bet it does."

"But what about the *Enterprise?* What will Jim do, just keep orbiting Gateway while I undergo this therapy and recover? Won't Starfleet Command notice that the *Enterprise* hasn't come home?"

McCoy grinned. "Admiral Morrow was so relieved to hear that we succeeded that he assigned us a little mission in the next quadrant to update the course of an ion storm discovered last year. It'll take just about four weeks, travel time included."

"You mean this Admiral Morrow knows about me?"

"Sure. Spock told him. You should've been there."

Zar raised an eyebrow as he envisioned the moment. "And Morrow agreed to let you ferry a civilian around for a month?"

McCoy grinned. "Bite your tongue. You're not a mere civilian, you're a visiting head-of-state."

"Oh, Goddess . . ." The gray eyes danced with laughter, then sobered. "You seem to have thought of everything."

"It's the least we can do. What about it, what do you say?"

Zar turned his palms up in a gesture of resignation. "Looks like I'm going to take a vacation."

"Okay, easy now . . . take it slow, Zar . . . that's it, just lie there for a second. How do you feel?"

Zar shook his head, trying to make the scene around him stop wavering. "Dizzy." He blinked, and his surroundings gradually steadied. He recognized the recovery room in sickbay, and McCoy's face bent over him. On the other side of the couch was the enormous Coridian nurse, and beside him, Spock. "Did it work? Have I really been unconscious for a week?"

"Yes, to both questions. How many fingers am I holding up?"

Zar squinted against the light. "Just one . . . and in a barracks, that gesture would earn you a sore jaw."

McCoy chuckled. "You'll do. Want to sit up?"

"Yes." With eight hands helping (two sets belonged to the

nurse), Zar sat up. The room spun around him for a second, then steadied. "Why do I feel so weak?"

"Because you haven't moved a muscle for seven days. You'll feel better the longer you're up. Hungry?"

"Ravenous."

After he had eaten, Zar demanded to try walking. "All right," McCoy said. "I guess that's the best way to convince you to take it easy. Urgh'kesht, don't let go of him."

"Yes, Doctor," the nurse said, obediently gripping Zar's left arm in three meaty red hands.

Zar inched his way to the side of the couch, felt the deck against the soles of his bare feet, then cautiously swung his weight forward and stood up. He couldn't repress a delighted grin. "The pain is gone!"

"Told you so," McCoy said, calmly. "Now take a step."

Zar lifted his left leg and strode forward—

—and was only saved from crashing down in an ignominious heap by Urgh'kesht's grip. The nurse held him upright as he swayed drunkenly.

"I can't walk!" Zar fought back panic. "Why not?"

The doctor folded his arms across his chest and regarded his patient imperturbably. "What's wrong is that for fifteen years you've been favoring that leg by walking incorrectly. You're going to have to relearn how to walk normally."

Zar thought about how long it had taken him to get around again after the initial injury. "But that'll take *months!*"

McCoy shook his head. "Not if you obey your kindly old doctor's orders. You'll spend part of each day with a regen unit on the leg, then do exercises on the physical therapy equipment, with Urgh'kesht, here. After that, you can exercise on your own—swimming would be good. Every day you'll be able to use it a little more . . . until you're back to normal." He frowned. "I'll warn you, it's always going to be a bit short. But it'll be so slight you may be the only one to notice."

Gritting his teeth, Zar tried another step, and this time managed to keep his balance, though all the muscles in his left thigh felt as though they were going into spasms. He took a deep breath, and a third step. Then a fourth . . .

As each day passed, he improved. On the third day, he walked unassisted to the gym and worked out on the equipment there, careful not to strain the leg. Then he cautiously lowered himself into the shallow end of the pool, and, teeth fastened in his lower lip, began the stretching and kicking movements Urgh'kesht had shown him.

After two days in the shallow end, he asked Spock to teach him to swim (a skill he had never acquired, due to Sarpeidon's ice-age climate). Within another week he was growing proficient enough to manage laps, and, as McCoy had predicted, this exercise proved to be one of the most beneficial.

Zar took his enforced "vacation" as seriously as any work he'd ever done. He drove himself to the limit in his workouts, but was careful never to exceed it . . . never to tax himself too hard. His daytime world narrowed to his leg and his general physical condition. He tempered and honed his body as he had the blade of his sword, knowing that his strength, agility, and reaction time might make all the difference.

His evening hours were spent going over the battle plans and maps he'd redrawn from memory, analyzing strategy, ground configuration, troop deployment, trying to plan for every contingency. When Spock and Kirk discovered what he was doing, the three spent hours discussing and refining possible tactics . . .

"This catapult here," Kirk said, pointing to a poker chip representing the assault engine. "If your map is accurate, you've got a small rise *here,* fifty meters further on. Right?"

Zar nodded. "All of Moorgate Plain slopes gradually downhill to the Redbank, but I see what you mean. If I change the catapult's position to the top of that rise, its range would be considerably extended . . ." He put out a finger and pushed the chip closer to the blue swath marking the Redbank. "But that little rise is steep . . . I'd need extra vykar and troops to pull it uphill—would it be worth it?"

Spock studied the pattern of troop deployment. "A good question. What type of ground is it?"

"Broken and rather rocky."

"Then I would estimate that the effort expended in getting the catapult up there would be too great to be offset by the greater range you would achieve."

Zar sighed. "You're right." He cocked an eyebrow at Kirk. "You know, Jim, I just thought of something. Since the Guardian is working again, we could always hop through and bring back a couple of consultants."

The admiral looked up, his hazel eyes brightening. "Good idea! Uh, let's see . . . what about Alexander? And Artos of Britain? Don't forget old Julius!"

Zar nodded. "Geronimo, of course. And Genghis. Patton?"

"Too recent for this kind of warfare. Though he used to brag that he'd fought at Marathon in a previous life . . . Don't you have anyone to contribute, Spock? What was the name of that famous pre-reformation Vulcan general? Voltan?"

"Voltag," Spock said, automatically, staring at both of them as though trying to reassure himself that they were pulling his leg. Zar and Kirk gazed earnestly back at him, the embodiment of innocence. Spock's eyebrow went up in dismay. "But . . . such an action would be disastrous to the integrity of the time-stream . . ." The Vulcan broke off, his eyes sharpening as Kirk's mouth began a telltale quiver. "I see," he said, distantly. "I hope both of you enjoyed your little joke."

The admiral began to chuckle. "You should have seen your expression." He gave Zar a sidelong glance. "Been a long time since I had him going like that. When I first knew him, Bones and I used to *kid* him—though I must admit, as time went on he learned to give as good as he got."

"Better," said Spock, flatly.

"Ouch," Kirk winced exaggeratedly. "Zar, I think we'd better get back to that battle plan . . ."

As the *Enterprise* performed her assigned mission, the Guardian continued to contact Zar every few days; distance seemed no hindrance to the time entity. Their "conversations" were fairly one-sided . . . Zar encouraged the ancient creation to tell him of the wonders it had witnessed and recorded, and it seemed pleased to comply. He "listened," and wondered.

"Jim tells me we're heading back to Gateway tomorrow," Dr. McCoy said, checking the settings on the regen unit strapped to his patient's leg.

Zar nodded. "That's what Spock told me. How did I do in those tests I took this morning?"

"The leg's coming along excellently. You've worked hard to condition it, and it shows. Now just don't mess up my handiwork by straining any muscles or getting a hunk chopped out of you, and I'll be very pleased."

McCoy crossed the physical therapy room, disappeared into his office, and returned with a cup of coffee. "Want some?"

Zar shook his head. "I've had my one cup. I can't afford to get too dependent on caffeine, since there's none where I'm going." He flexed his hands, noticing that the callouses on his palms were beginning to soften and peel. "What about my overall reaction time and muscle tone? My stamina?"

McCoy grinned. "Let me put it this way. If a rogue *vitha* was raiding my herds, I'd hire you to get rid of it."

Smiling, Zar relaxed. "Then you certify me fit for command?"

"Absolutely." McCoy hesitated. "I probably shouldn't bring this up, in case you've forgotten, but have you made a decision about that other matter we discussed? You've seen the results of those genetic tests I ran. You're fine."

"I hadn't forgotten." Zar stared fixedly at the diagnostic readings on the regen unit, as though he had never seen them before. "Last night I dreamed, Leonard. I dreamed about Araen's death, the way I have dozens of times before . . ."

McCoy settled back and took a sip of coffee. "Not surprising, after what the Originators did. Jim told me he's dreamed about his mother's death several times since he saw her image on Gateway." His face darkened. "Hell, I dreamed about Jocelyn—and that's something I haven't done in a *long* time. I can imagine how you felt, though."

Zar frowned miserably at his leg. "I don't know what to do, Len. I'm still afraid, the dream proves that, but lately I've been thinking that asking you to give me that hypo now would be like . . . like breaking faith with Wynn. As though I'd repaid her honesty with a lie. Not to mention that I'd be mocking her religious beliefs. I'm torn."

"You said Wynn wants children. How do *you* feel about it?"

Confused, Zar glanced up. "I explained why I was afraid—"

McCoy was already shaking his head. "No, that's not what I meant. Let me put it another way. Suppose your wife had a normal pregnancy and a healthy baby. Would you want the child?"

"Of course I would! Didn't I make that clear?"

"No." McCoy stared at him, unblinking.

Zar settled back against the padded couch and considered silently. "Hmmmm," he said, finally. "You're telling me, in your own inimitable fashion, that I'm being paranoid."

"Yes." After a second to allow his response to sink in, the doctor raised an eyebrow. "Now, obviously, there's a risk, I'd be a liar to tell you there isn't. But the danger to Wynn is no greater than for any other woman in your time period. And there is *nothing* wrong with your genes." He finished the last of his coffee. "Sometimes, it's not just a matter of taking risks yourself. Sometimes, you've got to be willing to let the people you love take them. You can't keep them in a steri-field."

"I see."

"Do you? Do you really?"

"I . . . I'm trying, Doc. I've lived with this guilt for so long . . . it's hard to let it go. At least when I was blaming myself, I felt as though I had some . . . control . . . over what happened." Zar shook his head, scowling. "That sounds crazy."

"No, it sounds human. Which is *not* an insult, no matter what your pop says."

Zar smiled faintly. "You two . . . still sparring, after all these years. I'm going to miss that."

He straightened his leg gingerly within the confines of the regen unit. "And I'll miss the stars. It's been wonderful to see them again, in all their myriad colors . . . every night before bed I've gone up to the observation deck and just sat there watching them. I never get tired of seeing the stars."

"Why don't you stay, then?" McCoy raised a hand to forestall Zar's protest. "Wait, I know what you're going to say. But you could go back and get Wynn, then bring her through the Guardian, too. You'd be doing her a favor."

"Would I?" Zar shook his head. "No, Leonard. Wynn would be a hopeless anachronism in this time . . . a priestess who'd devoted her life to serving a Goddess whose name has been forgotten for thousands of years. She'd never fit in. She's been brought up to believe in demons, just as sincerely as your society believes in science."

"You could help her adjust. She's an intelligent woman, she could learn."

"But would she ever be *happy?* I doubt it. Wynn is like Jim, she's a natural leader. In this society, she'd feel useless . . . powerless."

"Sounds like what you said about yourself back on Sarpeidon when we first tried to convince you to stay."

"Yes . . . but it's worse for her. Unlike me, Wynn *enjoys* being in command. Hell, if I could figure out a way to abdicate and devote myself just to teaching my people, I'd probably do it, because that's what I enjoy. My mother was a teacher, you know. And my grandmother, Amanda."

McCoy smiled. "So's your father, come to think of it . . . one of the most highly regarded instructors at Starfleet Academy."

An answering smile tugged at the corner of Zar's mouth. "Runs in the family. Maybe, if I make it through, I can gradually hand over the reins to Wynn."

They sat in companionable silence for several minutes, then Zar said, "I'm especially going to miss *you,* Leonard.

You know, we haven't had time for a poker game, yet. How am I going to pay my doctor's bill?"

McCoy grinned. "We've still got six days. I'll try and set something up."

"No, Len. I'm going back as soon as we make orbit around Gateway. Day after tomorrow."

"It's too early!" McCoy protested. "The leg's not quite ready. I was going to try and talk you into making it ten days or two weeks, rather than just another week!"

"The leg's fine. You said yourself that I've made excellent progress."

"But if you wait another ten days, I could be *certain* there's no residual weakness! As it is . . . it might go out on you if you strain it."

"I'll have to risk that. Leonard . . . I lie awake at night, thinking about the battle, imagining . . . you know. If I wait any longer, I'll go crazy. I've *got* to get this over with . . . one way or another."

Spock stepped onto the turbo-lift at the end of his duty shift. "Deck E, level 5," he said absently, mentally reviewing Naraht's report on the trajectory of the ion storm. The Horta officer ran his Science Department with admirable efficiency and logic. *A formal commendation is in order,* the Vulcan decided. *I will speak to Starfleet Command about it when we reach Earth . . .*

When Spock entered his quarters a few minutes later, he found Zar sitting at the desk before the terminal, staring at a blank screen.

The Vulcan was not surprised to find him there, since his son had been a frequent visitor during his father's off-duty hours, but now he knew immediately that something was wrong. Silent-footed, he stepped over to glance down at the label of the data cassette lying on the desktop.

In his own neat Vulcan script, it read:

SARPEIDON—HISTORY (GF)

Spock's breath caught in his throat, then he said, very quietly, "Did you watch it?"

Zar did not start when he heard the voice, and Spock realized that he had known his father was there all along. "No," he said, finally. "I couldn't get up the nerve."

The Vulcan reached over the other's shoulder to pick up the cassette. "There is no logic in subjecting yourself to a viewing. I intended from the first to tell you whatever I could that might enable you to avoid . . . this."

Zar nodded, still half-turned away. "I'd appreciate that."

Spock seated himself on the edge of his meditation stone, a long, polished slab of Vulcan granite—one of the few luxuries he permitted himself. He stared unseeing at the large IDIC wall-mosaic. "The details were difficult to discern, but it . . . happens . . . on a small hill," he said, at last. "There is . . . a blow to the head. I could not see the man's face, but he did not appear to be wearing much in the way of armor. His arms, for example, were bare."

"Asyri," Zar identified. "Many of them go into battle wearing only a bronze helmet, sleeveless bronze cuirass, a battle kilt, and bronze greaves from their knees to their sandals. Lots of vulnerable spots, but the light weight leaves them very quick." He rubbed his jaw thoughtfully as he turned to face Spock, and the Vulcan saw that he was clean-shaven, and that his hair had been trimmed.

"Could you see the weapon?"

Spock shook his head. "Some type of impact weapon. It resembled a short axe, but I could not be positive. Definitely not a sword."

Zar nodded impassively, then glanced up and met the Vulcan's eyes. "One more question, and forgive me in advance for being gruesome, but . . ." he shrugged, "there are worse things than death. Living with a crippled mind, for example. Was it a killing blow? Immediately fatal?"

"From the force of the blow and the resulting amount of blood, I am positive," Spock said levelly, "that no one could have survived it."

"That's reassurance of a sort, anyway," Zar said. "I recognize that it was . . . difficult . . . for you to speak of this, and I am sorry I had to ask. Thank you for telling me."

Spock nodded silently, avoiding his son's eyes. He relived

the desolation that he had felt while watching the battle sequence. *Stay here,* he wanted to say. *Don't let this thing happen.* But he could not speak; Zar had made his decision, and there was nothing . . . nothing . . . that he, Spock, could do.

The Vulcan had never felt so helpless.

When he looked up again, Zar was watching him, concerned. "Are you all right?"

"Yes." To change the subject, he said the first thing that came into his head. "Your beard is gone."

Zar felt his jaw again. "It feels strange, after all these years. I intended to clip it extra short, the way I always do before a battle—a beard long enough to grab can be dangerous—but I couldn't find any scissors. So I used your beard repressor. Doc gave me a haircut, too, for old time's sake."

"When are you going back?"

"Tomorrow morning, right after breakfast."

"I see." Spock kept his voice level with an effort. *So soon?* he thought, blankly. *But . . . I thought we would have another week, at least . . .* "McCoy says your leg is completely healed?"

"No, Leonard wants me to stay another ten days. He lectured me the whole time I was on the regen unit this morning about waiting . . . but I can't. The leg feels fine. I've even been fencing with Sulu."

Spock raised an eyebrow. "I heard about that. Those bouts are becoming one of the ship's major spectator attractions. Apparently you are considered well-matched opponents."

Zar shook his head ruefully. "Hardly. Hikaru—he's *fast*—fences circles around me with the foil and the épée." He rose and walked smoothly over to stand in front of the ancient Vulcan S'harien sword hanging on the wall with the other antique weapons. "I do better with the saber, because it has an edge, but the saber is Sulu's particular forte—no pun intended—so he wins there, too.

"But . . ." a wicked smile touched his mouth, "today

256

Scotty, who watched yesterday's saber match, produced two claymores—Scottish broadswords—and two bucklers, and dared us to go the best two out of three with *them."*

"What happened?"

"You should have seen Hikaru's face when he picked his up. The things were even longer and heavier than my bastard sword." (Spock raised an eyebrow at the nomenclature.) "The stance is different, too—more face-on, so you can swing two-handed, instead of sideways. Not surprisingly, I won every encounter. Scotty, who'd bet on the matches, cleaned up. He said he wanted to nominate me for honorary membership in the Scott clan."

Spock's eyebrow went up. "What was Commander Sulu's reaction to his defeat?"

"He told me he hadn't had so much fun in years. He wanted me to coach him in using a broadsword, but of course I'm leaving tomorrow. So Scotty volunteered to give him some pointers."

The Vulcan nodded absently. *Tomorrow . . .* he thought. *And after you go, I will almost certainly never see you again. There are so many things I want to say to you, but cannot . . .*

With an abrupt, angry movement, Spock got up and began pacing restlessly, hands behind his back. "You seem remarkably untroubled about what you may face when you return tomorrow."

"I think our encounter with those two disturbed superbeings overloaded all my scare circuits," Zar replied. His eyes met the Vulcan's, clear and candid. "And, it's odd, but I suppose people condemned to hang have the same reaction—there's a curious serenity that comes from knowing how, when, and where you're going to die. You know that, until then, nothing can touch you."

But something will *touch you. Something . . . someone . . . is going to* kill *you. If only . . . if only there were something I could do. If only I could convince you to stay here, where it is safe . . .* Spock realized that his reasoning abilities were compromised, due to personal involvement, but he could not help it. *If only I could . . .*

"Father." Spock looked up. "There's something I want you to know. Wynn told me that she thinks there is a way that I may avoid . . . what you saw. That was why she insisted that I come here to help you. It's possible that, with your warning and with my leg healed, I might be quick enough to dodge that blow."

Spock felt a spark of hope kindle within him.

Zar looked down at his hands. "I *want* to be quick enough, now. The lecture you gave me that night after the handfasting made me think, and I began to realize that what I'd been calling fatalism was mostly a bad dose of self-pity. Thank you for helping me see that."

The Vulcan smiled faintly. "I suspect that what happened afterwards with Wynn had more to do with your renewed enthusiasm for life than any words of mine," he said, dryly.

Startled, Zar glanced up, then, as Spock's words sank in, his eyes widened and he flushed hotly. "Damn," he muttered, chagrined. "Look what you've made me do. I haven't blushed in years."

"It is especially noticeable now that the beard is gone," his father observed, amiably.

Zar raised an eyebrow at him, then his teeth flashed in a reluctant grin. "I'll pay you back for that."

"I hope you get the chance," Spock said, seriously.

They exchanged a long, searching glance, then Zar handed him another cassette. "Before I forget, I want you to have this. I made it for you to show Amanda and Sarek . . . if you think they'd like to see it. You decide."

The Vulcan took the little square. "Thank you. I'm sure it will mean a great deal to them." He drew a deep breath, then struggled for words. "It is difficult for me to express . . . what seeing you again has meant . . ." He hesitated, then made a small gesture of frustration. "More than friendship, you know that . . ."

"Father . . ." Zar interrupted, softly. "I do know. I understand."

If only I could stop you from going . . . but I cannot. If only I could help you . . . but that is impossible. Impossible?

258

Spock's eyes narrowed in thought as the words he'd said so often to his students came back to him. *There are always possibilities . . . if only one can find them . . . always possibilities . . .*

"Have you had dinner?" he said suddenly, his mind working busily, analyzing the problem from all angles. *Possibilities . . .*

Zar was taken aback at the complete change of subject, but shook his head and answered, "Not yet."

"Shall we?" Spock asked. "I find I am suddenly hungry."

"Got everything?" Kirk called as he approached Zar, who was standing with McCoy in the corridor outside the transporter room.

Zar hefted the bag he carried. "New music and literature cassettes, plus the medical kit Leonard put together. All here."

"Not quite all," Kirk said, and produced a package from behind his back. "Bones told me you missed this. It's coffee."

"Thank you!" Zar took the large parcel, then sniffed it appreciatively. "This is wonderful."

Kirk grinned. "It's the least I can do for the man who got Scotty to paint my bridge doors red again."

The Sovren smiled back. "They look like old times, don't they?"

The admiral nodded, lowering his voice. "Of course, he says he'll have to repaint them to regulation spec before we dock, but I've certainly enjoyed them. Even considering the circumstances that brought us here, it's been great to be out from behind that desk."

"This is where you belong, Jim," Zar said, quietly. "You know that."

Kirk hesitated, then looked away. *Of course I know, damn it. But what can I do about it?* "Where's Spock? He should have been here by now. When he wasn't at breakfast, I figured he was going to meet us here. Maybe I'd better page him."

"No." Kirk could see hurt disappointment in the gray eyes, but Zar sounded adamant. "No, don't. We . . . said good-bye yesterday evening."

"Well . . . all right." Reluctantly, Kirk led the way into the transporter room, then set the controls, deliberately delaying in case the Vulcan changed his mind and decided to join them. *I can't believe Spock isn't going to say good-bye . . .*

"You take care of yourself, now," McCoy was saying, his voice harsh with emotion. "Don't strain that leg. Remember to keep up those exercises . . . don't forget to meditate . . . and remember to . . ." He broke off. "Oh, damn, I can't *stand* this." The doctor seized Zar in a brief, fierce hug, then was gone, out the door.

Kirk turned away from the console, holding out his hand. "I'll miss you, Zar. A lot. Take care of yourself, all right?"

Zar gripped his hand tightly. "You do the same, Jim. I'll miss all of you, too. And *her*—" He made an all-inclusive gesture at the bulkheads and console. "Take care of her."

"You know I will."

Kirk watched him step up on the pad, clutching his bag and package of coffee, then managed a final smile and wave.

"Good-bye, Jim."

The transporter whined, then Kirk was alone in the chamber.

When the admiral stepped out of the room, he found McCoy waiting for him in the corridor. The doctor's eyes were reddened, but he was outwardly composed. "You okay, Bones?"

"Yeah," McCoy grunted, in a "let's change the subject" tone.

"Have you seen Spock this morning?"

"No, but when I do, I'm going to give that coldblooded Vulcan sonofabitch a piece of my mind. Imagine him not showing up to say good-bye!" McCoy's sorrow vanished in a surge of righteous indignation. "Where the hell is he?"

"I don't know. He's not on duty. Maybe he's in his quarters." The admiral frowned, conscious of a growing unease. "Maybe we ought to see if he's all right."

When they reached the entrance to the Vulcan's cabin, Kirk identified himself, but there was no answer. "He's not here."

"Get Uhura to page him," McCoy suggested.

Instead, Kirk pressed the "open" button, and the portal slid silently aside. Vulcans never locked doors.

He walked into the room, feeling the higher temperature flow over his body, partially combating the sudden chill that struck him. "Something's not right, Bones," he said, looking around. "Something's different . . . missing . . ."

McCoy frowned. "Everything looks okay to me . . . 'course you spend more time here than I do, so you'd be the one to notice." He moved toward the intercom. "Want me to request a page?"

"Hold on a second," the admiral said absently, his gaze sweeping the room . . . bunk, neatly made with military precision; meditation stone; firepot in the alcove; IDIC mosaic; desk with the computer tie-in; all normal, all as they should be . . .

Kirk suddenly stiffened. "Oh, no. God in Heaven, no . . ."

McCoy grabbed his friend's arm, his grasp hard and frightened. "What's wrong, Jim?"

Wordlessly, Kirk pointed to the wall, at Spock's collection of ancient Vulcan weapons. Two of them that Jim had particular cause to remember were missing.

"It looks the same to me! What *is* it?" McCoy demanded.

"The *lirpa* and the *ahn-woon*," Kirk said, his voice tight with fear. "They're gone. He's taken them with him, Bones."

"Taken them *where?*"

"Sarpeidon, of course." The admiral's voice was hollow. "Spock's gone back to that battle, to try and save Zar."

Chapter Fourteen

ZAR PACED SLOWLY back and forth, the chill breeze stirring his hair. He was warm enough within the muffling folds of his cloak, but he shivered nevertheless. His stomach lurched, then tightened with nausea. *You'd think you'd be used to this by now,* he thought, gritting his teeth.

But it was always the same; before every battle he fought a silent conflict with his own insides, one that had nothing to do with the death-warnings he had received about those who were close to him. These other bouts were caused by nothing but pre-battle nerves. When the fighting began, they would vanish.

You'd think you were a raw recruit, he told himself disgustedly, *instead of the First-in-War. You'll be lucky to get through your "do or die speech" without disgracing yourself today.*

On the other hand, he reminded himself dourly, *this is probably your last battle, so if you can just make it through this time, it's likely you won't have to worry about making any more speeches . . .*

To distract himself from such thoughts, he mentally stripped away the darkness, reviewing in his mind the terrain where he and those under his command would soon be fighting.

He was standing on Moorgate Plain, a large, rolling

expanse of still-damp turf that sloped gradually downward toward the Redbank, which lay nearly half a kilometer before him. On either side, the plain heaved itself into larger and larger swells as it met the foothills of the mountains to the north and south. At his back, about two kilometers away, lay New Araen.

The Lakreo Valley narrowed as it approached the city, and Zar was counting on the noncombatants having ample time to reach the foothills and the mountain passes if the day went against them; his troops could hold the valley entrance for a long time.

But his strategy demanded room to maneuver, so their first encounter with the invaders would be here, on Moorgate Plain.

"Sire?" Cletas's voice reached him out of the darkness.

Zar could barely make out the outline of his Second-in-War; the night was overcast, black as the bottom of a well, and the camp torches were far behind them.

"Here, Cletas. Are we ready?"

"All troops in position, sire. We've made the changes in the catapult positions you ordered and redistributed the archers as you instructed. Yarlev and the cavalry are concealed in the hills, waiting for our signal."

"Good." Zar was about to say more, but another spasm of nausea knotted his stomach. He fought it down and began walking again, the Second beside him. Both of them stepped cautiously, careful to avoid the thinly camouflaged pits the troops had dug during the night to trap the enemy chariots as they raced up out of the river.

"It's hard, waiting, isn't it?" Cletas said.

"Yes." Zar looked across the Redbank, seeing the torches in the enemy camp. *There are so many of them . . . we're still so outnumbered . . .* He shuddered, and lowered his voice to ask, "Do you ever get the shakes before a battle, Cletas?"

"Every time," his Second said, cheerfully. "And it's equal odds whether I lose my breakfast or not. Remember our first fight together? That big troop of bandits, with the leader who was missing an eye and wore the necklace made of scalps?"

"I remember."

"When we rode into *that* one, I not only puked, I rode home on a wet saddle." The Sovren heard the grin in the Second's voice. "Never told anyone about it . . . until now."

Zar put a hand on Cletas's shoulder, feeling the flexible hardness of the Second's mail byrnie beneath his cloak. "Thanks, my friend. It helps to talk, doesn't it? I recognize your strategy . . . and believe me, I appreciate it. May Ashmara keep you safe today."

"Will She? Will I be safe?"

Zar drew in a breath. "So you know about that?"

"I've known for years. Ever since the Lady Araen died."

"I see. I've had no warning yet today, Cletas. So perhaps you'll make it through."

"Does that mean that you'll be safe, too, my liege?"

"I don't know. I can only tell about others, never myself."

They stood in silence for a while, hearing the faint but unmistakable sounds of the army massed behind them (soft curses, hiss of whetstone against steel, the restless blowing and pawing of a vykar, a few plaintive bars of music) and, before them, the even fainter *blup-blup* of the Redbank as it lapped its banks.

Zar was careful to keep his mental shield up, to listen only with his ears, never with his mind—he knew that letting his guard down for even a moment could prove disastrous. There was too much apprehension before a battle, and too much pain and fear during it. He had learned, of necessity, to keep his mind-shield raised automatically, but it represented another drain on his physical and mental energies.

Cletas sniffed the breeze coming down off the mountains. "I'll wager it'll storm by midday."

"Those clouds are thickening," Zar said, nodding. "It will be a late dawn, and a dark one. Still, there'll be light in another hour. I'd better go and get ready."

Slowly, the Sovren picked his way through the darkness,

back to the command tent. It shone pale gold, lit from within by lamplight. He nodded to the saluting guard, ducked through the open flap, and went in.

Wynn stood in the middle of the tent, double-checking the fastenings on her armor. Voba knelt beside her, lacing her new chain-mail byrnie. She wore no helm yet, but was otherwise fully armed. Her leg, thigh, knee, and arm guards were her old ones, made of the bronze-plated boiled leather—there had been no time to make plate steel ones to fit her.

"How do you like your wedding present?" Zar asked.

Wynn drew the new sword hanging on her left hip, and the lamplight sent amber runnels shimmering down the blued steel. "I love it. The length is just right, and the balance is superb. Although," she grinned at him as Voba stepped back and she swung the weapon in a constrained drill, mindful of the limited space, forehand, backhand, and chop, "I had trouble keeping a straight face when you presented the swords to Father and me in front of all the officers. You have to admit, a sword *is* a somewhat . . . *symbolic* . . . gift for a husband to give his wife." She raised her eyebrows at him suggestively.

Zar shook his head. "That significance never occurred to me," a slow smile tugged at his mouth, "at least not until I happened to notice Cletas's face. He looked as if he were strangling, trying not to laugh."

"That's because you don't have a dirty mind, my dear lord. Cletas and I do." She sheathed the sword without looking down at the scabbard. "It's a good thing you were wearing your helmet. I don't think anyone else saw you blush."

"That's twice in two days," Zar said, ruefully. Their eyes met, and he took an involuntary step toward her, wishing they could be alone—just for a few minutes. Since that first ecstatic embrace when he'd first come back, they'd been surrounded by others and too swamped by duties to exchange more than a quick smile and a few whispered words . . .

Voba cleared his throat, and Zar turned to see his aide-de-camp standing there, his arms full of mail and plate. He sighed. "You're right, it's time."

The Sovren glanced over the assorted pieces Voba was holding and made his selection. In recent years he had spent much of his time during battle mounted, directing troop movements rather than fighting, and had worn the armor of a light cavalry trooper so he could move fast. But he had no illusions about today: today they would all be involved in close-quarters, hand-to-hand fighting, before it was over.

The problem was to balance the weight of the armor against the protection factor. Knights during Terra's medieval period had worn suits of plate armor (often with chain mail beneath) that had afforded them excellent protection from blows and thrusts, but were so heavy that the warrior would only be capable of strenuous fighting for fifteen or twenty minutes at a stretch.

Now Zar chose a pair of chain-mail leggings—*chausses*—that were held up by a belt at the waist, then added his much-mended mail byrnie. Short-sleeved, it covered his torso to mid-thigh, extending over the tops of the chausses.

Then, frowning, he picked up a mail hood with an attached coif that hung down to protect the throat and neck. Ordinarily, the Sovren wore only his plate steel helmet with its distinctive scarlet plume, so his troops could recognize him easily, but, in view of Spock's warning, additional head protection seemed in order. *I'm going to roast in all this. Damn.*

Zar placed the hood and coif on the pile.

"Very good, sire," Voba said, nodding approval. The red-haired aide was always hinting that his commander needed more and heavier armor. "But what about rerebraces and vambraces?"

The Sovren nodded reluctantly, and selected the upper and lower arm guards made from plate steel. "Happy now, Voba?"

"That's much better, sire."

Zar pulled on the snug-fitting hose that protected the skin from chafing, then slid the chausses up like long stockings.

The only way to put on armor was from the ground up; he'd discovered that the first time he'd tried it the other way. Voba hopefully produced a pair of *demi-greviére*—plate steel shields to cover the front of the leg from ankle to knee, and Zar, grumbling under his breath, let his aide buckle them on. Then he shrugged on the quilted leather shirt and Voba laced his byrnie. Finally, he slid on a tight cap and drew the mail hood over it. He'd fasten the coif up around his neck at the last moment before engaging.

Finally he inspected, then belted on, his sword. Together, Wynn and Voba fastened on his arm guards.

Zar picked up his helmet, then slid his shield onto his arm. It was actually a combination of buckler and shield, in that it could be either slung on his arm by straps, or gripped in his left fist. As he'd explained to Kirk, it was essential for parrying blows.

He glanced at Wynn. "Ready, my lady?"

"Ready, my lord."

Together, they went out. Zar studied the sky, seeing a faint lightening in the east. The air was filled with the soft *ching* of armor and weapons being fastened on, and the nervous snortings of the battle-trained vykar. On the far side of the camp, he could hear faint clangs as two soldiers warmed up. His stomach tightened.

"I hate the waiting," he muttered, hardly aware that he'd spoken aloud.

"The best thing to do is to stay busy," Wynn told him, and drew her sword. "Shall we warm up?"

Zar nodded, pulled off his cloak, then set his helmet on it. His sword slipped into his leather and steel-gauntleted hand as naturally as breathing.

They touched blades in salute, then began slowly, gradually picking up the tempo, not hurrying, just loosening muscles, sharpening reaction time.

Forehand, backhand, parry, chop, thrust—Wynn, like the rest of her people, had little experience with using the point, so when Zar's blade touched her left breast even as he parried her swing, she halted. "You'll have to teach me to do that."

"Gladly." He spent a few minutes demonstrating, then they returned to the drill.

"Now you try one," he said, then deliberately left her an opening, prepared to leap back and parry if she tried too forcefully.

Wynn thrust at him, but missed a vital spot. "You've got the idea," he said. "Now it just takes practice."

She nodded, her face grim with concentration, then a second later her steel touched his shoulder. "Much better!" She stepped back. "I'd better stop while I'm ahead."

He sheathed his blade, then bowed slightly. "I enjoyed that," he said. "You're good with a sword."

"No, *you're* good," Wynn corrected him, moving close. "I can handle myself, but I'm not in your league. Especially now, with your leg healed."

Zar flexed his left thigh muscles cautiously, then nodded. "I'm trying not to put too many demands on it, but it feels wonderful to move freely again."

They had collected a ring of watchers. Wynn nodded at the soldiers gathered around. "Even better is the effect on the troops," she whispered. "Their spirits are high, now that half of the prophecy has already been fulfilled."

Zar had nearly forgotten the exact wording of Wynn's vision until she reminded him. Seeing Voba emerge from the command tent, he said, "The tent is empty, now. I don't want to say our good-byes out here."

Once inside, he dropped the flap, extinguished the lamp in the predawn grayness, and drew Wynn to him. He stood looking down at her, barely able to make out the pale blur that was her face. "We have only a few minutes," he whispered.

She touched his cheek. "So smooth," she murmured. "How did you get it so smooth?"

"Not with a blade," he told her. "More 'magic' from my time aboard the *Enterprise*. Do you like it?"

"I don't know. I'll need time to get used to it."

"Time . . ." He kissed her lightly. "If only we had more time . . . if only I don't—"

"Hush!" she cried, fiercely, her arms going up behind his neck. "Don't even *say* it. It's *not* going to happen."

"All right," he whispered, and kissed her with slow, passionate deliberation. She responded, holding him tightly, making a tiny noise in the back of her throat.

When he finally pulled away, she frowned up at him. "Kissing while wearing armor is stupid," she complained. "No fun at all."

"Then why are you breathing hard?"

She laughed softly. "Already you know me too well."

Zar touched her cheek. "It's time."

"Yes, I know."

Nursing a slashed arm against his side, the runner halted his heaving vykar, then saluted awkwardly, left-handed. "Sire! Commander Zaylenz requests reinforcements. Rorgan's archers have forced him to drop back, and his line is weakening."

Zar nodded. "Can you ride?"

"Yes, sire."

"Then tell him we are right behind you."

The vykar leaped away.

Zar beckoned to the next of the mounted runners who waited with him on the slope. "Instruct Second Cletas to lead three companies of reserve infantry to support Commander Zaylenz's line. Then find Commander Yarlev and tell him to dispatch a troop of cavalry through the foothills for a rear attack on the Asyri flank. Tell both of them I am going ahead immediately with a squad."

"Yes, sire!" His vykar, fresh and skittish, went racing upslope to the reserve units as though it might take flight.

Zar turned to find Voba at his elbow, holding out the reins of his commander's vykar. "Summon the guard. We can't let them break through."

He took the reins and vaulted up, momentarily relishing the fact that he hadn't needed to order his mount to kneel.

Moments later he was trotting downslope, shield slung and sword drawn, at the head of twenty infantry soldiers.

Rorgan and Laol's forces had begun their attack about an hour after dawn. Their chariots had splashed across the Redbank in seemingly unending waves, but the catapults and the pits had diminished their numbers dramatically. Still, there had been enough of them remaining to guard the enemy infantry as they, in turn, made their crossing.

As Zar rode downhill, he studied the field. Laol's forces were fighting furiously on the left, but his people were holding them, even driving them back a little. But before him, he could see that the Asyri archers were punishing the right flank of the Lakreo forces, which were slowly retreating upslope. Half a kilometer of ground between the Redbank and the clashing armies was bare except for the bodies of the dead and wounded. Zaylenz's troops were fighting bravely in ranks, in contrast to the savage but disorganized clumps of the invaders—but they were clearly weakening.

Zar signaled his mount to go faster as he saw the line grow thinner, waver, then a man fell with a shriek, and the Asyri were pouring through.

A second later Zar was in the middle of them, chopping hard at shoulders and throats, as his vykar leaped and charged, swinging its horned head viciously. A lance struck him in the side, but was deflected by his mail, then he caught another on his shield. A second later he felt something strike his left leg, and whirled in the saddle just in time to stab the man in his open mouth before the Asyri could swing again. Teeth rattled against the blade as he jerked it free.

His leg seemed to be all right, Zar realized, relieved, even as he automatically parried another Asyri's swing, then kicked the man in the throat with his mailed foot. The Asyri warrior staggered back and went down with a scream beneath the vykar's stamping hooves.

By this time the squad of Lakreo soldiers had joined the melee, and for several minutes the Sovren was too busy to think consciously. Despite their best efforts, they were still being driven back.

Suddenly Zar's mount stumbled on the rocky ground and

fell, pinning an Asyri beneath it. Zar freed his right leg and leapt clear as his vykar rolled over, crushing the man beneath it, then struggled back to its feet. The Sovren saw that the creature was lame, and whacked it across the rump with the flat of his sword to get it out of the way. Startled, it leaped upslope, and he lost sight of it immediately as he parried a low slash intended to hamstring him. A moment later his sword found the soldier's armpit, and there was another one he needn't worry about again . . .

Cut, thrust, parry, forehand, parry, backhand, parry, thrust again, then step back, don't skid in the muck or the blood . . .

Back—they were being forced back, up a steep slope on the far right side of the battlefield . . .

Thrust, parry . . . step back . . . and back again . . .

Zar was panting hard, but his arms still moved with sure precision, and he was vaguely grateful for those weeks aboard the *Enterprise,* those hours in the gym. But for them, and McCoy's healing his leg, he'd probably have been down long before now.

"Stand back! Remember my orders! The demon-spawn's mine!"

The roar in Asyri reached Zar as if from a great distance, faint compared to the din of the battle, the blood pounding in his ears, his heaving gasps for breath. The Sovren glanced around, puzzled, seeing that the Asyri warriors had drawn back into a rough circle, leaving him alone in the middle of it.

As he fought for air, he saw a big man, as tall as he was and built like a draft vykar, step out of the circle. *Who is that?* he wondered, without much curiosity, mostly concerned with trying to slow his breathing. Then he saw that the man carried his sword in his left hand; where his right hand should have been was a round ball studded with vicious spikes.

Rorgan Death-Hand, Zar realized. *The man responsible for the deaths of Wynn's husband and child.*

Out of the corner of his eye he saw Voba and the remaining members of the squad he'd led starting uphill toward him, and emphatically shook his head at his aide. *No. Whatever he wants, this may buy us sufficient time for Cletas and Yarlev's reinforcements to reach us.*

As Voba and the rest stopped obediently, Zar wondered how the rest of the battle was going. The only thing he was sure of was that Wynn was all right, since she was still there in the back of his mind, tucked away like a secret talisman against fear and loneliness.

"Do you know me, demon-spawn?" the Asyri leader bellowed hoarsely. "Even a demon has the right to know who it is that kills him."

Zar nodded silently, saving his breath, studying the way the other man stood, checking his bronze armor for vulnerable points. The Asyri chieftain wore a helmet, cuirass, scaled kilt, greaves, and a bronze arm-guard on his sword arm.

Rorgan addressed his troops. "I want the pleasure of killing him myself. This is an honor duel, so anyone who interferes with either loser or winner dies! Understood?"

The assembled Asyri warriors saluted. *Idiot,* Zar thought, dropping into guard position, watching Rorgan as the Asyri leader moved toward him. *In his place I'd have me dispatched from behind in two seconds and be on my way to New Araen. This single-combat, "he's all mine" notion is a load of vykar—*

The Asyri leader's bronze sword hissed through the air. The Sovren leaped back, parrying the blow on his shield, then slashed forehanded at Rorgan's arm. The man twisted, avoiding the blade by a handspan, and the mace swung down. Zar ducked, feeling those wicked spikes comb the plume on his helmet.

He may be a fool, but he's fast, *despite his size.*

They grappled for a moment, mace trapped against shield, blade against blade, and for the first time Zar was close enough to get a glimpse of the blue eyes and unlined features beneath the shadow of the Asyri leader's helmet. His heart sank. *And young, too. Damn. I've got twenty-five years on him, probably.*

272

The Asyri leader's huge-muscled arms bulged even more as he forced Zar's shield arm down . . . down . . .

Goddess, but he's strong . . .

With a deafening, wordless shout, the Sovren brought his mailed foot down hard on the other's booted toe, then, as Rorgan yelped, leaped back and away.

"You have no honor, demon-spawn! Stand and fight, coward!"

Zar backed away, circling, his eyes never leaving his opponent's. It had been years since he'd fought a left-handed opponent, and he had to adjust his stance accordingly. He couldn't afford to forget the mace, either. It was not only a formidable weapon, Rorgan could parry with it, too.

"I heard you married that slut of a priestess," the big man said, teeth showing in the stubble of his beard as he grinned. "But then, your mother was a slut who bedded demons, so I guess you're used to sluts, aren't you?"

Zar said nothing. Rorgan was trying to make him furious enough to attack mindlessly, but the Sovren had no trouble ignoring the insults. *I'm too old to fall for that trick,* he thought. *And you'd realize that, if you were smarter, and save your breath for fighting.*

With a wild howl, the man charged, his mace impacting on Zar's shield with staggering force. Zar had no choice but to use his sword to parry the other's cut. Their weapons *whanged* together, steel against bronze, then slid down each other until they were hilt to hilt. The Sovren had to shift his forefinger quickly to avoid losing it as Rorgan's blade ground against his. And as he did so, he hooked his heel behind Rorgan's and jerked upward with all his strength.

The Asyri went over on his back, but before the Sovren could reach him with a thrust, he rolled, coming up fast, his blade swinging in a deadly cut at Zar's neck. The Sovren ducked, taking the blow on his right shoulder, but the impact staggered him, and he nearly fell.

As he struggled to keep his feet, the mace punched into his side, sending him to his knees. Agony lanced through him, and, for a blinding second, he couldn't catch his breath. He saw motion out of the corner of his eye and ducked, automatically backhanding with his sword.

Luck was with him; the edge of the blade caught the Asyri leader on the thigh, biting deeply enough to wring an involuntary cry from Rorgan.

Zar gasped again, managing this time to catch his breath, though the air stabbed his left side like a dagger. He lurched to his feet and scuttled backward, trying to flex his sword arm.

"You're going to die here," Rorgan growled, advancing again, though he was clearly limping now. "I'm going to rip your guts out with my bare hands and use them to hang you off your own walls!"

Zar licked dry lips, stealing a glance at his surroundings. *Where the hell is Cletas?* For the first time, he realized that the ground beneath his feet sloped downward on all sides to Moorgate Plain, where the battle still raged.

I'm on a little hill . . . a hillock . . . just as Spock described it . . . this is it, then, the moment that he saw . . . He eyed Rorgan's mace. *And that must be the impact weapon that kills me . . .*

The Asyri leader came in again, swinging the mace hard, even as he slashed at his opponent's legs with his sword. Zar ducked and leaped forward, parrying with his shield, then slammed it into the man's midsection. Rorgan's breath went out with a grunt and he folded up at the waist so completely that they both went over onto the ground, with Zar on top. They rolled from side to side, gasping, kicking, pounding at each other's head and shoulders with the hilts of their swords.

Suddenly Rorgan dropped his weapon and slammed his gauntleted palm upward into Zar's face. White-hot pain exploded in the Sovren's eye and nose, and he dropped his sword, but he retained just enough presence of mind not to take his weight off the mace that he had managed to pin beneath his shield.

Gritting his teeth, the Sovren turned his head to the side and repeatedly slammed his helmet into Rorgan's face. The nose-guard of his helm protected the Asyri, but he jerked back involuntarily, shifting position, and suddenly Zar was able to bring his knee up viciously into his enemy's groin. The chieftain yowled in agony.

The Sovren tried to follow up his advantage, but before he could draw his dagger, Rorgan heaved beneath him and sent him tumbling over onto his back. Zar lurched to his hands and knees, the air rasping his lungs, his side stabbing fire, and scrabbled sideways for his sword, lying a meter away in the mud.

Even as he touched it, the mace impacted with his left shoulder hard enough to knock the buckler spinning from his grasp. Zar snatched up his sword and rolled away, but the Asyri had sagged back onto the ground, groaning. Zar staggered to his feet, blinking, trying to see where his shield had fallen.

Something's wrong with my eye, he realized dazedly, and touched his face with his free hand, noting detachedly that the fingers of his gauntlet came away bloody. He peered around him again, but could not find the shield.

I can't parry without it, he thought desperately. *One blow from that damned mace will break my sword.*

The Asyri leader was also back on his feet again, but now he was hobbling, his face drawn with pain and rage. "While you're hung from your own walls, dying, demon-spawn," he wheezed, "you can watch me with your slut. If you beg hard enough, I may be merciful enough to kill her after I'm done."

Rorgan came toward him, sword in hand, the mace held ready.

Zar had been thinking fast. *Only one chance,* he decided. *And it'll leave me completely open to a head attack. If I fail, that mace is going to do exactly what Spock described . . .*

As Rorgan moved in, Zar backed quickly away, altering his grip on the hilt of his sword, shifting to present his right side to the Asyri leader. He moved his left foot, turning it outward at a ninety-degree angle so he could use it to push off—*couldn't have done this before*—then, praying his aching shoulder would hold out, he leaped forward onto his right foot, his body uncoiling in a full-extension lunge, just as Sulu had coached him.

The sword-point plunged through the leather kilt, sinking deep into the Asyri leader's body. Rorgan dropped his weapon, staring down in shocked horror at himself as Zar pulled his blade free, then the chieftain's knees buckled, and he fell. Zar looked up, seeing the stunned expressions of the Asyri warriors, and, beyond them, Cletas and his troops coming downslope.

"Coward . . . afraid to kill me, demon-spawn . . ." came a choked whisper from his feet. The Sovren looked down to see Rorgan lying on his side, hands clamped to his belly, knees drawn up, writhing uncontrollably. Gut wounds usually meant a particularly slow and agonizing death.

For a moment Zar relaxed his mind-shield slightly, and the agony the Asyri was feeling flooded into him, making his knees buckle. Hastily, he shut out the other's pain, positive now that Rorgan had indeed received his death wound. But it would take him the rest of the day to die, probably.

"Do you want me to?" the Sovren asked in Asyri, thinking that Wynn would have something to say to him if he showed *this* man mercy. But he couldn't condemn anyone to the suffering he'd experienced in his moment of empathy with the chieftain.

Mad blue eyes glared up at him from a sweating, muddy face. "You . . . not enough courage . . . to give me honorable death . . . demon . . ."

Zar sighed as he drew Zarabeth's knife. "Don't thank me, then," he muttered in his own language. "But I'm doing you a favor, and it's going to get me into trouble with my wife." Quickly, he pulled back the Asyri leader's chin and drew the knife across the top of the throat, making sure he slashed both the internal and external carotid arteries.

Rorgan was dead by the time he'd retrieved his shield, halfway across the circle. Zar brought his sword up into guard position, struggling to catch his breath, feeling the grandfather of all stitches in his side, as he eyed the ring of warriors surrounding him. He began turning wearily in a slow circle. "Who's next?" he called, in Asyri.

Nobody seemed anxious to step forward. He let out a long sigh of relief (which hurt). *I can't believe it*, he thought. *I'm still here. I've won. Now, if we can only—*

Zar never felt the blow that struck the side of his head, and sent him hurtling down into immediate and unending darkness.

Chapter Fifteen

SPOCK MATERIALIZED out of nothingness on a rocky, brush-covered slope between two gigantic gray boulders. The Vulcan glanced around him, then gave a short, satisfied nod—the Guardian had, as requested, deposited him in the foothills bordering Moorgate Plain. He wanted to survey the battlefield from a higher elevation, in an attempt to locate Zar's position. He knew where his son *ought* to be—but that was no guarantee that he was there. The Sovren had planned to personally lead the first wave of reinforcement troops, so he could be anywhere along the front lines.

Spock had no difficulty locating the battle itself, even though he could not see it.

In the first place, he could hear it—the clang of weapons, the shrieks of wounded people and animals, war-cries filled with terror or triumph—even from some distance away, it was an appalling din, and the closer he drew, the more ear-shattering it became.

But the sound, horrible as it was, was as nothing compared to the smell—the mingled stench of blood, excrement, vomit, and death. The Vulcan nearly gagged the first time he rounded a boulder and almost stumbled over the sprawled body of a soldier, guts trailing behind him for meters, who was covered in a living curtain of insects that rose, buzzing angrily, from their feast.

He swallowed hard, clenching his teeth. Clamping down iron control, Spock stepped around the body and moved on, holding his lirpa at the ready.

He emerged from the foothills at the lower edge of the plain, not far from the Redbank, and for a moment stood staring in horror at the battleground before him. Moorgate Plain was a roiled sea of mud, smashed chariots, and bodies—animal and human, living and dead.

Spock had seen war and its results; had picked his way through colonies devastated by Klingon or Romulan attack, had ministered to dull-eyed refugees who were literally more dead than alive. But war in his time was usually cleaner. Phasers and disruptors killed instantly, neatly vaporizing the bodies.

The main fighting was still some distance ahead of him, near the mountain pass leading to New Araen. Storm clouds shouldered their way over the peak of Big Snowy as Spock began trotting toward the conflict, constantly scanning the horizon for a certain hillock, one forever fixed in his memory.

Often, he had to slow to a walk, trying to pick a way through the maze of caved-in pits, spilled entrails, gutted bodies, and weapons, some still clutched in severed hands or arms.

Whenever possible, he detoured around the bodies, but in places they were piled waist- and even shoulder-high, and he was forced to use the buffeting end of the lirpa to roll enough of them out of the way so he could step over them.

And the worst of it was, not all of them were dead.

"I'm sorry," he murmured, the first time an armored figure clawed at his boot, begging for water. Her shoulder was a hacked ruin. "I'm sorry, but I don't have any."

He moved on, trying not to hear them. But it was impossible. *"Water,"* they pleaded or demanded, mostly, and sometimes, *"help me,"* or *"kill me."* Some spoke in languages he did not know, but he understood their meaning anyway.

One wounded man, maddened by pain, lunged at the

Vulcan with a halberd, and Spock had to use the lirpa to knock him aside.

He was getting closer to the battle; the clang of weapons was louder, mixed now with the gathering rumble of thunder. And still he had not identified the little rise where Zar would fall.

Or had fallen.

Or was even now falling.

The Vulcan tried to go faster, slipping and skidding in the greasy muck that seemed to be composed of equal parts mud and spilled blood. It didn't help that the blood was almost the color of his own.

He found that he had to check some of the little hills from several different angles, which slowed him down further. *I may be too late . . . even now, I may be too late . . .*

He was on the fringes of the fighting now, and several times had to defend himself for a moment before he could run. But he was not wearing armor, and offered no challenge, so most of the combatants simply ignored him.

Which hill? There are so many. I'm on the side of the field where Zar was supposed to be directing the Lakreo forces, but suppose he crossed over to the other side? Am I too late?

Spock could tell that Zar's forces were being driven back, but the retreat was controlled, orderly. *The Lakreo and Danreg forces are inflicting heavy damage. If they can hold out long enough, they stand a chance of winning.*

He staggered and slid in the muck, catching himself with the lirpa. *Which hill? They all look the same!*

As he stared, a voice echoed in his mind: *Straight ahead. Hurry.* Such was the ring of authority in those warm, ringing tones that the Vulcan began to obey, even before he recognized the identity of the mind-touch.

The Guardian! But how can it know?

Still, he had no other guide, so he forged straight ahead, running hard now.

Which way, Guardian? he thought, as he passed another hillock, his breath catching fire in his chest.

To your left. Hurry. Hurry.

Spock bore left, trying to pick up his pace despite the rocks underfoot. He was in the midst of the front lines, but, strangely, many of the troops in this portion of the field were not fighting. Instead, knots of soldiers from both sides huddled in small groups with their comrades, staring up at one of the little hills. Spock zig-zagged around them, anxiously scanning the ground to his left—*nothing . . . nothing, am I too late?*

There! The one they're all staring at! That's the one!

Unwrapping the ahn-woon from around his waist, Spock dropped the lirpa and raced toward the hillock he'd recognized, putting on a burst of speed that made his heart feel as if it were about to explode. He could hear shouts of encouragement and the sounds of a struggle as he reached its foot, then, as he began to climb, all sounds abruptly ceased.

Gasping, the Vulcan scrambled the last few meters, finding himself on the edge of a circle of warriors. An armed figure stood in the middle of that circle, dripping sword up and ready, clutching a small, battered shield. Spock could not see the man's face, but from his stance and his chain mail, the Vulcan recognized Zar. A blood-drenched body lay sprawled at his feet. Spock heard his son call out a phrase in a language he did not recognize, then the Sovren pivoted slowly around.

As Zar's back appeared, Spock glimpsed a flash of movement to his own left—one of the Asyri warriors leaped forward, axe raised high, his movement the same as the one the Vulcan had witnessed on the screen of his tricorder.

"No!" The Vulcan knocked startled enemy soldiers aside as though they were straw men, and lunged after the Asyri. With every bit of skill he had in him, Spock lashed out with the ahn-woon, his target the warrior's raised weapon—

—and *missed.*

The ahn-woon whipped around the man's neck, instead, and even as the Vulcan jerked back on it, the flat of the axehead impacted with the Sovren's red-plumed helmet. The blow echoed in Spock's mind, as he saw Zar half whirled around with its force, glimpsed his son's bloody face, heard him grunt as the breath went out of him.

Zar's knees buckled . . . he fell forward . . . to lie, unmoving.

A dreadful calm settled over Spock. *I've failed. To come this close and fail . . .*

Absently, he looked down at the man he had pulled down, seeing that he was dead. The body was still twitching, but the Asyri's neck was obviously broken.

I did not intend to kill him . . . Spock thought, dully, but he could not summon any remorse for his action.

The handle of the ahn-woon slid out of his numb fingers, and he left it where it fell. Blindly, the Vulcan pushed his way through the Lakreo troops that were suddenly milling about, crowding the top of the little hillock.

As he reached the sprawled figure, Spock saw the dent in the right side of the battered steel helmet. He dropped to his knees beside his son's still body, and, gently but hopelessly, rolled him over onto his back. The face that came into view was a gory greenish mask, the right eye puffed nearly shut, the mouth split, the nose swollen and canted. Blood trickled from one nostril in a thin, steady stream . . .

Blood trickled . . .

Blood *trickled* . . .

Spock stared unbelievingly at the blood, watching it well, then drip—

If he's bleeding, he's still alive!

Hastily, he slipped a finger beneath the edge of Zar's helmet and touched his temple. He sensed the low-level mental activity even as he felt the pulse—weak and thready, but there! He put a hand over his son's mouth and nose, and after a moment, warm breath brushed his palm.

A gauntleted hand seized his wrist and yanked it away, even as a voice snapped, "What the hell do you think you're—"

Spock looked up, seeing that it was Cletas who had grabbed him. The Second stared at him, then let go. "I'm sorry, sir. I didn't realize who you were."

"He's alive," Spock said, reaching for his tricorder.

"Yes, I see," Cletas agreed, crouching on his heels beside the Vulcan. "Dead men don't bleed."

"We have to take him to safety." Spock glanced up, to find Voba kneeling across from them. He studied the tricorder's readings. "Concussion . . . possibly serious. He could go into shock, especially with the ground this cold and damp. We'll need a stretcher."

Voba snapped out an order to one of the Lakreo guards, and the woman saluted, then raced off.

I had better get that armor off, so he can breathe, the Vulcan thought. He began fumblingly to unfasten Zar's helmet, but the red-haired aide-de-camp gently pushed his hand away. "I'll do that, sir. I'm used to it."

"So much for the prophecy," Cletas muttered, glancing at the troops milling around them. "Damn it all, we were holding them . . ." he began swearing, a profane litany in a language Spock didn't understand.

"What prophecy?" the Vulcan asked.

Cletas busied himself helping Voba unlace the sides of the Sovren's byrnie. "Wynn's oracle," he said, distractedly. "She pronounced it to the enemy troops the afternoon before we captured her—'if he who is halt walks healed, if he who is death-struck in battle rises whole, then Ashmara will turn her face from us'—meaning that, unless he wakes up and walks out there, we've had it. If our troops think he's dead—and the word that he's fallen will be spreading like wildfire, it always does—that's going to take the spirit right out of them. The invaders will run over us like the Redbank in flood."

"'If he who is halt . . .'" Spock repeated, slowly. "But half the prophecy has already been fulfilled. Zar is no longer lame."

"Right enough," Voba said, "but now he's got to stand up and walk out there, where they can all see him . . . and there's no way that's going to happen—even if he lives, he'll not be on his feet for days."

Spock, his mind racing, thought of the silently staring

faces, defender and invader alike, and an idea came to him. The Vulcan met Cletas's gaze squarely. "Suppose he *does* stand up and walk out there?"

"But he—" The Second's eyes widened as sudden understanding flowed between them like a current. *"Yes! By Ashmara, it could work!"* He turned his head and shouted, "Guards! Guards! Stand close, here, shoulder to shoulder. On the double! I want a complete circle."

Quickly, they were surrounded, walled in, by soldiers. Cletas snatched up the blood-smeared helm. "Here, put this on. No—wait, you'll need mail first. Nobody will notice the breeches, but the mail—"

With frantic haste, he began ripping at the lacings of his own byrnie. "Voba, where's his red cloak?"

"I have it," the little aide said, calmly.

The Second dragged his byrnie, then his padded undergarment, over his head. Cletas shivered as fat raindrops spattered onto his bare shoulders. "Put this on. Don't bother lacing, you'll have the cloak to cover it. Here." He thrust the mail shirt and the quilted leather at the Vulcan.

Spock pulled the shirt, followed by the byrnie, over his head. He rose to his feet, feeling the unaccustomed weight of the armor settle onto his shoulders. "How should I do this?"

"Just stand there on the hillside and let them notice you," Cletas said, pointing, holding out the battered helmet. "Then take off the helm and let them see your face. The cloak, Voba."

The aide swung the red folds around Spock's shoulders. "You're thinner," Cletas fussed, pulling the mail into place.

"From a distance, nobody will notice that," Voba said, sounding positive. "Here's the sword, sir."

As Spock eased the scarlet-plumed helmet over his head, the aide hastily buckled Zar's swordbelt around him.

Cletas growled a soft order at the surrounding guards, and they all snapped to attention, saluting, as Spock stepped between two of them, out from behind the screen of armored bodies.

Several of the Asyri captives gasped when they saw him.

Trying to imitate Zar's walk, Spock strode boldly over to the side of the hill and stood there, silhouetted against the livid, dark-clouded sky, the scarlet cloak whipping behind him in the gusty wind. Thunder rumbled ominously.

He had been there only a few seconds when somebody noticed him and pointed, then an uncertain cheer began rising from the Lakreo forces. Spock waited another beat, then pulled off the helmet, tucking it under his left arm.

The cheer strengthened as more and more of the troops turned to look up, until it flowed up to him in waves of deafening jubilation. The Vulcan could see the Asyri and Kerren forces hesitate, then begin pointing up at him, obviously frightened. *They're almost ready to flee,* he thought. *But I need something else . . . Jim has a flair for the dramatic. What would he do?*

The answer came to him immediately, and he grasped the sticky hilt of the sword at his left hip, then drew it, holding the stained blade high in salute.

"Victory!" Spock shouted, so loudly his throat hurt.

A white crack of jagged lightning split the sky above him, followed a moment later by a deafening clap of thunder.

The enemy troops broke and ran.

"Easy, now," Voba cautioned. "Just slide him off, don't lift him."

Gently, Spock and the guards moved Zar's unconscious body onto the bed, then the aide dismissed the two soldiers.

"Now let's see the rest of the damage," the little man muttered, expertly slitting the quilted leather padding with his knife and peeling it off gently.

"You've done this before, I take it," Spock observed.

"I can assign a battle to most of these scars," Voba told the Vulcan grimly. "Hmm . . . no cuts . . . will you look at both shoulders . . . and the ribs . . . ouch, he won't be able to do much with that new wife of his for awhile will he?" the little man mumbled, mostly to himself.

"He took quite a beating," Orwin said, eyeing the huge,

emerald bruises and wondering where Zar had put the medical kit McCoy had spoken of giving him.

Voba snorted indignantly. "He gave every bit as good as he got. If Rorgan weren't lying there dead, he'd look worse . . . and *his* wives would be lucky if he was ever any good to them again."

Spock's mouth twitched, and he hastily cleared his throat. "You watched the fight?"

"We could see most of it, from where we stood upslope." Voba smiled reminiscently. "That was a fight, that was."

The door opened, and Wynn limped in, still wearing her armor. Blood had sprayed onto her face like darker greenish freckles, and the front of her mail was dull with it, but she seemed relatively unhurt, except for a stained rag knotted around her knee.

"How is he?" she asked, moving to Zar's side.

"I was just taking a good look at him," Voba said. "He's been out like a pinched candlewick ever since he was hit, over an hour ago, now."

Wynn gently parted Zar's hair and examined the swollen lump on the right side of his head, careful not to touch it. "Hmm." She rested her fingers on the pulse at his throat, then peeled back each eyelid to watch the pupil dilate, and finally lifted his upper lip to check the color of his gums. "Hmmm." Her brisk, unemotional manner reminded Spock vividly of Leonard McCoy.

"For the moment, his lifelink is steady," she pronounced, glancing up at them. "I wish McCoy were here. Or can you use the box-that-whirrs, Spock? The one that sees inside a body?"

"I already did," Spock answered. "And it agreed with you. He is in no immediate danger."

She looked pleased. "But we need to get this swelling down. Voba, send someone up to the high pastures on Big Snowy to bring back a big bag of ice and snow. Until then, we'll use cold-water compresses."

The aide scowled conspiratorially at the Vulcan. "Are healers where you come from as bossy, sir?" he whispered.

Spock nodded. "It appears to be a universal trait."

Voba left, muttering under his breath.

Wynn was pulling off her armor, wincing as she bent over to take off her greaves. "Are you all right?" Spock said.

"Not bad," she grunted, struggling to pull her byrnie over her head without unlacing it. "Shallow cut, but it bled a lot . . . lucky . . . any deeper, and I'd have been hamstrung . . ."

Wynn dropped the mail with the rest of her armor and disappeared next door, where he heard her snapping orders at someone, then she returned, minus her kilt, wearing a clean gray homespun skirt and a thin white linen shirt. She rolled the sleeves up briskly, poured water from the ewer into the basin, then began scrubbing her face, hands, and arms.

Spock watched her, surprised, and she must have picked up his reaction because she explained, "My teacher, Clarys, was the greatest healer my people ever had. One of the first things she taught me was that disease demons are attracted by dirt."

Spock raised an eyebrow. "That is one way of putting it," he conceded. "Was it she who discovered that cold brings down swelling?"

"No, that remedy has been around for generations," Wynn said, drying her hands, then returning to the bed. "I'd better wash his face before he wakes. It's going to hurt him."

She stood looking down at her husband for a moment, and for an instant Spock glimpsed a break in her cool, professional demeanor. "Thank Ashmara he's alive," she whispered, gently brushing his hair off his forehead. Then she straightened, all business once more. "Would you hand me that soap, please?"

"I know of something that would be even better than soap for driving away disease demons," Spock said. "It was in a bag," he measured off a space with his hands, "black in color, and Zar would have brought it back from the *Enterprise.*" He raised an eyebrow. "Did he tell you about the ship?"

"The space-wagon that flies between stars," Wynn said, nodding. "And I remember the bag you speak of. It's in the weapons cabinet." She pointed.

Spock located the medical bag, took out the medical tricorder and antiseptic solution. He opened the latter, then handed it to Wynn. "Use this."

She sniffed the container skeptically, wrinkling her nose. "Strong stuff."

"Disease demons cannot abide it," Spock said, perfectly straight-faced.

"I believe it." She poured some of the solution onto the bleached cloth she'd produced. "Stand ready, please. This may bring him around, and he must *not* be allowed to get up. He'd only faint, and perhaps injure himself worse, falling."

"I understand." Spock watched as she began cleaning the blood and filth off Zar's face, her touch sure and delicate. "What makes you think he will try to get up?"

She gave him a sideways glance. "Male patients usually behave in either of two ways: One, they're such babies that you want to shove them out of bed after hearing them whine and complain for ages; *or,* two, you have to sit on them to prevent them from trying to get up, so they can take care of everything they think is going wrong during their absence. I'll wager this one is the 'let me up' kind, but, of course, I could be wrong."

Spock raised an eyebrow. "Surely female patients are not always reasonable."

"They're not as apt to make fools of themselves by trying to get up immediately, but it's hard to make most of them rest long enough," she said. "The minute they begin to feel better, they get up, do too much, then end up relapsing."

By now Zar's face was clean enough so that Spock could see the cut above his eye that had caused much of the bleeding. *He'll have a scar beneath that eyebrow.* The skin around both of Zar's eyes was already turning greenish-black, and both lips were split.

The Vulcan examined the revealed features closely. "His nose is broken."

Wynn nodded. "When the swelling goes down, I'll try to straighten it out. It's going to leave a bump, though." Her patient stirred, then groaned. "He's coming around. Watch him." She hurried across the room to the washstand to empty the bloody antiseptic solution out of the basin and bring it back to the opposite side of the bed from Spock.

Zar's head turned restlessly on the pillow, then the less swollen of his eyelids lifted, and he squinted up at his father. When he finally spoke, his voice was a thready, stuffy-nosed wheeze. "I *dew* it . . . I'm dead 'n gone to Hell, right?"

The Vulcan hid his profound relief with an exaggerated sigh. "Very funny. How do you feel?"

"Terrible . . . can't see bery well . . . can't breathe bery well . . . hurts all over . . ."

"That is because you have two black eyes and a broken nose, a broken rib, plus numerous bruises, contusions, and a moderately severe concussion. But it seems as though you will recover."

The gray eye blinked, then sharpened suddenly. "The battle! By . . . my troops! Got . . . got to go see—" Panting, Zar began pushing himself up, trying to swing his legs to the side.

"No," Spock commanded, hastily locating two relatively unbruised areas and holding the patient down. "The battle is over. Your people won. And you are not going anywhere."

"But—"

"Lie still, or you'll get sick," Wynn admonished. She gave the Vulcan an "I-told-you-so" look.

"Wynn?" Zar whispered, putting out a hand. She gripped it. "Is there anything I can get you, my dear?"

He tried to swallow. "Water . . . so thirsty. We really *won?*" His good eye peered incredulously at first one, then the other of them as they nodded. "Casualties?"

"Remarkably light," Spock said. "Cletas is handling things in your absence. He said to tell you not to worry."

"Remember . . . fighting . . . trying to hold Zaylenz's line." Zar frowned. "My vykar was lame . . . is he all right?"

His wife shook her head. "I don't know. But I promise I'll ask Cletas to check," she assured him. "Here . . . just a few sips."

Zar gulped the water thirstily, then made a face when Wynn took the goblet away. "Rorgan and Laol?"

"Heldeon captured Laol," Wynn said. "And you killed Rorgan yourself, in an honor-duel, so they tell me."

"*I* did? Was that when I broke my dose . . . nose?" Gingerly, he reached up to touch his face, but Wynn prevented him.

Spock nodded.

"Too bad . . ." Zar mumbled. "Always was proud of this nose." His battered mouth twisted into a lopsided smile. "Inherited it from m' old man y'see . . ."

He passed out again.

Spock hunted through the medical kit and found an ampule of tri-ox. "This will help him breathe," he told Wynn, as he pressed the hypo to Zar's shoulder.

The patient recovered consciousness almost immediately. "Th' battle . . ." he said, seeming more alert than before. "Who won?"

"We did." Wynn smiled at him. "A complete victory."

Zar relaxed slightly. "Good . . ."

"Do you remember fighting with Rorgan?" she asked.

"I did?" The gray eye was puzzled. "Oh, yes . . ." He started to nod, but quickly stopped himself. "Remember bits 'n' pieces . . ." He looked sideways at Wynn, suddenly contrite. "I gave him a merciful death."

She shrugged. "We all make mistakes." Spock could not tell whether she was being sarcastic.

Zar grimaced. ". . . starting to come back. Tell Hikaru the fencing practice . . . came in handy. Used that lunge . . ." He sighed. "And tell McCoy . . . I kept his leg safe . . ." The gray eye began to close. "My sword?"

"I brought it back," Spock said. "Voba put it away."

"Good . . ." Zar lapsed into quiet for such a long time that the Vulcan thought he had passed out again, or fallen asleep, but then he stirred and muttered, "The battle . . . who won?"

"You did," Spock said, but Zar did not respond. The Vulcan cast a concerned glance over at Wynn.

She answered his unspoken question softly. "Happens all the time with blows to the head. They're confused at first, and their memories are patchy."

The Vulcan took out the medical tricorder and scanned its readings again. They reassured him slightly. There was no internal bleeding, no skull fracture . . . but his son's disorientation worried Spock.

Wynn leaned over to place a cold compress on the side of Zar's head, and the little instrument's readings altered abruptly as they registered her metabolism. Spock's eyes widened, then he deliberately scanned her again, his eyebrow rising. A faint smile touched his mouth.

The cold cloth roused the patient again. "Ouch . . ." Zar looked over at Spock. "What're *you* smirking about?"

"Vulcans," Spock said placidly, with utmost dignity, "never smirk. Incidentally, congratulations. To both of you."

Wynn gave him a puzzled glance. "On our victory?"

"Among other things," Spock said enigmatically, shutting off the tricorder and putting it back in the medical kit.

Zar seemed about to pursue the matter, but a sudden thought occurred to him and he struggled to get up again. "The wounded! Got to check whether they're—"

"No," Spock and Wynn said together, holding him down until he finally surrendered, gasping.

"Are you going to lie still now, you fool?" Wynn scolded. Sweat beaded her husband's face as he nodded meekly, then he paled, gulped ominously, put a hand to his mouth and mumbled, "Feel as if I'm going to—"

"I warned you," Wynn told him, with a grim smile, and held his head over the basin.

Spock awoke the next morning to find Voba putting another log on the fire. He straightened up stiffly, realizing that he'd fallen asleep in the chair beside the fireplace. His time sense assured him that it was still early.

Across the room Zar was asleep, breathing much more

normally. Wynn sat cross-legged at the foot of the bed, her back braced against the bedpost, her chin drooping as she dozed. They'd taken turns rousing their patient at intervals throughout the night, to make sure he *could* be awakened, but at some point weariness had obviously overcome both of them.

His back protested as Spock stood up. Voba was watching him. "How about some breakfast, sir?"

The Vulcan realized that he was extremely hungry; he'd forgotten to eat yesterday. "Yes, thank you, I would appreciate that. No meat, please. Cereal, or bread and cheese . . . fruit—any of those would be welcome. Actually," Spock admitted, "they would *all* be welcome. I am very hungry."

"Right away, sir."

As Voba left, Wynn stirred, rubbed her eyes, mumbled something Spock took to be a greeting, then went into her adjoining room. The Vulcan took the opportunity to stretch the kinks out of his back, then used one of the jugs of melted ice-water to wash up.

He felt better for being clean, and the cold water cleared the last of the sleep from his mind. Spock walked over to look down at Zar. The snow and ice compresses had helped; though still pale and bruised, his son looked much more like himself. He was obviously in a normal sleep.

The Vulcan touched his arm gently. "Zar?"

Both eyelids rose, then the gray eyes widened. *"Father? What are you doing here?"*

"Good morning," Spock said. "Are you hungry?"

Zar nodded absently, as if surprised to discover that he was. "You were here yesterday, weren't you? I remember you telling me we won." He blinked. "And you held me down."

"Yes, I did. You appear better this morning."

"I am. Will you tackle me again if I try to sit up?"

The Vulcan hesitated. "I think that would be all right. If you take it slowly."

Stiffly, his son pushed himself up, stifling a groan as he moved his ribcage. Spock hastily placed another pillow behind his back to support him. "Things were so strange, yesterday . . ." Zar frowned. "I couldn't think rationally most of the time. I remember asking you questions and not understanding the answers."

"Do you remember the battle, now? The fight with Rorgan?"

"Dimly. But," he looked over at the Vulcan, bewildered, "you're not supposed to be here! Why did you come back?"

"To save your life, my dear," Wynn said, emerging from the connecting door and crossing the room with her long, decisive stride. This morning she wore boots, breeches, and a sleeveless jerkin of tan leather. "If it hadn't been for him, my unfortunate prophecy would have come true."

Zar stared at her, then turned to look at Spock while Wynn leaned over to feel her patient's forehead, peer into his eyes, and check his pulse. As she straightened up, her husband caught her hand and pulled her down to sit on the bed beside him. "Don't go. I want you right here," he ordered, his fingers tight around hers. "Now, tell me what happened."

Wynn launched into an account of the battle and the events following the fight with Rorgan Death-Hand.

When she finished, Zar sat staring at the Vulcan in silence for a long time. Finally he said, "If there's a logical reason for your actions yesterday, I'd like to know what it is."

Spock looked down. "I told you before that I've discovered that some things transcend logic. This was one of them."

"But the time-stream! If I was meant to die yesterday, didn't your action compromise its integrity?"

The Vulcan shook his head. "I do not believe so. Changes made in the distant past—and 5,000 years is fairly distant—tend to be smoothed out over the years. The Mordreaux equations show that one's ability to alter events in the past is inversely proportional to the square of the distance in time one travels."

Zar shut his eyes for a moment, obviously visualizing the equation. Finally, he nodded. "I see that, yes . . ."

"Besides," Spock continued, "my examination of the time-stream, as I told you, showed peace coming to the

Lakreo Valley, and I doubt that your continued presence will change that destiny." The Vulcan raised an ironic eyebrow. "Or will you take advantage of your new, 'supernatural' ability to return from the dead, and wage wars of aggression against your neighbors?"

His son shook his head, ruefully. "You know better than that."

Spock nodded. "Yes, I do. But the main reason for my action was that I found that I could not stand by, that I *had* to try and help. Actually," he shrugged again, self-deprecatingly, "I missed with the ahn-woon. So, while I may have deflected that axe slightly, I suspect it was the mail hood that saved your life, not any action of mine."

"But if you and Wynn hadn't warned me, I wouldn't have put on that extra armor," Zar pointed out.

Voba chose that moment to arrive with the food, and they ate in silence. After his aide-de-camp had removed the dishes, Zar questioned him as to the status of the Lakreo wounded, was assured that Cletas and Heldeon had everything well in hand, then thanked the little man for his report. "I don't know what I'd do without you, Voba, I really don't."

The aide colored, mumbled something inaudible, then beat a hasty retreat. "He's always been like that," Zar observed, with a faint smile. "I wanted to make him Third-in-War a couple of years ago, but he refused. Said if I didn't have someone to look after me, I wouldn't last through the next winter. But he'd rather I just took him for granted, rather than thank him."

He turned his head to look squarely at Spock. "Are *you* going to let me thank you? I owe you . . ." his hand squeezed Wynn's, "more than my life. More than anything you did for me personally, when you impersonated me, you saved my people."

Spock allowed himself a faint smile. "Some of the credit for that belongs to Cletas. Without his help—and his armor—I could not have done it. I merely provided the . . . image. The doppelgänger."

Zar chuckled a little. "I wish I could've seen that. I'll bet some of those Asyri are *still* running. My reputation as the undying son of a demon is now so entrenched that I doubt I'll have any trouble with the neighboring tribes or clans for a long time."

The Vulcan nodded. "So now you can do more of what you wanted to do—teach, develop that printing press, and the paper to use in it—those things, instead of fighting continually."

"I'll probably always have to do more fighting than I care to, but you're right. Besides," he gave Wynn a sidelong glance, "I'm thinking about abdicating in favor of my consort, here. I'll let her give the orders, since she's so good at it."

She laughed, shaking her head. "I refuse to do all the work, my lord. Besides, in two days you'd be itching to take back the reins."

Spock rose to his feet. "I would like to stay longer, but I must return to my ship. It will not take the admiral long to realize that I have gone, and where. The last time I left without orders he threatened to push me out the airlock without a vacuum suit if I ever did it again."

Wynn slid off the bed and walked around it to face the Vulcan. "Farewell, Father-kin," she said, softly, her green eyes shining. "I will miss you. May Ashmara hold you in Her hand, always. And thank you."

Spock gave her a formal salute, "Peace and long life, Lady Wynn."

She nodded, then addressed Zar without turning her head. "And you, my dear lord . . . don't you *dare* get up, understand?" Then she was gone, the connecting door shutting behind her.

The Vulcan watched her leave, his mouth twitching slightly. "At times, she reminds me of a cross between Leonard McCoy and James T. Kirk."

His son smiled ruefully. "Frightening, isn't it? I'll tell you one thing . . . wild vykar couldn't drag me out of this bed until she gives me permission. I shudder to think what she'd do."

"Were you serious about abdicating?"

The Sovren shrugged. "I don't know. If I thought I could do so successfully, I'd abdicate in a minute. But that wouldn't be fair to Wynn. I suspect I'll be trapped here, doing a job I don't like, for the rest of my days.

"But I decided before I left the *Enterprise* that if I made it through that battle, things were going to be different, and they will be. I can gradually shift some of the load onto Wynn's shoulders—and I'm going to insist that the Council take a bigger part in the day-to-day business of governing." He glanced up at Spock. "Listen to me—I'm talking just to keep you here, which isn't fair."

"I asked," the Vulcan said, simply. He took a deep breath. "I wish I could stay, but you know that I cannot."

Zar sighed, nodding. "I'm already missing you. I'll . . . we'll . . . never see each other again, will we?"

"No," Spock said, hearing the roughness in his own voice. "No, knowing the restrictions placed on the use of the Guardian, I cannot imagine that we will. I . . . regret . . . that."

"So do I." Zar drew a long, shaky breath. "I . . . oh, damn, this is hard, isn't it?"

"Yes."

Spock swallowed, then silently held out his hand. Zar gripped it, and for a second, the words they could not speak aloud surged between them.

Then the Vulcan gave a slight backward pull, and the hard, calloused fingers clenched around his immediately let go. He glanced up, met the gray eyes one final time, then nodded. "Farewell, son. Peace and long life."

"Farewell, Father." Zar had to pause for a second. "Live long and prosper."

Spock did not trust himself to look back as he strode forward, feeling the Guardian's time-displacement seize him. A heartbeat later he was standing on Gateway's chill, sterile soil, hearing that eternal, moaning wind.

The Vulcan stood in silence for several minutes, then he took his tricorder out, aiming it at the time portal's central opening. "Guardian," he said, "thank you for helping me save him."

"He is my friend," the time-entity said, its inner glow awakening. "Have you a request, Spock of Vulcan?"

"Yes. Please show me the history of the planet Sarpeidon."

As the scenes began flashing before him, this last time, Spock stood with his head bowed, not trying to watch, letting the tricorder run until the final nova-burst of energy.

"Thank you, Guardian."

"You are welcome."

Then, mechanically, he turned off the instrument, took his communicator out of his pocket, flipped it open. "Spock to *Enterprise*. I am requesting beam-up."

Kirk's voice emanated from the little speaker, surprisingly gentle. "Spock? You sound . . . are you all right?"

The Vulcan swallowed. "I will be, Jim." He turned to look back through the Guardian, seeing in his mind's eye Zar's face, envisioning Wynn beside him . . . knowing he was no longer so desperately alone.

Good-bye, my son . . .

The transporter beam caught him, wrenching him into his component sub-atomic particles and waves, then he was gone.

Epilogue

JAMES T. KIRK raised his snifter of Saurian brandy. "A toast," he said. "To absent friends." *And sons,* he added silently, as the liquor slid over his tongue, warm and heady.

Spock and McCoy gravely raised their glasses and drank.

The three officers were sitting in the small lounge area in Kirk's cabin, the "night" following the Vulcan's return from Sarpeidon. The admiral could feel the faint, unhurried vibration of the *Enterprise*'s engines carrying him back to Earth, back to his duties there.

Kirk sighed and sat back in his chair, idly glancing around his cabin. He had come aboard too quickly to have brought much in the way of personal possessions; unlike Spock, he was not aboard the *Enterprise* enough to cause this cabin to be reserved for his exclusive use. But, despite its bareness, it was home, as no other place ever had been, or would be.

Soon, the admiral thought, *I'll be back in that bureaucratic tangle again. I hate the thought of it.* Still, it was his duty, and he'd spent his entire adult existence doing his duty. He could not envision a life outside Starfleet.

But if it hadn't been for Starfleet, and the Enterprise, *he found himself musing, Carol and I might still be together. David might be a part of my life.*

He finished the brandy, and then, with a slight air of

defiance, poured himself another and sipped. The warmth in his stomach was already spreading to the rest of his body.

Kirk remembered the boy's face as it had been when he'd last seen him as an adolescent. *Not much of me there. He definitely takes after Carol . . . coloring and everything. Don't think he liked me much—but that's not surprising. Kids are sensitive, and I felt so awkward that I'm sure he picked up on it.*

That had been what—ten years ago? At least. How old would David be now? To his shame, he could not remember.

Years ago, I was wrong when I agreed to let Carol raise David without telling him about me. I know that, now. Probably the biggest mistake of my life. But now . . . would it be fair to David for me to come barging into his life? Just because I need some sort of absolution? Would my contacting him benefit David—or would it just make me feel better?

Kirk sighed. *I used to know what was right; at least most of the time I did . . . or I thought I did. But the older I get, the more I question. And . . . regret . . .*

He frowned down at his drink. *Be honest with yourself, Jim. Contacting David now would probably cause him more harm than good.* His hand tightened on the stem of the brandy snifter. He frowned down at his glass, then took another sip. *Damn.*

Kirk looked up, met Spock's concerned gaze, and straightened, trying to adjust his expression into some semblance of normality. *He's been through a lot . . . he doesn't need to be worrying about you, too. Pull yourself together, Jim.*

"More brandy?" he offered.

"No, thank you," Spock said. "I have to go up to the bridge before retiring."

"I just wish I'd been there to see you wearing armor and waving a sword," Kirk told the Vulcan, for the fourth time, shaking his head over the picture his imagination conjured up. "The whole adventure is like something out of Tennyson, or Scott. Incredibly romantic and swashbuckling . . ."

"You sound like Miniver Cheevy, Jim," McCoy said, raising an eyebrow. "You forgetting the cold, the dirt, and the smells?"

Spock also raised an eyebrow. "Miniver Cheevy?"

The doctor gave the Vulcan a startled glance. "I don't believe it. You mean *I've* actually read something *you* haven't?"

"Apparently," Spock said, imperturbably. "What is the reference?"

"It's a poem by Edwin Arlington Robinson," McCoy said, "about a man who spent his entire life yearning after the age of chivalry in days of yore."

"I remember the last verse," Kirk said, and quoted:

> Miniver Cheevy, born too late,
>   Scratched his head and kept on thinking;
> Miniver coughed, and called it fate,
>   And kept on drinking.

"So, here's to the so-called 'good old days.'" Deliberately, the admiral raised his glass to the Vulcan, then took a sip.

"I . . . see," Spock said, and the worried shadow was back in the dark eyes.

Kirk shook his head. "Cut that out, Spock. You know me better than that."

"I suppose I do," his friend said, "but this mission has been a difficult one . . . for all of us."

"I'll say," McCoy agreed. "By the time we get back, the semester will be nearly over. They'll have found someone to replace me, by now. I'm probably out of a job."

The admiral smiled at the idea. "Why not hang around Earth for awhile, then? You could teach at the Academy, with Spock."

McCoy snorted. "Teach what? First-aid for young officers?"

"Actually," Spock said, meditatively, "you could be of use, Doctor. I sometimes find myself at a loss when it comes to evaluating the emotional reactions of my human cadets

—especially in stressful situations. I would value your advice."

The doctor's eyes widened. He turned to Kirk. "Did I hear him right? Did he really say what I thought I heard him say?"

The admiral chuckled. "C'mon, Bones. You know Spock has a lot of respect for your opinion."

"He's managed to hide it well," McCoy grumbled. "Well . . . I'll consider it."

"I'll be around more, too," Kirk said. "I'm going to tell Morrow as soon as we get home that I want to spend at least half my time teaching." He pounded his fist softly against the arm of his seat, for emphasis. "And *this* time, I'm making it stick."

McCoy suddenly leaned forward, his eyes intent on the Vulcan's hands. "What've you got there, Spock?"

The Vulcan held up the data cassette he'd been fingering. "Before I left Gateway, I took one more reading of Sarpeidon's history—I had it in mind to attempt an additional analysis of the effects of our mission on the time-stream. To see whether Zar's history had *really* changed."

"Why should you question that?" McCoy asked, quickly. "You said he was all right. That he wasn't that badly hurt."

Spock nodded. "But I do not know how malleable the past can be. It is always possible that I . . . we . . . changed very little. That the integrity of the time-stream repairs itself . . . or, as you might put it, Doctor, that fate refuses to be mocked."

McCoy snorted. "Bull. I believe that whatever happened, *happened*. And that, if we were part of it, then that's the way it was *supposed* to be. Like that incident with Gary Seven. When we checked the history files, we found out that that was what had happened all along."

The Vulcan's somber expression lightened a bit. "I had forgotten about that. Perhaps you are right, Doctor," he murmured. As they watched, he picked up the tricorder that lay on the table beside him and inserted the data cassette. Then, with studied deliberation, he pushed the "erase" button.

Kirk gave McCoy a startled, sidelong glance, and both of them looked back at their friend. "And, if the doctor is *not* correct," Spock finished, so softly his friends had to strain to hear him, "I find myself preferring not to know about it."

"He'll be fine, Spock," McCoy said. "He and Wynn'll probably have six kids and live to ripe old ages."

A reminiscent half-smile relaxed the Vulcan's stern mouth for a fleeting second, and he glanced down at the tricorder in his hand again. "You may well be right, Doctor . . ."

"Speaking of ripe old ages, Jim," McCoy said, a moment later, his blue eyes sparkling mischievously, "you've got a birthday coming up next month."

The admiral grimaced. "Don't remind me. I'm trying to ignore this particular one."

"What would you like for a present?" the doctor persisted. "Another antique for your wall collection?" He chuckled. "Spock, you should've filched that sword of Zar's while you had the chance."

Kirk grinned. "It was a beauty, all right. But he needs it more than I do." He considered. "I don't know . . . yes, I do." He sat up with an air of decision. "I'd like to spend my birthday out in space. Not a real mission, nothing desperate like that. Just a chance to be aboard the *Enterprise* again."

"There is a training and inspection cruise scheduled for next month," Spock said. "Perhaps you can arrange to handle the inspection yourself, Jim."

"I'll twist Morrow's arm," Kirk promised, cheerfully. A sudden thought struck him. "Spock, we've served together for all these years, and I don't even know when *your* birthday is."

"Vulcans celebrate name-days, rather than the anniversary of birth," Spock said. "But the actual date was . . ." he calculated for a bare second, "last week, actually."

"Then I owe you a dinner out," the admiral said, raising his glass in salute. "You pick the place. And a belated 'Happy Birthday' to you. Many happy returns of the day."

The Vulcan raised an eyebrow. "'Many happy returns of the day'?" he repeated, obviously puzzled.

"He means, 'may you enjoy many more birthdays to come,' Spock," McCoy translated. "Same as saying 'may you live long.'"

"Oh. Thank you, then," Spock said, rising to his feet. "I will consider where to go for dinner. But at the moment, I must check in on the bridge." The Vulcan picked up his maroon uniform jacket from where it hung over the back of his chair. After slipping it on, he fastened it, then squared his shoulders, tugging it down around his lean hips so it fit perfectly.

Kirk grinned, stretching his legs out in front of him, settling deeper into his seat. "Better you than me. I intend to be lazy the rest of the way home, and let you mind the store, Captain. R.H.I.P., you know."

The Vulcan nodded. "Enjoy it while it lasts, Jim," he said, a faint gleam of amused affection in his dark eyes. "Remember that before we can embark on the training cruise itself, all the command cadets must first take the 'Kobayashi Maru' test."

The door slid open before the Vulcan, and he left, leaving Kirk and McCoy alone. The admiral groaned quietly. "I'd forgotten about that. And I *hate* inspections."

McCoy raised an eyebrow. "Would you rather do paperwork?"

The Chief of Starfleet Operations grinned. "Hell, no. Paperwork gives me a headache, Bones. Literally."

"Really? I'd better check your eyes, Jim."

James T. Kirk yawned. "Tomorrow, Bones. We've got lots of time for that. Lots of time . . ."

The two old friends sat sipping their drinks and talking, while around them, enclosing and protecting them, her gleaming hull shrouded in rainbow shimmer and endless night, the *Enterprise* glided serenely toward Earth, and home.

1252.01